I0577308

TRYING TIMES FOR THE MILL GIRLS

CHRISSIE WALSH

Boldwood

First published in Great Britain in 2025 by Boldwood Books Ltd.

Copyright © Chrissie Walsh, 2025

Cover Design by Colin Thomas

Cover Images: Colin Thomas

The moral right of Chrissie Walsh to be identified as the author of this work has been asserted in accordance with the Copyright, Designs and Patents Act 1988.

All rights reserved. No part of this book may be reproduced in any form or by any electronic or mechanical means, including information storage and retrieval systems, without written permission from the author, except for the use of brief quotations in a book review. This book is a work of fiction and, except in the case of historical fact, any resemblance to actual persons, living or dead, is purely coincidental.

Every effort has been made to obtain the necessary permissions with reference to copyright material, both illustrative and quoted. We apologise for any omissions in this respect and will be pleased to make the appropriate acknowledgements in any future edition.

A CIP catalogue record for this book is available from the British Library.

Paperback ISBN 978-1-83633-412-5

Large Print ISBN 978-1-83633-413-2

Hardback ISBN 978-1-83633-411-8

Trade Paperback ISBN 978-1-80656-105-6

Ebook ISBN 978-1-83633-414-9

Kindle ISBN 978-1-83633-415-6

Audio CD ISBN 978-1-83633-406-4

MP3 CD ISBN 978-1-83633-407-1

Digital audio download ISBN 978-1-83633-410-1

This book is printed on certified sustainable paper. Boldwood Books is dedicated to putting sustainability at the heart of our business. For more information please visit https://www.boldwoodbooks.com/about-us/sustainability/

Boldwood Books Ltd, 23 Bowerdean Street, London, SW6 3TN

www.boldwoodbooks.com

In memory of my Mam, Dolly, and for all my family

1

ALMONDBURY, HUDDERSFIELD IN THE WEST RIDING, 1900

A mad March wind tugged at the window frames in the upstairs room at Far View House and the Virginia creeper scrabbled its fingers against the leaded-glass panes. Inside the darkened room in the large double bed, Verity Hardcastle moved restlessly as she slept.

In armchairs either side of the hearth, Ada Brook and Clara Medley sat drinking tea and waiting for their mistress to give birth. The two elderly women knew Verity well. Clara had been housekeeper in Far View House for more years than she could count, and had cared for the young Verity in the absence of her mother, and Ada had nursed Verity's father after he had suffered a stroke which had eventually caused his death. Now, they talked in low voices about a new life in the house, one they expected to arrive before dawn.

Verity had had her first contraction in the late afternoon, squealing as the pain seared through her body then panting with relief as it subsided. More had followed in the early evening, but since then, she had experienced nothing but a few twinges and now, close on midnight, her nurse and her housekeeper had little to do but hold whispered conversation as they kept watch.

Over in the large bed with high brass and iron ends, the bed in which she herself had been born, Verity was lying on her side, her long, chestnut hair scribbling the white pillows against which her flushed cheek was pressed. In her tangled dreams, her father was towering over her, his lips wet with spittle as he berated her for being 'a big, ugly lump. A gawky girl who no man would ever want to marry.' How many times had she heard those words?

She opened her mouth to deny them, and half-sleeping and half-awake with the cruel taunts still hurting, she let out a loud groan as an agonising pain tore her into wakefulness. The sheer force of it rolled her over onto her back, her long frame – overly tall for a woman – stretched out on the bed as the grinding torture wracked her body.

Ada and Clara sprang to their feet and hurried to stand at either side of the bed.

'There, there,' said Clara, smoothing her hand over Verity's fevered brow. 'It's the bairn just letting you know it's ready to come.'

'Lift your knees and wait for the next contraction then push when I tell you,' Ada said, pulling up the sheets and peering under them. When she came upright, she shook her head. 'Nothing to see as yet,' she murmured to Clara as Verity flopped back on the mattress.

Clara dipped a cloth into a bowl then mopped her mistress's face. Verity's eyes were closed and she lay perfectly still, readying herself for the next contraction. Several minutes ticked by without any further action and Verity appeared to be dozing.

'First timers always take longer.' Ada spoke with the authority of years of experience as a nurse and midwife.

'Aye, that's a fact, but I've never seen a woman as big wi' child as Miss Verity is,' Clara whispered. 'I reckon there's a big lad in there.'

Ada gazed down at her patient. She didn't doubt her own ability as a midwife – she'd delivered hundreds of babies – but suddenly, she felt uneasy. Should they send for the doctor?

'Aye, she is unusually big, but then she's a big lass, and Oliver's a strapping fellow.'

The strapping fellow in question was downstairs pacing the drawing-room floor and smoking one cigarette after another. He was about to become a family man; a man who had never contemplated marriage until he had fallen head over heels in love with Verity Lockwood. Oliver Hardcastle had been the manager of Jebediah Lockwood's failing worsted mill when first he met Jeb's daughter. Now he was her husband and soon to be the father of the child she was struggling to deliver.

He smiled wryly as he remembered the morning some three years ago when Verity had arrived at Lockwood Mill, and how he had dismissed her interest in saving the failing business as frivolous. Then, other than being Jeb Lockwood's daughter, she had no connection with the mill, and as far as he knew, her childhood years had been spent at boarding school and afterwards living with her aunt in Leeds until she came of age.

However, he had soon realised her sincerity and her genuine desire to save the mill from bankruptcy and the jobs of almost one hundred employees. Impressed by her determination, he had schemed along with her as to how they might just do that. Between them, they had hatched various plans behind Verity's father's back, and whilst he spent his days and nights drinking and gambling in the inns in Huddersfield, Verity and Oliver had worked together to combat Jeb's profligacy and rescue Lockwood Mill.

When Jeb suffered a stroke caused by a lifetime of carousing, Verity not only nursed him but continued her work at the mill, and when her father had eventually died, she became the heiress of the small but thriving worsted mill in Aspley Basin.

Memories of that time flooded Oliver's mind, and tired of pacing, he came to a stop in front of the hearth and watched the slow progress of the minute hand on the clock on the mantelpiece as he recalled how during their first year together, he had taught Verity everything he knew about running a mill and making cloth, and how in the long hours they had spent in each other's company, they had turned the business round.

And not only that, he had fallen in love with her and any misgivings he'd had about falling for 'his boss' had flown out of the window when he had found that love reciprocated.

By mutual agreement, they had kept their romance secret, and their courtship, if it could be termed as such, had been hidden from all who knew them, Oliver not wanting to be seen as a bounder marrying the Mill Mistress for monetary gain and acceptance into the upper classes, and Verity conscious that the more snobbish mill owners and particularly their wives would be aghast at her courting her mill manager.

As the mill began to prosper, Verity, having been born into the upper echelons of the manufacturing elite in the Colne Valley, had been readily accepted into its social circle. She had been thrilled by the invitations to attend the mill owners' grand houses, and thinking it was good for business, she had immersed herself in their company.

Now, as Oliver crossed the room to pour himself a glass of whisky, he remembered, rather bitterly, that he had never been included. A mill manager was working class.

A rueful smile twitched the corners of his mouth as, sipping his whisky, he mused on how Verity's introduction into the mill-owning fraternity had gone to her head and almost destroyed their relationship. She had embarked on a whirlwind of parties, unaware that some of the manufacturers were making a game of her. It was unusual for a woman to run a mill, and whilst she had learned her trade well under Oliver's guidance, and could hold her own when discussing mill business, her lack of experience in society and her naivety had allowed the unscrupulous Clarence Hargreaves to take advantage of her.

Clarence Hargreaves. The name still rankled.

Oliver slugged his drink then refilled his glass before plumping down on the couch.

As he lit yet another cigarette and anxiously listened for noises from above, he recalled how he had warned Verity that Hargreaves had wanted her not for herself but to save his own floundering mill from closure.

That memory brought to mind an incident that had occurred shortly before they had planned to announce their engagement, Christmas 1897. Verity had suggested that come the New Year, the mill workers who started work at 6 a.m. should start an hour later for the same pay. Oliver had angrily told her they couldn't afford to do that, and they had quarrelled.

She had stormed off to a Christmas party in the George Hotel and Oliver, regretting his anger, had gone after her, only to catch her in the arms of Clarence Hargreaves.

Oliver's lips twisted into a snarl as he replayed the scene.

He had already been told by a fellow mill man-ager that Hargreaves was pursuing Verity to get his hands on her mill and rescue his own that was in dire straits. Oliver had tried to shrug off the gossip but the seeds of doubt had been sown. Did the Mill Mistress truly love him? Or was he, as his mother had warned, simply being used?

On the day he'd dashed into the George Hotel, the rumours that Verity and Clarence were romanti-cally involved had suddenly become reality. Oliver had seen red. He wasn't by nature a violent man but he had thoroughly enjoyed the sound of Clarence's nose crunching under the weight of his fist and the sight of blood staining his fancy shirt.

That recollection brought a smile to Oliver's face, and as he emptied his glass, he reflected on how stu-pidly he had behaved in the aftermath. Believing she had made a fool of him, he had left the mill and gone to Cumbria without giving Verity the opportunity to explain that she detested Clarence, and that he had been kissing her against her will.

Fortunately for him, Verity's friend, Dolly Ar-mitage, chanced to meet Oliver's mother and tell her the truth of the situation. Evelyn Hardcastle had then passed on the information to her son. He had hot-footed it back to Huddersfield, just in the nick of time to save the mill from being burned to the ground. Had it not been for Dolly, he might still have been nursing his pride in Cumbria, Oliver told himself, as he got to his feet and resumed his pacing.

Later, they had learned that Hargreaves had sought revenge when Verity had spurned him, and he had paid a disgruntled overseer whom Verity had sacked for sexually abusing the young weavers, to set fire to her mill.

Oliver's heartbeat quickened as he pictured the blazing wool shed and Verity enveloped in flames. He'd saved her then, but by leaving for Cumbria without giving her a chance to explain that Clarence meant nothing to her, he had shattered her belief in him.

Now, shaking his head to dispel the memory of how close he had come to losing her, he crossed the room and opened the door, listening for sounds from above, considering himself to be a most fortunate man to have restored her faith in him.

Theirs was a true marriage of minds, and as Oliver waited to become a father, he thanked God for their happiness, asking him to speed the birth of their child and release his beloved Verity from the pain she was now enduring.

Up in the bedroom, when night was at its

thinnest, Verity bit down on her bottom lip as another contraction wracked her sweat-soaked body. They were coming regularly now and she was doing her utmost to comply with Ada's instructions.

'Keep breathing like I told,' Ada said, 'and you, Clara, support her by the shoulders.'

Verity took a deep breath. Her body heaved again and she let out an agonising wail that ended in a full-blown scream.

'Push now! Push,' Ada cried as a head covered in dark hair appeared and was swiftly followed by the body of a squirming boy child with a healthy pair of lungs. Tying then snipping the umbilical cord, she handed the baby to Clara.

'Eeh! T'Master'll be pleased it's a boy,' said Clara as she cleaned the baby, ready to place him in his mother's arms.

Verity fell back against the pillows, gasping for breath and her eyes wild.

Ada peered at the blood-stained mess between Verity's legs. Coming upright, she began smoothing her hands over Verity's swollen belly. Something wasn't right.

Verity's womb undulated under Ada's touch. Ada drew a sharp breath, her practiced palms and finger gently probing, and her mouth twisting with fear.

Clara leaned into the bed to hand the swaddled baby to his mother.

'Wait! Not yet, Clara. Hold on to him!' Ada's voice had risen an octave. 'There's another one in there!' Panic surged. 'Get Oliver to fetch Doctor Braithwaite. Tell him it's urgent.'

Clara dithered with the child still in her arms.

'Put him in the crib,' Ada snapped, and when Clara did as she was told, Ada said, 'He'll be fine, whereas...' Her fear for the life of the unborn child and its mother mounting, she shooed the house-keeper out of the room.

Utterly confused, Clara tottered down the stairs as fast as her aged legs would carry her. Without knocking, she burst into the drawing room. Oliver hurried towards her, an expectant smile on his face.

'Ada says get Doctor Braithwaite. It's urgent,' Clara squawked, collapsing against the doorjamb then clinging to it for dear life. *Another baby, that's what Ada had said.*

But before she could tell him, Oliver had pushed past her and, pale and distraught, he was dashing to the rear of the house. The pony and trap had been left ready in case of an emergency, one which he had prayed wouldn't arise. Springing into the driver's seat, he urged the little grey mare out of the stable yard and down Far View Hill.

The moon was hidden behind banks of thick, grey cloud and the road in front of him black as pitch. The howling wind tore at his hair and whipped the branches of the trees as he descended the steep incline into the heart of the village where, heedless of waking its sleeping inhabitants, he hammered on the doctor's door.

Meanwhile, as Oliver and the bleary-eyed doctor sped back to Fair View House, Ada was doing her utmost to ease Verity's distress. Ada knew from experience that a second child inside the womb had a better chance of survival if the mother rested between deliveries. At the same time as praying that the baby would change its position and that her patient wouldn't haemorrhage, she chastised herself for not realising that Verity had been carrying twins. *I should have known by the size of her,* she moaned.

Verity's eyes flitted from Ada to Clara who, having come back to the bedroom, was tending to the boy in the crib. 'What... what's happening?' she whispered.

'You've got a beautiful, healthy son, lass, but it's not over yet, so breathe slowly and don't push no matter how much you want to,' Ada told her through gritted teeth.

A son? I have a son. Verity struggled to comprehend what she had heard and fought to still the movements inside her. *Breathe slowly, don't push. Breathe slow...* Verity lay still and breathed slowly, her pale lips fluttering.

The sheets that had been smooth and white were rucked and stained, the room reeking with the smell of childbirth. The minutes ticked by. Ada glanced anxiously at the clock then back to Verity. Was she and the unborn child losing the will to live? And where was the blasted doctor?

Jeremy Braithwaite was haring up the stairs two at a time with Oliver at his heels.

'Better you stay out here, old chap,' Jeremy said, ducking into the bedroom then closing the door in Oliver's face. The young doctor was new to the village, and as he listened carefully to Ada, he thanked God that he had made a point of studying labour, parturition and delivery; his own mother had died giving birth to his younger brother when Jeremy was a boy. Placing his hands on Verity's abdomen, he began his examination.

The boy in the crib cried lustily, and with Ada's guidance, Clara fed him drops of sugar water. His crying ceased as his lips sucked on her little finger. Now, the only sounds in the room were the doctor's

urgent instructions to Ada, and their patient's anxious cries.

Twenty-five stressful minutes later, minutes in
which Verity had writhed and grunted, Jeremy eased
the tiny mite into the world. Placing his mouth over
the child's nose and mouth, he cleared its airways
then, dangling it by its feet, he gave its rump a gentle
slap. With a triumphant smile, he gave the baby to
Ada, its faint mewling cries growing louder as she
cradled the tiny child against her shoulder and
gently rubbed its back. Then he turned his attention
back to its mother.

Verity felt a pair of gentle hand touching the
parts of her body that had only been touched by herself or Oliver but she made no objection. The dreadful, tearing pains had eased and as her mind cleared,
Jeremy Braithwaite's pleasant face came into focus.
She managed a tremulous little smile and he returned it with an encouraging grin. Then, assured
that everything was in order, he stood back, rubbing
his hands clean and smiling broadly at Ada then
Clara, acknowledging the parts they had played, before he turned back to his patient.

'Well done,' Jeremy congratulated Verity. 'You
have a son and a daughter.'

'Two babies?' The new mother gazed in confused

awe at the large bundle in Clara's arms and then at the fragile little scrap that Ada was holding. 'Twins! I gave birth to twins?'

'That you did, lovey, an' a grand job you made of it,' said Clara, placing the boy in the crook of Verity's right arm, and as Ada tucked the little girl into Verity's left side, she said, 'She's small but she's perfectly healthy.'

Spellbound, Verity lay in a dreamlike state, the feel of her children's warm little bodies filling her heart with a love so overwhelming that she began to cry. Recognising them as tears of joy, Jeremy, Ada and Clara exchanged pleased glances. Ada began to hastily clear away the afterbirths, bundling them in newspapers and handing them to Clara to dispose of on the blazing fire. Then, as the midwife gently sponged between her patient's thighs, the fog that clouded Verity's brain slowly dissipated, bringing her surroundings sharply into focus. She saw the doctor packing his bag, and Clara's bent back as she stoked something on the fire, and felt the soothing swab of Ada's hand. But something was wrong! Someone was missing.

'Oliver! Where is Oliver?'

At Verity's anxious cry, Ada left off sponging and pulled Verity's nightdress down over her legs. Clara gave the bundle of papers on the fire a final prod, and the doctor hurried over to the door, his smile wide.

Oliver was pacing the landing when Jeremy stepped out to fetch him.

'Is it over?' he gasped. 'Is Verity all right? Is the child born?'

Jeremy grinned. 'Your wife and your babies are grand.'

'Babies?' Oliver stared, nonplussed.

'Aye, a bruiser of a boy and a dainty little girl.'

Oliver's jaw dropped and his eyes widened in wonder. He had been thrice blessed. Not only did he have a beautiful, marvellous wife, he now had a son and a daughter. His heart swelled and his eyes glowed with love and anticipation as he strode into the bedroom.

2

'What shall we call them?' Oliver asked Verity, his chest puffed with manly pride at having fathered two such beautiful specimens of humanity, a big, healthy, handsome boy and a little, pretty girl. His wife, having given considerable thought to the naming of her son, turned her luminous, dove-grey eyes on him ready, in part, to answer her husband's question.

The proud parents were in the nursery at Far View House, a splendidly appointed room with its two deep armchairs and two finely crafted cribs, a second one having been hastily ordered from Best's Furniture Shop on Queen Street. Each one bore the emblem of a Yorkshire rose that was the craftsman's signature, as did the drawers and cupboards that were filled with soft, white nappies and sheets. Hanging in the wardrobe were the long, white baby gowns trimmed with lace and ribbon that Verity had purchased from Rushworth's Bazaar during her pregnancy, a task that had given her the greatest pleasure. Now, as her husband cradled their daughter and Verity nursed their son, she answered him with alacrity.

'I want to call him Blaise, after Merlin's tutor in the Arthurian legends.'

Oliver laughed and asked, 'Why not just Arthur?'

'Because Blaise was one of the keepers of the Holy Grail, a martyr and a magically adept swordsman,' Verity replied, her smile enigmatic.

Oliver shook his head in bemusement. 'Then Blaise it is,' he said, wondering what on earth anyone else would make of such a name. 'And what about this delightful, sweet little creature?' he asked, caressing his daughter's creamy cheek then gently coiling a wisp of her red-gold hair round his finger.

'I'll let you choose.'

Silence fell as Oliver pursed his lips and furrowed his brow. Then, his countenance brightening, he said, 'I'd like to call her Briony.'

Verity brooked no opposition to Briony, but she was curious as to why he had chosen it.

'I read somewhere that it means to climb to the highest heights as it blooms,' he said. 'It's a thing of nature, and the colour of her hair sums up the beauty of the landscape in which we live. Those glorious autumn days when the moors turn russet and gold.'

'Poetry to my ears, my darling.' Verity laughed then said, 'How blessed we are.'

And so, Blaise and Briony Hardcastle were duly christened in All Hallows church, the vicar just one of the many in the congregation who were puzzled, amused or mildly shocked at Verity and Oliver's choice of such outlandish names.

'I suppose Albert and Susan aren't good enough for the likes of them,' one old dear was heard to comment as they left the church.

'Well, they'd not want to call the lad Jebediah in case he turns out like his grandfather, that drunken reprobate.' Her companion's reply was laden with sarcasm.

The other mill hands in hearing distance sniggered.

* * *

Verity delighted in being a mother to her two babies even though she herself had no memory of ever having been mothered. Her own mother, Leila, had always been too ill to devote the time and attention that Verity now gave to her own offspring. They, in turn, responded to her loving care by growing into healthy bundles of joy.

However, before long, it was plain for all to see that although the brother and sister had shared the same womb, they had acquired very different personalities. The Hardcastle's diminutive daughter was placid and obedient. She slept for long hours, and at feeding time, she sucked delicately at her mother's breast then fell asleep again. Her sweet, gentle nature endeared her not only to her father but also to Clara Medley and Briony's extended family: her grandmother, Evelyn Hardcastle, and her aunts, Rose and Maud. And as Verity nursed Briony, it evoked a tender feeling of love bordering on gratitude quite unlike that she felt for Blaise, who was awake at all hours roaring and wriggling, his chubby fists pummelling at Verity's breast as his hungry lips ravaged her nipples.

Strangely enough, this assault on her body stirred Verity into feeling a fiercely passionate love for her son, something altogether different from that she felt for her daughter. Whenever she gazed into his dark, restless eyes and at his firm chin and Roman nose, so like his father's, her heart swelled and her breath caught in her throat at the realisation that she, Verity Hardcastle née Lockwood, an ugly gawk of a girl as her father had often described her, was the well-spring that had given life to such a magnificent child.

Oliver, quick to spot where Verity's adoration was focused, centred his attention on his delicate little girl. In the nursery, always his first port of call when he arrived home from the mill, he would cradle Briony in his strong arms and lose himself in her dove-grey eyes and rosebud mouth. Meanwhile, his wife dandled Blaise on her knee in an attempt to pacify him as he grabbed at her hair and pawed at her face, bawling and clinging to her when she tried to put him down. In unwanted moments, Oliver found himself thinking of a limpet – or more uncalled for, a leech – as Blaise demanded more and more of his mother's devotion.

By the time the twins were five months old, their different temperaments were often the subject of conversations held by family and friends. Also remarked on was the attention their mother gave to one child, and not the other.

And so, on a beautiful autumn day just before noon, when Ada Brook made one of her regular visits to Far View House to check on the twins' progress and offer Verity some much-needed advice, she didn't look particularly happy. In the kitchen, taking off her gloves and accepting the cup of tea Clara offered, her tone of voice held more than a hint of concern as she asked, 'And how are things today?'

Clara pulled a face as she poured boiling water over the leaves in the pot. 'Same as usual,' she said, exasperation colouring her words. 'An' judging by the bags under Madam's eyes, she was up again most of the night with that rapscallion of a son of hers.'

Ada heaved a sigh then said, 'She can't go on like this. It's detrimental to her and the children. But will she listen? No.'

The two women continued to air their concerns about Verity, Blaise and Briony as they sipped their tea.

'She's a lovely little thing, an' no bother at all,' Clara said, smiling fondly as they commented on Briony's progress, 'but,' her lip curled, 'he's turning out to be a right handful. What with his tantrums, and bawling his head off if she puts him down, he keeps that poor lass on her toes day an' night.'

'And she submits to his every whim,' Ada said

with a despairing shake of her head. 'Even though I've told her time and again that the more attention she pays him, the more he will demand. I've seen it often enough. There isn't a baby anywhere that's not cute enough to know how to manipulate its mother, and Blaise is a master of exploitation for all he's not yet six months old.' Ada set down her empty cup and stood. 'I'll go up and see how things stand today, try and talk some sense into her, but I don't expect she'll listen.'

Clara lifted a pile of clean nappies from the end of the table. 'I'll take these up and ask her what she'd like for lunch. Not that she'll get chance to eat in peace.'

Ada tutted. 'I have told her she mustn't neglect herself, that she needs to eat plenty whilst ever she's breastfeeding, but I noticed on my last visit that she's looking rather gaunt.'

'An' no wonder,' Clara replied as they made their way up the basement stairs into the hallway then climbed the next flight up to the nursery. They heard the cacophony long before they reached it. When the two women entered, they exchanged meaningful glances.

Verity was sitting on a chair by the window, the buttons on her loose wrapper undone and one side of her nursing corsets open to reveal her breast. Shadows beneath her eyes resembled over-ripe plums, and her unwashed hair was scraped back unbecomingly, but the look on her weary face was one of patient admiration as, seeming oblivious to Briony's hungry little whimpers, she opened the other side of her corset and attached Blaise to her nipple. He stopped writhing and screaming and began to guzzle.

'Give him to me,' said Ada, marching over to the window and abruptly detaching the cantankerous boy. 'Your daughter needs feeding so do that whilst I settle this lad.'

Verity, taken aback by Ada's brisk removal of Blaise, cried out, 'But he hasn't had his fill.'

'He's hardly likely to starve,' Ada retorted as she hefted the chubby, big-boned baby up to her shoulder. Depositing him in his crib, she lifted his sister. Blaise wailed all the louder, his eyes fixed on his mother as she reluctantly allowed Ada to place Briony in her arms. The baby girl attached her rosebud mouth to Verity's breast. Clara looked on approvingly.

'Eeh, she's an angel is that one,' she cooed as Briony placidly sucked, her tiny hands tucked under her chin. Although Verity cradled her daughter and stroked her downy head lovingly, her eyes strayed to Blaise in his crib. Ada went and lifted him to her shoulder again.

When Briony's lips slackened and her eyes drooped, Verity handed her to Clara.

'Put her down to rest,' she said, and looking to where Blaise was pummelling Ada's cheeks with his fists, Verity commanded, 'Give him back to me. He's still hungry.'

Ada did as she was asked, and Blaise clamped his greedy mouth on Verity's breast. Verity winced as he pulled on her nipple but she bore the pain silently until Blaise released his hold. He burped loudly and with his head lolled against Verity's bosom, he dozed. Ada stooped to take him from his mother's arms but Verity stopped her with a look. Ada came upright, her expression grim.

'Mrs Hardcastle, I've said it before and I'll say it again. You're not doing yourself or your son any favours.'

* * *

On a Sunday afternoon in August, Oliver and Verity set out to pay one of their regular visits to his mother's house, Verity proudly pushing the pram through the village as they made their way to Evelyn Hard-castle's home at the foot of Almondbury Bank.

Oliver, equally proud, strolled along by Verity's side, every now and then tipping his hat to the ladies and shaking the hands of the men who stopped to admire the babies and the large, gleaming Silver Cross pram in which they were propped on cush-ions, one at either end. The sun shone down on the tendrils of Briony's red-gold hair that peeped from under her lacy bonnet, the ladies exclaiming she was a picture. It also shone on Blaise's angry red cheeks and his sullen mouth as, squirming and roaring, he tried to free himself from the blanket that restrained his movements. The admirers tended to look away in embarrassment, as did Oliver, but Verity happily re-lated her children's progress in answer to their questions.

The untended path across Dog Kennel Bank was a riot of colour with dandelions, scarlet pimpernel, yellow archangel, red sorrel, purple vetch and feathery green fescue grasses. As Verity breathed in their sweet, fresh scents, she felt glad to be alive, and her happiness stayed with her until shortly after they arrived at their destination. Oliver's mother had, as usual, laid on a spread of egg and onion sandwiches and home-made sponge cake, but Verity was so busy coping with Blaise that her plate was barely touched.

When the time came for them to leave, Evelyn couldn't resist saying, 'You can bring Briony anytime you like and leave her with us, she's such a pleasure to have about the place, but as for that one...' she wagged an accusing finger at Blaise, 'none of my children ever behaved so badly.'

Verity, who had always been of the opinion that her mother-in-law objected to Oliver marrying his boss as she had then been, seethed at the remark then shrugged it off as just another of Evelyn's jibes meant to let Verity know that she wasn't the sort of woman she would have chosen for him. And Rose, his older sister, hadn't helped by twittering how sweet Briony was, not unlike her friend, Lucy Whittaker's baby, who was 'an absolute dream.' Lucy, having failed to capture Oliver's heart, had married a bank clerk and just as cleverly produced a 'very adorable son, not in the least like yours,' Rose had added spitefully.

Determined not to let them see how hurt she was, Verity raged inwardly but when, as they made their way home, Oliver suggested that Blaise took after Rose, Verity strongly objected. He was nothing like Rose. She was a shrewish spinster with a vindictive nature; hadn't she tried to come between them in the early days of their courtship by telling Verity that he already was as good as engaged to Lucy Whittaker?

'And I hope you aren't suggesting that Briony takes after Maud,' she said tartly, because his younger sister was what Oliver's mother inferred to as 'lightheaded', Maud being a simple woman with a vacant expression in her eyes.

'Maud can't help the way she is,' he snapped. 'She was born damaged.'

Verity had the grace to look ashamed.

But throughout the following months, as summer faded into autumn and Christmas drew near, she remained blind to her rip-roaring son's wilfulness and turned a deaf ear to the advice that Oliver, Clara and Ada frequently gave:

'You're spoiling him.'

'He has to learn to know his limits.'

'He's deliberately trying your patience to see just how far he can go.'

'You'll live to rue the day.'

3

ALMONDBURY, HUDDERSFIELD IN THE WEST RIDING, JANUARY 1901

'Queen Victoria dead! Read all about it!'

The news boy's cry rang out as Verity and Oliver Hardcastle's trap slowed to a stop at the junction of the Somerset and Wakefield Roads.

Verity's gloved hand shot to her mouth. 'Oh, my goodness! Buy a newspaper, Oliver,' she cried, her voice rising above the noise of passing carts and wagons, and the anticipation and excitement she'd felt on the journey from Far View House fading fast. This was to be her first full working day at the mill since the birth of Blaise and Briony, and she had been so looking forward to it that now she felt somewhat cheated.

For the past ten months, she had devoted her time to nursing her babies, delighting in giving them the loving care that she herself had been denied. Although Verity had only vague memories of her own mother, she knew that Leila had been too sickly to attend to her and that it was Clara who had cared for her before Jeb sent her to boarding school. Determined that her own children would never know such deprivation, she had gladly stayed at home, but just lately, the lure of the mill had been calling to her with each passing day. And listening to Oliver's second-hand news as he related all the goings on in the mill about the business or the latest gossip from the girls, wasn't the same as being there; the mill was part of her heart and she felt as though she was missing out. Rather reluctantly, for she found it hard to leave Blaise even for a few hours, she had employed a nanny to help care for them, and satisfy her own needs. Mary Shuttleworth was a lovely, efficient young woman. The twins had taken to her like ducks to water and Verity, relieved to escape the confines of the nursery, had no qualms today about leaving them in Mary's care for the day.

Oliver beckoned to the news boy, tossed him a coin, then handed the copy of the *Yorkshire Post* to his wife. As she scanned the headlines, he flicked the pony's reins and they joined the stream of traffic heading towards Aspley Basin.

'Yesterday evening at six thirty on Tuesday the twenty-second of January, our beloved Queen Victoria died peacefully at Osborne House on the Isle of Wight surrounded by her family,' Verity read out loud as Oliver drove the trap along the wharf to the mill. Verity continued reading until they reached the mill gates: twelve feet high and crafted in heavy wrought iron, the arch above them spelled out *LOCKWOOD MILL*. Her heart swelled with pride.

The gatekeeper swung the gates wide then saluted the Mill Mistress. Verity smiled and called out, 'Good morning, Joe.'

'Thas heard the news then?' Joe asked as Oliver steered the trap into the cobbled mill yard and brought it to a halt.

'We have, Joe. A sad day,' said Oliver, jumping down and handing the reins to Joe before helping Verity alight. It was just past nine o'clock, the January morning bright but chilly and a coating of frost lingering on the cobbles as they made their way to the mill office.

'Do you think we should close the mill today out

of respect?' Verity asked Oliver as she slipped off her cloak and hung it on the hook in the office wall.

'No need for that. We don't want to fall behind with our orders. We'll close the day of the funeral.' He smiled to lessen the impact of his curt response. But it was his responsibility to curb Verity's enthusiasm for doing the right thing, as she saw it; business was business and she often let her heart rule her head. 'We'll fly the Union Jack at half-mast. That will do.'

Verity nodded, somewhat appeased. Four years ago, when she had first taken over her father's business, she would have argued that it was her mill, and she should be the one to make decisions. However, she had learned a lot since then about manufacturing fine worsted cloth, most of it under Oliver's guidance, and now that they were not only husband and wife but business partners, she stifled her impetuosity and let Oliver have his way.

'It's the end of an era, one that's seen many changes and much of them for the better,' Oliver remarked as he lifted a bundle of yarns. He began sorting through them, and Verity opened a ledger to check on the progress of their orders as they continued commenting on how Victoria's reign had seen the British Empire grow to become the first global industrial power producing much of the world's coal, iron, steel and textiles.

'Our industry has improved by leaps and bounds under her rule,' said Oliver. 'At one time, we'd never have dreamed of exporting our cloth to countries thousands of miles away. Now we do it regularly.'

'Yes, she was the figurehead who saw us through some extraordinary times.' Verity began ticking them off on her fingers. 'The Crimean War, the abolition of slavery, the Great Exhibition at Crystal Palace, and the wonderful advances in the arts and sciences. A great deal of change in our lifetimes, Oliver.'

'And we can expect more now that we have a new monarch,' he replied, picking up the yarns he'd selected then striding to the office door. 'I'm off to the dyehouse.'

After he had gone, Verity leaned back in her chair and gazed up at the office ceiling through half-closed eyes, her thoughts drifting. She'd experienced plenty of changes in her own lifetime, some of them unbelievably joyful and some heartbreakingly cruel. Her life hadn't always been as sweet as it was now.

She had been Jeb and Leila Lockwood's only surviving child, two of her three brothers stillborn and the third dead within a year of his birth. Verity had grown up in the sure and certain knowledge that Jeb, a callous and cruel reprobate, had never forgiven her for being a girl, and an ugly one at that, as he had so often told her.

Great big gawky girl. The words still stung, and she flinched as she recalled her father's harsh, guttural voice mocking her. Oh, how she had longed to have a mother to run to then, one who would comfort and protect her from Jeb's nasty jibes and his drunken wrath.

But she had barely known her mother. Leila, taking her doctor's advice, had spent all but three months of the year living in Cornwall in the hope that it would cure her tattered lungs, the air being much cleaner there than the smoke-laden, soot-filled clouds that hung over the industrial town that was Huddersfield. Unfortunately, it hadn't, and now as a grown woman, Verity presumed that her mother's absence had been perhaps more to escape her husband's cruelty than it was to improve her health. *Poor Leila*, she thought. *Did she love me? And would she have packed me off to a boarding school in Headingly, more than twenty miles away from home?* Somehow, Verity thought not.

Boarding school. Her memory of it was not unkind, but she had been lonely – particularly at holiday times, when the other girls had gone home and she had been left with only the Misses Dowling for company. But even that had been preferable to what came afterwards, when, within days of her mother's death, Jeb had sent her to live with his sister, Martha, and her unwelcoming husband, Joseph Boothroyd.

From the start, her Uncle Joseph had made it quite plain he didn't want her in his home. He'd complained bitterly about what he called her 'childish clutter' and avoided being in the same room as her whenever possible. What Verity would never know was that her childless aunt's husband had a predilection for young girls, and whilst he felt no compunction about dallying with underage village girls, he drew the line at doing so in his house. Verity's presence too tempting, he had demanded that Martha get rid of her, and Aunt Martha had reluctantly asked Jeb to take her away. Jeb, infuriated by his sister's request, had taken his daughter back to Far View House, and after two miserable weeks in which he had neglected her or cruelly chastised her, he had sent her to live with Leila's sister in Leeds.

At fourteen years of age, Verity had felt like a parcel that nobody wanted to receive.

Aunt Flora had taken her in rather unwillingly, and her three cousins – silly girls who made fun of her bookishness and her height and dowdy appearance – had made her life a misery. Throughout her unhappy childhood and teenage years, Verity had felt that she had nowhere she could call home.

I was a disappointment to everyone, she thought, shifting uneasily in the hard office chair and grimacing as she recalled that by the time she was twenty-one, Aunt Flora had tired of trying to find her a suitable husband – *not that I was looking for one,* she reflected – and having no money of her own and nowhere else to go, she had returned to Far View House. She gave an involuntary shudder at the memory of how unwelcoming her father had been, and that she had felt like a stranger in the house. Had it not been for Martha, who lived close by, life would have been unbearable.

If Aunt Martha hadn't warned me that my father was in danger of losing his mill and his home, I might not have stayed, she thought, her heart fluttering at the idea. *If I hadn't, I would never have met Oliver.*

A gentle smiled curved her lips. Darling Oliver. What a wonderful man he was. He had worked at Lockwood Mill since leaving school and had risen to the position of mill manager. For his own sake and that of all the workers employed in the mill, he had struggled against the odds to keep the mill solvent. *And he'd thought I was a foolish, upper-class girl inter-*

fering in the business on a passing whim, she mused, her smile widening as she recollected what Aunt Martha had told her: 'Take matters into your own hands, Verity. It's up to you to save the mill.'

And saving the mill was my epiphany.

Dreamily, she dwelt on how she had not only fallen in love with the mill and rescued it from the brink of bankruptcy, she had fallen head over heels in love with its manager. Then, much to the surprise and a certain amount of disdain from the other mill owners in the cloth-making heart of the woollen industry that was Huddersfield, she had married him.

Her heart gave a little jolt as she recalled how near she had come to not marrying Oliver. That thought brought to mind the detestable Clarence Hargreaves. He had wormed his way into her company, and Verity had spurned his advances at every turn – but Oliver hadn't known that. When he'd witnessed Clarence foisting a kiss on her at a Christmas party in the George Hotel, he had believed she was romantically involved with him. After delivering a blow to Clarence's nose, Oliver had left without giving her a chance to explain.

Oliver's sudden disappearance, and the struggle to keep the mill running without him, had left Verity devastated. That he hadn't trusted her enough to let her tell him that Clarence had forced himself on her had been beyond bearing. She'd pined for him constantly, but her faith in him had been badly shaken and it had taken a great deal of persuasion on Oliver's part to restore her trust.

What a fool I was then. I don't know how I could have thought so badly of him when all the time, I knew I could not live without him.

She stretched lazily, enjoying the memory of making up with him. She who had once believed that no man would ever marry her was not only the successful heiress of a thriving business but the wife of Oliver and the mother of twins. At twenty-five years of age, Verity considered herself blessed.

She was still musing on her good fortune when Oliver bounced back into the office.

'Ah, daydreaming again, I see,' he said, his sharp, blue eyes meeting a pair of the softest dove-grey, and his wife delivering a sharp rebuke that she was doing nothing of the sort.

'I was thinking,' she told him, smiling up into the handsome face of the man she loved with every fibre of her being.

She watched as he stripped off his jacket, exposing his broad chest and strong shoulders under a crisp, white shirt. At six feet tall, his fine physique and black hair that curled round his ears and in the nape of his neck still caused Verity's heart to flutter as it had done when first they met. Then, she had struggled with emotions that she had never before felt but now, sure in his love for her and hers for him, she no longer felt unattractive and out of place as she had so often done in the past. She got to her feet, her face almost on a level with his, and told him she was going to make her rounds of the mill.

Oliver watched Verity go, his eyes filled with admiration. In his opinion, she was beautiful although some might have disagreed. Her shapely figure was unfashionably tall, and her straight nose, high cheekbones and well-defined chin made her look haughty, but he knew that she was as lovely on the inside as he considered her to be on the outside. She had given everything she possessed to save Lockwood Mill from dissolution, not for her own sake but for the well-being of the workforce and their livelihoods. To Oliver, she was the most adorable woman in the whole world.

Verity strolled across the cobbled mill yard towards the weaving shed. Doing her rounds of the mill was one of her pleasures, one that she had undertaken every day when she first became the Mill Mistress. She attached great importance to getting to know her employees. From the start, she had believed that if she treated them with respect and ensured that their working conditions were safe and their wages fair, they would reciprocate by producing the finest worsted. And she had been proved right. Although her mill was small compared to some in the valley, it now had a good reputation for weaving top-quality cloth, and orders were plentiful.

Lingering at the weaving shed door, she recalled that inheriting the mill had not only given her a husband she adored, it had also granted her the wonderful friendship of Dolly Armitage. Dolly had been a weaver at the mill, and the friendship had begun when Verity discovered that Dolly could read: an attribute denied to many of the mill hands who had had little or no schooling. Verity had then had the idea to start reading classes for her workforce and give them the opportunity to better themselves. Oliver had laughed at the notion, and most of the mill hands had shunned the classes in the belief that she was sneering at their ignorance. At first, few had attended but Verity had remained undeterred. Along with Dolly's enthusiastic assistance, the number of pupils swelled from five to twenty-five in a matter of months. The classes were still running one evening each week, those who had learned to read teaching the newcomers. They never had fewer than twenty pupils eager to learn.

After that, whenever Verity had sought to make improvements, she had asked Dolly's advice and the sisterly bond they had formed remained strong to the present day.

Verity, extremely conscious of the hardships that most working-class women endured, had then introduced other ways to improve their lives. The weekly sewing sessions in the canteen were a great success, the more adept needlewomen showing the beginners how to use the two treadle machines that Verity had provided, and how to make garments from the off-cuts of the cloth they wove: the ends of pieces that would have been shredded for rags.

The canteen was another of Verity's improvements for it enabled the workers to eat their breakfasts and lunches in comfort whereas before, they had sat out in the mill yard on dry days, or at their machines if the weather was too cold and wet. Lockwood Mill was known throughout the valley for the benefits it offered its workers, and those who were employed there considered themselves lucky. Verity prided herself on knowing the names and backgrounds of all her workers, one that Oliver had fostered in his years as mill manager, and as she opened the weaving shed door, she realised just how much she had been looking forward to today.

The roar of the looms assailed her ears and the dust motes rising from the woven cloth swirled before her eyes. She paused, breathing in the familiar smell of wool and grease.

It was good to be back.

At the top of 'weaver's alley' – the wide aisle between the rows of looms – she paused to survey the thrashing looms and the women tending them. Fred Garthwaite, the overseer, hurried to greet her.

'Good to see thi back, Mrs Hardcastle,' he mouthed, the noise of the looms making it impossible to conduct an ordinary conversation.

'Good to be back, Fred, although the pleasure has been somewhat overshadowed by Queen Victoria's death,' Verity mouthed back.

Lip-reading was one of the many things she had had to learn and now it came easily to her. She asked Fred about the new jacquard patterns they were weaving and the quality of the yarn. He confirmed that everything was fine and Verity began walking slowly down the alley.

As she walked between the looms, friendly smiles and mouthed enquiries were exchanged.

'How are the babies?'

'Thriving. Getting bigger by the day.'

'Are they good sleepers? I never got a minute wi' mine.'

'I know what you mean.' Verity gave a mock-yawn.

'Two at one go. Tha must o' done some pushin'.'

Amid cheeky comments and gales of laughter, she strolled to the end of the alley, the weavers' sharp eyes meeting Verity's then darting back to their loom's flying shuttles in case a loose end marred the parallel perfection of the cloth they were weaving.

At the end of the shed where the rattle of the looms didn't drown ordinary conversation, she found Nellie Armitage hard at work showing the new apprentices how to weave. Nellie was married to Dolly's brother, George, and like Dolly and her husband, Theo, they were friends of Verity and Oliver. Verity paid no heed to the snobbishness that divided the social classes, something that her fellow industrialists frowned on. They showed their disapproval by withholding invitations to their garden parties and soirees, but Verity and Oliver cared not one jot; they knew who their true friends were.

'Have you come to see if we're doing the job right or did you just get fed up of changing nappies?' Nellie joked.

'A bit of both, Nellie. I've missed being here.'

'And how are Blaise and Briony?' Nellie's eyes twinkled with amusement. Both she and Dolly had been surprised by the unusual names Verity had given her children.

'They're grand,' said Verity. 'I've left them in Mary's capable hands for the day.'

They continued chatting about the twins and the mill for some time before Verity, pleased by all she had seen and heard so far, continued her rounds from the weaving shed to the spinning and the carding rooms then the baling room and the raw wool shed before finally going to the dyehouse.

George Armitage, the master dyer and under-manager at the mill, greeted her with a beaming smile. He was showing her a batch of green yarn and asking for her opinion on the shade of it when the mill hooter blared.

'My goodness, half-past twelve already,' Verity said, and leaving the dyers to have their dinner, she went back to the office, her heart warmed by the welcome she had received at every port of call.

'Will we eat in the canteen today?' she asked Oliver. 'I'd like to seeing as it's my first day back.'

'Then we will,' he said, reaching for his jacket

and asking, 'Did you find everything to your liking on your rounds?'

'Indeed, I did,' she chirped. Then giving him a condescending smile, she simpered, 'You've managed perfectly well in my absence, Mr Hardcastle.'

'Impertinent baggage!' said Oliver, playfully slapping her rump as they left the office to make their way over to the canteen.

Although the country had known for some time that the queen's health was declining, the newspapers keeping them abreast of her condition, it had come as something of a shock to learn that their monarch had died, and in the canteen, the workers talked of little else.

'Sixty-three years on the throne,' Isaac Holroyd, the head loom tuner solemnly declared, 'an' a good queen she was. She had more than her fair share of problems to deal with an' she dealt wi' 'em wisely.' He spoke with the authority of his own sixty years, aware that like himself, the younger mill hands had never known any other monarch.

'Aye, being t'queen's not all it's cracked up to be,' Fred Garthwaite opined.

'She'd never been the same since Albert died,' May Sykes said. 'She loved Albert.'

'And she never wore any other colour than black after his death,' Nellie remarked.

'Do you think we'll have to start weaving black serge?' Molly Binns asked. 'I hate working wi' black yarn. It muddles me eyes.'

'Is it true she had nine children?' an apprentice carder asked.

'Aye, she did,' Isaac confirmed. 'Bertie'll be king now, an' I reckon he'll not make a good 'un. He's cut from't same cloth as wa' Jeb Lockwood – a gambler an' a womaniser.'

'Aye, t'papers said it wa' his bad behaviour that drove Prince Albert to an early death,' May said with a shake of her head. 'An' now he's bahn to rule England, God help us.'

'Aye, t'papers call him the playboy prince. He's never wi'out a woman in his bed.'

'An' it dun't matter whether they're prostitutes, actresses or sum'dy else's wife.'

The young mill hands pricked up their ears at the tasty bits of gossip.

'He dun't sound fit to be king,' one lad commented, 'but his mother wa' a proper queen.'

'I read that she asked for her little Pomeranian dog called Turi to be brought to her at the last minute,' Lizzie Holt proudly informed them. A member of Verity's reading class, she was eager to let them know that she could read the newspapers.

'It's ever so sad, isn't it?' May sniffed back tears.

'Sad be buggered. She wa' eighty-one. She had a bloody good innings if you ask me.' Lily Cockhill stubbed out her cigarette as the mill hooter called them back to work.

Verity had been listening to their conversation and when dinner time was over, she went to the baling room and unearthed four large bales of black serge that had yet to be put on the market. Black garments now being the order of the day for many of the late queen's subjects, and possibly for several months by true royalists, she immediately contacted Levi Ruddiman, a Jewish tailor with several garment factories in Bradford and Leeds. He bought the lot.

The day was rewarding in more ways than one, but by six o'clock, as the workers made their noisy way out of the dark mill yard, Verity felt the need to be with her children. Closing the ledger in which she had been entering neat columns of figures, she turned to Oliver and said, 'I'm missing my babies. Let's go home.'

The frost that earlier in the day had rimed the roads had hardened, patches of black ice causing the little pony pulling the trap to step gingerly up Somerset Road. Although Verity was wrapped in her heavy, grey woollen coat with an astrakhan collar and her head covered with a thick, felt cloche hat, she was shivering by the time they reached Almondbury village. Oliver, his hands in stout leather gloves and the collar of his black overcoat turned up to his ears under his black bowler, carefully steered the trap into Westgate and past All Hallows church, its Gothic tower rearing up into a sky lit by a pale moon and handful of brittle stars. Lamps glowed behind the curtained windows of the houses lighting the way, but as the pony strained in its harness up the steep incline of Far View Hill, they were plunged into darkness.

When they arrived back at the house, Verity almost leapt from the trap and rushed indoors, straight upstairs to the nursery.

Mary placed two fingers against her lips as Verity entered the room. 'They're sleeping,' she whispered.

Verity couldn't hide her dismay. 'Did they miss me?'

'Not so's you'd notice, Madam. They've been as good as gold all day,' Mary replied as she gathered up tiny garments to take down to the laundry room. 'An' guess what. Master Blaise pulled himself up by the chair an' stood on his own two feet. Took two wobbly steps, he did.' Mary giggled. 'Just for a minute or so, he looked ready to run.'

The stab of envy and deep disappointment caught Verity under her ribs. She should have been here to witness her son's first steps. Tiptoeing over to stand between the two cribs, she looked at her son then at her daughter. Briony was curled up in a ball, her tiny fists tucked beneath her chin, but Blaise was lying on his back, his sturdy limbs outstretched. His eyes were closed, long, dark lashes feathering his cheeks, but Verity knew they were the brightest blue. Verity's heart swelled with overwhelming love for both of her children, but deep inside, she had to admit that the warm and tender love she felt for her little girl was different to the fiercely passionate love she felt for her son.

Oliver padded softly into the room and gazed into first one crib then the other, and seeing that his children were sleeping, he said, 'Best not to disturb them.' Looking at his wife then nodding his head at the door to indicate that they should leave, he left the room as quietly as he had entered, but Verity lingered by Blaise's crib.

'If they waken before my husband and I retire for the night, don't hesitate to bring them down to us,' Verity told Mary, and still feeling aggrieved at what she had missed, she added, 'I sorely missed them today, and whilst I'm sure they were perfectly happy with you, I've realised that being away from them for a whole day doesn't suit me.'

Mary smiled. 'Whatever you think best, Madam,' she said, heading for the door and the laundry room in the basement.

Even after Mary had left the nursery, Verity stayed for a while, willing her son and daughter to waken and need her. When they didn't, she went down to the dining room, where Oliver was waiting for her to join him for their evening meal. As Clara served them with lamb chops and cabbage, Oliver remarked that it had been perfectly 'all right' to leave the children in Mary's capable hands for the day.

Verity gave him an almost contemptuous look and, her tone verging on disbelief, she said, 'Blaise stood and took his first steps today, and *I* wasn't here to see it. There's nothing right about that, Oliver. In future, I'll only go to the mill for an hour or two now and then.'

Oliver saw her disappointment. 'A wise decision, my dear. The children's needs are more important than the mill.' He gave a wide, proud smile. 'So, the little chap took his first steps. I wouldn't have minded seeing that for myself,' he said, saluting with his glass of port.

'And so would I,' Verity replied with feeling, and resigned herself to letting her beloved mill take second place for the foreseeable future. Her children must come first.

* * *

On the day of Queen Victoria's funeral, Lockwood Mill, along with all the other factories and shops in the town, closed for business. Verity and Oliver commemorated the occasion by going to the service in St Paul's Church and later, with their children, to Greenhead Park to listen to the brass band. As Verity looked round at the crowds of mourners, the better off in their best black suits and capes and dresses, she jested, 'I bet half the people here are wearing clothes made from our black serge.'

'Not those who can't afford to buy it,' Oliver replied. 'George told me that several of our hands had brought garments to the dyehouse to have them dyed black.'

'How respectful,' said Verity, then paused, thinking that many of her employees had few enough clothes, let alone having to dye those they had black. 'I wasn't aware of that.'

Her sharp, accusing tone had Oliver raising his eyebrows. The suggestion that he had somehow neglected to inform her of this irritated him, but this evening wasn't the time for confrontation. And acutely aware of his wife's struggle to come to terms with her divided allegiance between motherhood and the mill, he sugar-coated his reply.

'You were probably busy elsewhere, my dear.'

4

FAR VIEW HOUSE IN ALMONDBURY, JULY 1913

Verity lingered in the open French doors of the sitting room, the sun warm on her face and the clean, sweet smell of newly mown grass filling the air. The garden was at its best at this time of year. Tall ash trees bent by an easterly wind gave shelter to a riot of red and white roses, and heavy-headed peonies fluffed their petals over the splashes of brightly coloured asters in the borders around the lawn. On days like this, she was wont to ponder on how quickly the past thirteen years had flown. It seemed no time at all since she had fallen in love with Oliver, saved her mill from bankruptcy and become the mother of a son and a daughter. Raising her family and running the mill had given her a great deal of happiness.

Leant against the doorjamb, Verity could hear the lazy humming of bees in the lavender and the squeals and shouts of the children playing at the far end of the garden. Nearer to hand, she heard the voices of the grown-ups seated round the table on the lawn.

Oliver was gesticulating with both hands as he described something to the men and women sitting with him, the words 'loom' and 'weaver' reaching Verity's ears and making her shake her head and smile wryly. Trust Oliver and Dolly, and Nellie and George to be talking about the mill whilst Theo sat patiently with his blond head rested on his hand under his chin and no doubt thinking about his own job as Sir Arnold Thornton's Land Agent at Thornton Hall. Mill talk didn't interest Theo.

Dreamily, Verity stayed where she was for a moment longer, appreciating the glorious weather, and thinking how pleasant it was to spend a Sunday afternoon in the garden in the company of good friends.

'Hey, Verity. Come here and settle an argument,' Dolly cried, the sun's rays catching her glorious red hair and turning it into a fiery halo as she turned her head and beckoned to her friend. 'Tell Oliver that it's nigh on impossible for a weaver to run four looms efficiently.'

Laughing, Verity crossed the lawn and sitting down at the table next to Oliver, she filled a glass with lemonade. 'It's Sunday afternoon, a day of rest, so we'll have no mill talk if you don't mind,' she said, fondling the dark curls that caressed the nape of her husband's neck.

'Well, if we've done with talking about looms, can we talk about something pleasant?' Theo glanced at Dolly. 'That means no mention of suffragettes.'

'You can't overlook the fact that Emmeline Pankhurst is still in jail and the government playing cat and mouse with the others by releasing them when they're sick then arresting them the minute they're well again,' Dolly said hotly.

Theo gave a loud groan.

'I still think of poor Emily Davison whenever anyone mentions horse racing,' Nellie said, ignoring Oliver and Theo's exasperated looks as she referred to the suffragette who had run in front of the King's horse at the Epsom Derby the previous June.

'She ruined a damned good day at the racing,' George commented.

'Trust you to say that.' Nellie scowled at her husband.

'Enough of that!' Oliver thumped the table. 'I agree that women must have the right to vote but to set fire to the cricket ground at Royal Tunbridge Wells was uncalled for, so we'll put an end to this topic of conversation. Agreed?' He looked from Verity to Dolly and Nellie.

'Fifty thousand women marched to Hyde Park to protest about the right to vote,' Dolly chirped, determined to get the last word.

'That's right,' Verity agreed. 'Some of them from our mill, Oliver.' She gave him a conciliatory smile. 'However, it is a dismal subject so let's be cheery and make plans for the Mill outing.'

'Good idea,' sighed Oliver, his relief patent. It was customary in the Colne Valley for the manufacturers to treat their employees to a day's outing, mainly at their own expense, although the mill hands contributed a penny each week throughout the year towards the cost.

'Where are you taking us this year then?' George asked as he poured himself a tumbler of lemonade from the large glass jug on the table.

'Barnsley. Locke Park. We've hired three chara-bancs. I would have liked to take them to Scarborough again,' Verity continued, 'but last time, they found the three-hour journey too long so they voted against it. Some of them have never travelled more than five miles from their own doorsteps, so I understand how they feel.'

'And Barnsley's less than an hour away,' Oliver added. 'We've done Roundhay Park twice, and canal trips to Mirfield and Marsden more times than I care to remember.'

'I enjoyed the picnics up on the moors. Scammonden's grand and Holme Moss's not bad but you need good weather, and you can't always rely on that,' George said.

The others nodded in agreement, fully aware that the Pennine moors could be bleak even in summer and that a washed-out picnic was no fun.

'Locke Park it is then,' said Dolly.

Verity was just about to praise the park's attributes when a tirade of raucous, angry shouting from the far end of the garden had them all turning their heads in that direction.

Blaise, thought Verity, wondering if she should have spelled it 'Blaze' in keeping with his fiery temper. He was bawling louder than any of the others as the children abandoned their makeshift game of tennis and made their way up the garden, squabbling noisily.

Briony was the first to reach their parents.

'Blaise is bossing us about all the time, and he doesn't play the game fairly,' she cried, dumping her elbows on the table then resting her flushed face in both hands as she looked at her father for his support.

Oliver felt a rush of love and sympathy. Briony Hardcastle had inherited her mother's best features. Her eyes were the same shade of grey, and her once red-gold hair had darkened to a light lustrous chestnut, but her diminutive frame favoured that of her maternal grandmother in that she was finely built and rather small for her thirteen years. Briony had grown up under the light of her twin brother and tended, like her mother, to be unsure of what people thought of her, but today, she was feeling brave in the company of Josh Beaumont and his younger sister, Sarah, and their cousins, Luke and Flora Armitage.

'He doesn't want the girls to play, and when we do, he hits the ball so hard, we don't have a chance to hit it back,' Briony continued, 'and he never once allowed Josh and Luke to win even when they did.' She turned and looked at Josh Beaumont and Luke Armitage, inviting them to add to her complaints.

They being visitors, and having been brought up to be respectful, exchanged wary glances with one another then with Blaise.

'What's all this about, Blaise?' Verity was frowning, but her tone was gentle.

Blaise shrugged and sneered. Verity looked away quickly. Then her eyes lit on Josh.

Josh was Dolly and Theo's eldest child, and like his father, he had a shock of blond hair and bright-blue eyes, the combination that many women craved. Quiet by nature, he liked roaming the countryside learning about plants and animals as he accompanied his father on his rounds of Sir Arnold's estate. And although he was a month older than Blaise, he was a good head shorter and of a much slighter build. He detested altercation as much as he disliked Blaise Hardcastle.

'He didn't agree with the way tennis should be played, Mrs Hardcastle.' Josh answered coolly and calmly, and at that moment, Verity wished that her son was more like him.

'That's because none of them know the proper rules,' Blaise yelled, flinging his racquet to the ground and looking daggers at his twin sister.

She swung round to face him and shouted, 'Yes, we do! But you kept changing the rules so that nobody else could win. You never give anybody else a thought. You always have to be the best.'

Briony's bravery was infectious.

'And he whacked Josh with his racquet,' Sarah volunteered.

'He wouldn't let me play at all.' Flora whined, 'and he would have hit Josh again if Luke hadn't stopped him.'

Luke Armitage, a stolid lad with dark-red hair and ruddy cheeks and the oldest of them by a couple of months, was seething inwardly. He itched to give Blaise a good kicking, but like his cousin, Theo, he held himself in check.

'What have you to say for yourself, Blaise?' Oliver fixed stern eyes on his son, his words so cutting, their delivery so sharp, they could have chipped ice. 'Did you spoil the game?' he asked, pushing back the lock of dark hair that flopped over his brow: a gesture that Verity had always found endearing, but now it angered her. Why was he speaking to their son like that before he'd heard his side of the story?

Blaise stared back, the stare verging on insolence. He was a dark, handsome boy who closely resembled his father in appearance, but whereas Oliver was patient and rational, Blaise was impetuous and given to thinking that he could do anything he so chose. Perhaps it was because he was unusually tall and broad for his age – or maybe it was because, like his mother, he had a love for acquiring knowledge through the books he read, a knowledge which he aired in a superior manner that frequently resulted in him irritating adults and his peers alike. This overt self-confidence and his enhanced stature often led to people who did not know him well into thinking that he was much older than his thirteen years. He liked that.

Now, Blaise continued to meet his father's gaze, his own unafraid as he said, 'Don't blame this on me. I can't help it if the others are too stupid and weak to play properly.'

Oliver sprang to his feet, his eyes blazing. 'You cheeky young pup! I'd a mind to give you a damned good—'

'Oliver! Please!' Verity's impassioned cry brought her husband up sharp. The other adults round the table watched passively, safe in the knowledge that their offspring wouldn't behave so badly, and Nellie feeling annoyed that Blaise had called her children stupid. But it wasn't the first time they'd witnessed such a scene; Blaise was notorious for riling Oliver and upsetting his mother, who had hastily placed herself between her husband and son.

'Blaise, dear, give the others a chance to play the game their way,' Verity appeased, at the same time wondering how it was that she had given birth to such a selfish, domineering child. At times like this, he reminded her of her father. Please God he wouldn't turn out to be another Jebediah Lockwood, she thought as she looked into her son's stubborn face. 'Now, I propose that you begin the game again and this time, play fairly.' She smiled from one child to the other. Five of them returned the smile.

'In that case, I'm not playing,' said Blaise. 'I'm going to my room to read.' He slouched towards the house.

Oliver exchanged an angry look with Verity.

'Good,' Briony declared. 'Now we can play what we want.' She picked up her racquet and ran to the end of the garden. The other youngsters trailed after her.

Verity's troubled eyes followed her son's departing back and she wondered why it was that she had such a positive rapport with the young boys who worked for her in the mill yet she didn't seem capable of having the same with her own son.

'Sometimes, I don't know where we got him from.' Verity looked helplessly at Dolly.

They had been staunch allies since first they met

when Dolly had worked at Lockwood Mill. Now they were the best of friends and shared their families' joys and woes like sisters.

'Goodness knows what he's going to be like when he's eighteen,' Verity continued, glancing from one friend to another in the hope that they would tell her she was worrying unnecessarily.

Theo obliged. 'He'll most likely grow out of it,' he opined. 'A bit of discipline is what he needs.'

'We've tried that already,' Oliver growled. 'It only makes him more pig-headed.'

They would have continued discussing how best to deal with Blaise had not a plump woman in her thirties appeared in the basement kitchen doorway. Her booming voice resounded across the lawn. 'Your tea'll be ready in ten minutes, Mrs Hardcastle.'

Oliver grimaced, and Dolly said, 'I see you've still not managed to train her.'

'Thank you, Bella. That will be lovely,' Verity called back, and turning to Dolly, she said, 'I've given up on that. What she lacks in finesse she makes up for with her marvellous cooking, and she has the patience of a saint.' She turned to her husband. 'Will you go and round up the children?'

Oliver set off for the bottom of the garden and Verity, Dolly and Nellie walked with Theo and

George towards the house and the open French doors.

Back in the kitchen, Bella Balmforth, cook and housekeeper, checked the side oven in which was a large cheese and onion pie that would go with the home-grown salad stuff that her father, Bert Medley, grew in the kitchen garden. On Sundays, the Hardcastles always had a roast-beef dinner served with Yorkshire pudding and vegetables at midday when they returned from church, and high tea in the evenings.

Bella liked working for the Hardcastles. They were kind, thoughtful people, never demanding too much, and they paid fair wages. Her parents, Clara and Bert Medley, had worked for the hateful Jebediah Lockwood from before Verity was born and Clara had looked after Verity before she had been sent away to boarding school and then to live with relatives. Bella frequently acknowledged that theirs had been a tough job compared with her own. Bert had regularly suffered the indignities Jeb subjected him to on the nights he had to carry him home, drunken and raving, and her mother had cleaned up the mess he'd made. Jeb Lockwood had been monster.

But there was none of that now. Oliver Hardcastle

was a decent, sober man and his wife the soul of kindness. Bella had taken over her mother's role as cook and general servant shortly after the twins' fifth birthdays, and with only a family of four to attend to and her own daughter, Susan, to help with the household chores and assist Verity with the children, life was easy.

Verity had been adamant that her son and daughter would not be sent away to boarding school as she herself had, and now they attended the local village schools. Miss Briony was no bother at all, but in Bella's opinion, her brother was altogether a different kettle of fish.

'You'd better go and tell Master Blaise his tea's ready,' she said to her daughter. 'He stamped up to his room a while ago in a right temper.'

Susan pulled a face. 'Spoiled rotten, that's what he is. A bloody good slap 'ud soon sort him out but the mistress's dead against that. I'll bet there are times when Mr Hardcastle itches to give him a good hiding.'

'Mind your tongue, Susan. It's up to them how they rear their children,' warned Bella, lifting the pie from the oven. 'But you're right in what you say. Miss Briony's a lovely little thing, but that lad upstairs will give 'em grief, mark my words.' She put the pie on the table with a thud. 'Off you go an' give him his marching orders.'

Susan ran up the back staircase. On the landing, she banged her fist against the door of Blaise's bedroom and strutted in uninvited. 'Your tea's ready,' she snarled.

Blaise was sprawled on his bed, reading. Without raising his eyes from the page, he said, 'Bring mine up here.'

'I will not,' Susan retorted. 'Your mother doesn't allow it.' *And I'm not skivvying for you when there's no need for it*, she told herself.

'I'm not coming down,' Blaise drawled, rolling over and tossing the book aside.

'Suit yourself. It's either that, or starve.'

Turning on her heel, Susan marched out and hurried down the main staircase into the hall just in time to see Verity leading her guests into the dining room. She debated whether or not to report that Blaise was refusing to come down, then dismissed the thought. She had little patience with the brat. Let him stew in his own juice.

A clatter of feet on the basement stairs heralded the arrival of Oliver and the other children. 'They washed their hands in the kitchen,' Oliver told Verity as they met in the hall. 'Where's Blaise?'

'He must still be up in his room. I'll go and fetch him,' said Verity as the others took their seats in the dining room.

Susan skipped down the basement stairs, wondering if his mother would have more success than she'd had.

'Blaise, darling, tea is ready,' Verity said as she entered his bedroom. 'Don't keep everyone waiting.'

Blaise deliberated between staying where he was or satisfying his rumbling belly. Hunger won and he rolled off the bed and onto his feet.

Verity breathed a sigh of relief. Thank goodness she hadn't had to beg. That all too often led to a nasty argument, and just lately, she'd had far too many with her son. She loved him passionately but she could not deny that he was a difficult boy.

Before he followed her to the door, he stopped at the large table in front of the window and moved two small, lead figures on the model battlefield. His collection of soldiers was his most prized possession and war games were his passion. He had already decided that one day, he was going to enlist in the army and fight. One day, he'd be a hero.

'I'm not sitting next to Josh or Luke, and I won't let them mess with my soldiers afterwards so don't ask me to,' Blaise said as they descended the stairs.

* * *

Later that evening, the Hardcastle children in bed and the visitors away to their own homes, Verity and Oliver were sitting on the couch in the drawing room, Verity's head resting on Oliver's shoulder. They had been discussing the mill, but as so often happened these days, the conversation turned to talking about Blaise. When it did, Verity sat up straight.

'That was very unsporting of him this afternoon, refusing to play with the others because he couldn't rule the roost,' Oliver said, getting to his feet and going over to the sideboard. He poured whisky into a tumbler. 'Would you like a sherry, dear?'

Verity said yes. Just lately, she often felt the need for a fortifying drink when they were discussing Blaise's behaviour. 'He's growing up so fast, poor darling. Thirteen's a difficult age. And being so much more mature than the others, he holds the opinion that he knows best,' she said, at the same time very aware that she was making excuses for him.

'He didn't show any sign of maturity when he stormed off to his room, or later when he wouldn't let Josh and Luke have a game with his soldiers.'

'Blaise has nothing in common with them. They're made of very different stuff.'

'Indeed, they are. They're mannerly and biddable whereas our boy is boorish and arrogant.' Oliver sounded weary and heavily disappointed. 'Where did we go wrong, Verity?'

'He's always been boisterous,' she said, feeling her husband's disappointment but loath to compare Blaise with Josh and Luke, and find him wanting. 'It's because he's so big for his age, and always has been. Maybe we expect too much from him. Why, only the other day, I overheard the postman asking him if he liked helping you run the mill. He looked shocked when Blaise told him he was only thirteen.' Her eyes moistened as she spoke.

'Maybe you're right. He's still a child inside, and perhaps we're to blame for his unpleasant behaviour. We've been too easy on him.' Oliver gulped a mouthful of whisky then swallowed it too quickly, the raw spirit burning his throat and making him cough. 'What do you think to sending him to boarding school? There are some—'

He got no further. Verity's horrified gasp became a wail. 'How could you contemplate such a thing?'

Oliver took a deep breath. 'As I was saying... there are good schools not too far away that would instil some discipline into him at the same time as giving him a good education.'

'Cold, cruel places full of bullies,' retorted Verity, her voice sharp and bitter.

'I think Blaise would be perfectly capable of standing up to them,' Oliver replied calmly, and thinking that it would be Blaise doing the bullying.

Verity set her glass down hard on the side table, sherry slopping onto its polished surface. 'I'm not going to discuss this any further. It's disgusting.' She sprang to her feet and glared into Oliver's face. 'I will not allow you to send our son away from home to live with strangers who care nothing for him. I know what it's like, and as long as I have breath in my body, he will stay here with his family who love him.' She swivelled on her heels and barged to the door. 'I'm going to bed.' The door slammed behind her.

Oliver ran his fingers through his hair then wiped his hand over his jaw. They rarely quarrelled, and when they did, it was, more often than not, about the way in which they should deal with Blaise. Slugging at his whisky, Oliver silently acknowledged that much of the blame for that lay squarely on his own shoulders. All too often, he'd allowed his love for Verity to cloud his judgement. He loved his son but he wasn't blind to his shortcomings – as was his wife – and it was up to him to do something about it.

Oliver wasn't a weak man. He stood fast in the face of adversity, firm in his beliefs. He was of the opinion that every person should be valued for themselves, and had proved that time and again in the running of Lockwood Mill. He had always made sure that the workers were treated fairly, and had fought with Jeb to ensure they always received their wages even when the old mill master had been bleeding the business dry to feed his lust for drink and gambling. But, over the years, Oliver, always mindful of Verity's own heartless rearing, had restrained himself from dealing with the boy as he saw fit, and he deeply regretted not taking a firmer stance. Had he done so, then they would not now be at loggerheads with one another. As he paced the floor, he also shamefully acknowledged that by sending Blaise to boarding school, he would be avoiding the task and leaving it to another man to discipline his son. This did not sit easily with him, but he was convinced it was for the best. However, he knew of old that Verity rarely gave in when she was presented with something she didn't agree with, and that her conviction to do the right thing was often stronger than his own.

He sipped reflectively on the remains of his whisky, remembering how in the early days of working together to save Lockwood Mill, she had fought to achieve the things she believed in. Things that he had thought were reckless and too costly: the extra day's holiday at Christmas for the mill hands, the canteen, the reading and sewing classes and other notions she'd had. They had all come about because she had insisted on them, and the mill had benefitted from them, the workers appreciating her thoughtfulness and repaying her with conscientious effort and loyalty.

He emptied his glass. Perhaps she was right, he thought, as he made his way to the door. Blaise should stay at home and he, Oliver, would spend more time with the boy, and gently but firmly instil respect for others and good manners into him. To let him grow up lacking those qualities was just as bad as letting him believe he could do as he pleased. Blaise had to learn how the world worked before he could find his own place in it, and it was a good father's responsibility to teach him. Exactly how he would go about it, Oliver wasn't sure. Dowsing the drawing-room lights, he climbed the stairs, his tread heavy with disappointment.

The bedroom was in darkness. Oliver undressed and climbed into bed. Verity turned her back on him, her tense shoulders letting him know she was still angry with him.

Across the corridor, tossing and turning between the sheets, Blaise was in the desert fighting a horde of Moorish tribesmen. He had wiped out most of them with his trusty sword but one ferocious-looking Arab was bearing down on him, his robes swirling and his scimitar raised. Blaise fell back, sinking into the sand, and his sword was ripped from his hand by the slashing scimitar. He woke with a start.

Covered in sweat and his heart clamouring, he lifted his trembling hands to his neck. His head was still in place. Gradually, his breathing slowed and he lay listening to the night sounds of the house: the slam of a door, heavy footsteps on the stairs, and the gurgle of water in the pipes. After a while, sleep evading him, he slipped out of bed and went over to the table under the window – his battlefield.

He had covered the table with a stiff piece of thick, brown paper on which he had drawn the contours of land in green and brown. Then he'd made hills from scrunched-up painted paper and stuck twigs into them to simulate trees behind which his soldiers could take cover. Listlessly, he began to move the little lead figures, reminded that earlier when tea was over, he had stubbornly refused to let Josh and Luke touch them. In his mind's eye, he saw Josh bite down on his lip to hide his disappointment as he had silently left the room. Luke had just shrugged then trailed after him.

In Blaise's opinion, Luke Armitage was a lumpish bore, and his sister, Flora, was too young for him to even consider. He didn't dislike Josh, or Sarah for that matter, and he loved Briony, but he was tired of being expected to play silly, childish games with puny girls and dull or soft-hearted boys when all he wanted was to let off steam on a rough and tumble battlefield. By now, he'd put blue-coated infantrymen to the front, Royal Welch Fusiliers behind them, and guardsmen in their bright-red jackets to the rear. Gaily painted Highlanders in their kilts flanked them on the left and to the right of them were the lancers on horseback. He picked up his favourite: a cavalryman on a sleek, black, high-stepping horse. Blaise loved the way the cavalryman's right arm could be raised and lowered and now he moved it so that his sword was aloft. Placing him carefully on his rectangular base at the front of all his troops, Blaise was ready to do battle.

But his eyes were drooping and he was feeling cold. Shivering, he climbed back into bed and snuggled down under the blankets. One day, he would be the bravest, most heroic soldier in the king's army, he told himself as he drifted into sleep.

In their large double bed with ornate brass and iron ends, Oliver gently clasped Verity's shoulder, attempting to turn her to face him. She resisted, her body rigid and her breathing pent. He nuzzled the nape of her neck, the sweet scent of her hair and warm skin arousing him and making him desperate to make his peace with her. Placing his hand on her hip, he moved it up and down in slow, soothing strokes.

He didn't think that his suggestion to send Blaise to boarding school was wrong, but he understood Verity's fears. Hers had been a grim childhood. Separated from her home and her parents and never having the love of either, she was committed to making sure that Blaise and Briony would never experience such pain.

He continued to stroke his wife's arm, and as he did so, he recalled how unworldly and innocent Verity had been when first he knew her. Now she was a confident businesswoman, a wife and mother, and whilst he respected her opinions and wanted her happiness, he had to make her see sense where Blaise was concerned.

'Don't let us go to sleep on a quarrel, Verity. We promised we would never do that,' Oliver whispered against the back of her head.

She didn't reply but he felt the tension easing from her body under his hand. Slowly, she turned so that her face was within an inch of his. He brushed his lips against hers.

When they first shared this bed, Verity had been terrified that she wouldn't know how to please her husband. Oliver had been gentle and patient. As her confidence in her own sexuality grew, she, like him, had become sensitive, generous and sensual and they still took great delight in satisfying each other's needs, their lovemaking always precious. Now, she felt her body thrill to his touch but she wasn't to be bought so easily.

'I won't allow you to send Blaise to boarding school,' she said.

'I know you won't,' Oliver replied softly then placed his lips on hers, his kiss passionate.

Verity couldn't help but respond. It wasn't right that they should quarrel over their son. They mustn't let the difficult patch they were going through do irreparable harm to their marriage. They'd work together to put matters right, just as they did at the mill. She turned on her back and as Oliver's lean frame covered hers, she raised her hips to meet his and gave herself up to the pleasures of the flesh.

5

ASPLEY BASIN, HUDDERSFIELD, AUGUST 1913

On a glorious sunny Saturday morning three charabancs waited outside Lockwood Mill's gate ready to take the mill hands on their annual outing. Standing in the cobbled mill yard, Verity watched the noisy crowd swell as latecomers rushed to join it, their faces breaking into relieved smiles when they saw they had arrived in time. Dressed in their best, they were going to Locke Park in Barnsley for a day of fun and leisure.

At the rear of one of the charabancs, Dolly, who had helped Verity organise the outing, was over-seeing the loading of picnic baskets and cardboard boxes that were piled high with sandwiches, buns and cakes that the women who ran the mill's canteen had prepared first thing. Crates filled with bottles of Tetley's Pale Ale for the men, and Mackeson's Milk Stout for the ladies, along with Vimto and Ben Shaw's lemonade for the teetotallers, were being loaded into another.

'Thank God it's not raining,' Dolly said to Verity when she came to ask if things were going according to plan.

'We're being blessed,' Verity replied with feeling, the months of June and July having been exceedingly wet. 'I prayed for it not to be a washout.'

'Well, it looks as though He listened for once,' said Dolly, raising her gaze to a blue sheet of sky before adding, 'And we'll not be needing these if the weather holds.' She patted the rolled-up canvas at the back of the open-topped vehicle that would be unrolled to protect the passengers should they be caught in a downpour. 'Now, as far as I know, everything's been loaded so all we need to do is get this lot aboard and we'll be off.' She waved a hand at the men and women who, chattering in loud excited voices, waited impatiently to be on their way.

'It'll be like herding sheep,' Verity said as, turning to her employees and her voice ringing with authority, she called out, 'Right! Everybody, take your seats.'

The eager passengers surged towards one or

other of the charabancs, friendly arguments breaking out as to who would sit where and with whom, and whether it was to be at the back or the front. As they squashed onto the long, wooden, low-backed benches, Verity and Dolly exchanged amused glances like mothers did over their brood of unruly children. Charabancs weren't known for comfort but today nobody seemed to care.

Satisfied that the workers were all on board, they walked to the one at the front, and as they did so, Dolly ran an admiring eye over her friend's outfit. 'And might I say, Mrs Hardcastle, that today, you're looking absolutely in the pink.'

Verity laughed at the old adage, her cheeks almost matching the colour of her silk, short-sleeved, square-necked summer dress trimmed with grey lace. Its slender skirt sheathed her tall figure beautifully, and a grey, wide-brimmed hat sporting pink feathers lent an air of frivolity to her overall appearance.

'Why, thank you, Mrs Beaumont,' Verity gushed, her barely concealed mockery making Dolly giggle. 'And might I also say, you yourself look charmingly nautical. Did you think we were taking a cruise on the canal?' She playfully flicked the corners of the white sailor collar edged in blue at the neck of Dolly's blouse.

Laughing out loud, Dolly playfully clapped her hand on the crown of the straw boater that was perched on top of her fiery-red curls and did a twirl. The sleeves of her white blouse billowed and her blue and white striped skirt flared out as she performed her version of a sailor's hornpipe.

Verity caught Dolly's hand and jigged with her, at the same time saying, 'We're keeping everybody waiting. We need to get a move on.'

'Then it's anchors aweigh, captain. All aboard for Locke Park,' Dolly bawled, her green eyes flashing with merriment as the mill hands roared their appreciation at the two women's antics. Verity and Dolly obliged with another twirl before, hand in hand, they skipped over to where Theo was waiting patiently with their children.

It had been agreed that Blaise and Briony, as heirs to the mill, must accompany them, and that Josh and Sarah, along with George's children, Luke and Flora, should also be included. Taking charge, Verity shepherded the youngsters to the charabanc at the head of the line where seats at the front had been reserved for them. As the children clambered aboard, Oliver hurried out of the mill yard to join his wife and Dolly. He'd been checking that the boilers were damped down and the sheds were securely locked.

'Is everyone here? We don't want to leave anyone behind,' he asked just as George and Nellie Armitage appeared at his elbow.

'Aye, it looks like it. Me and Nellie have checked all the charas and ticked 'em off,' George told him, flourishing the list that contained the names of all the employees who had paid their dues and opted to go on the outing. As Master Dyer and Mrs Weaver, George and Nellie took their responsibilities seriously.

'And they were told we'd leave at nine sharp and it's twenty-past now,' Nellie said, 'so if they're not here by now, they'll not be coming. Them already here didn't seem to think anybody was missing.'

Oliver smiled at Nellie's long-winded explanation then shouted to the drivers who were standing smoking by the charabanc furthest from the gate. 'Right, lads. We're ready for off. Locke Park, and don't spare the horses.'

The drivers nicked their cigarettes and went to their respective vehicles.

What followed next was some shifting and scuffling as the children's parents organised who would sit where on the long benches. Verity and Oliver and Dolly and Theo sat on the front bench with Briony and Sarah. Behind them, George and Nellie sat with little Flora, Luke and Josh and Isaac Holroyd, the head tuner. It wasn't until Verity looked about her to make sure everyone was comfortable that she realised Blaise wasn't amongst them.

'Where's Blaise?' she asked, her voice sounding slightly panicked.

Josh gestured with his thumb. Blaise had taken himself to the back of the charabanc and was sitting with the young lads who worked at the mill.

Verity looked anxiously at Oliver, her eyes asking what they should do.

'Leave him,' Oliver growled. 'He's all right where he is.'

Once they were all settled, the drivers revved their engines and headed out into Wakefield Road. The traffic going in and out of the town was busy and slow-moving, the passengers jolted this way and that at a sudden stop or a quick start as the drivers negotiated their way from Aspley to Moldgreen, but they didn't care. Feeling like lords and ladies, the mill hands waved to passers-by and called out, 'We're off to Locke Park.' The envious bystanders smiled wistfully and waved back as the cavalcade of three charabancs bowled along Wakefield Road to Dalton then Waterloo, and out into the open countryside.

When they came to the water meadows at Fenay Bridge, Verity gave a wistful little smile and asked Oliver, 'Do you remember when we brought the children to picnic here when they were small? We haven't done that in a long time.'

Oliver said yes, he remembered, and sighed. He knew Verity was disappointed that Blaise had chosen not to sit with them, and it annoyed him; trust the lad to spoil her day.

The mill hands craned their necks as the chara-bancs trundled through the little village of Shelley and then onto Shepley. As they drove past The Sovereign Inn, a well-known watering hole, they cheered; they were halfway to their destination.

'Pity we got here before opening time,' a burly carder shouted. 'I could murder a pint.'

At the back of the charabanc, out of earshot of his family and their friends, Blaise was enjoying himself. He'd been given a tentative welcome by most of the young lads who worked in the carding room or at scouring and as doffers, but he being the boss's son made some of them feel uncomfortable. To ingratiate himself, Blaise adopted a rougher manner of speech, cursing every now and then as they did, and laughing raucously at the lewd remarks about the girls sitting close by.

'I quite fancy that one with the big tits,' Blaise said cockily. He pointed to a well-endowed girl with a mop of frizzy, fair hair.

'Oh, you'll get nowt from Jessie. She's as tight as t'thread on a bobbin,' an older lad sneered. 'An' anyway, you're too young for her.'

'Aye, but he's t'bosses son. She might be tempted for a bob or two.'

Blaise puffed out his chest and sat back, enjoying the banter. Further down the charabanc, the older mill hands were chatting happily.

'I'm glad we're only going as far as Locke Park,' Mona Hepplethwaite confided in Bertha Strong. 'It'll nobbut tek an hour to get there. Last year, when we went to Scarborough, I wa' dyin' for a pee long afore we got to York.'

'Aye, so wa' I,' Gertie agreed. 'Me bladder's not what it used to be, but I'll not have to worry about that today. An' it's a lovely day for it after all t'rain we've had.'

'Aye, if t'sun keeps on shinin' like this, I'm bahn to tek me stockin's off an' tuck me skirt into me knickers. Get some sun to me legs,' Lily Cockhill informed them.

'I should think you're not, Lily,' Maggie Broadbent objected. 'We don't want you shamin' us in front o' them Barnsley folk.'

'I don't give a bugger what them from Barnsley think,' Lily shouted back.

'Somebody told me there's a lake there,' Mary Booth said, 'an' if there is, I'm goin' for a paddle, so I'll be tuckin' me skirts up an' all.'

'Be careful you don't drown, Mary,' one of the lads called out.

'I'll drown thee afore I drown mesen, you cheeky young bugger,' she called back.

When some of the boys lit cigarettes and dragged on them like old troopers, Blaise ached to do the same. But, afraid of his parents suddenly turning their attention to him, he had to forego the offer of a Park Drive or a Woodbine. Even so, he felt awfully grown up, and as the lads told jokes and swapped titbits of information about the girls they fancied, Blaise imagined that this was what it would be like when he joined the army.

The charabancs cruised through Upper Denby then Cawthorne, May Sykes enviously cooing, 'Eeh, it 'ud be lovely to live out here,' as they sailed past pretty cottages with tangles of roses round the doors and bright borders of marigolds edging the little front gardens. A rumble of agreement met her remark. The mill hands, used to living in the densely populated streets built in the shadows of huge mills, gazed out over the fields as they travelled through Hoyland Swaine and on to Silkstone.

'I'd not want to live too close to one o' them,' Nellie said, pointing to a monstrous mountain of detritus that loomed threateningly behind a row of small terrace houses black with coal dust. The mill hands, their curiosity aroused, stared at the giant slag heaps and the stark, towering structures of the collieries' pithead winding gear for now they were in the heart of the coal-mining district, and for most of the day-trippers, this was foreign territory. For some it was the furthest they had been away from home.

Lily Cockhill started to sing 'Be My Little Baby Bumble Bee' and everyone joined in. Then, the mood catching, they sang 'Everybody's Doing It' and 'Who Were You With Last Night?'

Verity smiled as Oliver's rich baritone voice rang in her ear, and telling herself she was being foolish by worrying about Blaise, she buried her disappointment; today was for enjoyment in the company of people she loved.

They were still singing when they reached Dodworth.

'Not far now,' the driver called out and the singing petered to a stop as heads turned this way and that. The charabancs chugged up Keresworth Hill and when they drove through Locke Park's impressive gateway, a resounding cheer went up from everybody on board.

* * *

'Isn't this just perfect?' Dolly was sitting with Verity's and her own family on rugs spread out under the shade of a huge horse chestnut tree. Beside them were the wicker hampers that Bella and Susan had filled and that were now rapidly emptying as the hungry men, women and children helped themselves to ham, cheese or egg and cress sandwiches, butterfly buns and ginger biscuits. In front of where they were lounging was a huge expanse of green sward now dotted with groups of happy mill hands also enjoying their picnics.

Oliver, his long, lithe frame stretched out on the rug, turned to the children sitting round about him and said, 'You all know about Stephenson's famous steam locomotive, don't you? Well, did you know that the man for whom this park is named was the driver of the "The Rocket" at the opening of the Liverpool and Manchester Railway.'

'They named this park after a train driver?' Blaise sounded surprised.

'He wasn't an ordinary train driver,' Theo informed them. 'He was a great engineer, up there with the likes of Stephenson and Brunel.'

'That's right, and this is where he lived,' Oliver continued. 'After his death, his wife, Phoebe, gave the land to the public in his memory. The inhabitants of Barnsley and those like us from further afield can now benefit from taking their leisure in the ornamental gardens and on long woodland walks, or on the boating lake.'

'Can we go and explore?' Briony's excited request spoke for all the youngsters except Flora. She never went far from Nellie's side. On hearing that they could, they leapt to their feet and ran towards a flight of shallow steps near to where they had been sitting. They led up to the circular domed tower that was over six-hundred feet tall and built in an eastern style. On reaching it, they dodged in and out of the classical columns that surrounded the tower's base then raced up the spiral stone staircase to the two observation balconies above.

Blaise, having parted with his cronies from the

carding shed to eat lunch with his family, crept up behind his sister and pretended to try and push her over the balcony's balustrade. Briony looked down from the dizzying height and shrieked.

'No, Blaise! Don't!'

'Just kidding,' he said, laughing and letting her wriggle free to run over to where Sarah, Josh and Luke were gazing out over the distance and the boys trying to name the places they could see. Bored, Blaise sauntered to the spiral stairs and went down. When the others went to follow, they found him blocking their way at a narrow twist in the staircase.

'Oh, for goodness' sake, let us past,' snapped Briony, who was leading the way.

'Don't be a spoilsport,' Sarah shouted.

'Come on, Blaise. Don't act the fool,' Josh cajoled.

Blaise gave an ugly laugh that turned into a squawk as Luke, shouldering his way past the other three, gave him an almighty shove that sent him reeling down the steps. Blaise seethed as he followed them out of the tower.

'Over here,' Oliver called out as they approached. 'You're just in time to run in the fourteens and under.' The races were always part of the annual outing and a straggling line of boys were already waiting to be off. Josh and Luke took their places. Blaise cast an eye over the competition. Some of the twenty or so runners were small for their age and looked under-nourished, and only a few were as tall as himself. Smiling smugly, he strutted to join them. He'd show them and his father who was best.

George raised his right arm. 'On your marks. Get set. Go,' he shouted.

The crowds on the sidelines cheered and urged their favourites on as the boys, legs flying and arms pumping, surged down the field. Blaise tore down the grassy track, running for all he was worth. A swift glance to left and right told him that he was in the lead, and sure of victory, he laughed out loud and his pace slackened. Too late, he felt the rush of air as a lad built like a whippet raced past him and over the finishing line, Josh hot on his heels. Stunned, Blaise came to an abrupt halt, only to be barged in the shoulder by Luke, who shambled past to finish third.

Theo declared the boy from the scouring room as the winner, Josh second and Luke third. They stood to collect their prizes from Verity. 'Well done, lads,' she said, casting a deeply sympathetic smile in her son's direction. Blaise, feeling utterly crushed, skulked off in the direction of the woods. His mother saw him go, her heart aching for him. She had so hoped he would win and be happy. She wanted to run after him, but it was her duty to spectate the older lads and mens' races, so she watched them disconsolately then forced a smile and a few words of congratulation as she handed the winners their rewards: bars of Fry's chocolate cream for the younger competitors, and ten cigarettes for the men. When it came to the women's turn, she who had always taken part in the past pleaded a headache, and declined.

'I'm sorry to hear that,' said Dolly, 'but it'll give me a better chance of winning.' And picking up the hem of her blue and white striped skirt, she took her place then raced down the field to finish a close second behind Maggie Broadbent.

The racing over, the mill hands went off to explore the park, the more adventurous opting to take a boat out on the lake. Verity and her party strolled along the Serpentine Walk and through the grounds, admiring the ornamental gardens and the statuary. When they came to the ABC steps, Briony and Sarah exclaimed their delight. The flight made from shallow stone slabs had the letters from A to Z carved into each tread and the girls ran up then down, singing the alphabet as they went. At the foot of the steps was a massive granite boulder. Josh and Luke, still on a high after their achievements in the running race and emboldened by the praise of their respective parents, took turns leaping on top of it and shouting, 'I'm the king of the castle!' Then they chased the girls round it, their merry laughter painful to Verity's ears. *Blaise should be with them.*

Blaise had walked through the trees until he came across some of the boys he had sat with on the charabanc. They were each armed with stout sticks and playing a game that was something akin to sword fighting. Blaise picked up a sturdy end of a branch and joined in. This was more like it. Brandishing his weapon, he lashed out at an opponent, who fought back valiantly until his stick split in two. For the next hour, Blaise was neither bored nor miserable. Adrenaline flowed as, yelling and lunging, the boys battled until they were exhausted. They threw themselves down in the bracken and lit cigarettes. When Blaise was offered a Park Drive, he accepted and laid with his back against a tree, puffing like an old hand, and trying his best not to cough.

All too soon, the fun and games and the exploration of what the park had to offer came to an end as Oliver and Theo strode around signalling that it was time to go. 'It's like herding sheep,' Oliver commented, unaware that he was echoing the very same words his wife had used at the outset of the trip as he chivvied a reluctant gaggle of mill hands across the grass to the driveway where the charabancs waited.

'The only difference being that sheep follow one another,' Theo replied, breaking away to chase after a gang of young lads heading in the wrong direction. Eventually, from all parts of the estate, the weary but happy mill hands gathered, ready to make the homeward journey.

'It's been a lovely day,' Bertha declared. 'I feel right rested for it.'

'I could live in a place like this,' Mona rhapsodised.

'Aye, them gardens are magnificent,' said Isaac. 'Did you see t'size o' them chrysanths?'

'I did. I can't grow owt like that i' my back yard,' a man from the dyehouse complained. 'And did you see t'size of his statue? That chap Locke must o' been important.'

'He must if he lived in a house wi' a garden what has a lake in it.'

At the mention of the lake, Lily cried, 'I thought we wa' goin' to sink when we wa' in t'middle of it. That little boat wa' no wider than my arse, an' it wa' dippin' up an' down summat shockin'.'

'Aye, she thought she wa' aboard *Titanic*,' her husband joshed.

'That wa' no laughing matter, an' nowt to joke about,' Isaac said sombrely. 'Over a thousand people lost their lives.'

The memory of the unsinkable ship that had collided with an iceberg the previous year caused a lull in the chatter, but only for moment.

'I had a drink from that lovely big water fountain, and do you know, the water tasted better than that what comes through our taps in Maple Street,' said May Sykes.

'Aye, but I'll bet it didn't taste as good as a pint. I wa' cravin' for one after winnin' that race, but all t'beer wa' finished,' whined a long-legged fellow from the baling room.

'You had your bloody share of it afore t'race, Syd,' a voice reminded him.

Syd spun round, aggrieved. 'I din't see thee wi'out a bottle in thi hand,' he snarled, but before a fight could break out, the order came to board the charabancs.

Verity's anxious eyes ranged over the crowd. Where was Blaise? *Please God, don't let us have to go searching for him,* she prayed, knowing that Oliver would be angry if they had to. It was followed by a huge sigh of relief when she saw Blaise ambling towards her. Dirty and dishevelled, he came to her side.

'Whatever have you been up to?'

'Having the best time, Ma,' he chortled, and tucking his arm into hers, he rested his head against her shoulder. The loving gesture made her heart swell. She breathed in the earthy, smoky smell of him and stroked his tousled hair. When he raised his gaze to meet hers, she saw that he really did seem happy. She'd been worrying needlessly.

They climbed aboard the charabanc, and to Verity's delight, Blaise opted to sit next to her and they chatted amiably about the things they had seen and done in Locke Park, Blaise deliberately omitting to mention the fight and the smoking in the forest.

The shadows lengthened and the heat went out of the day as they journeyed back to Huddersfield. The mill hands, much quieter than they had been on the outward journey, were content to talk amongst themselves or doze, their energy spent.

Verity turned to Oliver. 'It's been a perfect day, hasn't it?'

Oliver nodded and said, 'May we have many more of them, my dear.'

6

HUDDERSFIELD, SPRING 1914

The summer faded into a glorious autumn then a mild winter, and life in the Colne Valley was going on apace. In the last months of the previous year, trade in the cloth-making industry had been slack, but things were steadily improving and much to Oliver and Verity's delight, the mill had received several new orders for the worsted cloth they wove. This also pleased the mill hands who had been working short time, their wages drastically reduced when they were laid off for one or two days each week.

'Thank God we're back workin' full-time,' Lily Cockhill said to Maggie Broadbent as they entered the weaving shed one Monday morning in April. 'I got behind wi' me rent an' that mucky bugger of a landlord told me I'd have to square it with him some other way if I didn't pay up.'

'Oh, aye. Did he want you to lean over t'sink an' lift your skirts? Me mam used to do that when she wa' behind wi' t'rent,' Maggie replied as she tied a turban over her greasy, black hair, and not in the least fazed by divulging the gross but not unknown manner in which desperate women got by in hard times.

'Course he bloody did, but I saw him off rightly, an' now I don't owe him a brass farthing,' Lily said, savagely tying the strings of her pinny. 'They're all the bloody same, them landlords. May Sykes told me that him what owns them houses in Rose Street wa' dippin' his wick every day comin' up to Christmas an' tellin' them women what live there he'd turn 'em out if they didn't let him have his way.'

'That's downright wicked,' Maggie scorned and would have said more had not the mill hooter let out its piercing wail. The two tough, hard-working women hurried to their looms, thankful that now work was plentiful they didn't have to worry about where the next penny was coming from. Mrs Hard-castle had told them and all her employees that the mill had orders to see them through until autumn and that more were likely to come in as the year progressed so, as the grinding roar of machinery bounced off the weaving-shed walls and the shuttles flew back and forth, they were ready to fulfil them.

In the mill office, Verity, having dealt with the post that had arrived a short while ago, added yet another new order to the list in the ledger in front of her. Things were definitely looking up. She sat back, musing on how life appeared to be treating her and her family kindly. Blaise and Briony, having recently celebrated their fourteenth birthdays, were thriving, and although she sometimes worried about the long hours her son spent alone in his room, he was giving his parents little cause for concern. Briony, as usual, was her sweet, sunny self and whilst her mother did not feel the same fierce love for her daughter as she did for her son, she truly appreciated the happiness that Briony created.

Oliver stepped into the office, back from attending to a problem with the boilers. 'What's brought that smile to your face?' he asked when he saw the delightful curve of his wife's lips and the warm glow in her eyes.

'I was just thinking how lovely it is to have a daughter as wonderful as Briony,' she said.

Oliver gave a bemused grin. 'She is lovely, and

always has been,' he said, wondering if it was only now that Verity had come to realise what a blessing their sweet-natured daughter had always been. He'd loved her from the moment he had held her fragile little body in his arms, and there were times when he struggled to feel the same depth of love for his son. But then, he reminded himself, Blaise often gave him just cause. Even so, it troubled him.

'My mother always says that daughters give you their love for a lifetime, whereas sons give their hearts to another woman,' he said, knowing that this was true in his own case, and feeling confused as to where this conversation was leading.

'She would say that,' Verity replied tartly, as Oliver's two spinster sisters who still lived at home with Evelyn Hardcastle sprang to mind.

Oliver, eager to abandon a conversation about his mother and sisters, and the animosity his wife justifiably felt for them, said, 'I've fixed the boiler. It was a leaking valve.'

'Oh, well done,' Verity praised, and just as loath as Oliver to dwell on a subject that involved Evelyn Hardcastle and her daughters, she readily began discussing the boiler and other things concerning the mill.

'I'm interviewing two young girls later today. If they're suitable, I'll set them on in the weaving shed,' she said. 'One of them is the girl from Barnsley that Dolly's mother is taking in as a lodger. Apparently, the poor girl's family are experiencing hardship and she's coming to Huddersfield to find work. Dolly suggested I might find her useful here.' Verity stood and put on her jacket, ready to do the rounds of the mill.

Oliver wondered how he would feel if he had to send Briony away from home to help support her family. It wasn't a pleasant thought.

'It must be a terrible wrench for any mother to have to part with her daughter,' he said, but Verity had already left the office and was making her way across the mill yard.

* * *

'Goodbye then, love,' Amelia Skeldon said as she hugged her daughter for one last time.

'Don't forget an' write to let us know how you're settling in.'

'I won't,' Juliet promised, trying to hold back tears as she picked up the bag at her feet. 'The bus is coming,' she said, giving her mother a brave smile.

It was Monday morning, shortly after nine o'clock, and they were standing at the crossroads beside the war memorial in Dodworth, waiting for the bus that would take Juliet from the village on the outskirts of Barnsley to Moldgreen in Huddersfield. She gazed into Amelia's forlorn face, blinking through the tears that clung to her long, fair lashes. The bus trundled to a halt. 'So long then,' Juliet mumbled, and afraid to look back she climbed aboard. Amelia waved until the bus was out of sight.

Juliet took a seat at the front of the bus and when the conductor came to take her fare, she said, 'A single to Moldgreen, please.' He spun the handle on his ticket machine, the clickety-click rattling in Juliet's brain, and as the ticket popped out, she asked, 'Will you let me know when we get to... to Somerset Road? It's... it's near Huddersfield.'

The conductor, a chap with a big nose and a kind smile, heard the wobble in her voice. He smiled down into her anxious, pretty face. 'I will, love. I'll keep an eye on you.'

He went and stood on the platform and Juliet stared straight ahead as the bus continued on its journey. Minutes later, it arrived at Silkstone, a village she was familiar with because her aunt lived there. Two elderly men that she thought looked like farmers got off; *they must have been to the market in Barnsley*, she thought, and watched the conductor reach out to take a heavy basket from a woman with three small children before helping them climb the steps.

'All aboard,' he chirped, ringing the bell, and as the mother chivvied her brood down the bus, the conductor carried the basket to where the woman and children were sitting. After collecting their fares, he sauntered back to stand on the step, whistling cheerfully.

How was it, Juliet thought, that everyone else was going about their business in the usual way and she was sitting here with her nerves as tight as the strings on a violin and her heart breaking?

The bus chugged along, stopping and starting, passengers boarding and alighting and Juliet looking out of the window at the tree-lined roads and the hedgerows thick with ragged robin, dandelions and rosebay willow herb. On it travelled, past farmlands where lazy cows munched on the sweet summer grass, and into hamlets and villages whose names she had heard of but had never visited.

'Cawthorne, next stop,' the conductor sang out, and Juliet looked enviously at the pretty cottages and gardens tumbling with climbing roses and bright with flowers of every hue. They were a far cry from the house she had left behind in Hudd Royd, a poky little hovel built in the shadow of a giant slag heap, its flagged yard and windowsills black with coal dust. Home before that had been a decent pit house, but the owners of Red Brook Colliery had evicted them after the miners' strike. If her dad hadn't lost his job down the pit, she wouldn't be sitting on this bus, she thought miserably.

On through Denby Dale with its massive arched railway viaduct and down into Shepley then Kirkburton, Fenay Bridge and Waterloo.

'Not long now, love,' the conductor said as he came and stood by her seat. Juliet tensed. Looking from one side of the road to the other, she noticed that they had left the greenery behind and that both sides of the road were lined with a higgledy-piggledy mish-mash of drab, soot-stained terrace houses, shops and huge mills, their many windows glinting in the sunlight. She had never before been so far from home.

'Here you are, love, Somerset Road,' he said, pinging the bell then lifting her bag. Juliet stood, her legs stiff and her insides hollow as she followed him to the platform. The bus ground to a halt and she stepped down to the pavement. The conductor handed down her bag. 'Best of luck, love,' he said, thinking that she looked as if she'd need it.

Juliet looked this way and that, trying to get her bearings. Her cousin, Katie Smith, had written her a letter with instructions of where to go and she took the creased page from her pocket:

Cross Wakefield Road to Silver Street. There's a hardware shop on the corner. The Armitage's house is the very last on the left with a green door.

Shoving the letter back in her pocket, she dithered on the kerb, waiting for a gap in the busy traffic. Carts, lorries and cars rumbled past and a noisy tram clanked its way along shiny, metal lines, sparks flying. They didn't have trams in Dodworth and Juliet wondered what it would be like to ride on the top deck of one; maybe she'd find out if she stayed in Huddersfield.

The traffic thinned and, taking her life in her hands, she nipped from one side of the road to the other, her breath caught in her throat. A few paces took her to Silver Street. There was the hardware shop on the corner. Changing her bag from one hand to the other, she set off walking. The street was much longer than she had anticipated, the rows of houses on either side all the same except for the curtains or the colours of the doors. She didn't need to check the house numbers; Katie had said it was the very last house on the left.

When she reached it, she stood and assessed the donkey-stoned doorstep with its clean, white diamond pattern then the window, behind which were crisp, snow-white net curtains. *She must be a proud housekeeper like my mam*, she thought, and curious to know what lay beyond the gable end of the house, she walked a little further. A large expanse of wasteland stretched before her with a factory of some sort on it, and beyond that, a sparkling river on whose banks were towering mills, their chimneys puffing out grey smoke that spiralled up to the clear, blue sky. Although the mills looked rather forbidding, she hoped that soon enough she would find work in one of them like her cousin, Katie, and earn enough money to send home to her impoverished mother.

Retracing her steps, Juliet knocked on the green door.

'Oh, you found us all right then.' Florence Armitage opened the door and smiled warmly. 'Come in, love, we were expecting you. I've just this minute made a pot of tea.' She led the way down a narrow passage into a neat, cosy kitchen. 'Put your bag down and take off your coat. We'll sit at the table and drink this before I show you your room,' she said, filling two cups and placing one in front of where Juliet was sitting. 'Now, your Auntie Molly told me that you're the same age as her Katie and that you're called Juliet. Is that right? It's a pretty name.'

Juliet nodded. 'That's right.' She blushed. 'Me mam once saw a play with a girl called Juliet in it and named me after her,' she divulged, her chagrined expression letting Florence know that she might have preferred a more common name.

'The play must have been Shakespeare's *Romeo and Juliet*: two star-crossed lovers who had a sad ending,' said Florence.

Juliet blinked her surprise. She hadn't known that.

'I love reading and while I haven't read many of his plays, I have read that one,' Florence said, giving Juliet an enquiring look that asked if she too was a reader.

Juliet didn't know what to say to that so she said, 'It's very good of you to give me lodgings, Mrs Armitage. I promise I won't be any trouble.' She hid her face behind her cup and sipped nervously.

'I'm sure you won't, love. When Molly told me

you were looking for a place to stay and somewhere to find work, I thought you might as well have the room that used to be George and Dolly's. It's been lying empty ever since they left home.' Florence refilled Juliet's cup. 'Our Dolly left home when she married Theo Beaumont, the Land Agent at Thornton Hall. They live on the estate, and our George lives on Carr Pit with his wife, Nellie,' Florence continued. 'And I've got four lovely grandchildren, two lads and two lasses. Our Dolly has Josh – he's fourteen – and his sister, Sarah's twelve. Our George's boy, Luke, is fifteen, and then there's little Flora. She's just turned eleven.' All this was delivered with pride, although Florence was only imparting the information to put Juliet at ease.

The more Juliet heard, the more she began to relax. Her landlady wasn't at all what she had expected. Her Aunt Molly, who worked in the pickle factory with Mrs Armitage, was rough and ready so her mam had told her, but this woman was mannerly and she must be well-educated if she read books by what-his-name. She drained her cup and decided she would like living in Silver Street.

'Do you want to use the privy before we go upstairs?' Florence asked and got to her feet.

Grateful for her thoughtfulness, Juliet said she

did, and Florence showed her out into the yard. The small brick building smelled of fresh limewash, and the relief she felt as she emptied her full bladder blossomed into hope. Coming to Huddersfield was turning out to be far better than she had thought possible.

When Juliet went back into the house, Florence led the way upstairs to the bedroom that overlooked the wasteland and the river. 'It's lovely,' Juliet said on her breath, comparing it with the small room in Hudd Royd that she had shared with her two younger sisters and little brother, a cramped space that offered little comfort and never saw the light of day under the shadow of the slag heap. Her eyes roamed from the prettily dressed single bed to the dark wooden furniture polished to a lustrous sheen. All this would be hers if she found a job.

'Right, I'll leave you to unpack,' said Florence, heading for the door. 'I'll be making a bit of dinner at midday for when Mr Armitage comes home. You can have some with us if you like. Until then, make yourself comfortable and come down when you're ready.'

'Thanks ever so much,' said Juliet, her voice rich with sincerity, and left alone, she wandered round the room, opening the dressing-table drawers and wardrobe doors before carefully putting her few belongings inside them. Then she went and stood by the window, gazing out at the mills on the riverbank. There was almost an hour to fill before midday and she wondered if she should use it to go in search of work. She'd ask Mrs Armitage. Maybe she could tell her where to start looking.

Florence was mixing batter in an earthenware bowl when Juliet entered the kitchen. She looked up with a smile. 'I'm doing Yorkshire pudding to go with the veg and gravy left over from Sunday's dinner,' she said, beating the thick, creamy liquid until it bubbled then pouring it into a large, flat tin.

'I was thinking I should go and start looking for work,' Juliet said. 'I thought you might be able to give me directions to...' She sounded so lost that Florence's heart went out to her.

'Don't worry your head about that, lovey. I've had a word with our Dolly. She's a friend of the owner of Lockwood Mill. When I told her you were arriving today, she told me that you're to go down there this afternoon and if Mrs Hardcastle thinks you're suitable, you can start in the weaving shed tomorrow.'

Juliet gasped. 'That's where my cousin, Katie, works... and you've made arrangements for me...' She couldn't find any more words to express her delight and gratitude but her brimming eyes and flushed cheeks said it all.

'Aye, it made sense to ask about for you. When your Auntie Molly told me you needed a job, and that she couldn't put you up in her house what with it splitting at the seams, I told her I'd help you out. We all need a bit of help sometimes if we're to make a go of things.'

Florence's tone was matter-of-fact but she felt glad to be helping this young girl that she had taken an instant liking to. She'd have wanted somebody to do the same for her Dolly had things been different. But her Dolly was well fixed now, and glancing across at the quiet girl who once again looked lost and homesick, she felt pity for her. Keeping up a lively conversation and continuing with her chores seemed the best way to put the poor lass at her ease so Florence put the Yorkshire pudding in the fireside oven and told her what to expect at Lockwood Mill. Then, checking that the pudding was rising, she said, 'You can mash them potatoes for me, if you like.'

This simple act made Juliet feel even more at home, and they worked together until the clock on the mantelshelf struck twelve. Five minutes later, the door opened and in walked Clem Armitage. A tall, handsome man with salt and pepper hair that had once been fiery red, he dwarfed the room with his presence. He nodded at Juliet and said, 'I see you got here then.'

Juliet smiled her reply. Florence filled three plates and they sat down to eat.

'So... you're here to work in the mill then. Are jobs hard to come by over your way?' Clem asked as he poured the rich, brown gravy over his Yorkshire pudding.

'Aye, there's plenty of jobs in Dodworth for lads who want to be colliers but there's not much on offer for girls. I've been working as a daily maid for a lady whose husband had a business in Barnsley, but the wages were next to nowt. I turned sixteen last November and Mrs Althrop was still paying me the same wage I'd started with at fourteen. Me mam never has enough money to pay the rent an' feed and clothe us all,' Juliet replied with asperity before lowering her voice and saying, 'You see, me dad can't get set back on at the pit.'

'And why can't your father go back down the pit?' Clem thought it most likely that the man had been injured; mining was a dangerous occupation.

Juliet's cheek reddened. 'He was arrested during the miners' strike a couple of years ago,' she said. 'He's only just got out of prison and there's not a pit nearby that'll give him a job. They say he's a trouble-maker.'

Clem looked somewhat shocked by her forth-rightness and the bitter tone of her voice.

'I remember that strike,' he said. 'The miners were out for weeks. What did he do to get put in jail?' He seemed genuinely interested and sympathetic.

Juliet set down her knife and fork. 'The colliers were only asking for better wages and safer working conditions, 'cos it's a dirty, dangerous job, but the rotten mine owners wouldn't meet their de-mands,' she said hotly. 'When the colliers refused to work and the pits shut down, the cheating mine owners brought in scab labour.' Her voice was heavy with disgust and her pale-blue eyes had turned to steel. 'Me dad and the other men pick-eted the pit and fought to keep the scabs out. That's when the police singled him out for causing what they called a "public affray". It was the owners who told the police to arrest him because he was the Union leader, but he was only fighting to protect his job.' She sounded as though she had made these claims in defence of her father many times before.

Florence too was rather taken aback. Her pa-thetic little lodger had suddenly turned into a firebrand. She shook her head. 'It sounds like a proper bad business.'

'It is,' said Juliet grimly, 'but my dad's not giving in. He's still a Union man and he says he'll bring 'em out on strike again until they get they want. Workers have rights, an' it's up to them to make sure the bosses treat them fairly, you know,' she concluded emphatically.

By now, both Florence and Clem were of the opinion that Juliet and her father were agitators of the first water, and whilst they sympathised with the miners, Juliet's outburst made them both feel a little uneasy.

'Well, if Mrs Hardcastle sets you on in the weaving shed, you won't have any cause for complaint there. Lockwood Mill's one of the best-run mills in the valley and the workers are always treated fairly,' Florence said. 'Now, finish your dinner and I'll make a pot of tea.'

'I don't know anything about weaving,' Juliet said anxiously, her spirits sinking.

'You won't have to. They'll train you on the job,' Florence assured her as she filled the teapot from the kettle that seemed to be permanently on the boil. They drank their tea, and then Clem went back to work.

'What does Mr Armitage do?' Juliet asked as she helped wash and dry the dinner plates.

'He's a carpenter. Did you notice a factory on the land beyond the house? Well, that's where he works: Ellis's cabinet makers and joiners.' Florence sounded proud.

'And you work in the pickle factory with me Auntie Molly.'

'Only three days a week now. I'm in charge of making the pickle so if I smell of vinegar, you'll know why,' Florence said as she put the last of the clean dishes back into the cupboard. 'Now, you go and tidy yourself up and then I'll walk with you down to Lockwood's, show you the way so you don't get lost.'

Dressed in just their frocks and cardigans – no need for coats on such a warm, sunny day – they walked at a brisk pace along Silver Street and out into Wakefield Road, Florence commenting on the various shops and factories as they made their way to Lockwood Mill. 'This part of the road we're walking down is called Storthes, and over yonder is King's Mill.' She pointed to a huge edifice on the left then swung her arm back to point to the right. 'That's Brierley's Mill, and the smaller one behind it is Lockwood Mill.'

Juliet's gaze followed Florence's pointing finger

but all she seemed to see were mills, mills, and more mills, their tall chimneys pumping out clouds of thick smoke. By now, they had crossed the bridge over a fast-flowing spate of water that Florence said was the River Colne, and a few paces later, they turned right into a cobbled street that led to a pair of stout gates. The wrought-iron arch above the gates read *Lockwood Mill*.

'Here we are,' Florence said. 'I'll leave you to go in on your own while I carry on up into the town to do a bit of shopping. I'll see you when you get back. Best of luck.' She walked back over the cobbles and Juliet hovered by the gate.

'Are tha comin' in or what?' a crabby-looking man asked her.

'Yes, please,' she said as he pulled open one of the gates to let her through.

'If thas lookin' for t'Mill Mistress, she's in t'office,' he said, pointing to a low stone building not too far from the gate. Juliet thanked him and walked across the cobbled yard, the thrum of machinery reaching her ears and the greasy smell of raw wool pene-trating her nose.

Verity liked what she saw the moment Juliet knocked on the door and stepped inside. The girl was clean and tidy, her bright-blue eyes alert and her fair hair pulled back from her pretty face and braided in a long plait that hung almost to her waist. Dolly had been right to ask her to give the girl a chance. The mill was doing good business and they needed more weavers.

Verity stepped from behind her desk, stretching out her hand in welcome.

'Good afternoon. I'm Mrs Hardcastle and you must be the girl who's come to stay with Mrs Armitage,' she said, her mellow voice friendly and putting Juliet at her ease.

'Juliet Skeldon,' she replied, grasping Verity's outstretched hand.

'Juliet. That's a pretty name. Is your mother an admirer of Shakespeare?'

There it was again: the mention of someone Juliet hadn't a clue about.

Verity smiled. 'So, Juliet, you want to learn how to weave. Fortunately for you, we have a vacancy for a trainee weaver, and if you come with me, I'll take you to the weaving shed to show you what the work entails.' Verity walked out of the office and Juliet followed her.

She hadn't known what to expect, but it certainly wasn't the cavernous shed filled with row upon row of roaring looms. Overhead, low-hanging leather belts were attached to the drums and pulleys that powered them. Dust motes clouded the air. At each loom, women leaned in dangerously close to the thrashing machinery as something with pointed ends whizzed back and forth, trailing a length of yarn between more lengths of yarn that stretched from the bottom to the top of the loom. Juliet stared in amazement. Her ears began to throb and her mouth went dry. The cacophonous noise drowned Verity's next words, and Juliet dithered, uncertain as to whether she could ever work in a place like this.

Taking her by the elbow, Verity led her over to a plump, pleasant-looking woman wearing a flowered overall, her hair covered in a turban. Juliet noticed that all the women were similarly clad. Then the Mill Mistress bent forward so that she was speaking directly into Juliet's left ear. 'This is Mrs Nellie Armitage. She'll show you the ropes.'

The woman gave Juliet a warm smile then moved closer to Juliet's right side. 'You must be the girl that's come to live with my mother-in-law. Her son, George, is my husband,' she shouted.

Juliet nodded, her eyes lighting up and letting Nellie know she had heard of George.

Nellie grinned. Florence had obviously filled her in on the family history.

'I'll leave you to it, Nellie,' Verity mouthed.

Nellie took Juliet down to the far end of the shed where two looms stood idle and the noise was less deafening. Raising her voice, Nellie began to explain how the loom worked. Juliet learned that the long strings were the warp and they were fastened to the heddle at the top of the loom and to the footer at the bottom. The pointed thing was a shuttle, and the yarn it threaded through the warp was called the weft. The yarn was wrapped round things called bobbins and the thrashing things were called beaters. Warp, weft, heddle, shuttle, bobbin, beaters: Juliet committed them to her memory. She needed this job, and by the time the lesson was over, her head was buzzing with unfamiliar words and sights and sounds.

When she and Nellie walked back down 'weaver's alley', Juliet caught sight of her cousin, Katie. Katie waved and her lips moved, but Juliet had no idea what she was saying. When they reached the door and stepped outside, the quietness in the mill yard shocked her even though her ears were still ringing.

'You'll have to learn to lip read if you want to hold a conversation in the shed,' Nellie said as they crossed the yard. 'Your cousin, Katie, was telling you that she'd call round to Mrs Armitage's this evening.'

Juliet was surprised by how much they already seemed to know about her: Mrs Hardcastle had been expecting her, and Nellie knew that Katie was her cousin. She put that down to Mrs Armitage and her daughter Dolly; they'd paved the way and she was glad of it.

'Wait here. Mrs Hardcastle will want a word with you,' said Nellie, popping into the office then coming out a few minutes later. 'She'll see you now,' she said and trotted back to the weaving shed.

'Come in, Juliet,' Verity called from her seat behind the desk. Juliet stepped inside. A tall, dark, handsome man in his forties stood in front of a filing cabinet, sifting through the folders it contained. He turned and smiled.

'This is Mr Hardcastle,' said Verity, nodding her head in his direction.

Juliet returned his smile.

'Well, Juliet, do you think you can learn to be one of our weavers?' Verity cocked her head to one side, her enquiry brisk.

'Oh, yes,' Juliet gushed. She had to, didn't she, if she wanted to earn money to send home to her mother? But deep inside, she was feeling overwhelmed by the task that lay ahead of her.

'In that case, you can start tomorrow, six o'clock

sharp. Bring an overall, and a scarf to cover your head. We don't want that pretty hair of yours getting tangled up in the loom, do we?' Although Verity said this with a wry smile, Juliet couldn't help shuddering.

'Looms can be dangerous,' Mr Hardcastle said. 'You have to take care when working them. Watch your hands and your head when you're leaning in, and never be in too much of a rush.'

Juliet's confidence was in tatters but she tried not to let it show. She was here to earn money to support her family. Her father had slaved down the pit working in the most hazardous conditions to put bread on the table, and she resolved to do the same in the mill.

'Is there anything you'd like to ask, Juliet?' Verity gave her an encouraging look.

Juliet's mind was still on the injustice her dad had suffered. Jutting her chin and looking directly into Verity's eyes, she tersely asked, 'Do the weavers have a Union?'

Verity was somewhat taken aback by the question and the steely glint in Juliet's eyes. Only a moment ago, the girl had been sweetly polite. Now she looked bitterly aggressive.

'They do, and some of our women are members,

even though the men don't make them welcome,' Verity calmly said, but the quick glance she exchanged with her husband said, *We'll have to watch this one.*

'And are you in favour of the Unions, Juliet?' Oliver asked lightly.

Juliet swung round and fixed her gaze on him. 'My dad says that we need the Unions to see that we're treated fairly. The miners fight for what's right and they won't give in until they get what they want.' Her strident delivery had Oliver raising his eyebrows and looking closely at her.

'You'll find that none of the workers in Lockwood Mill are treated unfairly,' Verity intervened, her voice icy and her face stern. 'I think that will be all for now, Miss Skeldon. Tomorrow morning at six.' A curt nod at the door indicated that the interview was over.

'Thank you, Mr and Mrs Hardcastle. I'll do my best to please.'

Juliet's demure reply made the corners of Oliver's mouth twitch, and when she had left the office, he said, 'I do hope she isn't going to be trouble.'

'So do I,' Verity said with feeling. She was beginning to wish she hadn't been so eager to listen to Dolly and Florence and the sad story that Molly at the pickle factory had painted. Lockwood Mill had always had a fairly reasonable affiliation with the textile unions, of which there were many, representing all aspects of cloth-making, and she wouldn't want it to be disrupted by a girl who seemed all too ready to spread dissension.

'I'll tell Nellie to keep a sharp eye on her,' she said.

7

'Did the children get off all right?' Dolly asked Theo as he strode into the kitchen of their home on the Thornton Estate. It was Monday morning, and this being the first day back after the Easter holiday, he'd just returned from running Josh and Sarah to their respective schools in the estate's trap: Josh to King James' Grammar School and Sarah to the Misses Steele's Academy for Girls.

'They did,' he replied, sitting down at the table and filling a mug with tea. As Sir Arnold's Land Agent, Theo had been granted a rather grand house befitting his position on the estate, and Dolly had delighted in making it their home. With its four bedrooms and a bathroom on the upper floor and a spacious sitting room, dining room, study and kitchen below, it was certainly a step up from her parents' home in Silver Street.

Dolly had a natural flair for creating beautiful spaces and the kitchen was bright with artful displays of dried flowers in copper pots on the windowsills and her own paintings decorated the walls. 'I'll join you before I go over to the big house,' she said, taking the chair opposite Theo's and lifting the teapot. 'Lady Sybil's hosting a gathering of ladies from the church. They're making new tapestries for the hassocks and she asked me if I would sketch some designs.'

Theo looked pleased. He liked it that his own wife and his employer's wife had a good working relationship. Lady Sybil often called on Dolly to assist her in all manner of ways, many of them to do with the charitable work she did in the community as befitted her station, or whenever she was entertaining friends or local dignitaries. Dolly took it all in her stride.

She had first come to Lady Sybil's notice some fifteen years ago when Dolly had been visiting Theo's father, Joshua Beaumont. He had been the Land Agent at that time, and Theo learning his trade. Initially, Joshua had objected to his son's desire to court a mill girl for at that time, Dolly had worked as a weaver in Lockwood Mill. He had thought that Theo could do much better for himself. However, once he had met Dolly and found her to be an intelligent, educated young woman with a talent for drawing and painting, he had changed his mind. When Lady Sybil had come across Dolly making a pastel drawing of the manor house that had perfectly captured the colours of the Virginia creeper in all its autumn grandeur, she had immediately asked to buy the picture. Dolly had given it to her, and an acquaintance had been made. After that, Joshua's esteem for Dolly had doubled and he welcomed her as his daughter-in-law. Joshua was now retired and living in Scarborough with a landlady who, Dolly had mischievously suggested, might be more than just that, and Theo had said, 'Good luck to him. He deserves a bit of love after the way my mother treated him.'

Theo's social-climbing mother had left his father for a wealthy man and his parents had divorced when he was young. At first, she had taken Theo to live with her and her new husband. He had been unkind to Theo, and eventually, they had packed him off to boarding school. His had been an unhappy childhood and when he was older, he had chosen to live with his father who by then was the agent on the Thornton Estate. He thanked God he had made that decision for by doing so, he had met Dolly, the love of his life.

Now, as they sat drinking tea, he asked Dolly, 'And have you any ideas for the hassock designs?' He already knew the answer. Dolly would have done her homework.

'Yes, I visited All Hallows and made some drawings,' she said blithely, as though it was all so simple. 'The ladies can choose from them or use their own ideas.' She shoved her sketchbook across the table for Theo's perusal.

'They're very good, Dolly,' he said, studying her drawings of the Kaye's and Ramsden's coats of arms, two of the most prestigious families in Huddersfield, 'and is this a griffin?' He pointed to the drawing of a large mythical bird.

'Yes, it's one of the gargoyles on the tops of the spouts, and these are the patterns in the altar screen.' She flipped a page to reveal the intricate drawings. 'I'm pleased you like them. I hope they meet with Lady Sybil's approval.' Dolly closed the sketchbook and put it in a large canvas bag then got to her feet. 'Will I collect Josh and Sarah from school, or will you?'

'I'll go. I have to make some calls in the village,' said Theo, pulling on his keepers' tweed jacket and his face creasing into a frown. 'And I just hope that when I get there, I don't find that Blaise has taken his revenge on Josh.'

'Why would he do that?' Dolly's arms were half-in and half-out of her cardigan sleeves, and she left them dangling as she looked at him with surprise. Yesterday, they and their children had visited with Verity and Oliver and she hadn't been aware of anything amiss.

'Before we left last night, Oliver told me he was going to severely reprimand Blaise. He's been behaving badly at school, bullying the other boys – one of them being our Josh.'

Dolly's eyes blazed. 'Our Josh never said anything to me about it.'

'He wouldn't,' said Theo with a hint of pride. 'Our son fights his own battles.'

'Verity didn't mention anything either. She must be worried sick.'

'She didn't say anything because Oliver hasn't told her. The headmaster sent for him and he kept it secret. He said he didn't want to upset her.' Theo raised his eyebrows and shook his head, making it clear he didn't agree with the way Oliver managed things. 'He's still regretting not sending the lad to boarding school.'

'Oh, Verity 'ud never agree to that,' Dolly cried. 'She told me she would never forgive Oliver if he sent Blaise away.'

'Aye, and Oliver knows that, and he loves her too much to go against her.'

'That's because she had such a miserable up-bringing. He over-compensates for that reason, especially where Blaise is concerned. She sees no wrong in him, and poor Oliver finds it difficult to see him in a good light.' This time, it was Dolly's turn to give a despairing shake of her head. 'It's only natural that a mother should love her son, but there are times when she seems besotted with him.'

'Besotted or not, I won't have her son bullying ours, but if Oliver's kept his word and given Blaise the rounds of the kitchen, he might be feeling angry enough to blame it on Josh.'

'I know what you mean,' said Dolly, looking anxious. 'It wouldn't be the first time he's taken his spite out on one or other of the children when he's been told off.' Her lip curled as she recalled past incidents then lifting her bag and slipping the handles over her shoulder, she added, 'He's a right handful, isn't he? Verity and Oliver have their work cut out.'

'The trouble is they've been far too lenient,' Theo opined as he headed for the door. 'I've not forgotten what he did at the Easter party.' His face twisted in disgust. 'If my son had thrown Briony's new pet kitten up into a tree just to prove that it would land on its four feet, I'd have taken the strap to him.'

'Our Josh would never do such a thing. He loves animals,' Dolly protested, following him outside and down the garden path, 'but as for Blaise, you never know what he'll do next, and that was a particularly cruel thing to do. Poor Briony was hysterical.' Then, her voice rising with incredulity, she asked, 'And what did Verity do? She gave him a little lecture on kindness to all creatures. Pshaw! And Oliver had to climb the tree to rescue the poor mite from the branches. But you know what, I could tell that he was fit to wring Blaise's neck. Maybe last night, he really did lay the law down, and gave Blaise what for.'

'I wouldn't put money on it,' Theo growled. 'Not if Verity had her say.'

'Aye, and I'll guarantee that she'd make excuses for him,' Dolly agreed, pausing at the gate where they would go their separate ways. 'And Oliver's that mindful of what an awful childhood she had that he goes along with her idea that their children will never be subjected to any sort of chastisement, not even a little slap now and then.'

'I can't say I agree with thrashings, but there's some truth in that old saying, spare the rod and spoil the child,' Theo said sagely. 'But look, I have to go. And Blaise is their problem, not ours.'

'He is when he takes out his spite on our Josh,' Dolly admonished, and her green eyes flashing dangerously. 'And if there's been any trouble today, Blaise Hardcastle will get the sharp edge of my tongue.'

'I'd be tempted to use more than my tongue,' Theo retorted dryly. 'Now, you get off and enjoy yourself with the church ladies and I'll go and see to the horses.'

Shortly after half-past three in the afternoon, Susan drove the donkey cart down the hill from Far View House. It was her job to collect Blaise and Briony from school, their parents both at the mill until six o'clock. The hedgerows were coming into bloom with bright clusters of yellow gorse, and celandines and primroses scattered in the lush new grass and she breathed in their fresh sweet smells as she travelled along the country lanes. She liked this hour of the day free from the kitchen and out in the open air. She had missed her jaunts into the village whilst the children had been at home over the Easter holiday. Added to that was the pleasure she took from being seen in Almondbury dressed in her smart, grey uniform and driving her own transport. She was hopeful that she might see some of her old friends from school, girls who, like her, were in service but had none of her privileges.

Her heart soared as she drew level with a house in Wormald Street and saw Dora Lucas down on her knees, scrubbing brush in hand, bucket at her side. Dora was scouring the steps.

Susan slowed the cart to a halt. 'Bit late in the day for doing that, Dora,' she shouted.

Dora scrabbled to her feet, her drab, brown dress and black apron wet at the hems.

'T'Missis gave off stink an' said I hadn't done it proper. She's made me do it again,' she groused, wiping a damp lock of hair from her brow.

Susan grinned down from her superior position on the cart. 'Ah, well, I'm just glad it's not me has to do it, Dora,' she said, hiding the fact that she had scrubbed the steps at Far View that very morning. Smiling smugly, she flicked the donkey's reins before breezily saying, 'Ah, well, I must get on an' collect my little charges,' making it sound as though she was their governess rather than a maid-of-all-work like Dora.

Dora enviously watched her go then gave the bucket a savage kick.

Susan drove the cart past All Hallows church, and steering it into St Helen's Gate, she brought it to a stop outside a large, two-storey house where Briony spent her days in the care of the Misses Steele. Two middle-aged spinsters, their establishment catered for fifteen or so girls aged between eleven and sixteen, where they studied literature, history and geography and acquired the indispensable female accomplishments of sewing, music and art.

The girls in their neat, grey uniforms were lined up in the hallway, ready for leaving.

'Good afternoon, young ladies,' the sisters chorused as, standing on either side of the door in their stiff, black bombazine skirts and white shirtwaists, they bade their pupils goodbye.

'Good afternoon, Misses Steele,' the girls sang as they filed demurely out into the afternoon sunshine, some to walk home and others to the traps parked alongside the road.

Briony skipped down the path, her chestnut hair bouncing as she ran to where Susan waited.

'Susan! Susan! I won a prize for being the best at reciting the poem we had to learn in the holidays,' she gabbled, holding up the little book of poetry so that Susan might admire it. Her pretty face was flushed with success, and she did a little twirl before going and patting the donkey. 'Look, Bluebell.' She repeated what she'd just told Susan. Bluebell lowered her head and showed the same amount of interest in the prize as Susan, which was barely none.

'Get in the cart. We need to fetch Blaise.'

'Miss Steele said I read my poem beautifully,' Briony persisted.

'Hurry up! He'll go wandering off on his own if we're not there in time.'

Deflated, Briony climbed aboard. Nobody was interested in her prize. Blaise was all anybody ever thought about.

Susan jerked the reins and they travelled a little further down St Helen's Gate then turned into a leafy lane that led to King James' Grammar School. Bluebell obediently trotted on, oblivious to the hordes of noisy boys streaming towards them. Blaise wasn't one of them, and by the time they reached the gate, only a handful of boys were to be seen.

'Can you see Blaise?' Susan asked, her eyes raking the playground and then the ancient, ivy-covered building with its arched windows and bell tower.

'No, I can't, and I don't care,' Briony said haughtily.

They sat and waited, gazing at the now empty playground and the school's closed doors, Susan's anxiety rising by the minute. She was under Mrs Hardcastle's strictest orders to bring Blaise straight home each day in order to prevent him getting up to mischief. Blaise was aware of this and on several occasions in the past, he had gone into the village and hidden, knowing that Susan would be frantically searching for him.

'We'll have to go look for him,' she snapped, pulling on the reins and, yanking poor Bluebell round far quicker than she cared for, they retraced the lane.

Back in St Helen's Gate, Susan remembered that the last time this had happened, she had found him hiding amongst the gravestones in the cemetery beyond All Hallows.

'Get down and help me find him,' she ordered Briony, bringing the cart to a stop near the cemetery.

Sulkily, Briony did as she was asked.

In the graveyard, they roamed between the headstones, calling out his name, but their search was fruitless. Back aboard the cart, they toured the nearby streets, asking if had anyone seen him. By now, Susan's patience was at an end and she turned the cart towards Far View Hill. 'The little bugger can rot for all I care,' she muttered under her breath, but her insides were roiling. He was her responsibility, and the master and mistress would have something to say if he wasn't at home when they arrived back from the mill.

'He's must have dodged past us an' we didn't see him. He's most likely made his own way back,' she said to Briony as she drove the cart up the hill, the reins clammy in her hands.

Briony, utterly indifferent as to her brother's whereabouts, was leafing through her poetry book and didn't bother to reply.

'Oh, that's a lovely book, Briony. Well done,' cried Bella as Briony rushed into the kitchen to show off her prize. Briony glowed. At least someone was showing an interest.

Sadly, the interest was short-lived as Susan chivvied her mother into the pantry and hissed, 'Is Blaise home yet? Have you seen him? I couldn't find him.'

Mother and daughter exchanged a fraught, whispered conversation. 'You'll have to go and look for him again,' Bella said as she poured a glass of milk for Briony. 'The little sod can't have gone that far. Go now, before they get back.'

* * *

Immediately he had been released from the classroom, Blaise Hardcastle had raced down St Helen's Gate, his feet flying as he put distance between himself and the school. Today had been awful, the headmaster bawling him out for being a lazy oaf and his classmates making fun of him at breaktime in the playground. He'd quickly silenced them with a few well-aimed kicks and punches before being dragged inside by Mr Walker and made to sit in a corner with his face to the wall for the rest of the day. And if that wasn't bad enough, he was still burning from the dressing-down his father had delivered the previous night.

Oliver had chivvied him into the drawing room and closed the door, his face dark with anger as he began to lecture him on his unacceptable behaviour. Then, when he thought Blaise wasn't paying attention, he'd grabbed him and given him a thorough shaking. Blaise hadn't liked being manhandled, and when Oliver had threatened that he would send him

away to boarding school, he'd liked that even less.
Blaise had then gone in search of his mother, but before he got to her, his father had hauled him upstairs
and forbidden him to leave his room. He'd kicked at
the locked door, but his mother hadn't come to his
rescue.

Pa was in a right twist last night, he thought, recalling how his teeth had rattled when Oliver shook
him. He'd never done that before, and for one awful
moment, Blaise had thought his father was about to
beat the living daylights out of him. It had been quite
shocking, and he suddenly felt hot and bothered at
the memory of it.

Slowing his pace, he mooched down Fenay Lane.
The air was heavy, and beneath the trees that over-
hung the verge, clouds of gnats swarmed about his
head. He flapped his arms to ward them off then took
off his jacket and swirled it like a matador. This made
him feel even hotter and when he came level with a
herd of cows plodding into a field, he stopped and
leaned against a wall, watching the farmer slapping
their plump flanks or poking them gently with a
stout stick if they stepped out of line. The last cow
ambled through the gateway and Blaise continued
walking carefully to sidestep the steaming cowpats
that they had left behind on the road.

'Dozy creatures,' Blaise said to himself. 'Nobody will ever push and prod me into doing something I don't want to do.' He smirked inwardly. *Pa can roar all he likes but he doesn't frighten me. Mama will never send me away.*

Up until now, he had had no clear idea of where he was going, but he reckoned that he was on the very edge of the Thornton estate. Tired of the sun beating down on his head, he climbed over a wall and into the shade of the woods. Last year's beech mast crunched under his boots. Blaise put his jacket on. It didn't occur to him that he was trespassing for after all, Theo Beaumont was the agent here, and he was a family friend. Blaise was on the warpath.

Pretending to be a Redcoat hunting down Red Indians, he crawled through the thickets, pausing every now and then to stab his enemies with a sharp stick he'd picked up along the way. The trees petered out and before him, he saw an open piece of ground and on it, a circle of vardos. A flash of excitement made his blood pulse: gypsies.

He dropped to his knees, and like a Cherokee warrior, he crept nearer to the vardos. At the edge of the clearing, a lean lurcher with a brindled coat and a long tail came bounding towards him. It pushed its snout in Blaise's face, sniffing furiously.

Blaise leapt to his feet.

The dog barked.

A young woman came out of the nearest vardo, a small child under her arm. The dog ran to her, and she looked in Blaise's direction. When she saw him, her dark eyes narrowed and she took a few steps closer.

'What do you want?' She pushed back a tangle of jet-black curls from her face and gave him a threatening glare. The barefoot child was now on the ground, staring at Blaise, who was staring back. Both the child – he couldn't tell whether it was a boy or a girl in its ragged smock – and the woman were as brown as berries and their eyes as black as pools of tar.

'Bridie,' the young woman shouted. 'Come ye out here an' take a look at this fine fella.' Her tone was harsh.

An old woman appeared in the vardo doorway. Spotting Blaise, she stepped out and walked over to where the young woman stood. The skin on her face was like worn leather and reminded Blaise of the seats in his father's old trap. Grey hairs straggled her chin. Her currant-bun eyes gleamed as she peered at him. 'Well, haven't we got ourselves a fine an' dandy wee visitor, Noreen? What brings ye here, son?'

Her accent was such that Blaise struggled to understand her. He tugged at his jacket then brushed off bits of twigs and leaves. Straightening his shoulders, he looked boldly from one woman to the other, feeling rather superior; after all, they were gypsies.

'I came to see your homes,' he said rather haughtily, a sudden urge to go inside one of the brightly painted caravans inspiring him. 'And I'm thirsty. I'd like a drink of water.'

The young woman glared at his impertinence, but the older woman said, 'Away an' get the young master a drink, Noreen.' She gave Blaise a gummy smile that showed the stumps of blackened teeth. 'An' make sure an' use one o' the best cups,' she called as Noreen sulkily climbed the steps into the caravan. When Noreen came back with a pretty flowered cup crafted from the finest bone china, she shoved it ungraciously into Blaise's hand.

He drank thirstily. Had he gone straight home, he would have had milk and biscuits by now to tide him over before dinner. His belly rumbled and he wondered if he should ask for something to eat.

His presence hadn't gone unnoticed and by now, he was being scrutinised by a group of women and girls of all ages and children much younger than himself. Dark eyes looked him up and down. Blaise regretted that his white shirt had lost its crispness and that the knees of his black serge trousers were dusty. Still, he must look awfully grand to them, he thought, noting that most of the girls and the little children were barefoot and their garments tattered. The women wore men's boots, the hems of their skirts and the collars and cuffs on their embroidered blouses frayed.

'Might I have something to eat?' Blaise asked, his tone imperious as he handed the cup to Noreen.

She squared her shoulders, the look on her face scornful she said, 'No, we have nothing for ye.'

But once again, Bridie overruled her.

'Sure an' let the young gentlemen take his fill; 'twill do no harm.' Then speaking rapidly in a weird language that Blaise didn't understand but Noreen did, Bridie convinced her to put aside her objections. Noreen smirked, her dark eyes flashing wickedly as she climbed the steps into the vardo. She returned a few minutes later with a hunk of crusty, dark-brown bread and a sliver of cheese.

Blaise stuffed the bread into his mouth then nibbled at the cheese. It tasted rank but he didn't care. His hunger temporarily staved, he strutted around the camp as though he was a surveyor, a gaggle of little children at his heels. They were fascinated by this strange boy in his white shirt with its stiff Eton collar, and his grey tweed jacket and fine leather boots. One little girl reached out and stroked his sleeve. Blaise knocked her grimy hand away.

By now, the shadows were lengthening. The women were tending the fire pit, stirring its slumbering embers and piling sticks on the hungry flames. The blaze licked the bottoms of large, blackened pots suspended over the flames, water bubbling as the women tipped onions, potatoes and greens in with the rabbit meat that had been simmering since earlier in the afternoon. There was a sense of expectancy in the air and Blaise soon found out why.

The dogs arrived first. Long, lean lurchers, beady-eyed black and white collies and white and tan Jack Russells with sharp noses and pointed teeth bounded into the compound, their tongues lolling. They were followed by six or seven boys, some about Blaise's age and the others older by two or more years. These lithe lads wearing shabby shirts and trousers that showed their bare, brown skin made him feel overdressed and lacking in virility.

The men came behind. Big, brawny men lugging a cart piled high with scrap metal and odds and ends. Suddenly, the camp resounded with the noise of barking dogs, shouts and yells as the women greeted their menfolk.

Blaise scuttled back to the safety of Bridie's vardo.

'Come sit ye by me, bonny lad,' Bridie urged, patting the step she was sitting on. 'Noreen will be after bringing ye a dish of stew for to taste your wee mouth. A growing lad like ye needs to keep up his strength.'

Blaise sat down. He wondered if he could become a gypsy, say goodbye to the boredom of school and the silly rules he was expected to abide by, give up the restraints of being clean and tidy and well behaved, and travel the roads like the boys gathered round the fire. Whilst he was musing on the possibility, Noreen brought him a dish of rabbit meat and vegetables. He tucked in, the meat tender and the gravy thick and pungent. With his belly full, he had no desire to go home, and he lolled against the vardo's open door until Bridie said, 'Ye can take a look inside our wee home, if ye like, young sir.'

Blaise needed no second bidding. Inside the vardo, he was amazed by its clean, tidy comforts. Low beds were covered with brightly coloured blankets, and narrow shelves along the walls held shining brassware and delicate porcelain ornaments. He sank down on one of the beds, letting his imagination run wild as he pictured a life on the road travelling here and there until Bridie called out, 'Seen enough, have ye?'

His reverie dissipating, Blaise stepped outside.

The sun was low in the sky, the blazing fire casting dancing shadows as the gypsy women handed round mugs of something that streamed through a spigot attached to a large wooden barrel. Noreen carried a brimming mug over to Blaise. 'Here ye are, take a sup o' this to wet your throat,' she said with a smirk.

Blaise drank deeply. The bitter liquid was cool and exotic and he emptied the mug. Noreen refilled it. An old man began to play a skirling tune on a battered squeeze box and the children jigged round the fire as the porter from the barrel flowed into their father's cups and down their throats. Blaise drained his mug again.

The men and women began to dance, and Noreen grabbed Blaise's hand, dragging him into the cavorting circle. At first, he felt foolish but as the porter settled in his stomach and then went to his head, he whirled and capered with the rest of them, feeling like a man of the world. Noreen spun him this way and that, and when he breathlessly protested, she filled his mug with porter again and again, saying, 'Ye are a prince among men,' and, 'Oh, but ye are the handsomest fella I ever set eyes on.'

'This is the life for me,' he told himself, as he whooped and leapt and drank, the fire hot on his cheeks and the stars in the sky glittering in their thousands as they pricked the purple sky. Flashes of colour and cavorting shapes swirled before his eyes and his feet wouldn't obey him. He staggered and fell. Bridie and Noreen dragged him inside the vardo.

8

'What do you mean, he hasn't come home?' Oliver's face was like a thundercloud.

Susan quaked.

'I searched for him everywhere an' he was nowhere to be found, Mr Hardcastle.' She threw back her head to prevent the tears that welled in her eyes from falling. It wasn't her fault, and she wasn't going to let the master make her shed tears for that horrible little brat.

'But where can he be?' Verity's distraught cry bounced off the walls of the kitchen. 'It's now almost seven. He's been wandering for nearly three hours.'

'Why didn't you send word to the mill as soon as

you knew he'd gone missing?' Oliver glared accusingly from Susan to her mother.

Bella's plump cheeks reddened. She hung her head and muttered, 'We thought he'd be back before you and the mistress arrived home. We didn't want to bother you.'

'Bother us! He's our son,' Verity screeched. 'Blaise is but fourteen years old and you left him to roam the countryside without a thought for his safety. Anything could have happened to him.' She clutched at Oliver's sleeve. 'We must organise a search party.'

Aye, an' if he wasn't your son, at his age, he'd be out working to earn his keep, not being lifted and laid by the likes of me, Susan thought sourly.

All this time, Briony had been sitting at the table nursing her grievances. Neither her mother nor her father had shown any interest in the prize she had won for her poem. Trust Blaise to spoil her moment of glory. He always won everyone's attention. Now they both looked at her and she lifted the little book. 'This is my prize for being—'

'Did Blaise say anything to you as to where he was going?' her father interrupted.

Briony's spirits sank and, shaking her head, she set the book aside.

'We're wasting time, Oliver. We need to notify the

police and get help to look for him. He could be in danger,' Verity said, almost choking on the words, and her face filled with dread.

Oliver turned baleful eyes on Susan and Bella, who were clinging to one another and contemplating losing their jobs. 'If he returns whilst we are away, send word immediately to the police station. And in the meantime,' his scowl deepened and his voice oozed sarcasm, 'try not to lose our daughter.'

Briony flipped the pages of her prize and watched in silence as her parents hurried from the kitchen, her mother ashen-faced and her father struggling to suppress his rage. Just at that moment, Briony told herself that she didn't care if they never found her blasted brother.

Oliver had recently purchased a car, a shiny black Austin, and he silently thanked God for this speedier mode of transport as he drove at reckless speed into the town. After a brief visit to the police station, they made their way to the Thornton Estate.

'Theo might know of Blaise's whereabouts; he might have gone there to see Josh,' Oliver said, 'and if not, he'll help us look for him.' He sounded far more hopeful than he felt. He also thought that he was to blame. Had last night's sharp reprimand forced the boy into running away? He glanced at his wife. She knew nothing about what he had said and done to Blaise, but if this was the reason for his disappearance then...

'But surely Dolly wouldn't have let him stay until this hour. She would know we'd be worrying as to where he was,' Verity cried, the hopelessness in her tone giving voice to Oliver's true feelings, and every turn of the car's wheels heightening her distress.

Theo, sitting at the table by the window in his own kitchen eating his evening meal with his family, was surprised when he saw the car draw up outside. 'It's the Hardcastles,' he said to Dolly, getting to his feet.

Dolly jumped up and ran to the door to welcome them, aghast when Verity almost fell from the car, tears streaming down her cheeks and crying, 'Is Blaise here? Have you seen him? Blaise is missing!'

Dolly caught her friend in her arms and held her close, at the same time shouting, 'Josh, do you know where Blaise is? He didn't go home after school.'

Josh clattered his knife and fork onto his plate and, looking bemused, he walked to the door to be met by a hail of questions from Verity and Oliver.

'I saw him in class and in the playground,' he said, not mentioning the fight or that Blaise had been made to sit in the corner for the rest of the school day, 'but I didn't see him when school was over. I called for Sarah and we came straight home with Pa.'

Verity's eyes fixed on Sarah, still seated at the table. 'Have you seen Blaise?'

Sarah shook her head then said, 'Josh told me he was fighting in the playground and the master was very cross with him.'

Oliver's heart sank. The telling-off had clearly not had the hoped-for effect on Blaise.

A spike of hope pierced Verity's heart and she clutched at Oliver's sleeve. 'Do you think the master's kept him behind? That he's still at school?' Her grey eyes shone with renewed hope.

Oliver gave her an incredulous look. 'What, detained him until this time? It's almost three hours since school finished.' The words came out scornfully, his rising panic for his son's safety making him careless.

'It was just a thought,' Verity muttered, hurt by Oliver's harshness.

'We're wasting time,' Theo butted in. 'I'll go and round up the labourers and we'll start a search, some men to the village, others to the town, and we'll do the estate. He can't be far away. Maybe he's hurt himself and is waiting to be rescued.'

Verity's scream let him know he'd said the wrong

thing, but knowing the lad as he did, it wouldn't surprise him to learn that Blaise had got into difficulties whilst trying to prove his invincibility. It wouldn't be the first time.

Theo fetched his horse, and as he rode to the farm to round up the labourers, he mused on Blaise's earlier mishaps: falling from a tree to prove he could climb higher than Josh, that had resulted in a broken arm. Provoking a swan with a sharp stick then ending up floundering in the canal and Oliver forced to jump in and rescue him. Setting fire to a haystack in a field close to Far View. *Good God!* thought Theo. There were so many incidents that it made the mind boggle. He spurred the horse onward.

Meanwhile, back at the Beaumont's house, at Josh's suggestion, he and Oliver had gone to search a nearby coppice where the boys had made a camp the previous summer, leaving Dolly to calm her distraught friend.

'Please, Verity. Do try and pull yourself together. You and I and Sarah will search the gardens and when Theo returns with the men, they can go further afield,' Dolly told her.

Verity shrugged helplessly; she didn't feel as though she could hold up much longer if her son wasn't found – and soon. She pictured him lying injured after attempting some dangerous pursuit, or worse still, dead.

When Oliver and Josh came back alone, she let out a wailing cry. Oliver hurried to her side, gripping her in his strong arms as if to imbue her with his strength.

'We'll find him, Verity. Have no fear. I'll bring him back to you.'

He was still holding her when Theo and the men arrived. 'I must go now. Time is of the essence,' he said, and almost forcibly disentangling himself from her clutches, he went to join Theo, who was talking with one of his farmhands.

'Sam tells me there's gypsies camped in the lea meadow by Fenay Beck,' said Theo. 'We'll go on foot through the woods and ask at the camp, have they seen him.'

'Thank God it's still daylight,' Oliver said as, shouting Blaise's name every now and then, they made their way through the trees. At the edge of the wood and within sight of the lea meadow, they paused and, looking across the distance, they saw the glow of a fire and the vardos. Oliver set off running towards the camp, Theo pounding after him. As they dashed into the camp, the singing and dancing came to an abrupt halt.

The gypsies greeted them warily. It was plain by their dress and air of authority that Oliver and Theo were men of some importance and as they listened to Oliver's urgent questions, the gypsies shuffled uncomfortably, their dark eyes darting unspoken messages one to the other. Bridie sat firm on the vardo step with Noreen beside her.

Then, a huge, muscular man stepped forward, his demeanour ingratiating. 'Ah, tis sorry I am to learn of your troubles, good sirs, but we can be of no help.' And made mellow by the porter that he had consumed, he began to wax lyrical about young boys being the bane of a father's life.

Oliver cut him off by repeating a description of Blaise and curtly asking were they sure that Blaise hadn't come this way.

'Tis only our own lads as ye can see, sir,' Bridie wheedled, afraid to admit that Blaise was lying drunk inside her vardo and fearing that her plan to deal with Blaise in her own way now seemed unwise. 'Be sure an' know that if we come across your boy, we'll bring him straight to ye, sir,' she placated, shifting uneasily on the step, afraid that Oliver might ask to search inside the vardos.

Meanwhile, Theo was prowling round the camp, peering through the open doorways of the vardos, but it was almost impossible to see anything inside the dark interiors. Theo, aware that his footsteps were being dogged by two beefy men, their expressions sullen and their fists clenched, made his way back to Oliver. He didn't fancy engaging in fisticuffs with these fellows. He and Oliver were outnumbered, and more than likely the gypsies were telling the truth. Even so, he felt the need to show his authority.

'Be off with you at first light; you're trespassing,' he barked. 'And be sure to take your rubbish with you.' He gestured at the piles of scrap metal.

'We will indeed, sir. Ye'll not see hide nor hair of us come dawning,' the gypsies' spokesman said. His affable manner, coupled with what seemed to be a genuine concern for the missing boy, had Oliver believing that they didn't know of Blaise's whereabouts.

'Come on, Theo, we'll get the car and search the town.' He began walking away and Theo fell into step beside him. 'With luck, the others will have had more success and Blaise will be at home by now.'

'Let's hope so. Those gypsies are scoundrels but I think they were being honest when they said they hadn't seen him.'

Hurrying back through the wood to Theo and Dolly's house, they found Verity sitting with her head in her hands, her face stained with tears. Oliver dreaded having to impart the news that they still hadn't found Blaise.

'We're taking the car into town to continue the search. I'll check with the police, and maybe the others have already found him,' he said but his heart wasn't in it.

'Ask did they check the canal,' Verity said hollowly, an image of Blaise's body floating on the oily waters making her shudder. Oliver felt the urge to embrace her but he held back, afraid that they both would crumble to dust in their misery.

'You go,' Dolly said. 'I'll see to Verity.'

It was close on midnight when Oliver and Theo returned. Verity knew immediately by their bleak expressions that Blaise was still missing. Great, shuddering sobs wracked her frame and Oliver held her to his chest.

'The night patrol will continue looking for him,' he said and, lost for words and his tread as heavy as his heart, he led his wife out to the car.

Dolly and Theo followed, Dolly giving Verity one last warm embrace, saying, 'He'll turn up, love. Blaise is more than capable of taking care of himself. He'll not have come to any harm.' She let go of Verity and turned away to hide the doubt plain on her face.

Verity wanted to believe her with all her heart, and as she slumped in the car seat and Oliver took the wheel, she prayed with all her might that Dolly was right.

When they arrived back at Far View House, Bella was waiting nervously for them. She had sent Susan home. Bella burst into tears, wailing and condemning herself when she learned that Blaise was still missing. Regaining some composure, she gabbled, 'I gave Miss Briony her dinner an' stayed on an' saw her to bed, Mrs Hardcastle. I'd not leave her on her own.' If she had hoped to appease her mistress, she failed miserably.

Verity's icy glare silenced her. 'If you had notified us immediately he didn't come home, we would have found him by now, Bella.' Her grating voice had Bella crying again. 'Go home; there's nothing you can do here.'

Oliver poured two stiff whiskys, adding a little water to the one he handed Verity.

She gulped a mouthful, the strong spirit catching in her throat then burning her empty stomach. 'I won't sleep,' she said soulfully. 'You go to bed if you like.'

Oliver took her arm, almost lifting her from the chair and, lifting the whisky bottle with his free hand, he led her up the basement stairs and into the drawing room. A fire burned low in the grate and he replenished it then went and sat beside Verity on the couch. They sipped in silence, each lost in their own thoughts.

I should have taken a firmer hand when he transgressed instead of letting him run wild. I shouldn't have threatened to send him away to school. I should have spent more time with him, shown more interest in the things that interested him, Oliver thought, his blood running cold at the idea that Blaise might be lost to them forever.

Verity recalled the first time she had held Blaise in her arms, his dark eyes looking into her with all the trust in the world. He'd been such a strong child from the moment he was born, bigger by far than his dainty sister. There had always seemed so much more essence in Blaise than there was in Briony, and although she loved her daughter dearly, her feelings for her son were greater by far. She felt overwhelmed by his strength of character and loved him all the more for it, excusing his wilfulness as a sign of something special and the beginnings of the great man he would one day be. Tears trickled down her cheeks as she contemplated the dreadful fact that he might never achieve his greatness.

'I should go and look in on Briony,' Verity said, standing shakily and appalled to realise that she had not gone to her before now. Oliver seemed to feel equally guilty.

'Good God, yes.' In all the turmoil, he hadn't given a thought to his placid little daughter.

They climbed the stairs and tiptoed into Briony's bedroom. She lay on her side, her rich-brown hair ribboning her pillow. Verity felt a spike of guilt mixed with overpowering love as she gazed down at Briony's sweet face. Gently, she stroked her smooth brow.

Briony's eyes flew open. 'Did you find Blaise?' she whispered lazily.

'Not yet, but we will,' Oliver said. 'He's just playing one of his silly games.'

'He'll come home when he's hungry,' Briony mumbled and, turning over, she appeared to fall back into sleep. Her parents watched over her for several minutes and, agreeing that there was little to be gained by making her worried, they crept from the room and back downstairs.

So, Blaise is still hiding somewhere, Briony thought sleepily. *He'll be doing it on purpose to frighten Ma and Pa.* A sudden, awful thought made her shiver. What if he'd run away and never came back? She might not like him much of the time but deep down, she loved him because he was her twin, her other half. She lay awake for some time dwelling on those thoughts until an uneasy sleep claimed her.

Back in the drawing room, Oliver and Verity sat through the long night barely speaking, sometimes dozing, and when they did talk, they tried their utmost to be positive.

As the pearly light of dawn cast its pale rays through the windows – no one had cared to close the drapes – Oliver roused himself.

'I'll go to the police station then to Theo's. Take up the search again.'

'I'll come with you,' Verity said, getting to her feet and smoothing her crumpled skirt then faltering as, once again, she remembered that her daughter would be left alone in the house. 'You go. I'll stay here in case Briony wakens before Bella arrives.'

Leaving Verity on tenterhooks, Oliver drove the car to the police station in Northgate, heedless of his speed and that he was unshaven and minus his shirt collar.

The policeman on duty offered his commiserations. The night patrol had searched the canal, the back alleys in the town, and the surrounding countryside without any success.

Oliver drove the car straight to Theo's.

'We'll have a better chance of finding him in daylight,' Theo said, pulling on his keeper's coat and calling to Dolly that he was going with Oliver to look for Blaise. Dolly ran out of the bedroom, her red hair in tangles and her eyes heavy. She too had barely slept.

'No news?' Hearing that there was none, she asked, 'How's Verity?'

'Hasn't slept a wink. She's devastated, Dolly.' Oliver's face crumpled.

'I'll get dressed and go straight to Far View. I'll take Josh and Sarah with me.'

'I'll come with you, Dad,' said Josh, coming from his bedroom fully dressed.

Oliver, Theo and Josh went in the same direction as the day before, tramping through the woods, calling out Blaise's name, and searching for evidence of where he might have been. In the full light of day, they were able to see where the branches had been broken and the grass trampled.

'Somebody came this way very recently,' said Theo.

When they reached the lea meadow at Fenay Beck, the vardos had gone, the ground rutted and the ashes of the fire scattered. Cowering in the shelter of an overhanging willow tree, they found Blaise. He was naked and shivering, his face streaked with dirt where his grubby hands had tried to stem his tears. He whimpered pitifully as his father and Theo approached.

'Oh, my boy! My boy!' Oliver cried, scooping Blaise into his arms and hugging him as though he would never let go.

Blaise felt his father's tears wetting the back of his neck and he let his own tears flow. Sobbing, he told Oliver how the gypsies had given him drink and that he remembered nothing until he'd woken lying on the ground where they had found him.

'I'm sorry I ran away, Pa,' he hiccupped. 'I'll never do it again.'

Oliver took off his coat and was about to wrap it round Blaise when Blaise spied Josh standing with his father and staring at him with big, round eyes. Thoroughly mortified, he let Oliver bundle him into the coat and carry him from the field.

9

In the week following Blaise's unfortunate escapade at the hands of the gypsies, life in Far View House had undergone a sea change. His mother, her relief at his safe return bordering on hysteria, had been so overjoyed that she instantly forgot the pain and anxiety he had caused.

'Welcome back the prodigal son,' Susan had muttered to her mother. 'She hasn't killed the fatted calf but she's damned near done everything but.' She still blamed Blaise for his mother's cold attitude towards her.

Verity had been horrified by the humiliation that her son had suffered and demanded that Oliver notify the police so that they might go after the gypsies and charge them with assault. He had done this, but the police had far more serious matters to deal with than chasing across the countryside after a band of travellers, and nothing came of it.

When he had been brought back to the house bundled in his father's coat, his mother had fallen about his neck, clasping onto him with gratitude and grief and he had tasted her salt tears as she smothered his face in kisses. Blaise had been overwhelmed with guilt at the trouble he had caused and deeply shamed by being found in such an undignified state. The feeling stayed with him.

For the first week after the incident, Blaise did not attend school, Verity keeping him at home and hardly letting him out of her sight. She pampered him with his favourite ice creams, a shopping trip to buy more lead soldiers, and was forever clutching him to her bosom and fondling his hair and his face, her relief at having him restored to her poignant.

Oliver went to the mill without her and when he came home in the evening, he spent his time with Blaise, the better part of many evenings taken up by playing mock-battles with Blaise's army of soldiers. Oliver sat watching, fascinated, as Blaise moved the tiny figures across the tabletop, the comparative taxonomy and meaning of which was known only to him. It made Oliver feel like an intruder and he would dearly have liked to know what his son was thinking. For his part, the boy quietly acquiesced to all this attention.

Blaise had made it quite plain that he didn't want to talk about the gypsies, and his parents accepted that it was better to let the episode fade from memory rather than discuss it over and again. When Briony pressed him to tell her what had happened, he had said it was too horrible to even think about it, and she being of a kindly nature had let it go.

However, when Blaise returned to school, the first thing he did was to take Josh Beaumont to one side and ask him had he told any of the other boys that the gypsies had stripped him and left him naked in the lea meadow at Fenay Beck. Josh assured him that he had not, saying it would be unkind to spread such an awful story.

After that, Blaise had looked at Josh through new eyes. He had also settled down to his schoolwork, his headmaster impressed by his diligence. Verity and Oliver revelled in their son's new attitude, marvelling at his quiet demeanour and glad to be free of his tantrums. And the longer Blaise continued in this manner, the more certain his parents were that they could rely on his good behaviour.

As the summer of 1914 unfolded, it was only the weather that was uncertain. Extremely hot dry days suddenly resulted in violent thunderstorms and flash flooding. The baling room at Lockwood Mill had to be hastily emptied as water poured in and threatened to damage the bales of fine worsted that were waiting to be delivered. The River Colne threatened to flood its banks, and the heat in the weaving shed was sometimes unbearable. Verity took all this in her stride, and although she never knew what to expect from the changeable weather, Blaise had changed and she was contented. He was pleasant and well behaved at school. He showed respect for his elders and whenever he spent time with Josh and the girls, he no longer dominated the occasions with his boorish behaviour. And in light of Josh Beaumont's kind and thoughtful tact, Blaise now looked upon him as a true friend.

Although Blaise secretly admitted that he had been the perpetrator of his own downfall, that it was his foolish belief in his own importance that had led to him being humiliated by the gypsies, he had not lost his fighting spirit. Instead, he carefully suppressed his rebellious nature to please those that he knew loved him, but deep down, he vowed that never again would he let anyone degrade him and that he would, one day, do exactly as he pleased and show the world what he was really made of. He had already decided that his future lay with soldiering, maybe the King's Royal Hussars or the Blues and Royals, both cavalry regiments with a glorious history. Of one thing he was certain: he wouldn't spend his life running a small cloth mill in the Colne Valley. But all this he kept close to his chest.

And so, as summer progressed, the handsome, clever Blaise and beautiful, sweet-natured Briony gave Verity and Oliver Hardcastle much to be thankful for. Like any family fortunate enough to have wealth and comfort at their disposal, they were basking in the pleasures of owning a thriving mill with a willing workforce, and being the proud parents of a healthy, biddable son and a charming daughter.

* * *

'How are things at the mill?' Dolly asked Verity half in jest, for although her days as a weaver at Lockwood Mill were long over, she still had an interest in its affairs.

'Well enough,' Verity replied somewhat hesitantly, her brow puckering as she poured Dolly a glass of iced lemonade. It was a gloriously warm afternoon at the end of June and they were sitting on the terrace outside the French windows of the drawing room at Far View House. It being a Sunday, the Beaumonts had come as they often did to spend their leisure time with the Hardcastles. Oliver and Theo were out in the garden, Oliver seeking Theo's advice as to what he should do about an elm tree that appeared to be dying. The children were upstairs, Blaise and Josh in Blaise's bedroom manoeuvring their troops across the tabletop battlefield, and Briony and Sarah across the landing sharing girlish secrets and giggling as they tried on Verity's hats.

Dolly had seen Verity's frown and always having her friend's best interests at heart, she now pressed her to say more. 'Your words said things were fine but your face told a different story. So, what is it?'

'I'm not sure.' Verity pursed her lips and shook her head. 'I suppose I've been living in a bubble of happiness ever since Blaise was found, and really everything seems fine, but for the past two or three days now, I've had this feeling that something's not right... and that I'll waken up one morning and find that it's true.'

'Is it to do with Blaise?' Dolly's anxious questions were accompanied by a squeeze of Verity's hand. She knew all too well how much Verity cherished her son.

'No, not at all,' said Verity with a little smile. 'He's so pleasant and well behaved, I have no worries there. It has nothing to do with family matters. We couldn't be happier.'

'Thank goodness for that,' Dolly said as she helped herself to more lemonade.

'You might think I'm foolish, Dolly, but everywhere I go outside my own home, I can feel this air of general unrest, as though the world is ill at ease with itself.' Verity's cheeks had pinked as she made her confession, and when Dolly giggled, they turned bright red.

'Oh, dear me, sorry for laughing, but you sound like one of those old soothsayers who predict doom and gloom,' Dolly chortled.

'I do, don't I.' Verity joined in the laughter. 'But ever since the spinners in Halifax came out demanding an extra shilling a week, and the doffers and the twisters made the same demands, there have been strikes and rumours of strikes, and I worry about our mill.'

'But Lockwood's has no need for complaint. You've always paid above the going rate, and you have good relations with the Unions,' Dolly protested.

'We do, and we're one of the few mills in the valley that has a canteen for its workers and a sickness scheme, but that doesn't stop the agitators who always want more.'

'And who's causing bother in your mill?' Dolly's curiosity made her green eyes flash.

'You're not going to believe this,' Verity said, her face a picture of dismay, 'but it's Juliet Skeldon, the girl your mother took in when she came from Barnsley looking for work.'

'Juliet?' Dolly looked askance. 'And how's she doing that?'

'By spreading dissension and finding fault with the way I run my mill. Why, only the other day, she tried to persuade the weavers to walk out because it was too hot to work in the shed.'

Dolly grimaced. 'Does she think you can control the weather? Hot or cold, you have a job to do, and you just get on with it.'

'I tried telling her that,' Verity said, her irritation mounting. 'We'd already opened all the doors and windows and given them plenty of water to refresh themselves, and even extended the breakfast and dinner-time breaks by fifteen minutes with no loss of earnings.'

'There's not many mills in the valley would do that,' Dolly sympathised. 'Maybe you should sack her.'

'Don't think I haven't considered it,' Verity replied with asperity, and her features softening as she went on to say, 'but then I'm reminded of the pitiful story your mam told us about how impoverished Juliet's family is, and that she's their only means of support.'

'Aye, there is that, and your kind heart always rules your head,' Dolly said. 'And let's face it, she's only a lass with jumped-up ideas. She doesn't really pull any weight.'

'I suppose you're right,' Verity reluctantly agreed, 'but she can be extremely annoying. The women don't like her because she pesters them to go to the Union meetings. The older women tend to ignore her, and the younger ones with children are too busy keeping homes and families to find time to attend the meetings, but even so, Juliet's intent on stirring things up. You know as well as I do that it's the men who run the Unions, and that they object to the women joining, but Juliet's managed to worm her way into favour.' Verity leaned forward in her chair, the look on her face derisory and her weary tone of voice changing to that of a gossip as she said, 'According to Nellie, Juliet's very flirtatious with the men, and they being men, they lap it up. It seems she's as free with her kisses as she is at making her ridiculous demands.'

'My goodness! She sounds like a right handful,' Dolly gasped. 'And she must have as many faces as a church clock. When I met her at my mam's, she seemed like a nice, quiet girl.' Dolly paused. 'But come to think of it, my mam did tell me she's not as sweet as she first thought, and Dad mentioned that she bangs on about workers' rights too often for his liking.'

'Oh, she does that all right,' said Verity with asperity. 'Last week at a meeting, she forwarded a motion that workers who arrived at the gate after the hooter has gone should not be locked out until breakfast time.'

Dolly gave a half-smile. 'Personally, I always thought that was most unfair.' Then realising what she'd said and not wanting to appear disloyal, she hurriedly added, 'but I know all the mills do it.'

'They do,' Verity replied, wringing her hands and her emphatic response begging for Dolly's understanding, 'and Lockwood's has to be careful to keep in line with the other mills in the valley. Otherwise, we risk alienating ourselves with them, and that's not good for business.'

'I understand that, Verity, but you have to look at it from the point of them that work in the mills,' Dolly said. 'Not all the mills are as fair as yours. That's why they need the Unions to fight their corner.'

'But we've always treated our workers more than fairly. You know that, Dolly, and I don't like the idea of them being persuaded into believing any different,' she continued with a hurt tone. 'My main objective ever since I inherited the mill was to ensure that we had a happy workforce earning decent money. Yes, the hours are long and the work taxing, but that's the way it is and if we don't run the mill in that way, we'd go out of business with the loss of over a hundred jobs.'

'You know that, and I know that, Verity,' said Dolly, her voice rising as she attempted to settle her friends worries. 'So... what if a chit of a girl who's free with her favours has the Union men listening to her? They're just playing with her. *They'll* do what *they* want in the end, not what Juliet Skeldon wants. You're getting this out of all proportion.'

'And the Unions grow stronger by the day.' Verity passed the remark musingly.

This rather dismal conversation came to an end with the arrival of Oliver and Theo.

'Theo says that large elm at the end of the garden will have to be chopped down,' Oliver announced as he flopped into a chair beside Verity.

'But it's such a lovely tree,' she protested, pouring Oliver and Theo glasses of lemonade.

'It's rotten, Verity. Tree rot like that can spread and before you know it, you won't have a windbreak to shelter the house from the easterly winds.' Theo spoke with the authority of a land agent who knew about such things.

'In that case, I'll be sorry to see it go,' Verity said. 'It must be a hundred years old or more. It must have been growing there before my great-grandfather built the house.'

'Think what it could tell us if trees could talk,' Dolly commented, her eyes twinkling.

'It would tell us that my great-grandfather, Ezra Lockwood, worked his fingers to the bone to build his mill and this house, and that my father, Jebediah, was hell-bent on squandering the lot,' Verity said, her bitter tone letting them know that she still hadn't forgiven her father for his nefarious lifestyle, and his cruel treatment of her.

'And would have done had you not stepped in to

save it, my love.' Oliver's voice was rich with admiration.

'We did it together,' Verity replied, reaching out and patting his arm. 'I could never have done it without you.'

The loving looks that passed between them were so heartfelt that Dolly found her own heart swelling and she thought how lucky she and Verity were. Two women from opposite ends of the class system who, because of Lockwood Mill, had become the firmest of friends, and both of them married to good men and blessed with beautiful children.

Dolly's thoughts on how fortunate they were to have such lovely families were interrupted when, as if by magic, a noisy clamour in the drawing room announced the arrival of Blaise and Josh, with Briony and Sarah at their heels. All talking at once, they made a beeline to their parents.

'We played the Boer War,' Josh cried, his cheeks ablaze with excitement. 'I won the toss of the dice. I was the British and Blaise was the Boers. He out-manoeuvred me twice but I won in the end, didn't I?' He turned to Blaise for confirmation.

Blaise nodded. 'You did. You won fair and square, Josh.' He still felt obliged to him for keeping secret his humiliation at the hands of the gypsies and he had deliberately let Josh, by far the most inexperienced player, win the battle.

Their parents smiled indulgently, happy to see their sons getting on so well.

'And what did you young ladies get up to?' Theo asked the girls.

'We were trying on Mama's hats and Sarah says she's going to wear the one with purple feathers when she is introduced into society,' Briony told them.

'What might that society be, Sarah?' Dolly's eyebrows had risen to her hairline.

'The people who come to Sir Arnold and Lady Sybil's parties,' Dolly and Theo's daughter replied, her pale-blue eyes and expectant smile sweetly innocent. 'I want to be like them and I'll have to dress properly if I'm to be invited into their company.'

'You have high expectations, darling,' her father replied, loath to tell her that it was highly unlikely that as the daughter of one of Sir Arnold's employees, she would ever receive such an invitation.

'And what about you, Briony?' Oliver asked, his eyes alight with amusement. 'What hat will you wear?'

'I chose that black hat with the stiff brim. I'll wear

it when I join the suffragettes,' she said, her tone ringing with confidence. To confirm her intentions, she raised her arm and cried, 'Votes for Women.'

The grown-ups exchanged meaningful glances, their minds working overtime as they tried to comprehend the futures their daughters had obviously planned for themselves: a debutante mixing with the cream of society, and an ardent campaigner for women's rights and the vote.

Before they could further contemplate, Bella appeared in the drawing room announcing that tea would be served in five minutes. The children cheered and followed her out of the room, Verity calling after them not to forget to wash their hands.

'Suffragette indeed. And there was I thinking that Blaise was going to be the problem,' Oliver whispered in Verity's ear as they made their way to the dining room.

After tea the children went into the small sitting room to play halma. Oliver and Theo relaxed in the drawing room with glasses of port and the wireless playing in the background. Verity and Dolly, taking advantage of the warm evening and the glorious sunset, walked in the garden.

'You'll never guess who I saw yesterday,' said

Dolly, her arm linked in Verity's as they strolled down the garden to look at the diseased elm tree.

'I imagine you saw lots of people so you might as well tell me who and save me having to make futile guesses.'

'Amy Dickenson.'

The women let the name hang in the air.

'She had a lad of about fifteen with her,' Dolly continued, 'so I suppose he's her son, the bairn she tried to claim was our George's.'

'And the child the gossips tried to lay at Oliver's doorstep,' said Verity.

'Aye, the scheming baggage caused no end of bother.'

'She did,' Verity agreed. 'Your poor George fearing his reputation would be tarnished, and the rumours running like wild fire all because the father of the child wore a hat like Oliver's.' She paused, recalling how she herself had doubted Oliver. 'I was left thinking he'd run away to Cumbria to be with her, and not just because he'd seen that hideous creature, Clarence Hargreaves, foisting his kisses on me.' She broke off the head of a dead rose in the border and tossed it into the hedge. 'I wonder how he's faring in prison?'

Dolly shrugged. 'Firing your mill was a dastardly act. He deserves everything he got.'

'Is Amy back for good, do you think?'

'I couldn't say. Life's not been kind to her, though. She's lost what looks she had, but the lad's handsome enough. Tall and dark-haired. He must favour his father, whoever he was.'

'Only Amy knows that,' Verity said as they turned and retraced their steps back up the lawn to the house. When they arrived at the French windows into the drawing room, they found Oliver and Theo deep in conversation, their voices animated and their expressions serious. In the background, the man on the wireless was delivering the weather forecast.

'The Archduke Franz Ferdinand and his wife were assassinated in Serbia this morning,' Oliver told them as the women stepped inside.

'Oh, my goodness, how dreadful,' cried Verity, clapping her hand to her chin and plumping down on the nearest sofa.

'Who exactly is the archduke, and why would anyone want to kill him?' Dolly didn't mind showing her ignorance in front of her husband and friends. They all knew she had little interest in politics.

'He's the heir to the Austro-Hungarian throne,

and the Bosnians strongly object to the power the Austrian-Hungarian Empire has over their country. Those neighbouring states have been at war for years,' Oliver informed her.

'Who did it?' Dolly asked, sitting down beside Verity.

'They've arrested a disgruntled young Bosnian nationalist called Gavrilo Princip,' said Theo, 'but that'll not be the end of it. He wouldn't have been working alone. He's only nineteen – a student, so they said.'

'Only nineteen?' Dolly echoed, aghast.

'How did it happen?' Verity asked, her face crumpling as she added, 'And you say they killed his wife as well?'

'That's right,' said Theo. 'The Archduke and his wife, Sophie, were travelling in an open-top car in a motorcade and the assassin jumped on the running board and shot them both at point-blank range.' He sounded shocked by how easily they had both been killed.

Verity and Dolly gasped at the awfulness of it.

'But was no one guarding them? If, as you say, there was trouble between the two countries then surely, they would have needed some protection,' Verity exclaimed.

'The entire event seems to have been a complete shambles,' Oliver said, taking up the strain to describe what they had heard on the wireless. 'They were there to inspect the military barracks in Sarajevo, and the motorcade had already come under attack when bombs were thrown at it.' He rumpled his hair in frustration. 'For some stupid reason, they continued with the visit, and when they arrived in the city centre to open the State Museum, it seems that everything was in such disarray that the killer was free to carry out his dastardly deed. Sophie died instantly and the archduke a short while later.'

'Did Sophie have any children?' Dolly wanted to know, and when the two men nodded, she said, 'Poor motherless souls.'

'Aye, it's a bad business all round and no doubt we'll be dragged into the consequences,' Theo opined.

'How does it affect us?' Verity's voice was sharp.

'Aye, terrible as it is, why would something that happened hundreds of miles away have anything to do with us?' Dolly sounded utterly confused.

'It's all to do with alliances,' Oliver explained. 'The Austrians will want revenge and will look to the Germans to support them. The Russians will back the Serbs, and seeing as Britain has an agreement with Russia, France and Serbia to come to their aid in times of trouble, we could find ourselves drawn into a war we never asked for.'

'A war!' Verity and Dolly chorused.

'Yes! Like I said, the entire thing is a bloody shambles, if you'll pardon my expression, ladies.' Oliver ran his fingers through the lock of hair that fell over his forehead.

'Dear me, how awful. Don't mention any of this to the children,' Verity begged. 'We don't want to frighten them needlessly. It might all come to nothing.'

'I hope you're right,' Theo said lugubriously.

'My thoughts exactly,' said Oliver, as over at the sideboard, he refilled their glasses with port. 'Sherry, ladies?' He gestured with the carafe.

'I think we're both in need of a strong drink; make mine a brandy, Oliver. What about you, Dolly?'

'I couldn't agree more. Brandy for me too.'

Verity sipped her drink, the strong, sweet spirit warming her throat but not her heart as she recollected the bad feelings she'd been having for some time now. Was that air of unrest that she had sensed whenever she was in the town or at the mill about to become reality? Her blood sprang up as she envisaged what the country at war might be like. Would men like Oliver and Theo have to fight to protect their families if foreign soldiers threatened their safety? She shuddered at the thought of it.

Trials....of the

as..d what the century at war might be like. World
....mble Oliver and Theo have to fight to protect
....their families if forced to.... would balance out....
....She thought and....he thought....

10

On the same Sunday afternoon at the same time as the Hardcastles and the Armitages were at Far View House, Juliet Skeldon was walking along Silver Street feeling rather bored and very lonely. It was almost a year since she had left her home in Dodworth to come to live in Huddersfield with Florence and Clem Armitage, and whilst she was grateful for the comfortable accommodation and her job, she wasn't entirely happy. Living with a middle-aged couple, no matter how kind they were, made her feel old before her time.

She didn't completely mind toiling over a noisy loom for five-and-a half days every week, the wages were fair and the working conditions better than most, but it wasn't the kind of work she would have liked, had she had any choice. It did, however, mean that she could send much-needed money home to her mother each week, and reaching the end of Silver Street where it met Wakefield Road, she walked up to the postbox outside the post office in Storthes and took an envelope from the pocket of her new blue dress. The little plopping noise the letter made as it landed inside the box brought a little smile to her rather sad face. With any luck, her mam would have it by Tuesday at the latest, in time to buy groceries for the week and pay the rent on Friday. The thought made her feel guilty. She usually posted the money on Friday evening after she received her wages so that Mam would get it on Monday morning in time to go to the open market in Barnsley where she could buy food there much cheaper than she could at the village shops in Dodworth.

But on Friday, Juliet had been sorely in need of something to raise her spirits, and so she'd hung on to her wages with the intention of treating herself to something new. Then on Saturday afternoon, she'd gone into the town and bought the blue dress, some stockings and a pair of sandals from a second-hand stall in the market. Her purchases had left her purse somewhat depleted and now, glancing down at her shiny, brown sandals and the smooth, rayon stockings covering her ankles, she felt even more guilty.

The reason for her unhappiness was twofold. She missed her mother and home, and she had failed to make friends with any of the women she worked with. Her cousin, Katie, had been friendly enough at first but she'd distanced herself from Juliet when she began haranguing the women to attend the Union meetings. Fearful of losing her own friends, Katie had made it quite plain that she didn't want Juliet tagging along with her whenever the girls met up after work. And to make matters worse, some of the women seemed to think that the natives of Huddersfield were superior to the people from the mining villages around Barnsley and they made fun of her. On Friday, May Sykes had referred to her as the 'black-arsed one'. When Juliet had looked angry and confused, May had sneered, 'Tha knows, them wi' rings of coal dust round their mucky backsides.'

'Aye, an' I'll bet there's more than one of our men as had a feel o' that black arse,' Lily Cockhill had added.

The other women had rumbled their agreement. Juliet knew they objected to the way in which she played up to the men, but if she were to uphold her father's beliefs – and her own – then a few kisses and cuddles were a small price to pay for being let into the Union meetings. Even so, she knew in her heart that whilst they sometimes let her put forward a motion, like the one she had made about not being locked out until breakfast time if a worker arrived after the hooter had blown, they didn't really take her seriously. They had their own agenda.

Now, as she clopped on towards Aspley Wharf, the pleasure she had taken from her shopping spree had worn thin and her new sandals were threatening to blister her heels. *Damn Lockwood Mill and all those awful women who work there,* she thought sourly as she clattered down a steep flight of stone steps and on to the canal towpath.

The canal's oily waters shimmered in the glow of the afternoon sun, rosy red and orange reflected in its mirror. Juliet thought of Dodworth and the swimming hole at Miller Dam. She'd gone there with her schoolfriends on hot summer days, jumping into deep, cool water wearing a swimsuit her mother had knitted from scraps of different coloured wool. She laughed softly as she recalled how, when it got wet, it got longer until it almost reached her knees. She should have gone home this weekend and handed over what was left of her wages after paying Mrs Armitage for her keep instead of selfishly treating herself.

She'd visited her family six times since leaving home, and it had been lovely to spend time with her brothers and sisters, walking along The Bottoms and up to Stainborough Castle in the afternoons, and at night giggling in the bed she shared with Rhoda and Wendy and little Cecil. She hadn't been lonely then. But the best part had been when she had handed over her wages in person, the look of love and gratitude on her mother's face making her heart swell with pride. Her dad was still seething with rage at being banned from working down the pit but even his bad temper didn't detract from the joy she felt at being at home. She listened to his rants and at the Union meetings she attended, she repeated his words. One day, she would make him proud of her, she told herself as she strolled along swiping at the heads of lacy, white cow parsley that grew on the towpath.

A barge loaded with bales careened slowly down the canal pulled by a huge shire horse and its handler who were walking steadily on the towpath. One of the two burly bargees on its deck waved to her and Juliet waved back. She wished she was with them.

She'd never sailed on a barge; Dodworth didn't have a canal. It had slag heaps.

Clem had told her that the canal was called after Sir John Ramsden, the man who had ordered it to be built, and that in one direction it went through nine locks before it reached Cooper Bridge, and in the other, it ran through the Standedge Tunnel for miles under the Pennines. That would be an adventure, she mused, feeling desperately in need of one.

When she came abreast of another large shire horse munching on the grass, Juliet stopped to pat its warm shoulder. The horse didn't object, and she was reminded of the pit ponies that worked underground in the mines. On one or two days each year, they were brought to the surface, and she'd gone with the other children to play with the ragged little creatures, many of them blind and lamed. The memory angered her. The rotten pit owners were to blame for treating them so badly. *And they treat the miners just as bad,* she seethed as in her mind's eye, she pictured how her dad had looked when he came off a shift, his skin black with coal dust and his knuckles and elbows bruised. But that had been when they had let him work before they'd sent him to prison. Now, he was pale and puffy, and his limbs which had been as strong as steel were scrawny. To dispel the sad thoughts, she nuzzled her cheek against the shire's soft hide, taking some comfort from its pungent, earthy smell. Then dropping a kiss on the end of the horse's velvety nose and giving it a final pat, she crossed the path to where a brightly painted barge was moored alongside.

Paintings of castles and red and white roses decorated the doorway into the cabin, and she wondered what it was like inside. Glancing round to make sure no one was about, she jumped down onto the deck. The door opened easily and she stepped into the small space, amazed to see that it was like a complete little house: a narrow bed, a little cooker, a sink and a table on which sat a tin with *Huntley and Palmer* written on it.

Biscuits. Her tummy rumbled, even though it was less than three hours since she'd eaten Mrs Armitage's tasty Sunday dinner of beef served with Yorkshire pudding and cabbage. Prising off the lid, she helped herself to a ginger nut then sat on the narrow bench gazing out of the little window as she munched and pretended that she was sailing home. Lost in reverie, she didn't immediately hear the thud of boots on the towpath. The barge swayed as heavy feet landed on the deck.

Juliet froze. Her mouth, already dry from eating the biscuit, suddenly felt as parched as if she had been eating sand.

'Hitch her up,' a voice shouted. The barge juddered. The timbers creaked, and the lantern above Juliet's head swung gently on its hook as the barge gave a lurch then steadied itself.

'Hitched up and ready to go,' a different voice shouted, followed by another thud on deck. To her horror, the mill that she'd been staring at through the window disappeared from view. The barge was moving. Fear turned to excitement. This was a real adventure.

Juliet moved closer to the window and saw a man leading a horse on the towpath. It looked like the one she had patted only a short while ago. She sat watching the scenery slide by and her heart in her mouth as to how she would explain her presence.

She was just about to go on deck and make her excuses when the cabin door opened. Blinding rays of sunlight shot into the gloom and all she could see was a dark, hulking shape in the doorway.

'Bugger me!' the shape exclaimed. 'Eh! Jim. We've got a bloody stowaway.'

A head appeared behind the shoulder of the man

in the doorway and stared at Juliet. She knew what a stowaway was, and she felt like a pirate in a story her schoolteacher had read to them. He had stowed away in search of treasure.

'Hello,' she said boldly. 'I hope you don't mind but I ate one of your biscuits.'

The bargees burst out laughing.

'Come on, get on deck. Let's have a proper look at you,' the one who had found her said. He was grinning widely. He liked the look of this cheeky girl with her pale, fair hair and blue eyes.

Juliet got to her feet and followed them, feeling not in the least afraid.

They were both muscular young men in their late teens or early twenties. The oldest-looking one had wispy, brown hair and slightly prominent front teeth. The younger man had a shock of thick, black curls and laughing eyes. Juliet's gaze lingered on his bared arms and chest. He was quite handsome.

She patted her hair and smoothed her dress then a gave the bargees a mischievous grin. 'Where are we going?' she asked carelessly.

The men looked at one another in amazement. They were quite discombobulated at finding a pretty girl with a cocky attitude aboard their barge.

'Who are you?' the younger man with black, curly hair asked. 'An' what's more, what are you doing on our barge?'

'Juliet Skeldon – and I was just curious to see what your barge looked like inside.'

'Well. I'm Fred, an' he's Jim,' he said, flicking his thumb at his mate, 'an' you've no bloody right to be here.' He turned to address Jim. 'We'd best go back to Aspley an' put her ashore. We can't take her with us.' Then he shouted to the man leading the horse. 'Hey, Syd! Hold on there. We've a problem.'

Syd did as he was asked and the barge slowed to a stop.

Jim frowned. 'We don't have time,' he protested. 'Not if we're to get the stuff an' be back here in time for t'wagon to pick it up. Harry'll not want to be hanging about, an' I'm not for losing a few quid just because this little madam wanted to see what a barge looked like.'

'You don't have to turn back because of me. I can go wherever I want, and I wouldn't want you to lose your wages by wasting time so I'll come with you.' Juliet gave them both an irresistible smile as though that settled the matter.

'Aw, bugger it! Let her come,' he said signalling to

Syd to carry on. The barge juddered as the horse took the strain and they were on their way again.

Juliet, unaware that she'd been clenching her fists whilst they made their decision, felt her hands relax. She grinned, and walking casually to the side of the barge, she perched on the rail, letting the light breeze ruffle her long, fair hair.

All this time, Jim had been at the helm and the barge gliding further and further from Aspley. Fred lit a cigarette then went to have a muttered conversation with Jim. Juliet hung over the barge rail, watching it push reeds and floating debris aside as it slunk through the silent water. Her blood pumped in her veins and she felt overcome with elation. When a barge going in the opposite direction glided by, she swung round, shouting, 'Ship ahoy.'

At the first lock, Fred leapt ashore to open the gates and Syd unhitched the horse. Jim kept the barge dead centre as they nosed inside. Juliet's tummy plummeted as the water dropped to reveal clumps of slimy weed like writhing snakes clinging to the lock walls. Then they were through and when Fred jumped back on board, he came and stood by Juliet. 'Well then, let's be knowing a bit about you, Juliet Skeldon. Where are you from?'

'Dodworth, near Barnsley,' she said, 'and I'm a weaver at Lockwood Mill.'

'Lockwood's, eh? Lucky you! We work for Brierley's. I've heard tell Lockwood's are good to work for,' Fred said.

'They're all right,' said Juliet carelessly, 'but there's not a mill or a pit in the whole country that couldn't be fairer to them that works for 'em.' Her tone had become heated.

Fred grimaced. 'You're right about that. It's one law for the rich an' another for the poor buggers that makes 'em rich.'

'It is. But the Unions will bring 'em to heel. You just wait an' see.'

'Oh, so you favour the Unions, do you?' Fred looked surprised.

'Aye, I do. Me dad was a Union man at the pit he *used* to work at,' Juliet said bitterly.

'You sound angry.'

'I am.' Juliet then went on to tell him about her dad, and how he was now unemployable. 'So, you see, that's what brought me to work in Lockwood Mill,' she said. 'An' I don't like it, but I'll carry on where me dad left off and make sure that the bosses meet the Union's demands whether they like it or not.'

'Good for you. I'm a Union man meself,' said Fred. 'The more there are of us, the more power we'll have to make the buggers sit up an' sing to our tune.'

Juliet smiled. She liked Fred.

By the time they had negotiated three more locks, she had lost her fear of the rise and fall of the barge in between the dank, slimy walls. When Fred went into the cabin and made potted meat sandwiches, she found she was enjoying herself tremendously. Sitting talking with the like-minded men was good for the soul.

They reached their port of call at a warehouse on a quiet stretch of the canal. Two tough-looking men were waiting for them beside several bales wrapped in hessian. Fred and Jim took them on board then exchanged a few whispered words with the other men before climbing back on the barge. The sun was setting and a fiery blaze lit the water as they careened back the way they had come. As they glided under a stand of willows weeping their long, green fronds over the canal and casting dark shadows on the barge, Juliet thought that she had never seen anything more beautiful. Then, curious as to why they were working on Sunday, Juliet asked what it was they were doing.

'It's for us to know an' nobody else.' Fred winked and tapped the side of his nose.

Juliet suspected that they were up to no good, and that their cargo was most likely stolen. It wasn't unknown for mill hands to make a bit on the side by thieving, but she didn't care. The mill owners had more than enough.

When they arrived back at Aspley and moored the barge on the wharf, another mysterious exchange was made, and the bales loaded into the back of a waiting wagon. Syd unhitched the horse, and saying he was taking her to the stables to be fed and watered for the night, he set off walking it towards a long low building. He returned within minutes and brushing his hand together and smacking his lips he said, 'I could murder a pint. Are you ready?'

Fred handed Juliet onto the towpath and the four of them mounted the steps to the road. She prepared to say goodbye, saddened that her magical journey was over, but before she could thank them for a wonderful afternoon, Fred said, 'We're going to the Boy and Barrel for a sup of ale. Our Jenny'll be there. Do you fancy coming wi' us?'

Juliet jumped at the chance. 'I'd love to,' she gushed.

They began walking up into the town, Juliet between them, her heart singing.

When they arrived at the public house in the Beast Market, Jim asked, 'Are you old enough to be going in licensed premises?'

'Course I am,' Juliet lied. Who cared that she was a few months short of her eighteenth birthday. She was with friends and it felt wonderful.

11

During the month of July, a few weeks after Verity had told Dolly that everywhere she went outside her own home, the world seemed to be ill at ease with itself, she discovered that her feelings of foreboding had not played her foul. After the assassination of the Archduke and his wife, international tensions were mounting and the Balkan states were in upheaval. As the crisis continued to ferment, there was much speculation as to how and where it would end.

'Do you think the trouble in other parts of Europe will affect us?' Verity asked as she sat with her husband and Dolly and Theo one Sunday evening in the drawing room at Far View House. They had just listened to the six o'clock news on the wireless, and what they had heard did not bode well for a peaceful settlement any time soon.

'If Germany keeps its promise to support Austria and Hungary in a conflict then I fear our alliances might well drag us into the whole sorry mess,' Oliver replied gloomily.

'I agree,' said Theo.

Dolly frowned. 'Oh, yes. I remember you telling us that the day the Archduke and his wife were assassinated,' she said, 'but then it didn't seem to be that important.' She looked at Verity, her frown deepening.

'But I thought the Serbs had agreed to Austria's ultimatum to meet their demands,' Verity cried, looking to Oliver for assurance. 'Didn't the Serbs agree to purge their army and stop the press issuing anti-propaganda about Austria?'

'They did, my love, but they refused to give up their sovereignty, and since then, Austria has broken off all diplomatic relations with them. It certainly looks as though they're heading for a full-blown war.'

'I'm afraid it does,' said Theo. 'Our government has called for a mediation conference, but so far, they've been ignored, and the Russians are already mobilising their troops.' He shook his head despairingly, his blond hair flopping over his forehead.

'But that's dreadful!' Dolly's green eyes flashed angrily. 'They have no right to ignore our government. We don't want their rotten war.'

'Nobody wants a war,' Verity exclaimed. 'I blame these stupid alliances. Why should we fight other countries' battles?'

'Because if we came under attack from an enemy, we would expect our allies to come to our aid, and they expect the same from us,' Oliver said with asperity. He stood and walked over to the sideboard. 'Anybody for another drink?' he asked. 'We can talk all night about the situation, but nothing we say or do will alter anything.'

'That's because you men like war,' Verity said, her tone bitter. 'If women ruled the world, there would be no fighting.'

Dolly nodded in agreement as she accepted her glass of sherry.

They each sipped their drinks in quiet contemplation of the future.

* * *

'Gone! Gone where?' Dolly asked as she sat down at the table in her mother's kitchen in Silver Street. It was a Friday morning, the last day in July, and she had called to see Florence on her way to meet Verity at the mill. 'When did she go?' Dolly continued, accepting the cup of tea her mother handed her.

'Sunday. She walked in here bold as brass last Saturday night and announced that she was leaving to go and live in Rose Street with a girl called Jenny and her brother, Fred. I don't know who they are, but she must be well in with them.' Florence sat down at the table and gave her daughter a look of bemusement. 'The very next morning, she packed her things and off she went.'

'It seems to me that Juliet Skeldon's a law unto herself, the ungrateful madam.'

'Aye, well, she's not been too happy living with us. We're too old to be company for her,' Florence excused. 'And she doesn't seem to have made any friends at the mill.'

'I'm not surprised to hear that,' Dolly retorted. 'Verity says she's a trouble-causer always trying to stir up the other lasses to make complaints when there's nowt to complain about.'

'I know what you mean. She had two sides to her, did Juliet. Sweet and demure one minute, and like a raging bull the next. She got on your dad's nerves the way she went on about workers' rights and the Union. I can't say I'm sorry to see her go; it was just the suddenness of it that took me aback. But there you are,' said Florence, rubbing her hands, 'we did our bit by giving her somewhere to make a start.'

'You did, Mam, an' I hope she was grateful for it.' Dolly stood and lifted her bag. 'Now, I'd best be off. I'm meeting Verity at eleven. We're finalising things for the mill outing.'

Florence looked askance. 'I'm surprised you can even think about day trips, what with Germany rampaging into Luxembourg. Mr Asquith says we'll be in the thick of it if Germany doesn't withdraw its troops. I just heard it on the news.'

'Oh, Mam, I know how bad things are. We talked about nothing else all weekend, and if the Prime Minister says we're joining the war, then we are.' Dolly sounded exasperated. 'But life has to go on, Mam. We can't just stop doing what we've planned to do. And anyway, it might all be a storm in a teacup and fizzle out before it really involves us.'

'Ugh! I wish I had your optimism, Dolly Beaumont. You live in cloud cuckoo land.'

'Always look on the bright side, that's me,' laughed Dolly, 'and like I say, if we are going to war then we'll just have to make the best of things.' She opened the door and bounced out into the street. Florence raised her eyes to the ceiling.

Dolly walked quickly along Silver Street and then down Storthes to Aspley Basin and Lockwood Mill. Verity was in the mill office and as Dolly entered, she met her with a smile.

'Thanks for coming. Come and sit here by me and look to see if I've forgotten anything,' she said, pushing the pages on which they had previously listed their plans across the desk.

'My mam's shocked at us planning a day out what with a war looming over us,' Dolly said, taking a seat next to Verity. 'And what's more, she's feeling a bit peeved that Juliet Skeldon suddenly upped and moved out.'

'Oh, where did she go? She can't have gone far. I saw her at her loom not an hour ago.'

'She's moved in with some friends of hers.'

'It can't be anybody from our mill. She's not at all popular with the other women.'

'Well, whoever she's gone to live with, they're welcome to her,' said Dolly. 'Now let's go over this itinerary. I'm glad it's Locke Park again.'

'Yes, they enjoyed it last time, and it's not too far

away. If this glorious weather keeps up, they'll enjoy the gardens and the lake.'

The two women set about checking the list: charabancs ordered, picnic hampers to be prepared by Gert and May in the canteen, and prizes for the racing and games. Taking so many people on an outing such as this was like manoeuvring an army, and they didn't want to leave anything to chance.

When it seemed that they had covered everything, it was time for lunch and they were preparing to leave the office just as Oliver appeared. He had been attending to problems with the carding machines.

'May I escort you ladies over to the canteen to partake of the finest Lockwood Mill has to offer,' he said, holding his arms akimbo.

Verity and Dolly laughed, and linking arms, they walked across the cobbled mill yard. In the canteen, they were met by smiling faces and nods of welcome.

'Eeh, Dolly, good to see you.'

'Have you come back to work in t'weavin' shed?'

Dolly laughingly fielded the greetings of her old colleagues. 'She won't have me,' she said, nodding at Verity. 'She says I'm a time-waster.'

The workers roared with laughter. They all knew what firm friends the Mill Mistress and Dolly were, and their own relationships with their employers were such that they felt free to join in the fun.

'That's right,' Verity said. 'She begged me to take her back but I told her we couldn't afford her.' As she spoke, her eyes alighted on Juliet Skeldon. She was scowling.

Inevitably, the joshing fizzled into talk of the impending war, with the workers asking Oliver and Verity their opinions on how it might affect the mill. They answered as positively as they could, saying it would be work as usual, and hopeful that it wouldn't affect the supply of raw wool, chemical dyes and other such stuff.

'Do *you* really think we'll have to go an' fight, Mr Horsfall?' The young lad from the scouring shed looked at Isaac for affirmation. The elderly head loom tuner was considered something of an afficionado on matters to do with the running of the country.

Isaac rubbed his grizzly jaw. 'We'll know soon enough, lad. Mr Asquith's asked the Germans to respect Belgium's neutrality an' withdraw their troops,' he said grimly. 'If they don't then our country will be at war.'

For a moment or two, a solemn lull fell over the

canteen which then erupted into more noisy questions, opinions, and hopes and fears.

* * *

The following day, the trip to Locke Park went ahead as planned, but without the joie de vivre there had been when they had made the same journey the previous year. All this talk of war had put a damper on things and the mill hands, for the most part, were mulling over how it might affect their own livelihoods. Those who were old enough to have lost loved ones in the Boer Wars commiserated with one another, and the younger ones considered the prospect of their husbands and sons being called upon to defend the country.

It was a scorching-hot August day, hotter than they had ever known, and usually, they would have welcomed it had circumstances been different, but the intense heat only added to their languor as they walked around the park or half-heartedly ran races and played games. On the homeward journey, Dolly commented that perhaps they should have heeded her mother's advice and cancelled the outing, but Verity disagreed. In her opinion, it was important to carry on as normal for as long as it was possible. Nobody could say what the future might bring. She'd even optimistically suggested that common sense would prevail, that the conflict could be brought to an end by peaceful negotiation. Whether or not she truly believed that didn't deter her from pressing the point. All she knew was that life had to go on.

The next day, Sunday, the news was even more depressing. Germany demanded to pass through Belgium; the Belgians refused. The Germans ignored their refusal, and on Monday, they declared war on France and invaded Belgium.

When Verity and Oliver arrived home from the mill on Tuesday evening, they like thousands of other British families sat glued to the wireless. Germany had already violated Belgium's neutrality and their invasion of that country had tipped the balance. At 2 p.m. that afternoon, Sir Edward Grey had delivered Britain's ultimatum for the Germans to withdraw by 11 p.m. British time (midnight in Germany). But the German army was hell-bent on marching into France, and by all accounts was making great progress.

'A German victory in Western Europe, and particularly in France, would establish their control over the English Channel,' Oliver told Verity. 'That would pose a severe threat to our security, and to trade.

Many of our supplies come by that route. The British Navy have been mobilised to protect the French coast, but whether they're successful remains to be seen.'

'If we lose control of the English Channel, we won't be able to export our cloth to Germany,' said Verity, her voice wobbling as she thought of the major orders of fine worsted that her mill sent to that country.

'Once they're our enemies, they'll not want it,' Oliver growled.

They sat listening to news reports with sinking spirits, and by 11 p.m., the British deadline remained unanswered. Close on midnight, Britain declared war, and Verity and Oliver went to bed with heavy hearts.

The following morning, the Hardcastle family in Far View House and the workforce at Lockwood Mill knew for certain that England was preparing to take on the might of the German army.

Blaise was excited by the prospect of his country going to war, and with the delivery of the morning papers, he scoured the pages of *The Times* and the *Leeds Intelligencer* with zeal. *The Times* headline blaring *Britain at War?* filled him with patriotic fervour, and reading such phrases as *To save her good*

Name; To save her life and empire; To save the freedom of the people all over Europe; Fight for your life; Fight for your honour; Fight for mankind, made his blood surge. He would dearly have liked to dash upstairs and don a uniform, pick up his guns and march into battle. But he was too young to enlist and, crushed with disappointment, all he could do was read about it.

After weeks of speculation and mounting tension, by September, Verity's fears that her mill would be seriously affected had somewhat abated. There seemed to be very little change in the world of commerce, and there was a general consensus that the war would be short-lived. It was maybe this belief that leant a certain kind of glamour and a sense of adventure about joining the forces. Recruitment centres had opened all over the country, and a flood of posters appealing to the consciences of young men were displayed in every town and city. Lord Herbert Horatio Kitchener, the Minister for War, stated that the British army needed an additional 100,000 men, and by the third of September, his plea had been partially answered when 33,000 men enlisted in one day. This included several of the younger male mill hands from Lockwood Mill who, lured by the patriotic fervour that was prevailing throughout the country, had handed in their notice. The lads had grinned sheepishly as they told her they were leaving, but she could tell they were happy and excited by the thought of a smart uniform, shiny buttons, and a chance to travel. She wished them well, taking care to hide the horrible feelings she had about the war, and thanking God that her son was too young to enlist. And as she did her rounds of the mill, in the spinning room and the weaving shed, she commiserated with the mothers and wives of the young men who had enlisted, her anxiety for them mounting by the day. It was then that Verity realised change was definitely afoot, and it would certainly affect the way in which she would have to run her mill.

* * *

One day, when Verity went into town with Blaise to buy him new boots, they came across a crowd in the Market Place singing 'Rule Britannia'.

Blaise slowed and tugged at her sleeve. 'Let's join in,' he urged, pushing his way into the throng and lustily breaking into song as he stood to attention, his face alight. Verity stood silently watching him and feeling uneasy. As the anthem petered to a stop, she called for him to come away. The feeling persisted as they walked along John William Street past the posters of General Kitchener's pointing finger and the slogan, *Your country needs you* and an image of John Bull asking, *Who's Absent?*

I am, Blaise thought, *and if this war lasts, I'll answer Kitchener's call. Ma might consider me to be a child but I have the mind of an adult and I'll do as I please.* He would have lingered by each poster had his mother not chivvied him across the road and into St Peter's Street, protesting, 'For goodness' sake, Blaise, we haven't got all day.'

They hurried down the length of the street, and as they were about to turn the corner into Byram Street, the pungent whiff of burning assailed their noses. Rounding the corner, they saw that the boot-maker's shop windows were no more, and the gaping, jagged holes in the smashed, blackened glass allowed them to see that a recent blaze had destroyed the interior. Half-burned boots and shoes littered the floor, some still smouldering amidst the debris of charred timber.

Verity clapped her hand to her mouth, aghast. 'Good Lord. Poor Mr Schneider.'

Blaise shrugged and said, 'It looks like we won't be buying my boots from here, Ma.'

Then Verity spied the owner of the crockery shop next door standing in his doorway.

'What happened here?' she called out. 'When did...' She gestured at the ruins.

'Last night,' Henry Nixon said, walking towards her. 'A gang of lads full of drink did it, so the police told me. They'd already daubed his windows wi' red paint two nights before.'

'Daubed his windows?'

'Aye. "Germans out," they'd written. He didn't heed the warning.'

'But he's been here for years; he and his son are lovely people.'

'Aye, they might be, but they're Germans. The whole damned row could have gone afire if t'fire brigade hadn't been on hand. I could have lost my shop.' He sounded more concerned for himself than he did for his neighbour.

Verity eyed Henry with distaste, shocked by his selfish lack of compassion. 'Were they harmed?' she asked, her heart going out to the gentle, elderly boot-maker and his polite son.

'Nay, they got out in time, the missis an' all. They've packed up and gone, as far as I know. And good riddance. He never did me a bad turn, but you don't want their sort on your doorstep at a time like this. You don't know what they'd be up to.'

'Supplying people with good-quality footwear,'

Verity snapped, 'just as they have since my husband was a young boy.'

Blaise stopped scuffing his boot toe against the pavement edge and said, 'They're Germans, Ma. They could be spies for all you know. They got what they deser...'

His mother's withering glare silenced him, but it didn't wipe the sneer from his face.

'Aye, you don't know who you can trust these days,' Henry agreed, giving Blaise an admiring glance. 'Get rid of the lot of 'em, that's what I say.' Blaise gave Henry a wide grin.

'I suppose you've already enlisted, a grand, big lad like you,' Henry continued. 'What regiment did you join?'

The enquiry had Blaise puffing out his chest, his pride at being recognised as a soldier hopelessly dashed when his mother snarled, 'He's not yet fifteen. He's too young to fight.'

Blaise's shoulders slumped and he mooched off down the street, his hands thrust deep in his trousers' pockets. Verity turned on her heel and hurried after him. When she caught up with him, they crossed the road by the Parish Church and in Cross Church Street, they purchased a pair of stout, black boots that in Verity's opinion were nowhere near as good quality as those she had intended to buy from the German bootmaker. She was further aggravated when the shop assistant attending them said, 'These'll stand you in good stead when you're marching. These boots are better than army issue.'

Verity paid the bill and stormed out of the shop. Blaise, now wearing his new boots, stomped along the pavement ahead of her, feeling rather pleased with what he'd seen and heard that morning. He wondered who the lads were who had fired the German's shop, and thought he'd like to join them. He might not yet be able to enlist, but he could rout out the enemy in his own town.

* * *

The weeks passed by, and come Christmas, those who had pontificated that the war would be over by then, changed their tune. Although the British Expeditionary Forces had succeeded in preventing the enemy's race to control the English Channel, the Germans had captured Hill 60 in Ypres, a major disaster, and the war raged on.

Resigned to the fact that no end was in sight, Verity and Oliver struggled to keep the looms turning, but as spring 1915 approached, it became more and more difficult to carry on as usual. Supplies dwindled, exports failed to be delivered, and orders were so few that the mill hands were back to working short-time, three days on and two days off. And suddenly, it seemed that everybody's husbands, sons and brothers were soldiers or naval recruits.

'We've lost a spinner, three wool scourers, and two lads from the dyehouse this week,' Verity told Oliver one Monday morning in March, two days after Blaise and Briony had celebrated their fifteenth birthdays. The party had been a scaled-down affair with just the Beaumont and Armitage families as guests, and whilst it had been pleasant enough, the happy feeling it generated had dissipated as soon as she'd arrived at the mill. Now, she pushed the ledger across the desk for his perusal. 'Add that to the hands who've already enlisted and our workforce is worryingly low,' she continued, her dove-grey eyes darkening as she gave her husband a despairing look.

'George says he can manage without the lads from the dyehouse for the time being, and what's left of our raw wool stock is already scoured,' Oliver said, running his fingers through his hair then rubbing his hand over his jaw. 'Let's face it, Verity, we've so little work on at the moment, the hands that have enlisted will hardly be missed. Every mill in the valley is facing the same problem. Yesterday, James Crowther told me that the cloth he exported to a regular client in Hamburg before Christmas still hasn't been paid for, and now he doubts it ever will.'

Verity's face creased with consternation. Germany was one of the cloth-making industry's most important overseas markets. 'And are we owed money by any of our German customers?' When Oliver answered in the affirmative, her shoulders slumped. Just lately, she had neglected to keep a strict eye on the ledgers that recorded the mill's finances, and now she felt guilty at having left Oliver to bear the brunt of the day-to-day running of the mill, but her concerns had been focused on another matter: Blaise.

On the surface, he appeared to be toeing the line as he had done ever since the unfortunate incident with the gypsies. He was no longer rude or confrontational with his parents, was pleasant to Briony and respectful to Bella and Susan. He attended to his schoolwork and his master had no further complaints as to his behaviour towards the other boys, and he had maintained his friendship with Josh Beaumont. At other times, he spent hours in his bedroom whose walls were covered with war posters and maps tracking the advances or retreats of the British army, fascinated by the war. However, his mother couldn't help feeling that there was an undercurrent at work, one she didn't care to admit to.

Several times over the past few months, he had asked permission to go out in the evening to meet up with Josh, something he had never before shown an interest in. One night, when he'd returned home late looking dishevelled, Verity had enquired lightly, 'Whatever do you and Josh get up to?'

Blaise had been shifty and mumbled, 'Oh, you know. The usual things.' Josh Beaumont had been just as cagey, his initial surprise when she mentioned his meetings with Blaise quickly masked by a few bland platitudes. Verity had then determined to ask Dolly what the boys got up to, but she was so busy at the mill that it had slipped her mind.

When she voiced her suspicions to Oliver, he told her she was imagining things and that he was far more concerned with keeping their business afloat. He'd been approached by a contingency of male mill hands who had informed him that they intended to volunteer if the war continued much longer, that they considered it their duty. 'Young, healthy men like us shouldn't be standing idly by whilst others are fighting for our freedom,' the spokesman had told him. Yet again, Verity chastised herself for her neglect of mill matters. Had they approached her, she might have talked them out of it.

Two weeks later, she realised that her plea would have been futile. On 7 May, a German U-boat sank the RMS *Lusitania* off the Head of Kinsale. Over a thousand civilian lives were lost. Outraged by such a despicable act, men who had yet to enlist flocked to the recruiting stations, and Verity's workforce was seriously depleted.

'Not that it matters,' she said one evening as she and Oliver sat at the desk in the study at Far View House juggling with the affairs of the mill. 'Our trade is slowly grinding to halt. We can't make cloth without the materials we need, and even if we could, we can't sell it. Our overseas market has gone to pot, and our inland deliveries are hampered now that the mobilising of the troops has taken over the railways. We'll just have to sit it out and do the best we can to stay afloat.'

Oliver, keenly aware of how much the mill meant to her, put down his pen and laid his hand on hers. 'And we will, Verity. We will.'

12

Briony crept from her bedroom and along the landing to Blaise's bedroom, careful not to disturb her parents in their room across the corridor. Entering without knocking, she caught Blaise in the act of stowing a heavy wooden club in the bottom of his wardrobe.

He sprung upright, his expression ugly.

'Where were you this evening?' Briony asked. 'And what were you doing?'

'Scouts,' Blaise growled.

'No, you weren't. Josh says you hardly ever go to the Scouts,' Briony accused.

'What has that got to do with him, or you, for that

matter? I don't have to answer to you for what I do. You're not your brother's keeper,' he sneered.

'I don't want to be,' Briony scoffed, 'but I have it on authority that you're running with a gang who're wrecking properties in the town that are occupied by Germans.'

Blaise flinched, the shocked look on his face admitting his guilt. Then, quickly gathering his wits, he began to bluster. 'Who told you that? It's a load of rubbish.'

'No, it's not. Mary Liversedge says her older brother knows for a fact that you were one of the boys running away from the pork butcher's shop that was wrecked two nights ago. He's in the fire service, and he wouldn't lie about something like that.'

'Case of mistaken identity,' Blaise bluffed, his nonchalant response making Briony think that maybe her schoolfriend's brother was just stirring trouble. But when Blaise stepped closer and grabbed her by the front of her nightdress, almost yanking her off her feet, she knew Robin Liversedge hadn't been telling lies.

'You keep your poky little nose out of my affairs,' he hissed, shaking her violently before shoving her away. 'Get back to your own room, and don't you dare go snivelling to Ma and Pa or it'll be the worst for you.'

Feeling awfully vulnerable in her state of undress, and having suffered many times at the hands of her twin, Briony ran from the room.

After she had gone, Blaise threw himself down on the bed, his ears pricked as he listened for signs that Briony had gone to blab to their parents. When nothing happened, he lay silently cursing Robin Liversedge and his big-mouthed sister. Maybe he'd have to curtail his forays for the time being. He screwed his face at the thought of missing out on the thrill he took from destroying a German business. After the incident at the boot-makers', he'd hung about the streets in the rougher end of the town until he'd managed to fall in with a gang of lads and men who perpetrated the rotten deeds, each sortie with them more satisfyingly brutal; he was fighting the war in his own way.

Back in her own bedroom, Briony climbed into bed, but she did not sleep. Instead, she mulled over whether or not to betray her brother. It didn't sit easy with her; he was her twin, her other half, and she had always believed in the special bond that had been formed in their mother's womb. Sometimes, she thought of them lying entwined as they'd waited to be born, her tiny body shielded by big, strong Blaise: two peas in a pod – but not at all the same.

Almost from the start, she had learned how different they were, not simply by gender or size but in their everyday dealings with the world. Whereas she was sweet-natured and placid, and content to accept that there were rules by which one lived, Blaise took pleasure in flouting them. But for all their differences, she loved him, and had lied, defended and forgiven him time and again. Deep inside, she felt that there was something about her brother that set him apart from Josh and Luke, and the other boys of her acquaintance. Now, as she pondered on his latest escapades, she was torn between loyalty and the need to keep him safe. Sliding down under the eiderdown, she told herself she'd give him a good talking to tomorrow, point out the error of his ways and the shame such behaviour would reflect on his family, and with that, she fell into a deep sleep.

* * *

Briony wasn't the only one who was having a restless night. Juliet Skeldon was lying in her bed in the room she shared with Jenny Moorhouse in the house on Rose Street. Through the thin wall, she could hear the rumbling snores of Jenny's brother, Fred, and his mate, Jim Whitworth. She had been living with them since the previous August now, and whilst the house wasn't as clean and comfortable as her lodgings with Florence Armitage had been, or the food as plentiful, life was much more interesting and exciting.

Like tonight, she thought, tossing onto the flat of her back, a sheen of sweat coating her skin when she looked back on what she had done not two hours ago. It had been her job to deflect the attention of the nightwatchman at the warehouse Fred and Jim had robbed. It wasn't the first time she'd acted as bait for their nefarious dealings, and she took pride in successfully luring the unsuspecting victims away from the mills or warehouses they were paid to guard. In fact, she'd almost perfected the art of attracting a man's attention then leading him on to believe that there was the promise of much more than a casual chat with a girl who just happened to be wandering by at a loose end.

Tonight, along with Jenny, Fred and Jim, she'd boarded the barge belonging to the men's boss and they had sailed down the canal under cover of darkness. A short way off from the warehouse they had targeted, Juliet, Fred and Jim had disembarked onto the towpath, leaving Jenny and Syd to steer the barge further down the waterway. Then, whilst the men hid nearby, she had walked up to the warehouse doors, and waited. She didn't have long to wait before the doors opened and a lanky chap wearing a leather cap and overall came outside. She withdrew a cigarette from the packet she was holding and stuck it between her red lips.

Holding her breath, and her nerves tingling, she gave him time to take his cigarettes and matches from his overall pocket then sashayed up to him, hips swinging and her smile wide.

'By, am I glad to see you,' she said, standing close and fluttering her eyelashes. 'I'm busting for a fag, but I've lost me matches.'

Once he'd recovered from his surprise to find a pretty blonde outside his door, he promptly struck a match and lit her cigarette. Juliet dragged on it. 'You're a lifesaver, love. I thought I was going to have to walk the rest of the way gasping for one. An' just my luck, I come across a good-looking fella like you to save me bacon.' She flicked her long, fair curls with her free hand and smiled up into his face.

He gave her a lopsided grin. 'What you doin' here anyway at this time o' night?'

She shrugged and turned her mouth down at the

corners. 'I wa' walkin' wi' me boyfriend but we fell out an' he left me to walk back on me own.'

'That wa' a rotten thing to do. I'd not walk off on a girl like you.'

Juliet linked her arm through his and leaned against him. She felt his long, thin body quiver. 'Aye, but they're not all gentlemen like you.' She freed her arm then slipped both arms up and clasped them behind his neck. 'Did anybody ever tell you you've a lovely smile? What's your name?'

'Arthur. What's yours?' By now, he was thoroughly aroused.

'Freda,' she lied. 'Free to do whatever I like.' She planted a smacking kiss on his lips.

'Let's go inside,' he gulped, stumbling into the warehouse and pulling her with him.

He would have had her there and then behind the door, but she skipped away from him, laughing as she ran to the back of the long building, dodging between the huge bales of raw wool that were stored there. Making a noise like an Indian warrior, Arthur gave chase.

Stealthily, Fred and Jim crept up to the warehouse's open door, and seeing no sign of the nightwatchman or Juliet, they speedily helped themselves to the six bales nearest the door by putting them on a trolley and wheeling it out to the towpath where Syd and Jenny, having turned the barge round and brought it back to the warehouse, were waiting for them.

A piercing whistle split the night air, and the amorous nightwatchman, locked in Juliet's embrace and doing his utmost to raise her skirt, suddenly found himself violently upended. As he went sprawling across the bales, she slipped from under him like an eel making its way up river, and dashed out to the towpath. Fred hauled her onto the barge, and it glided silently down the canal to Aspley Basin.

Now, as sleep evaded her, the thrill of duping the nightwatchman had palled, and she thought about what her mother would say if she knew that the money Juliet posted, or handed over on her regular visits home had been earned not from working extra shifts in the weaving shed but from thieving. Even so, she thought, as she turned on her side and drew up her knees in an effort to capture sleep, it was worth it to see her mother's delight and her father's proud smile; there was food in the larder, the rent was paid and the bairns were well clothed. She couldn't have provided that on a weaver's wage, and until the mill went back to employing her more than two or three days a week, and the Unions forced the mill owners to raise the piece rate, she'd boost her earnings with a bit of slap and tickle.

* * *

Almost a year to the day since war had been declared, Verity was sitting at the desk in the mill office, her expression doleful as she drew her pen across the page in the ledger in front of her, deleting one name and then another. How many of her weavers was she to lose to the munitions factories, she fumed, crossing out two more names. Whilst she understood that the women could earn better wages making bullets and hand grenades, she was angered at their disloyalty. Although orders for cloth were fewer than they had ever been, and raw wool, yarns and synthetic dyes in short supply, her mill was still functioning, and it grieved her to see looms standing idle.

A noise at the door had her pushing the ledger aside and rising to meet the postman.

'Morning, Mrs Hardcastle,' he said, slapping a bundle of envelopes on her desk. 'I hear them bloody Zeppelins are still causing havoc in London. Killing innocent people's not right, is it?'

'It's absolutely dreadful, Jack,' Verity agreed. 'I

just hope they don't find their way up here. That's the last thing we want.'

'Aye, well, there's nowt much they'd want to bomb round here, 'cept for t'British Dyes, that is,' Jack said dourly, then as an afterthought, 'or L. B. Holliday's.'

'Oh, don't say that, Jack. They supply us with our synthetic dyes now.' Verity sounded positively aghast. 'We always bought them from Germany before the war because Read Holliday couldn't compete with their prices, but now the British government's taken over the chemical works to manufacture explosives, Lionel Holliday has established his own dye works with the ten thousand pounds they paid him,' she informed.

'Whew! Ten thousand pounds. That's some cash,' Jack exclaimed. 'An' does he mek 'em as cheap as t'Germans did?'

'Not quite,' said Verity, pulling a face. 'But it does mean we can buy the dyes we need.'

'Aye, I suppose so, but I don't know why t'gover'-ment had to choose his place to mek explosives. It's inviting trouble. British Dyes be buggered. We'll all be blown to kingdom come, you just wait an' see.' On that sour note, he heaved his postbag onto his shoulder and stomped out of the office.

The government had bought out Read Holliday to establish the British Dyes because labour conditions in the north of England were favourable, and railway and canal communication, along with the easy availability of coal, electricity and water, made it an ideal site. Yet, having a huge factory on your doorstep that produced monstrous explosives was somewhat unnerving.

Jack could well be right, Verity mused. A manufactory like that was an ideal target. She began sifting through the post. Picking out a stiff, brown envelope bearing the insignia of the Board of Trade, she drew in a sharp breath and was just about to open the seal when Oliver walked in. She waved the envelope in his face, her smile hopeful.

At the start of the war, the British Army had been caught on the hop when thousands of men had enlisted, and had had to resort to issuing new recruits with surplus navy-blue uniforms that were worn by postal workers. Now they wanted uniforms made from khaki cloth – the sludgy, grey-green colour thought to be ideal camouflage for the troops. It had been estimated that contracts were required for 500,000 yards of khaki and 2,000,000 yards of silver flannel. The cloth manufacturers knew from past experience of the Boer Wars and other Victorian campaigns that armies had to have uniforms, and to secure a share of the contracts for the mills in Huddersfield and the Colne Valley, a deputation of manufacturers had paid a visit to the War Office to urge the authorities to place orders as soon as possible.

However, the Army Contracts Department's bureaucratic administration had made application a very slow process. More recently, officials from the Board of Trade had visited several mills in the valley, one of them being Lockwood Mill – much to Verity and Oliver's delight – but as yet, they hadn't been offered a contract. The large mills had been the first to be granted orders to weave cloth in khaki and silver-grey. Immediately, the price of cloth shot up, some local army depots buying cloth at any price. Now, Verity's hand trembled as she held out the stiff, brown envelope.

'Open it,' Oliver urged, his eyes alight with anticipation.

Verity did so, and let out a whoop. 'We've won a contract,' she cried, her eyes sparkling and her smile wide. 'Twenty thousand yards of woollen khaki.'

She waltzed round the desk and, grabbing Oliver, she jigged with him in the confined space, singing, 'Twe... e... enty thousand yards, twenty thousand ya... rds' to the tune of 'Be My Little Bumble Bee'.

Oliver laughed out loud. 'And here's me thinking you didn't listen to the songs the weavers sing at their looms.'

Verity stopped dancing. 'You know me, Oliver. I've ears everywhere in my mill.'

'And eyes,' he said, laughing again.

The workforce at Lockwood Mill met the news of the contract with cheers that almost lifted the canteen roof. This meant that jobs in all departments were secure, for they supplied the weavers with the yarn they needed to weave the khaki.

'Eeh, an' there wa' me thinkin' we might all be out of work afore long,' Lily Cockhill said when Verity announced that their jobs were secure for the future.

'Aye, mebbe now the Union'll put pressure on an' demand better wages,' Juliet sneered. 'After all, we can't keep the government waiting.'

May Sykes turned angrily on Juliet. 'Aw, shurrup, you an' your bloody Union. Mrs Hardcastle'll see we get fair pay. She allus gives a bonus when an order's completed before time. We've nowt to complain about.'

Juliet scowled. 'Aye, but she still pays men more than us women for doing the same job.'

'All t'mills do, mardy arse. You're never bloody satisfied,' Lily snapped.

Verity couldn't hear the women's conversation, but she presumed from the heated looks on Lily's and May's faces that Juliet's remarks had been contentious. Her eyes narrowed as she gave Juliet a stern glare. The girl met her gaze, her eyes challenging, but Juliet was the first to look away. Verity seethed inwardly. Then, recalling Dolly's words telling her that Juliet was just a skit of girl with big ideas, and that she should pay her no heed, she curved her lips into a defiantly triumphant smile.

'Now, let's give the army what it wants,' she cried to the assembled workers. 'It's business as usual at Lockwood Mill.'

13

'I have to go back to the mill,' Oliver announced, pushing his pudding plate aside and untucking his linen napkin from his waistcoat. 'I need to check on that last batch of yarn the spinners completed today. We need to start the next order tomorrow if we're to meet the deadline.'

The weavers at Lockwood Mill had already woven hundreds of yards of khaki to meet the contract for the British army, and it was important that the shade and quality of the yarn was consistent with that already produced.

Verity gave him a sympathetic smile and reached across the table to pat the back of his hand. 'Poor darling, the hours you work get longer and longer.

But I suppose we should be thankful for the contract. It's keeping our workforce in full employment.'

'And making us a tidy profit,' Oliver said, his eyes twinkling as he got to his feet and looked first at Briony and then at Blaise. 'I'll bid you goodnight, children. You'll no doubt be in bed when I get back.'

'They may not,' said Verity. 'I'm taking them with me to Thornton Hall. Dolly and I have to attend a meeting of the Female Friendly Society this evening, and Blaise and Briony can spend an hour or two there with Josh and Sarah whilst their mothers do good deeds.' She gave a little sigh. 'And what with all the recent bereavements in the town, we have plenty to do. Far too many families are struggling with the loss of husbands, fathers and sons.'

Both she and Dolly were patrons of the society whose charitable works assisted the poor in times of sickness, bereavement and hardship, and they considered it their duty to assist the war effort in any way they could.

'Yes, it's a bad business. The grieving families need all the help they can get,' said Oliver, shaking his head at the cruel waste of lives.

'And we'll give them it,' Verity replied briskly. 'Now, off you go to the mill.'

Oliver stooped and plopped a kiss on his wife's

cheek then addressed his son and daughter. 'Enjoy your evening at Thornton Hall.'

Briony gave him a sweet smile but Blaise groaned out loud.

'Do I have to go?' he groused. 'I have an essay on Keats I want to finish.'

Oliver glanced from his son to his wife, his eyes asking for her opinion.

Verity pursed her lips. The boy was fifteen, quite old enough to be left alone in the house for a couple of hours. Even so...

'Why not?' she said, swallowing her misgivings and trying not to dwell on her son's past unruly behaviour; he hadn't caused them any problems of late. 'If Blaise is keen to attend to his schoolwork, then who are we to deny him?' she said airily.

Blaise grinned. 'Thanks, Ma. I really do want to do old Keats and his Grecian Urn justice.'

His mother gave him an adoring smile.

'That's settled then,' said Oliver. 'Your mother and Briony will go to Thornton Hall, and you, young man, can write your essay.' His stern glare did not escape Blaise's notice.

When Blaise was sure that the coast was clear, he went up to his bedroom, not to work on his Keat's essay but to don his disguise, as he thought of it. Out

from the back of his wardrobe, he took a black balaclava and an old jacket that had once belonged to
Bert Medley, the handyman, and that several weeks
before, Blaise had found in the potting shed. He
dressed quickly, and turning up his coat collar and
pulling the balaclava over his head to hide his face,
he left Far View House and raced down the hill into
Almondbury. It being August and the time not yet
half-past seven, it was still light, and he didn't want to
risk being recognised in the village. He didn't stop
running until he reached the bottom of Somerset
Road. As he walked over the bridge at Aspley, he
could see Lockwood Mill. He just hoped that whatever business his father was attending to kept him
there until late. He hurried up to Shore Head,
making his way to where he assumed he would meet
the gang of lads he'd accompanied on a few sorties
already, and he thought of as his friends. In Blaise's
opinion, routing treacherous Germans was good fun
and destroying their businesses necessary if the
British were to win the war. Who would suffer at
their hands tonight? he wondered as he strutted into
the narrow passage that accessed one of the yards at
the bottom of King Street.

Each yard housed a cluster of shabby buildings,
some being dwellings and others where a variety of

trades were carried out: silk-spinners, carpenters, hosiers, rag merchants and tinners to name but a few. The lads were lolling against the walls of a tannery, the air thick with the stink of animal hides soaking in a mixture of oils, lime and salts. Usually noisy and bustling with activity, the yard was reasonably quiet at this time of day, the workers finished, and only a handful of scruffy children playing around the water pump. Two blousy women stood gossiping in a doorway, and a couple of mangy dogs chewed over the stinking carcass of something evil.

Blaise slowed his pace and strolled up to the gang, at the same time wryly imagining his mother's horror if she were to find out that he was frequenting such a place. She might not object to helping the poor and needy who lived in yards like this, but she'd have forty fits if she knew her son was mixing with them.

The lads silently watched his approach, their expressions baleful and not at all welcoming. Blaise's step faltered. The leader of the gang, a burly lout called Scuff, flicked the butt of his cigarette onto the cobbles, eased his back off the wall and stepped forward.

'Bugger off,' he snarled. 'Get back to where you belong.'

Blaise came to a sudden halt. His cheeks reddened. In the past, they'd been glad to see him, eagerly accepting the coins he doled out to buy sweets and cigarettes or bottles of ale.

'Aye, tek your hook,' a wiry little lad known as Spider yelled. 'We know who you are.'

'Aye, we do, an' we don't tek kindly to bein' told lies. You don't come from Carr Pit, you lying bugger. You're Hardcastle's lad, him what owns Lockwood Mill,' Scuff bawled, rushing at Blaise then delivering a flying kick that caught him in his groin. Blaise doubled over as an agonising pain shot through his crotch. For a brief moment, he attempted to retaliate, but realising he was sorely outnumbered, he turned tail and fled.

Hampered by the fire in his loins, he ran as fast as he could down the narrow passage, jeers and hallooing ringing in his ears. He had almost reached the street when he heard the shout, 'After him, lads. Don't let the bugger get away.'

Fearful of what they would do if they caught him added impetus to his feet, and heedless of his aching groin, he ran back the way he had come. His heart was hammering and his breath coming in short gasps but he could still hear the thudding feet and the yells of his pursuers. Head down, blind to where his feet were taking him, he kept going.

At Aspley Basin, at the point where the main road met the cobbled sideroad leading to his parents' mill, Blaise could still hear the lads hot on his heels. *The mill! I'll go to the mill. They'll not dare follow me in there.* So certain was he that safety was at hand, he didn't see the car exiting the sideroad until...

Too late, Blaise skidded to a stop, but the car's jutting headlight administered a swinging blow to his hip and sent him spinning.

The car slewed, its brakes screeching and the driver cursing as a dark shadow thudded against the front bumper. Blaise fell to the pavement and rolled over onto his back. Oliver flung open the car door and leapt from the driver's seat. Out on the pavement, his eyes stood out on stalks as he looked down into the terrified face of his son.

'Good God in heaven!' Oliver gasped. 'What the...?'

He fell to his knees, his mind in turmoil. *Had he killed his own son?* The horrific thought had him shaking, and his hands trembled as he began to asses Blaise's injuries.

But Blaise pushed him away and shuffled into an

upright sitting position, muttering, 'I'm all right, Pa. I'm not hurt.'

Still on his knees, but assured that Blaise had suffered no serious injuries, Oliver slowly stood up and, staring down at him, he dwelt on what the consequence of the collision *could* have been, and then on his son's irritable, almost insolent response to it. Cold fear turned to burning rage, his face masked in fury.

The pursuers, seeing the master of Lockwood Mill towering over their prey, hared back the way they had come, leaving their quarry slumped on the pavement.

Oliver grabbed at Blaise's jacket and yanked him to his feet. 'Explain yourself,' he growled, shaking Blaise until his teeth rattled. The same teeth that Blaise frantically gabbled through as he concocted one lie after another.

'I worked on my essay... I felt in need of fresh air... I took a walk into town... those thugs set about me... tried to steal my money...'

His father, noting the way Blaise was dressed and wise to his son's dishonesty, didn't believe a word of it. 'Get in the car,' he barked, giving Blaise a hefty shove. 'We'll discuss this at home.'

* * *

Verity and Briony arrived back at Far View House to find Oliver in a rage and Blaise slumped sulkily in a chair in the drawing room.

'But darling, whatever made you go into the town?' Verity cried, her voice high with anxiety and her expression distraught to think that her son had put himself in danger.

'Oh, Ma,' Blaise whined, 'I worked so hard on my essay that my head was ringing. I thought a breath of fresh air might do me good.'

'But why not the garden instead of the town? And... and why are you dressed like that?' she asked, puzzled as to why he was wearing what she recognised as one of Bert Medley's old gardening jackets. Blaise was still wearing the balaclava rolled up above his brow and now he tore it off his head and stuffed it down the side of the chair.

'Lies. All lies,' Oliver snarled. 'He's been up to no good, that is obvious.'

Verity paled. 'Oh, Oliver, don't be so hard on him,' she begged. 'The poor lamb could have been seriously hurt. You can see he's traumatised.'

Briony, saddened to see her mother so distressed, pushed aside any loyalty she felt for her brother and cried, 'He is lying, Mama. He's been running with a gang of thugs who burn the Germans out of their businesses and—'

She got no further. Blaise leapt from his chair and ran at her, shouting, 'Keep your snivelling trap shut, you treacherous bitch!'

Briony staggered back into her father, who caught her and held her close.

Verity let out an agonising wail. 'Tell me it's not true,' she implored, catching hold of Blaise's arm and forcing him to face her.

He hung his head, a deep-red flush suffusing his neck and cheeks.

Seeing this as an admission of his guilt, his mother flopped into the nearest chair and buried her head in her hands.

'Now see what you've done,' Oliver roared, letting Briony go and lunging at Blaise. 'You are a gutter-snipe,' he bawled, clamping both hands on Blaise's shoulders. 'We thought you'd grown out of your fool-ishness but all the time, you've been going behind our back doing just as you damned well please.' He tightened his grip, shaking his son back and forth. 'You don't give a toss as to the hurt you cause but this is the last time you'll step out of line. As from now, you will do exactly as I say.' Raising his hand, he slapped Blaise hard across one cheek with his palm and then the other with the back of his hand.

Blaise gasped, his eyes wide with shock. He looked across at his mother but she was sobbing noisily, her face still in her hands.

'Get to your room and stay there until I send for you,' Oliver growled.

Blaise slunk from the room, but not before he had given Briony a glare that said she'd pay for her treachery. Heavy-hearted, Briony went to comfort their mother then after a while, she too went to her room, leaving her parents deep in discussion about her errant brother.

* * *

The next morning at breakfast, Oliver faced his son and told him how things would be from now on. 'In your free time, you will be confined to the house. You will attend school and work hard, and after lessons, you will be collected from there each weekday and brought to the mill. When you're there, you will be put to work, learning the trade that pays for your fortunate way of life.'

This time, Verity raised no objections to her husband's decision. She just gazed sadly at Blaise, her disappointment so raw, he felt as though he could reach out and touch it.

'But... but I'm not interested in the mill,' he groused. 'I want to—'

'You will do as your father says,' Verity interrupted through gritted teeth. 'The mill will be yours one day. You should be grateful for that.'

Blaise shrugged. He'd pacify them for now, but as far as he was concerned, the mill could go to hell. He had other plans.

* * *

The following day, her head aching with the events of the previous evening, Verity interviewed and set on six new weavers. One of them, Amy Carter, was a woman of her own age. Her rather faded prettiness and the fact that she was a widow with a seventeen-year-old son appealed to Verity's kind heart. She was completely unaware that Amy Carter, as she now called herself, was the Amy Dickenson whom George Armitage had courted before he married Nellie, and that she had been the girl that the rumourmongers suspected of having a child by Oliver Hardcastle.

Satisfied in the knowledge that now the weaving

shed would be working to full capacity, she sat back in her chair in the mill office musing on the mill's new-found prosperity now that they had the contract to supply khaki for uniforms, and smiling at the slogan on the poster she'd pinned to the office wall.

No cloth should be made for fine gentlemen
until all our soldiers are clad.

This wartime boom was being enjoyed by all the mills in the Colne Valley, and although there was some anxiety over the supply of raw wool from Australia – the shipping lanes under threat from the German navy – the manufacturers were managing to keep production going with locally produced wool. But even as Verity mused on her mill's good fortune, in the back of her mind were worrying thoughts of her son. To allay the problem of Blaise's latest escapade, she left the office and toured the mill, looking in on the spinners to assess the quality of the yarn, then to the dyehouse, where George assured her the khaki dye was consistent. When she went to check that the new weavers were being trained to use the new looms in the recently extended weaving shed, she was somewhat consoled by the diligence of her employees and the happy smiles on the weavers' faces. Weavers were paid a basic wage plus piece-work rates based on the yardage of the fabric they wove. The less complex the pattern, the faster it went through the loom and the more money the weaver earned. It also simplified the job of the twisters and the drawers-in who fixed the warp, and made the loom tuners lives easier.

'Weaving plain khaki serge is a doddle,' Lily Cockhill told Verity as she stopped by her loom. 'I earned twenty-five bob last week and I'm aiming for a bit more come Friday.'

Verity walked away, pleased that her employees had something to smile about.

At four o'clock, Oliver arrived at the mill with Blaise, having collected him from school just as he had threatened to do. Blaise was sullen and unresponsive when his mother greeted him, her enthusiasm for indoctrinating him into the workings of the mill doing little to raise his interest.

'We'll start with the wool scouring, show you all the processes that are involved in making fine cloth,' Oliver said heartily, leading the way across the mill yard.

Verity stood in the office doorway, her eyes on the

backs of the man and boy she loved best in the world. Blaise was almost as tall as his father, though not as broad, and the shape of his head and his thick, dark hair so resembled Oliver's that the surge of love and pride she felt as she watched them go was only slightly marred when she compared Blaise's reluctant tread with Oliver's eager stride.

* * *

Wool scouring, combing, carding, dyeing and spinning, would it never end? With each passing day, Blaise dreaded his enforced visits to the mill. Three weeks on, and he was heartily sick of the stink and the tedious instructions long before his father introduced him to the work in the weaving shed.

The thrashing of the looms drowned Oliver's voice – not that Blaise was paying him any heed – but as he followed him down 'weaver's alley', he perked up as the women looked up from their looms and acknowledged him with smiles.

They liked the look of this handsome young man. He was tall and lean of waist and hip but with strong, muscular shoulders which filled his well-cut, grey jacket, woven from Lockwood's finest worsted.

His hair was thick and black as coal, the curls about his ears and the nape of his neck giving him a rakish glamour. His sharp, blue eyes, the colour of sapphires, were framed with finely arched eyebrows and long, dark lashes above his high cheekbones, and the casual stance of his long, lounging body and the insolent lift of his head left them in no doubt as to who he was: the boss's son and heir.

Blaise returned their smile and began enjoying himself.

Many of the weavers were girls of his own age, some of them very pretty even though unbecoming turbans protected their hair, and their figures were hidden beneath baggy cross-over aprons. He could tell by their eyes that they admired him and his ego swelled.

When his father stopped to exchange words with the loom tuner, a grizzly man with greying hair, one particular girl took her eyes off her flying shuttle long enough to favour Blaise with a saucy smile followed by a cheeky wink.

Her eyes were the brightest blue, and her forehead sported a fringe of pale-blonde curls.

Blaise grinned back, instantly smitten. The girl smiled again then pouted her lips as if to blow him a kiss. He felt his heart flutter. Who was she? he wondered. How could he get to know her? He could hardly make such an enquiry from his father.

Just as he was contemplating on this, Nellie Armitage the Mrs Weaver appeared at his side. Blaise's heart soared. Nellie was his mother's friend and he liked her; she was fun was Nellie. She was also in charge of the weavers. She'd provide him with answers.

'Hello, Blaise. Come to learn the trade, have you?' she asked, putting her lips to his ear so that she could make herself heard. 'Or come to do your old man out of his job?'

Blaise grinned and cockily nodded as though he agreed before pretending to show an interest in the looms that were churning out yards of khaki cloth. With their heads close together so that they could hear one another, he asked questions and Nellie answered, but all the time, his eyes were on the girl with the bright blue eyes. Then, his curiosity burning, he pointed her out and said, 'Who's she?'

Nellie looked surprised. 'Juliet Skeldon. Why?'

'I thought I recognised her. She looks like a girl from Briony's school,' Blaise lied.

'No, she comes from over Barnsley way,' Nellie

shouted in his ear. 'She's a bit of a hothead. A cheeky madam full of her own opinions.'

Blaise liked the sound of that.

When Nellie left him to speak to Oliver, Blaise continued looking in Juliet's direction until he caught her attention, his eyes and his winning smile conveying his feelings. Juliet was quick to acknowledge him. Holding up six fingers, she mouthed the words 'gate' and 'wait'. Then, with her mouth hanging open expectantly and her blue eyes wide, she cocked her head to one side to see if he had understood.

Blaise frowned, the creases in his brow suddenly smoothing and his own eyes widening as, understanding the message, he nodded affirmation. She'd be by the gate when she finished work at six o'clock. His heart thumped against his ribs.

'Sorry to leave you standing, but Isaac had a problem that needed my attention,' Oliver said as he and the loom tuner returned to where Blaise was standing, his eyes still fixed on the object of his desire.

Blaise almost jumped out of his skin. Had they seen him communicating with Juliet? He breathed a sigh of relief when his father passed no remark and bade the loom tuner farewell. As he and Blaise left the weaving shed, Oliver asked, 'Well, what do you think?'

'I found it fascinating, Father. I'm looking forward to spending more time at the mill.'

Oliver's jaw dropped, and quite taken aback by Blaise's enthusiastic reply, he clapped his arm across his son's shoulder and hugged him. 'Good man. I knew you'd get the feel for it.'

They walked across the mill yard to the office talking about the different aspects of cloth-making, Oliver rejoicing and Blaise feigning interest: *Roll on six o'clock.*

Verity was delighted when Oliver reported their successful afternoon in the weaving shed. 'I just knew it, Blaise,' she cried. 'You couldn't fail to be drawn to it. It's in your blood, darling.' She threw her arms round him, kissing him on both cheeks.

The mill hooter blasted out a piercing wail. The mill yard throbbed with the noise of clogs on cobbles and loud chatter. Blaise's heart was beating almost as loudly. Leaving his parents still enthusing over his unexpected liking for the mill, Blaise ducked out of the office and joined the mill hands hurrying to the gate where Juliet was waiting for him.

'Hello,' he said, his cheeks pinking as an unusual wave of shyness enveloped him. He'd never taken much interest in the girls Briony sometimes brought to the house. He thought them rather vapid, but this lovely creature standing before him with a pert smile on her pretty face promised to be neither dull nor lacking in depth.

'Hello,' Juliet replied, looking him up and down, amused by his obvious nervousness. She'd taken off her turban and now she flicked at her long, blonde hair and gazed coquettishly up into his face. Blaise swallowed.

'I'm Blaise Hardcastle,' he said, feeling rather foolish.

'Oh, I know who you are,' Juliet said archly. 'You're the son and heir, and nearly as handsome as your old man.'

Blaise laughed. He liked her accent. Much broader than that of Huddersfield people.

'Will we be seeing more of you at the mill then?' Juliet asked with a come-hither look.

'I... I suppose so,' Blaise replied, his cheeks growing redder. He was aware of the curious looks the other mill hands were giving them as they passed by and he began to sweat.

'You need to steer clear of her,' an older woman called out.

'Aye, she's bad news, Master Blaise.'

'Take no notice of them,' Juliet snapped, conscious that they were drawing unwanted attention. 'Just tell me some place else we can meet. That's if you want to.'

She gave him a hopeful smile and Blaise's heart lurched.

'I'd... I'd like that,' he stammered.

'Well, be quick an' suggest somewhere?'

Fazed, Blaise rattled his brain his brain to think where and when. 'By the steps that go down to the towpath,' he said, nodding his head in the direction of the canal at Aspley Basin. 'Tomorrow night at eight?' He was almost breathless with anticipation.

'I know where you mean. I'll be there.' Juliet beamed at him, and spotting Verity and Oliver coming out of the office, she said, 'See you,' and hurried away from the gate.

'See you,' Blaise blurted and turned to greet his parents. 'Are we going home now?'

His father said they were, and as they drove back to Far View House, Verity asked Blaise, 'Were you standing at the mill gate saying goodnight to the workers like I used to do when I first took over the mill?'

Blaise leapt on the idea. 'I did, Ma. I remembered

you telling me and Briony you did that, and I thought I should carry on the tradition.'

'Oh, Blaise, you're such a sweet boy,' his mother cooed.

Blaise's lips curved in a sardonic smile as he turned his head and gazed out of the car window. *Good old Ma, always easy to fool.*

14

'Blaise, darling, don't eat so quickly,' Verity chided as he shovelled a forkful of potato and minced meat into his mouth. It was the evening after Blaise had met Juliet at the mill gate and the family were sitting down to dinner, the hands on the grandfather clock in the dining room at Far View House pointing to ten-past seven.

'Sorry, Ma.' Blaise gave a contrite little smile then looked across the table at his father. 'Sir, please may I beg your permission to go to the Scouts this evening?'

The humble request hung in the air, and Oliver narrowed his eyes as he considered it. Scouting was a

worthwhile pursuit. It instilled discipline and useful-
ness, and Blaise could do with conforming to both
those things.

'Scouts, eh?' Oliver, aware that Blaise hadn't attended their meetings for more than a year, wondered what had renewed his interest.

'Yes, Pa. Josh tells me they're doing war work now.
They're being instructed how to put peach pits into
gas masks tonight, and I'd like to help,' he said with
enthusiasm, hopeful that the lie sounded convincing
and noble.

'Don't talk with your mouth full, dear,' his
mother corrected before giving him an admiring
smile and saying, 'That's very worthwhile, Blaise.'

Oliver was still looking doubtful, and Briony cast
her brother a suspicious glance.

'I told Josh that if I was allowed to go, I'd meet
him at half-past seven,' Blaise continued meekly. 'I'd
really like to, and I don't want to be late.'

Oliver nodded, but he was still frowning. Maybe
the lad should be allowed to go even though it was
breaking the rules he himself had issued less than a
month ago. Something good might come of it.

'All right,' Oliver said slowly. 'You have my permission, but no nonsense,' he warned as Blaise gab-

bled his thanks. 'In fact, I'll run you both there,' he offered.

Blaise quailed. That was the last thing he wanted. 'Thanks, but there's no need. I said I'd meet him at Helen's Gate and we'll walk into the town together.' He clattered his cutlery onto his empty plate. 'No pud for me, Ma. I'll be off,' he said, getting to his feet.

'If you're sure,' Oliver said, feeling rather weary and relieved not to have to get the car out again, and satisfied that Blaise was going off to do something useful for the war effort. The visits to the mill seemed to have brought about a change in his son's attitude. Perhaps Blaise was learning to be more responsible now that he had seen how hard people had to work for a living.

Briony's eyes drilled into Blaise's own. 'Sarah didn't say anything to me about you meeting Josh and going to the Scouts,' she said caustically.

'That's because Sarah doesn't know everything, you ninny,' Blaise snapped, dashing from the room before Briony could further delay him.

'Don't speak to your sister like that,' Oliver barked, but Blaise was already in the hallway pulling on his jacket, ready to go and meet Juliet.

* * *

'You made it then,' Juliet said as Blaise arrived at the steps leading down to the towpath. She was perched on the wall, her long, blonde hair loose about her shoulders. Blaise thought she looked extremely pretty in her candy-striped frock and white cardigan. He told her so. Juliet blushed and wondered what he would say if he knew that her outfit had been purchased with her share of the money from the last robbery she'd committed with Fred and Jim.

Taking Blaise's hand, she led the way down to the towpath. She was feeling rather triumphant and wished that the weavers she worked with, especially those who ostracised her, could see her walking out with the bosses' son.

'Now, tell me all about yourself,' she coaxed, squeezing his hand. 'What do you do when you're not at the mill, and how old are you?'

'Seventeen,' Blaise said stoutly, and then rather vaguely, 'I'm studying.'

Juliet knew he was lying. She'd asked Maggie Broadbent, who worked on the loom next to hers, all about him. Still, it made no difference to her. He was a young man with money and position and she was going to use him to her advantage.

They walked and they talked, Blaise telling her of

his intentions to join the Blues and Royals amongst other things, and Juliet deliberately playing down her impoverished background. When she told him that her mother was an avid reader of William Shakespeare and that she had been named after the girl in the play *Romeo and Juliet*, Blaise had replied that he knew the play, and that he thought it was the perfect name for a girl as beautiful as she was.

'I just hope we don't have to kill ourselves like they did,' he said.

Juliet didn't know the story, and didn't care. She giggled and said, 'Oh, it'll not come to that. Me an' you are survivors.'

All too soon, it was time for Blaise to go home. Holding hands, they retraced their steps on the towpath, Blaise asking when could they meet again, and Juliet telling him she'd be there for him whenever he wanted. At the foot of the steps up to the road, they paused, gazing into each other's faces, Blaise's expression that of a lovesick puppy, and Juliet's elated.

When she kissed Blaise, his knees turned to jelly and his stomach lurched. He liked the feel of her soft lips wetting his mouth, and as he breathed in her warm, earthy smell tinged with the faint scent of lavender, he knew he was in love.

* * *

The war that almost everyone in Britain had thought would last but a few months raged on. The allied forces in the trenches on the Western Front and in Gallipoli continued battling against the might of the German army, and nearer home, enemy Zeppelins inflicted damage on London, Great Yarmouth and King's Lynn. Throughout Britain, people were feeling the bite of the destruction of their homes and places of employment, and mourning the loss of their loved ones who had died fighting for king and country.

Although the war magnified and intensified the problems that women in the Colne Valley encountered every day – bad housing, poverty and food shortages – these were issues that they had contended with before the war. But now, as the mills churned out cloth for uniforms, the women were experiencing a new-found prosperity: regular employment, overtime with extra wages and bonuses that gave them the glorious feeling of independence and raised their self-confidence; the war was good for them.

'Sometimes, I think that our women are totally

disregarded by the government,' Verity complained to Dolly one day in early December. Dolly had called at the mill to collect her and go to a meeting of The Women's Relief Society of which they were patrons. 'Just because we don't make shells and bullets or tend the wounded shouldn't mean we are completely overlooked. Our troops need uniforms as much as they need weapons,' she continued as she distractedly wiped her hand over her cheeks and chin.

'You work too hard, Mrs Hardcastle.' Dolly's reprimand received a weary smile.

'We have to keep going. We've just been given a new contract for grey-blue serge to kit out the Royal Flying Corps, so I suppose I shouldn't moan,' said Verity, reaching for her coat and slipping it on, 'but I never seem to have a minute to relax these days.'

'Tell me about it,' Dolly scoffed. 'Lady Sybil has me at her beck and call all hours helping her to rally the knitting circle and the bandage winders. We've knitted socks and scarves enough to equip the entire Yorkshire Regiment, and I personally have wound ten miles of bandages.' She laughed at herself and her efforts. 'Still, we don't see half as much of one another as we used to do before the war, and I miss our get-togethers. Theo's run off his feet dealing with the cattle on the estate that the government take to slaughter to feed the troops, but seeing how they've commissioned most of the horses, he has less to do with them. I hardly see anything of him some days.'

'I'm the same. Oliver's buried under a load of paperwork that the government demands and making sure the orders are delivered on time. But we mustn't gripe. It could be far worse. They could be in France or God knows where fighting this awful war,' Verity said, putting on her hat then picking up her handbag. 'Right, I'm ready to go.'

'How are things at home?' Dolly enquired as they stepped out into the mill yard.

'Rather good,' said Verity. 'Briony is involving herself in all manner of war works. They have a knitting circle in school and she's now adept at turning a heel on the socks she knits. Far better than I can.' Verity giggled. 'And she told me that she tucks encouraging little notes into each sock to let the soldiers know they are not forgotten.'

'Good for her. She's such a sweet girl. And what about Blaise?'

'Working hard. When he's not at school, Oliver sets him to work in the mill, and he spends at least two or three evenings a week with the Scouts. Last week, he was going round the houses selling war bonds, and before that, he was stuffing peach pits into gas masks. It's marvellous to see him happily making himself useful.' Verity gushed.

'Josh has been out selling war bonds as well,' Dolly said as they walked up Kirkgate, 'but most of his evenings are taken up helping his dad on the estate, and Lady Sybil's roped Sarah into packing comfort parcels to send to those poor sods in the trenches.'

By the time they reached the library rooms where the meeting was to be held, they had caught up with news of their respective families and were ready to partake in a discussion of how they might help the needy of the parish.

At the meeting, Mrs Blamire, the lady chairman, praised the ladies for the success of their Christmas campaign. They had supplied the troops with cheering gifts that Verity, Dolly and the other members had begged from the shopkeepers in the town: boxes of chocolates and sweets, biscuits and other such things to add taste to the soldiers' usual fare of bully beef, watery stews and stale bread. Congratulations delivered, she then set about what they would next do, and when the meeting came to an end, Verity suggested that Dolly should accompany her back to the mill for Oliver to take them back to their respective homes.

They arrived in Lockwood Mill's yard just as the last wail of the mill hooter signalled the end of the working day. The doors to the weaving shed flew open and a gaggle of women emerged, eager to go to their own homes to attend to children and the household chores awaiting them. Among them was Amy Carter.

'What's she doing here?' Dolly's eyebrows shot up, her voice high with disapproval. She pointed to the slim, fair-haired woman hurrying to the mill gate.

Verity frowned. 'She works in our weaving shed,' she said. 'She's Amy Carter.'

'Née Dickenson,' Dolly spat. 'She's the trollop that tried to blame our George for the baby she had out of wedlock.'

Although Verity was aware that George had once courted a girl who had deceived him, she had never met her. 'I didn't know who she was when I set her on,' she protested. 'Surely, if that's her, why haven't Nellie and George said anything to me?'

'That's what I'd like to know,' Dolly exclaimed, and seeing George coming up the yard from the dye-house, she called out to him. He came towards her, a jovial smile on his face.

'Hello, Sis, have you come to see how the other

half works?' George often mocked Dolly's status as the wife of Sir Arnold Thornton's Land Agent, making fun of her friendship with Lady Sybil even though Dolly was still the same sweet woman she'd always been.

'No, I'm just after asking Verity what Amy Dickenson's doing here, after all the rotten trouble she caused. Verity didn't know who she was when she set her on, but what I don't understand is why neither you nor Nellie has ever mentioned it.' Dolly's green eyes flashed with annoyance. She loved her brother and still felt angry about Amy's duplicity.

George shrugged. 'We recognised her immediately even though she's aged since we last saw her, but we both agreed to make nothing of it. Verity has a right to employ anybody she chooses, and me and Nellie don't give a toss about what happened all those years ago,' he said, letting his sister and his boss know that his and Nellie's love for one another couldn't be harmed by the reappearance of Amy Dickenson. 'She calls herself Carter now so I suppose she must have found some silly sod to marry her,' he continued and grinned as he added, 'Mind you, Nellie makes her pay for the rotten trick she played on me. She only ever lets her work on an old loom, and she's been known to make her wait till last to get her loom warped.' He laughed. 'Our Nellie's a bit like an elephant; she never forgets.'

'Well, you just steer clear of her,' Dolly warned. 'She's one nasty customer, and you of all people should know that if anybody does.'

George laughed again and turned to Verity. 'Our Dolly thinks I need her to look after me. She forgets it used to be t'other way round.'

Verity gave him a grateful smile, relieved that he wasn't in the least offended by her oversight. But the memory of the rumour about Oliver possibly having fathered Amy's child stayed with her, and as Oliver was driving her home after leaving Dolly at Thornton Hall, she recalled what had been said. Some of the women at the mill had spread gossip about the man Amy had been two-timing George with, saying that he looked like Oliver and that he wore a wide-brimmed hat like the one Oliver used to wear. These days, he wore a bowler, and as she glanced sideways at his handsome profile and the firm set of his jaw as he steered the car up the hill to Far View House, she wondered if he too had known who Amy Carter was, but like George and Nellie, he'd chosen not to mention it. The question burned to be asked, but with Blaise sitting in the back seat, she held her tongue.

Later, when they were sitting in the drawing room, Blaise away to a Scout meeting and Briony with Sarah at Miss Hinchcliffe's dance class, Verity repeated the conversation she'd had with Dolly and George about Amy Carter.

'I had no idea who she was when I set her on,' she said, 'and neither Nellie nor George thought it worth the mention.' She paused. 'Did you know her then, Oliver?' she asked, her voice deliberately light.

He shook his head. 'Can't say that I did,' he replied, sounding rather disinterested, and his casual response allaying Verity's fears. Silently, she chastised herself for fostering such awful notions; she was as bad as the rumourmongers.

'Blaise is really stepping up to the mark these days,' she said, keen to change the subject. 'He's taking his responsibilities at the mill willingly, and he rarely misses a Scout meeting.' Her dove-grey eyes gleamed with love and pride. 'I'm of the opinion that our son is proving to be a fine young man.'

'Yes, I'm inclined to agree with you. He was positively bouncing with enthusiasm when I set him to work in the weaving shed this afternoon,' Oliver said.

His proud parents exchanged satisfied smiles then began to discuss business.

* * *

Earlier that day, Blaise had been collected from school and brought to the mill by the recalcitrant old gatekeeper, Joe. The old man objected to the task. To his mind, the arrogant young pup was capable of walking a distance of not even two miles, and he'd made his feelings plain. Blaise had cockily reminded him that he was the son and heir, and that the first thing he'd do when he was in charge would be to sack Joe: a meaningless threat because he had no intentions of becoming a cloth manufacturer. His sole purpose of coming to the mill was to be near Juliet, his passion for her still burning.

When he'd arrived at the mill, he'd jumped down from the trap with such alacrity, his father had taken this as a sign that Blaise was keen to further his knowledge of making cloth. 'Good to see you, son,' he said, clapping his hand on Blaise's shoulder and leading the way across the mill yard.

Yesterday, he had arranged for Blaise to work in the weaving shed so that Isaac, the loom tuner, could instruct him how to warp a loom. Now, as his son strutted into the shed, Oliver's heart swelled. He took out his pocket watch, a gold hunter that Verity had given him for his thirty-fifth birthday, and flicked it open to check the time before returning it to his waistcoat pocket. Then, smiling with satisfaction, he produced his cigar case, selected a cigar, lit it and breathed in the smoke with lingering pleasure.

Blaise strolled down 'weaver's alley' to where Isaac awaited him. On some days, he and Juliet were only able to share no more than conspiratorial smiles, but on at least one if not two nights in the past three weeks, they had engaged in their secret trysts on the towpath or in Juliet's bedroom where, no matter how bitter were the cold winter nights, Blaise's blood was heated almost to boiling point by her amorous advances. Tonight, he would meet her again.

Wily and devious by nature, he had formulated the perfect ruse for his meetings with her. Just as he had told his parents, he met Josh at seven and went with him to the Scout hall, but by a quarter to eight – having shown scant interest in putting peach pits into gas masks or learning how to read maps – he had vacated his post and raced off to meet Juliet.

Josh, by now wary of enquiring into Blaise's affairs, and erring on the side of past experience, asked no questions and told no one of his friend's strange behaviour. However, this didn't prevent him from speculating that whatever it was Blaise was doing, it wasn't something that was above board.

Now, in the weaving shed, as Blaise feigned interest in the warping of the loom, his mind was on what was to come later. Oliver watched as Isaac showed Blaise how the warp was threaded. He was the apple of his eye and the darling of his mother's heart, but if Oliver's life had depended on it, he could not have told him so. Instead, he praised him mightily when he had successfully completed a task, his pride in his only son kept well hidden beneath his own stern exterior.

When it was time for Blaise to leave the weaving shed, he caught Juliet's eye and gave her a wink and a nod that let her know he would see her at their appointed meeting place. She winked back, her smile saucy.

* * *

Later that same day, he met Josh as usual at Helen's Gate and they strolled into the town discussing the latest success of 'Town', as the local football team was affectionately known. They had recently beaten Derby County four goals to one.

'Those two goals Crossley scored clinched the game,' said Josh in praise of his favourite player.

'Personally, I think Elliot's the best player,' Blaise replied without much enthusiasm, his mind else-where as he anticipated what he and Juliet would do when they met.

When they arrived at the Scout hall, Blaise delib-erately chose to work with a different group to the one Josh was in so that he could slip away without having to explain himself. They hadn't been working long when Blaise sidled to the door and made his escape. Josh watched him go, and his curiosity unex-pectedly getting the better of him, he made hurried apologies to the Scout master and ran after Blaise.

He followed him down Shore Head to Aspley, careful to keep a distance between them.

At the steps down to the towpath, Blaise slowed his pace as he came level with a girl. Josh spied on them from a shop doorway as they exchanged a few words then when they resumed walking, he trailed after them. Feeling like a sleuth in a Conan Doyle novel, he watched as they entered a house in Rose Street. Then he walked slowly back to the Scout hall, wondering who the girl with the long, blonde hair and curvaceous figure was, and what Blaise was doing in her company. He could tell she was working class by the way she dressed, and the house he presumed she lived in on Rose Street, like his Granddad and Grandma Armitage's house in Silver Street, were homes for mill and factory workers. Maybe she was a girl who Blaise had met at the mill. If so, he didn't for one moment think that Verity Hardcastle would approve.

* * *

Blaise paid scant heed to the shabby hallway and dingy staircase as Juliet led him up to her bedroom in the house in Rose Street. Instead, he concentrated on her pert bottom and shapely hips as they mounted the stairs, his heart pounding with anticipation. At the top of the stairs, they came across Fred. Blaise gave him a surly glance, jealous to think that the girl he loved shared a house with the brawny bargee. Fred grinned, his leery eyes saying he knew what they were about to do in the privacy of Juliet's room. Blaise felt his cheeks redden.

'Tha can get done for leading bairns astray, tha knows,' Fred sneered, poking a finger at Juliet's chest before, laughing harshly, he clattered down the stairs.

'Take no notice of him; he's just jealous,' Juliet

said as she led Blaise into the sparsely furnished room. The lime-washed walls were cracked and stained and the rickety chest of drawers and frayed curtains lent little ambience to their love nest but Blaise had long since got over what he might once have considered squalid. The delights that Juliet delivered cancelled out any feelings of revulsion about his surroundings.

She put her arms round his neck and kissed him, a long, deep kiss that made Blaise's head swim, and that Juliet delivered without any inner passion other than that it was part of her cunning plan.

They flopped back onto the bed and, clothing loosened and hands groping, they stroked and kissed body parts that, up until now, Blaise had thought of as extremely private and only to be touched by their owner. Doing the things she had taught him, he nuzzled her breasts, sucked her nipples and fondled her secret places, his fingers wet and sticky. She clutched his manhood, feverishly massaging it till, his heart pounding and his blood throbbing, he cried out in the throes of ecstasy. Panting, he sprawled on the crumpled bedspread, a soporific smile on his young, handsome face. Juliet smirked with satisfaction then wiped her hands on the sheet. Blaise, in his youthful innocence, was easy to please.

Juliet settled back beside him, unconcerned, as though she had carried out a mundane task which neither pleased nor displeased her. It had to be done for her scheme to bear fruit. She was playing the long game and when the time was right, she would strike, sure in the knowledge that she held the winning cards in her hand.

15

ALMONDBURY, HUDDERSFIELD 1916

The drawing room in Far View House rang with laughter as the Hardcastle family and their friends, the Beaumonts and the Armitages, welcomed in the New Year. The room, still sporting its Christmas garb of a twinkling tree bedecked with multicoloured baubles, and white winter chrysanthemum and ivy garlands on the mantelpiece lent a festive air to the proceedings as the assembled company nibbled on sweetmeats and played charades.

Briony looked delectable in her first grown-up evening gown, its wide, square neck showing off her creamy skin and its high waist and straight skirt making her appear taller. The dark-green velvet overlaid with a white guipure lace bodice complemented her chestnut hair that her mother had plaited then wound about the crown of her head. As she strutted across the Turkey rug, her raised arm holding an imaginary placard, Oliver thought it wouldn't be long before she was breaking some young fellow's heart.

Luke Armitage, a heavily built, rather dour lad short on conversation, now worked alongside his father in the dyehouse at Lockwood Mill. He had little interest in silly games but he couldn't take his eyes off Briony. An embarrassing twitching in his pants had him folding his hands over his lap. She was far too good for him, for God's sake. He shouldn't be having feelings like that.

When Briony came to a stop, she adopted the manner of someone giving a rousing speech then asked her audience, 'Who am I?'

'Oh, that's so easy, Sis,' Blaise drawled. 'You're Emmeline Pankhurst.'

'So I am,' Briony replied, delighted that her enactment of the woman she greatly admired had been recognised. 'I was going to do Emily Davison but I didn't want to get down on the floor and spoil my dress,' she said, referring to her favourite suffragette.

'And throw yourself under a horse just to let

everybody know just how stupid you are,' Blaise scoffed. 'Silly woman!'

'Suffragettes are neither stupid nor silly!' Sarah intervened. 'They're brave and clever, Blaise Hard-castle. You seem to think that us girls have no brains at all. Well, I'll have you know that we do.'

Blaise gave a nasty laugh. 'Not if you go round throwing yourself under horses. It's a waste of time and money educating girls.'

'No, it's not,' Briony snapped, and loosely quoting her favourite woman author, she went on to say, 'Charlotte Brontë believes that women need exercise for their faculties as much as their brothers do. It's narrow-minded to say they ought to confine them-selves to making puddings and knitting stockings.'

'You never made a pud or knitted a sock in your life,' Blaise hooted.

'I did too,' Briony shouted back, her cheeks blaz-ing. 'I helped Bella make the sponge you ate at lunch, and Sarah and I have knitted dozens of stockings for soldiers. So there!'

'Charlotte Brontë must be clever to write those books, and I suppose there are lots of women with just as many brains as men,' Josh remarked amiably in an attempt to prevent Blaise from firing any fur-ther insults. It had the desired effect.

Blaise suddenly thought of the skilful ways Juliet used to give him so much pleasure and grinned. 'You're right, Josh. Some girls are incredibly knowledgeable.'

'I think Briony has brains as well as beauty,' Luke mumbled.

Briony threw him such a dazzling smile that he felt a stirring inside his pants again.

George and Nellie beamed at their taciturn son's kind remark.

'My sister? Brains?' sneered Blaise. 'She's as daft as a brush.'

'What does that old saying mean?' Briony asked, more curious than offended. 'Brushes aren't daft. They're useful.'

As their offspring engaged in their youthful spat, their parents exchanged amused or somewhat anxious glances, Verity hopeful that her son wouldn't go too far, and Oliver ready to rein him in if he did. Theo and Dolly smiled at one another when their son brought the heated conversation to a peaceable end, and laughed out loud as he took his turn at miming the story of the three little pigs.

Shortly before midnight, Oliver replenished everyone's glasses: port for the gentlemen, sherry for the ladies, and blackcurrant cordial for the children.

As they raised their glasses, Oliver gave thanks for the prosperity of the past year and for keeping their families safe. Then Theo toasted the troops fighting in the trenches and said that he sincerely hoped the world would soon be at peace. The solemnity that these little speeches incurred cast a shadow on the evening, and after they had emptied their glasses, they sat talking in hushed voices.

Luke pondered on how to engage Briony in conversation without sounding foolish. Failing to come up with any witty ideas, he sat and watched her as she talked with Sarah.

Blaise walked over to the window that looked out onto the garden, and drawing back one of the rich-red velvet drapes and securing it with the thick, corded tassel to a brass hook in the frame, he gazed out into the blackness, his mind on Juliet. New Year's Day being a Saturday, she had gone home to spend the weekend in Dodworth with a crisp ten-shilling note in her pocket that Blaise had given her, and that Oliver had given him as payment for his labours in the mill. In the past two weeks, their meetings had been brief and disappointing, Juliet making excuses that she was busy with Union business, and Blaise forced to attend the many Christmas and New Year functions that his family engaged in at this time of year. He was missing her dreadfully, and now he wondered with a heavy heart if she was tiring of him.

Josh, aware that the adults were taking little notice of their children, and that Briony and Sarah had their heads together discussing some girlish interest, made his way over to where Blaise stood. 'Who's the girl who lives in Rose Street?' he asked in a low voice.

Blaise whirled round to face him, a guilty flush suffusing his neck and cheeks.

'What girl? What are you talking about?'

'The girl I saw you with before Christmas. The one you went into a house in Rose Street with. Is she a mill girl?'

'What if she is,' Blaise hissed, his eyes flashing to where his mother sat talking with Dolly. 'If you must know, seeing as how you have obviously been spying on me, she's my girlfriend, and I'd thank you to keep that between us.' He glared at Josh.

'I wasn't spying on you,' Josh replied coolly, even though he knew it was a lie. 'I just happened to see you with her and I'm curious, that's all.' He gave Blaise a smile that he hoped his friend would interpret as a man-to-man gesture. 'So, you've got a girlfriend, have you? Lucky sod.'

Blaise puffed out his chest and said, 'Yes, I have.' Then, the temptation to boast too much to resist, he rolled his eyes and patted his groin before adding, 'And she's absolutely marvellous. You won't believe the things we get up to.'

'Oh, I think I would. I'm not completely innocent, you know,' said Josh, his eyes narrowing lasciviously although in truth, he'd never even kissed a girl, let alone done the things that Blaise was intimating. 'I gather your ma and pa don't know about her?'

'Good God, no!' Blaise said, his eyes shooting in their direction again then back at Josh. 'You won't say anything, will you?'

'Not to anyone. You have my word on that,' Josh said, of the opinion that whatever murky dealings Blaise Hardcastle involved himself in was his own business. He did however think that it could only end in disaster. 'I'd be careful, if I was you,' he warned.

'I am,' Blaise said boldly, clapping his hand on Josh's shoulder. 'Our secret, eh?'

Josh nodded, the grim set to his mouth going un-noticed by Blaise who, grinning broadly, said, 'Shall we go and join Luke the Lugworm and the old folks and our simpering sisters?'

* * *

There were no signs that the war in Europe was abating, and 1916 seemed set to follow the pattern of the previous years. With battles raging at the Western Front, and in Gallipoli, Italy and North Africa, the bid for supremacy was taking its toll. Heavy casualties demanded the British government introduce imposed conscription on men aged between eighteen and forty-one to join those already fighting for king and country.

'Thank God you're too old to be called up,' Verity said to Oliver, her words gushing out with relief when they heard the news. They were sitting in the drawing room listening to the wireless on an evening at the end of January, the garden outside the window blanketed under a recent fall of fresh snow.

'Yes, being forty-four has some advantages, although I'd willingly go if I thought it would bring an end to it,' he replied grimly, shaking the newspaper he was reading. 'The death notices grow longer by the day. Lads we employed who'll never work or play again. What a terrible waste.'

Verity heaved a sigh. 'I've lost count of our grieving widows and mothers. Every day, there's someone needs comforting. Why, in the last two weeks alone, Annie in spinning, and Mavis and Gladys in the weaving shed lost their sons, and

Mabel in the mending room lost her husband. She's left with five children to rear.' Verity's eyes filled with tears as she contemplated how she would feel if she were to lose her son or husband.

'I know, I know, darling,' Oliver growled, touched by her compassion which equalled his own. 'But we're doing all we can to alleviate their distress.' He was referring to the widows and orphans fund the mill contributed to, and time off with pay that Lockwood Mill allowed their bereaved employees.

'My heart goes out to our women,' Verity said. 'They toil for long hours every day then go home to make meals out of whatever their meagre rations allow. Many of them keep their older children off school so that they can join the queues for bread and such first thing in the morning because by the time our workers finish, there's nothing left to be had in the shops.'

'Aye, the men in the trenches are paying the ultimate price but civilians are also fair game when it comes to war. If the Germans can't shoot us, they'll try to starve us,' Oliver bitterly agreed. 'And we should be thankful that we haven't been subjected to any of their blasted Zeppelin raids.'

'That's true. When those warships bombed Scarborough, the war seemed very close at hand, but two years on, it seems that the enemy's ignoring us, thank goodness. Apart from the shortage of things in the shops and the difficulty we have in obtaining supplies for the mill, we could almost be forgiven for thinking that we don't have a fight on our hands.' Verity gave her husband a bemused little smile.

'That's because we have a different battle to deal with,' Oliver said, the wry look on his face letting his wife know he didn't relish the fight. 'The Unions are hotting up for an all-out scrap that will certainly rock the boat.'

'Ah, yes. We mustn't forget the Unions,' Verity groaned.

* * *

In the wider world, the demand for men, material and money had grown more strident in the past two years of conflict. In the Colne Valley, the General Union of Textile Workers that represented the mill workers, and in particular the weavers, were quick to take advantage of the precarious situation and were busy making their own demands.

The manufacturers were reaping the benefits of lucrative government contracts and the Union seized the opportunity to insist that their members had the right to increased wages, bonuses, and shorter working hours: all the things they had fought for long before the war. Now, believing they had the upper hand, they issued threats to the mill owners, telling them that the withdrawal of labour from a dissatisfied workforce could have a disastrous effect on their productivity. How would they fulfil their government contracts for khaki, flannel and woollen blankets if the workers went on strike?

Verity and Oliver, like all the other mill owners in the valley, were now faced with the problem of how to satisfy the Unions and still turn a sustainable, healthy profit. With so many men answering the call of duty to fight for king and country, the workers at Lockwood Mill were predominantly women, and as the Unions made their voices heard, the women who had previously rejected membership now clamoured to join, lured by the promise of increased wages and shorter working hours. This was music to Juliet's ears.

There was further cause for rejoicing when in January, at Huddersfield Town Hall, the Yorkshire Trade Council voted to demand that the government should introduce an eight-hour working day and grant equal pay for women. Historically, the men had always been paid more than their female counterparts, even though they were doing the same job. A woman weaver earned between nineteen and twenty-two shillings per week, whereas a male weaver was paid twenty-seven to twenty-nine shillings. But now, with fewer men in the workplace, the women were taking on duties that before the war had not been expected of them. This being the case, they demanded equal pay.

Juliet had regularly attended Union meetings. She flirted with the young men in her bid to be accepted, and remained undeterred when the older men ignored or derided her contributions to the matters in hand. When they told her, 'Tha'd be better off keepin' my bed warm than wastin' thi time here,' or to, 'Bugger off back to t'kitchen' – for that was the place the men thought women belonged – she retaliated fiercely to their ribald remarks, telling them that they had no fire in their bellies. If they had, they'd fight like the miners did and, like her own father, be jailed for their beliefs instead of pussy-footing round the bosses with their fruitless proposals. Having bearded the lion in its den, she was now grudgingly accepted, and the newly joined women members looked to her as their leader even though some of them did not like her. Juliet didn't care one way or the other. Her friendship with Blaise was going according to plan, and her desire to up-hold the fight for better wages and conditions that her father had instilled in her was burning brightly.

Now, tonight, as she made her way to the Somerset Arms public house where the Union meetings were held, she was ready to continue the fight. She had to go carefully, taking little steps like a tightrope walker as she avoided the patches of ice gleaming blackly on the pavement. The February air was bitingly cold and stung her cheekbones like the blade of a knife but when, up ahead of her, she saw the women who had recently joined the Union making their way to the pub, she was warmed to the marrow. Quickening her pace, she caught up with them and when they made her welcome, a surge of power flooded her veins.

'How do, Juliet.' Maggie Broadbent linked her arm in Juliet's. 'What's it to be tonight then?' Maggie had been one of the first weavers to give Juliet her support, and now she was an ardent Union member.

'To make us selves heard,' Juliet replied. 'Make 'em believe our votes count now that there's so many of us.'

The women cheered, and with their ringleader urging them on, they marched into the pub behind Juliet, who sashayed across the taproom as though she owned it. Following her example, the women filed into the back room, ready to make their demands known. Tonight, equality was at the top of their agenda.

The chairman, Bert Higginbottom, and the secretary and the treasurer were seated behind the long table at the front of the room. Facing them were rows of chairs, most of them already occupied, and the occupants all men. The tension in the room heightened as the women pushed their way between the rows to find seats.

'Aw, bloody hell. I came here to get away from t'Missis, and you soddin' lot have to come an' spoil it,' growled a chap with a shiny, bald head.

'We've as much right to be here as you have,' Juliet told him curtly.

'You don't pay as much as we do in subscriptions so you've less bloody rights,' he argued, pressing the point that women paid less for membership.

'Aye, and we get less benefits if we're on short time or on strike,' Juliet reminded him.

'Aw, shurrup! Like I said, I came here to get away from one woman's carping. I don't have to listen to you.'

'I bet she were glad to see t'back of you,' Maggie

scoffed as she plumped down in the empty chair next to him.

'I'd like to see t'back o' you interferin' buggers, pokin' your bloody noses into what's men's business,' an elderly overseer with a grizzled chin and no teeth chuntered.

Like most of the men in attendance, he was well past fifty, and only a handful were below that age. They were the ones with poor eyesight, flat feet or failed health, considered unfit for war duty. A few were married or widowed with children. They also were exempt, but now that the government had made it compulsory for men aged between eighteen and forty-one to enlist, their peers were either in training camps or fighting on the Western Front.

Juliet's cold, blue eyes glinted as she addressed the men. 'Less of your bloody cheek,' she snapped. 'We're here to give our support, and you should be glad of it.' She sat down next to Maggie, and following her lead, the other women shuffled into the vacant chairs.

Bert Higginbottom called the meeting to order, and as usual when the women were in attendance, the air was fraught with arguments.

'I don't see why I should be paid less than them

for doin' t'same job,' May Sykes complained as they discussed the matter of equal pay.

'Aye, but tha doesn't do t'same job, does tha, May? You can't lift your beam off your loom when it's full. It's us men has to do it for thi,' a cocky young lad with a squint in one eye shouted.

'Aye, you only do half the bloody job, so why should you get paid the same as us?' the bald-headed fellow agreed. 'An some of us tune us own looms. You don't do that either.'

The chairman banged his gavel, and as order was resumed, May subsided in her chair, silently admitting that the women still required strong men to carry out certain tasks.

Juliet jumped up from her chair. 'Permission to speak,' she said, looking over at Bert. Through half-closed eyes, he nodded his acquiescence, and she took a deep breath. Then using the words she'd heard her father say over and over again, she raised her voice.

'We might not be strong enough in body, but we women are strong in spirit. We want better pay and shorter hours just as much as you do, so let's stop fighting one another and unite with one voice,' she rallied, her eyes shining with fervour.

The men shifted uneasily in their seats but they let her have her say.

Realising she held the floor, Juliet was taking full advantage of it. 'I want to tell you a story my dad told me. He's been a Union man all his working life, and knows more about the struggle than you lot have had hot dinners.' Her eyes drilled the seated men to make sure she held their attention, and seeing she had, she continued, 'Some of you hadn't even been born when it happened, but you older men might remember something about it. In 1875, thirteen women in a mill in Batley formed a committee to protest against the owners cutting their wages. They asked the miners' union in Wakefield to help them raise funds so that they could pay their rents and feed their families... something you all have to do... and then they went on strike.'

The emphasis she put on the word 'strike' made her audience sit up. They glanced from one to the other then back at Juliet. Juliet's heart thudded as the delicious feeling of power flooded her veins. She was in control, and she wasn't finished yet.

'When the men they worked with saw the support that the women were getting from the miners and all the mill hands in the district, they joined them,' she continued. 'That's what my dad called *soli-*

darity, and that's what *we* need... *solidarity!* All in it together!'

Steadily, her bright-blue eyes roved over her audience, but her heart was pounding and her palms were clammy as a sense of relief that they had listened flooded through her veins. The silence that had met her delivery now changed to a muttering and then a rumbling as the men and women voiced their approval. Juliet's taut lips parted in a triumphant smile.

Her audience began to talk all at once, and Bert hammered the table with his gavel before pandemonium threatened to take over the proceedings. Called to order, the hubbub subsided. Bert's eyes roamed the room, and when he began to speak, his tone was wistful as he gave Juliet a wry smile.

'I wa' ony a lad when that happened, but I've not forgotten about it, lass.' he said. He looked away from her and addressed the workers in a stronger voice. 'It stuck in my mind, 'cos when those women stood up for their rights, the bosses realised they were losing more than thirty pounds a day for every day that the strike went on. An' what did they do?' Once again, his eyes roved his captive audience, and warming to his theme, he shouted, 'They caved in and begged 'em to come back to work on their own terms.'

There was a rumble of approval and Juliet felt dizzy with success. Careless of going against the protocol of the meeting and interrupting Bert, she jumped up onto her chair and yelled, 'Strike! Strike! Strike! If we threaten to strike, we have the bosses at our mercy. With all the government contracts they have to meet, they can't afford to refuse us.'

Heads nodded, eyes gleamed, grins widened as the mill hands got to their feet.

'Strike!'

'Solidarity!'

'All of us together!'

'All for one, and one for all!'

The shouts and yells bounced off the walls. Bert hammered with his gavel for silence.

'Now, calm yourselves down, an' let's tek a vote.'

16

Verity gave a huge sigh of sheer frustration as Bert Higginbottom left the mill office. She couldn't remember a time when she had felt so oppressed. Problems seemed to be mounting at an exponential rate, and after having had to reason with Bert for almost an hour, she felt as though she was losing control of all that she held near and dear.

Dealing with Bert made her feel like tearing her hair out. Instead, she tucked a long, chestnut tendril that had escaped from her neat chignon behind her ear then leaned back in her chair and closed her eyes. If the weavers went on strike as they were threatening to do, the mill would be unable to meet the deadlines for the government contracts to which they were committed. The war *had* brought prosperity to mills like hers, but it had been earned the hard way and she was wearied by the never-ending struggle.

These days, much of her time was consumed by meetings with Bert Higginbottom, who mediated for the weavers – the workers who, if they went on strike, represented the biggest threat to production – and if she wasn't wrangling with Bert, she had to make herself available to the spinners, the carders and the dyers, who were also asking for increased wages.

They were all champing at the bit to achieve their demands. Perhaps the most vociferous in their fight for equal pay were the women weavers. It pained Verity to be at loggerheads with the women she had looked on as friends, and she was tired of having to meet with them and listen to their exhortations. And if dealing with meetings in her own mill wasn't bad enough, she was expected to attend those called by the other mill owners in the valley.

Of course, she had Oliver's full support, but he was more often than not engaged in the constant necessity to obtain raw wool, yarns and dyes, and all the things required to keep the production of cloth functioning. A drought in Australia was severely affecting exports of raw wool, as was the danger of German submarines on the precarious sea crossing, and even though the British government was buying the entire wool-clip in the United Kingdom, Oliver was run ragged as he sourced materials to keep the mill functioning.

Verity's unpleasant thoughts were interrupted as the mill hooter split the air and signalled the end of the working day. Her eyes flew open. Six already, and Oliver not yet back from Bradford where he had been buying yarn.

Stretching to ease her stiff neck and shoulders then getting to her feet, Verity went and stood at the office door as the workers streamed out of the sheds and into the mill yard. Many of them acknowledged her with a cheery goodnight as they made their way to the gate, but she pondered on their duplicity; could these same men and women who she thought of not just as employees but as friends so easily cast aside their loyalties and stop production, which might ruin her mill? Hadn't she always tried to do her best to ease their labours by providing things for their benefit? Safe working conditions, a canteen where they could eat in comfort, doctors' bills and funeral costs settled, and rewarded them with bonuses when productivity had exceeded expectation. She had always had their best interests at heart – a heart that Oliver often told her was far too generous – and now it seemed as though they were throwing back in her face the kindness she had so readily fostered.

The mill yard fell silent as she gazed after the mill hands' departing backs, and still she stood, shivering in the chill night air and feeling utterly depressed. Across the yard, the mill languished in an eerie blackness, grey wisps of smoke drifting soundlessly upwards from its chimney, and the thrum and roar and rumble of machinery stilled for the day. This is how it would be if the Union insisted on strike action. The fear of that sent icy fingers rippling down her spine.

And where was Oliver?

When she saw the gleam of a car's headlights coming towards the mill gate, her spirits were temporarily raised. Oliver brought the Austin to a stop on the cobbles in front of the office door then alighted. She could tell by the look on his face that his search for the yarns they needed had been unsuccessful. It was just one thing after another, Verity told herself.

'What are you doing standing out here in the cold?' Oliver asked as he came to her side.

'Worrying myself to death.'

'Then let me take you home... Forget about this place and its troubles for a few hours,' he said, pushing past her into the office and unhooking her coat. Gently, he draped it round her stiff shoulders then helped as she threaded her arms into the sleeves. Although her coat was fashioned from thick, grey wool and had a wide fur collar, she still felt chilled to the bone.

Oliver picked up a ledger he needed and dowsed the light. 'Homeward,' he said, cheerily chivvying her into the car before taking his place behind the wheel.

Verity huddled deep in her seat and Oliver spun the car round with alacrity. After a brief stop at the gate to bid Joe goodnight and to check that the night-watchman had reported for duty, they were bowling along the roads that led to Almondbury, and home. In Somerset Road, the bare-limbed trees sur-rounding the Ramsden estate loomed starkly against a lowering sky, their witch-like branches blackening Verity's mood, and when they reached the village, the rosy glow behind the curtained windows of the houses did nothing to raise her spirits. Verity half-listened to Oliver telling her about his lack of success in Bradford, for she knew deep inside that along with the dilemma at the mill, there were other problems awaiting her at Far View House. Today, after Joe had collected Blaise from school and brought him to the mill, Verity had instructed Joe to take him straight home. She'd had neither the patience nor the energy to deal with her sulky son.

Ever since Christmas, Blaise had been in a foul mood, taking his temper out on anyone who crossed his path. He had been vile to Bella, complaining that his breakfast bacon was cold, that his shirt hadn't been properly ironed, and that her sponge pudding was soggy. Bella had been close to tears. And when her daughter had been cleaning his room, he had accused her of prying into his personal affairs, and Susan, being made of sterner stuff than her mother, had told him he was a spoiled little brat with a dirty mind. They had almost come to blows. He had been spiteful to Briony, making fun of her allegiance to women's suffrage, and criticising her appearance, which he said was so prim and proper that no one of the opposite sex could possibly find her attractive. Poor Briony had wept, the insult twice as hurtful coming, as it did, from someone whom she thought should love her. She, of course, was completely unaware that Blaise was unfavourably comparing her with Juliet, for it was she who was the cause of his aggravation.

Juliet was too busily involved with Union business to spend time with him, so she said, but he was nursing the awful feeling that she had grown tired of him, that he wasn't man enough for her. To offset this feeling of inadequacy, he'd given her money and a pearl necklace that he'd pilfered from his mother's jewellery box – one that she never wore and wouldn't miss. It infuriated him to think that Juliet would rather go to meetings and haggle over boring matters to do with the mill than entertain him.

Had Verity known that her son's irascible and sometimes appalling behaviour was due to a weaver from her own weaving shed having withdrawn her favours, she would have felt even more miserable. In fact, she would have been shocked to the core. In her eyes, Blaise was still an innocent, if complex, boy who was finding it difficult to bridge the years between childhood and manhood. She had no doubt he would do that eventually, and splendidly, but for now, she felt overwhelmingly saddened by his intractability and the effect it was having on her family.

'Here we are. Home sweet home.' Oliver's cheerful announcement interrupted his wife's dour thoughts as he brought the Austin to a halt at Far View's front door. She climbed out of the car feeling vaguely hopeful that once she was in her own home sitting comfortably by a blazing fire after having digested one of Bella's hot, tasty dinners, she would be freed from the ice-cold shell encasing her.

'Dear God! What's going on?' Oliver cried as he entered the hallway, Verity at his heels.

Briony stood at the foot of the stairs, her burning cheeks stained with angry tears and her hands outstretched as she screeched, 'Give it back, you rotten monster!'

Blaise, his stance arrogant, tauntingly flourished a magazine just out of Briony's reach. On the cover was a picture of Emily Davison depicted as an angel, complete with a halo and wings. Briony made a grab for it. Blaise jumped back then began ripping the magazine apart. Pages fluttered to the floor. Laughing nastily, he stamped his foot on the image of the dead suffragette, obliterating her angelic face and wings under the sole of his boot.

'Stop that at once!'

Oliver's roar had Blaise turning, and when he saw his father's livid face and his mother's distressed expression, he toed the remnants of paper towards his sister, muttering, 'Here, have your stupid magazine.'

Briony rushed at Oliver, throwing herself against his chest. 'He stole my... magazine... the one with...

Emily on the cover... He knows I treasure it,' she sobbed.

'Oh, Blaise. How could you?'

At the sound of Verity's horrified cry, and the sight of the tears brimming her eyelashes, an ugly redness crept up Blaise's neck then into his cheeks. For a fleeting moment, he felt ashamed. Then, shrugging it off, he said, 'It was only a ridiculous magazine.'

His mother flashed him a look of utter contempt that hurt him more than he expected. He charged upstairs, the slam of his bedroom door reverberating through the house. Briony, her equilibrium somewhat recovered by the comfort of her father's arms, watched him go then turned her eyes on her mother.

'Oh, darling. I am sorry,' Verity said, taking a by now rather soggy Briony by the hand and pulling her close to her chest. 'I know it's unforgiveable, but do try to understand. Blaise is going through a bad patch and he...'

'Stop that, Verity! I'm tired of making excuses for him,' Oliver barked, his disappointment in his son palpable. Just lately, he had thought the lad was learning to be a decent human being. 'Now, I don't know about you, but I'm hungry. Let's have dinner.'

He marched into the dining room and Bella, who

had been hovering halfway up the basement stairs listening to the fracas, and waiting to serve dinner, darted back to the kitchen.

'He's been at it again,' she said to Susan.

Her daughter didn't need to ask who. Whenever there was upset in Far View House, it was always that brat, Master Blaise, who caused it.

'He's always up to summat, an' none of it for the good.' Susan snorted. 'Have you seen t'state of his sticky underwear? He's either fiddling wi' himself summat rotten to get 'em in that state, or more likely he's found some poor lass to give him a helping hand.'

'Ooh, Susan!' Her mother's eyes widened. 'You shouldn't be noticing such things.'

'I can't not. I have to wash the dirty little bugger's pants, don't I?'

'Let's have no more talk like that. Dish that soup up while I fill these tureens.'

In the dining room, Blaise flatly refusing to join them, despite Verity's pleas. She sat down with Oliver and Briony, but they had lost their appetites and most of Bella's onion soup, fish pie, and stewed apples and custard was sent back to the kitchen, barely touched.

'So much for all my efforts,' Bella grumbled. 'It's

hard enough to make decent meals what with everything on ration, and then find it's not appreciated.' She began scraping the leftovers into dishes to take to her mother's house later on; in her opinion, good food should never be wasted, and Lord knows it wasn't easy to buy the stuff she'd just served up.

'Them as has it all never appreciate owt,' Susan snarled, clattering dishes into the sink.

But Verity didn't feel as though she had it all when, a short time later, Oliver ordered Blaise to come down to the drawing room. Surly, and not in the least repentant, he stood shuffling his feet and looking bored as his father gave him a dressing-down.

'I will not tolerate such spiteful behaviour towards your sister, nor your rudeness to Bella and Susan, and as for the pain you are inflicting on your mother, it goes beyond words.' Oliver shook his head, exasperated. 'You will apologise to each of them, and you can start by asking your mother's forgiveness.'

Blaise looked relieved; apologising was easy, even when it wasn't sincere.

'I'm truly sorry, Ma. I hate myself for upsetting you. I'm all mixed-up at the moment,' he said, willing his dark eyes to gleam moistly as he gazed into hers.

A sad, conciliatory smile curved his lips, and Verity's heart melted.

But Oliver hadn't finished, and went on to say that his pocket money was suspended, and he was banned from leaving the house in the evenings.

'But what about the Scouts?' Blaise panicked at the thought of not being able to meet Juliet. He turned a pleading face to his mother. 'Tell him, Ma. The work I do there is essential to the war. I can't let them down. I've sold more War Bonds than anybody else,' he lied.

Verity's resolve easily weakened whenever her beloved son begged for her to come to his aid. She gave her husband an equally pleading look. 'It seems a shame to deny him that, Oliver. He's already devoted so much time and effort...'

Oliver's eyes glinted dangerously as he turned them on his wife. Why did she always go against him where Blaise was concerned? It seemed that they, who agreed on most things, would never see eye to eye when it came to disciplining their son, and now Oliver's anger was such that he felt close to losing control. Relinquishing the urge to punch something, he barged out of the drawing room to seek solace in his study.

'Thanks, Ma,' Blaise gushed as he hugged her.

The gesture, totally unexpected, for Blaise rarely demonstrated his feelings in this way, brought Verity close to tears.

'Oh, darling... do... do try to... behave more reasonably,' she said, and desperate to prolong the embrace, she wrapped her arms round him, pressing him to her breast.

17

As winter faded and daylight hours lengthened, things were moving apace both at home and abroad. In France, Germany had attacked Verdun in what was to become the longest battle of the war, and at sea, ships bringing vital goods to Britain were at the mercy of U-boat blockades. In the Colne Valley, the mill owners continued to hold out against the Union's demands for better wages and equal pay.

'Will we have to strike, do you think?' May Sykes asked the women weavers sitting in the canteen at Lockwood Mill one morning at the end of February.

'Bert says he's getting nowhere with Mrs Hardcastle. She's prevaricating at every turn. She says she has to go over the finances before she can agree to giving us equal pay, and that she's consulting with the other mill owners on the matter,' Juliet said pompously as she repeated what the Union chairman had told her. Just lately, he had taken her under his wing and was using her to keep the women informed. Their cooperation was vital if a strike was to be called.

'Aye, the owners allus stick together when it comes to doing us out of our rights,' Maggie Broadbent grumbled. 'Mrs Hardcastle'll not do owt without their say-so.'

'She did in the past,' an older woman reminded them. 'She gave us an extra day at Christmas when t'day itself fell on a Sunday. That caused a right stink wi' t'other bosses in t'valley, din't it, Violet?' She looked to her elderly colleague for confirmation.

'Aye, she did, but that wa' afore she married Hardcastle. She's not as soft these days. Mind you, he's not bad to work for, but he's allus been more careful than her when it comes to it. Oliver goes wi' his head, whereas that lass goes wi' her heart.'

'Her heart'll tell her what to do this time round,' Juliet said with a smirk. 'When she hears what I've got to say, she'll fall over herself to give us equal pay, I can guarantee that.'

Maggie gave Juliet a quizzical glare. 'What the

bloody hell are you on about? Anybody 'ud think you were running the Union the way you talk.'

'Maybe I know things you don't,' Juliet said, her eyes glittering wickedly.

Maggie, annoyed that Bert had chosen Juliet to lead the women, and irritated by her cocky attitude, couldn't resist letting Juliet know that some of the women still looked down on her because she was an in-comer from a pit village near Barnsley.

'Aw, shut your gob, you black-arsed cow,' Maggie spat, and the fight that was about to ensue was prevented by the blast of the mill hooter.

Juliet strutted out of the canteen, impervious to the slight. She felt with certainty that she could make Mrs Hardcastle see things differently.

* * *

Verity was feeling slightly more hopeful these days, and as she and Dolly walked to Silver Street to visit Dolly's mam, Florence, she told her friend about the latest meeting she'd attended in the George Hotel where the mill owners had gathered to discuss the bugbear regarding equal pay.

'We reached the conclusion that if we all refused their demands, the Unions would have no leverage...

They won't be able to play us off one against the other.'

'That's as maybe. But can you trust 'em? They'll all do as they please in the end. You don't want them to call a strike. Remember the strikes in 1912 when the blacklegs went into work and them that agreed with strike action fought tooth and nail to keep them out,' Dolly said, her voice high as she recalled the fights outside the gates of some of the other mills.

'I do,' said Verity, shaking her head and her expression grim as they turned the corner into Silver Street. 'Fortunately, our mill wasn't one of them. Mills like Lumb's actually let those opposed to the strike live in the mill just so they could keep production going. I'd hate for us to have to do that but as you say, we can't trust the Unions. And the mill owners are no better. There's Brierley's asking for their workers to be made exempt from call-up, but Walter Sykes at Zetland Mill has given notice to all his men who are old enough to enlist. None of us agrees on anything these days.'

Dolly, her lips curled at the anomalies, pushed open the door of her mother's house and they walked through into the kitchen. 'If that's not forcing their hand, I don't know what is.'

'Who's forcing whose hand?' Florence asked by

way of a greeting then waving a hand at the table, inviting them to sit before she lifted the kettle.

Verity sat down heavily and pulled a face. 'We were talking about all the disagreements there are between the mills and the Unions,' she said wearily.

'Aye, I've heard some of the mills are paying their hands less than the hourly rate for the government contracts,' Florence said, and sniffed to show her disgust. 'It's no wonder the workers are kicking up stink when the system's so unfair.'

'Lockwood's isn't! We always pay our employees fair rates,' Verity protested as, with a little smile, she accepted the cup of tea Florence handed her.

'Aye, I know *you* do, but you've got to look at it from their point of view, Verity.' Florence passed a cup to Dolly then sat down at the table. 'It's a changed world, and you've got to accept that,' Florence continued. 'If you believe what you read in the papers about women making bullets and driving trains, you'd think that women had never held down jobs before the war, but us women in the North of England have always worked. It's nothing new.'

Verity and Dolly nodded their agreement.

'But now they're demanding recognition for their labours, and you can't blame them,' Florence went on. 'And it isn't as if the mill owners can't afford it,' she said, looking pointedly at Verity. 'You have to admit, you've all benefitted from the war.'

'That's right, Mam. They have,' Dolly said, her green eyes alight with fervour. Although she hadn't worked in the mill for many years, she still had a sisterly compassion for the weavers she had once worked alongside.

'I hear what you're saying, and I'm inclined to think you're right, Dolly, but it doesn't make my job any easier. I'm sick of this blasted war.' Verity was close to tears.

'Nay, don't let it upset you upset, lass.' Florence placed a comforting hand on Verity's and patted it. 'Try and look on the bright side.'

'I'm trying to, Florence.' Forcing a wide smile, Verity said, 'Look, let's talk about something cheerful. Blaise and Briony will be sixteen next week, and I'm going to have a party at the house. I've told Bella to see what she can rustle up in the way of food, but things are in such short supply, she'll have her work cut out.'

'I'll pitch in with some apple pies. There's still some pureed apples in the ice box that Theo made for me,' Dolly said, grinning at the thought of the little brick house that her husband had built beside her back door and regularly kept stocked with ice he took from the Thornton estate's large ice-house.

'And I'll give you some pickled onions and beet-root,' said Florence. Her cupboard was always well-stocked with jars she brought home from Shaw's factory.

'That'll be lovely,' said Verity, listening as her friend made further suggestions and thinking how Dolly and Florence were always on hand when she needed them. But then, they didn't have a mill to run, she thought sourly. Pushing the unwelcome reminder aside, she began to discuss the party with as much enthusiasm as she could muster.

* * *

A mad March wind had suddenly sprung up with scudding clouds threatening a downpour. Briony's pony, sensing the change in the weather, became skittish and his mistress was regretting having stayed too long at Outlane. She had been visiting a school-friend, Anne Blakeborough, who lived on a farm at the edge of the moor, and like Briony, she was a keen rider. They'd had an exhilarating gallop over the heather to Rocking Stone Hill then gone back to the farmhouse for tea and cakes before Briony set out for home.

Briony had been given the little mare that she called Emily for her twelfth birthday, and although she was now an accomplished horsewoman, the gusting wind and darkening sky was making Emily behave in an altogether unaccustomed manner. One moment, she was trotting along nicely, only for her to buck suddenly and shy to the side of the path, almost unseating her rider. Briony gripped the reins so tightly, her knuckles were white and her knees aching as she tried to steer Emily homewards.

She had travelled a good part of the way and was just riding along the road by Royds Hall when Emily came to an abrupt halt and shook her head violently. Briony pitched forwards. The reins slipped through her fingers, trailing onto the ground beneath the mare's hooves. There was nothing she could do but dismount, but as she stooped to gather the reins, she had no sooner taken hold of them than Emily reared up on her hind legs, the hooves of her front legs pawing the air dangerously close to Briony's head. She screamed and fell backwards on the path, the breath knocked out of her. In her dazed state, she heard a voice with a distinct foreign accent shouting, 'Oh, my Lady! You are in trouble? May I help?'

The stranger leapt and grabbed at the pony's bridle, swinging the mare away from her.

Shocked by such rough handling, Emily jinked and pranced for a moment or two then submitted to the strong hands holding her fast.

Briony looked up into a pair of warm, brown eyes in a handsome but concerned face. She flushed her annoyance at being found in such an ungainly position and on trembling legs, she staggered to her feet. The mare, now standing quietly, looked decidedly contrite. Briony stroked her neck and whispered soothing words before addressing the stranger.

'Thank you, thank you so much. You came just in time,' she gushed.

'You are not hurt?'

The warm, brown eyes looked Briony up and down then lightened with relief when she shook her head. 'No, just somewhat shaken.'

'I was fearful for you. You had a narrow escape,' her saviour said in broken English.

'I wouldn't have had, had it not been for your timely intervention,' she replied, her voice rich with gratitude. 'For some strange reason, my horse is behaving oddly,' she continued, and feeling discombobulated by the very attractive looks of the young man patiently holding her horse, she gabbled, 'I think it's the wind that's disturbing Emily. Usually, it never bothers her.' Then aware that her hat was askew and her hair tangled across her reddening cheeks, she set about tidying her appearance.

He stood by, thinking how attractive she looked in her dark-green riding habit with its flowing skirt and close-fitted jacket, the bunch of white lace at her throat appearing all the whiter against her pretty, flushed cheeks.

'Yes, you have very strong winds in your country, and very much rain,' he replied, giving a Gallic shrug, 'but that is not what has made your horse be-have badly. It is this!' He pulled out a sharp sprig of gorse that had somehow lodged itself under Emily's saddle. 'There! She will give you no more trouble,' he said, rubbing the mare's shoulder at the spot where the gorse had stuck into her hindquarter.

'Oh, dear me! How could I not have noticed it?' Briony cried with anguish. 'It must have got there when I was riding over the moor. I should have re-alised something was hurting her.' She patted Emi-ly's neck then offered her thanks again.

The young man stuck out his hand and gave a courtly little bow. 'My name is Marc Hendricks and I live and work here at Royds Hall.'

He gestured towards the mansion standing back

off the road at the end of a long drive in the spacious, tree-lined grounds, and at the large wooden huts located nearby. Briony knew that the Hall had been a reception centre for Belgian refugees who had fled their own country when the Germans invaded it, and that it was now one of the many military hospitals that had been established in the Colne Valley to serve the casualties of the war.

'Are you from Belgium?' she now asked, intrigued by his strange accent. 'Are you a doctor in the hospital?'

Marc gave a little laugh. 'Yes, I am a Belgian, and no, I am not yet a doctor. I had to leave my country when the Germans destroyed our way of life. I work in the hospital as an orderly, doing anything I can to help those poor injured men who have fought so bravely to rid us of the Kaiser's army.' His smile had faded and he looked distressed at the mention of his homeland and the patients he cared for. 'But one day, I hope to resume my studies and qualify as a doctor,' he said stoutly, his eyes brightening and his smile returning. 'And I tell you all this about myself, and I still do not know your name.'

'Briony Hardcastle of Far View House in Almondbury. And this is Emily.' She patted the pony's nose.

'I am honoured to make your acquaintance.'

'I don't know why. You must think me very foolish for not being able to control my horse, but she's usually so placid, I'm not used to her being skittish.' She turned to Emily, who was standing quite contentedly cropping the grass on the verge. 'She seems to have calmed down now so I had better be on my way.'

'She is calm because she is no longer in pain. It was not the wind but the gorse that troubled her. And see,' he said gesturing with his long slender hand, 'the wind has gone away. It came with a fury just for a short while and I am glad that it did. If it had not, I would not have met you.' His smile was warm.

Briony blushed as she glanced around her. She had been too fascinated by her new acquaintance to notice that the wind had dropped. Marc Hendricks was a lovely young man.

Reluctantly, she repeated herself. 'I had better be on my way. Thank you once again.' She gave him what she hoped was a captivating smile.

'Perhaps I should walk with you. The wind may blow again,' he said, his eyes inviting her to accept his offer. 'I am free today, and I only have seen what is here,' he gestured to Royds Hall and his immediate surroundings, 'and if I walk with you, you can show me more of your beautiful countryside.'

Briony hesitated. He was a stranger – and a foreign one at that. Yet, he seemed harmless enough. And it would be a kindness, make him feel more at home, if she introduced him to places further afield. Besides, she wanted to get to know more about him, so she said, 'I'd appreciate that. I've still a mile and more to go and it will be my privilege to have your company.'

Walking one on either side of Emily, they made their way towards Almondbury, Briony naming the places they passed through and pointing out things of interest even though there wasn't much to offer other than the impressive Wesleyan Chapel at Thornton Lodge and Primrose Hill's Baptist Church. Marc asked her about herself, and she told him her family owned a textile mill, that she had a twin brother, then about her schooling and her interest in the suffragette movement. He listened attentively and made appropriate comments, but Briony was far more interested in learning more about her companion and tactfully steered the conversation that way.

'It must have been very hard to leave your home and family,' she said.

'It was, but we could not stay. The Germans, they came with their soldiers and marched into my city to destroy us,' he said, his anguish apparent.

'How awful! I've heard how horrible they can be. Some of my schoolfriends have brothers who are fighting in France,' she said. 'My father talked about the invasion of Belgium and how the German army used your country as a gate into France.'

'Yes, and Antwerp is an important city. We are a big port for shipping on our River Scheldt. It flows to the North Sea and the Channel that separates your country from mine.'

'I've heard of Antwerp,' Briony said. 'It's famous for its trade in diamonds and making silk, isn't it?'

'That is so,' said Marc, the light in his eyes showing his admiration for Briony's knowledge as he looked over the mare's head into her face. Briony flushed with pleasure. 'And when the Germans came,' Marc continued, 'we believed we could halt them for we are a heavily fortified city, and we had the help of the British navy and its soldiers, but...' He gave another of his Gallic shrugs, his hands raised palms upward, and his face crumpled as he told her how brutal the German soldiers had been. Briony paled, horrified, as Marc described how people had been dragged from their homes and shot in the street. That friends and neighbours had been taken away, never to be seen again, and how the invaders had commandeered food supplies, leaving the inhabitants of Antwerp to go hungry. The picture he painted was one of chaos, destruction and death, and it took Briony's breath away.

'Oh, you poor souls. I can't imagine how dreadful that must have been.' She stopped walking and suggested they sit down to rest. Leaving Emily to crop the grassy verge, they sat on a low wall alongside the road. 'And were any of your family...?' She couldn't bring herself to use the words 'killed' or 'taken away'.

Marc shook his head. 'Thankfully, no. The Germans bombarded our homes with shot and shell and their hideous Zeppelins. Forced us to flee with whatever we could carry. I brought my mother and my sister to safety in England, but my brother... he stayed to fight for our country. He is very brave, but I am not. I do not want to kill people; I want to heal them.'

Briony could see that it pained him to say this and her heart went out to him. She reached out and gently placed her hand on his. He covered it with his free hand and for a long moment, they sat without speaking.

Although Briony had claimed she couldn't

imagine how Marc had suffered, she thought what it might be like if bombs rained down on Far View House and she and her family were suddenly forced to run for their lives. She'd have to leave behind all her books, her pretty dresses and the things that mattered most. Terrified by the thought, and loath to cause him any further pain, Briony pointed to the high hill in the near distance. It was bathed in a pale, watery light, the sun low in the sky.

'That's Castle Hill,' she said, eager to change the subject.

Marc raised his gaze and looked at the high ground on which stood a tall four-square edifice, black against the sun's dying rays.

'I can see it from my bedroom window,' Briony enthused. 'The tower on top of it was built to celebrate Queen Victoria's Golden Jubilee. That was three years before I was born, and long before that, it was ruled by an ancient queen called Cartimandua. She was a great warrior who protected the people who lived in Almondbury.'

Marc smiled at the childish enthusiasm with which she told the story, grateful that Briony had sensed the need to lighten their conversation even though he felt much better for having it. It had been cathartic to relate the horrors he and his family had endured, especially to one who had listened so sympathetically.

'Antwerp did not have a warrior queen. Instead, we had a giant called Antigon who chopped off the hands of the river's boatmen until the hero, Brabo, served him with his own medicine. He severed the giant's hand and threw it in the river. *Werpen* in my language means to throw, and that is why my city is called Antwerp.'

Marc laughed, and Briony joined in, glad she had made him feel happy.

'I don't have much further to go now,' she said, saddened that their journey was coming to an end. 'Will you be able to find your way back to Royds Hall?'

'You have been a very good guide, and I will remember the places you brought to my attention. I will look out for them,' he replied, feeling rather disappointed that she did not want him to accompany her to her door. 'Thank you for widening my knowledge of what I must now think of as my home for the time being. I have enjoyed our time together. Maybe we will meet again.' His smile was hopeful.

Briony fiddled with Emily's reins to hide her confusion. She would dearly have liked to invite Marc back for dinner, but she was unsure what sort of a reception he might get. Blaise would no doubt sneer and make unpleasant remarks about men who ran away from their country instead of staying to fight, and her parents would be wary of her making friends with a young man they didn't know. She knew that her father still considered her to be 'his little girl', and whilst she adored Oliver and in many ways was closer to him than her mother, she often found his attitude towards her irritating. He seemed not to realise that she was a young woman with a mind of her own, capable of making wise judgements and intelligent enough to make her own decisions.

Throwing care to the wind, she said, 'Tomorrow is Sunday. I usually take a walk this way in the afternoon. If you are free, perhaps I will meet you here.'

Marc's face split into a wide smile. 'At what time should I be here?' he asked, resting his hands on Emily's neck and gazing into Briony's eyes, his own alight with fun.

'Half-past two,' Briony told him. 'Now, will you help me remount?'

Marc cupped his hands. Briony placed her foot in them and with his help she levered herself up to the saddle. 'Thank you, kind sir,' she said smiling down at him, and pressing her heel into the pony's flanks and saying, 'Walk on, Emily' she clip-clopped away down the road feeling rather audacious. But by the time she reached the bottom of Far View Hill, she worried that she might have given her new Belgian friend the impression that she was a little bit too forward.

Marc's tread was light as he walked back the way they had come. He had found a friend, and a most delightful friend at that. It would make his enforced stay in England all the more pleasant, he was sure of that. He would ask his English colleagues what they knew about Miss Briony Hardcastle of Far View House in Almondbury.

18

Verity was in the dining room at Far View House checking the napery and cutlery, plates and glasses on the long table that was covered with a pristine, white linen cloth. Finding that everything was in order for the buffet supper she was hosting, she turned her attention to the arrangement of chairs and side tables, making sure there was sufficient seating and space to move between them. Tonight, they would celebrate Blaise and Briony's sixteenth birthday with a small gathering of family and friends, and satisfied there was nothing more she could do, she made her way down to the basement kitchen.

In the past few days, Verity, Bella and Susan had

raided the pantry and store cupboards in search of the provisions needed to feed their guests. In these lean times with so much on ration and so little available in the shops, it required inventiveness to put on a feast. Mason jars had been emptied of the previous year's preserves, apples and pears from their own trees and baked into tarts and pies, and potted meats made into savoury treats.

Now, as she entered the kitchen, she met with an array of their best efforts spread out on the counters and tables, waiting to be transported up to the dining room. Bella gave her a lopsided smile, and gesturing with a spatula, she asked for Verity's opinion on the cake she had just finished icing. With flour in short supply, Oliver's mother, Evelyn, had eased the strain on Verity's rations by contributing a large sponge cake, and Bella had transformed it into a birthday cake.

Verity looked at the wobbly, green letters and numbers on the white iced background. 'It's grand,' she said, 'but I don't think it will bear putting sixteen candles on it,' glancing at the pile Bella had laid alongside it. 'Let's just go with a few around the edge.'

'Right you are, Mrs Hardcastle,' Bella agreed. 'I'll just let the icing harden afore I stick 'em in.' She wiped her hands on her apron then asked, 'What do you think to these?'

Dolly had given Verity two large jars of bottled peaches grown in the hothouse at Thornton Lodge, and now some of the luxurious slivers of fruit topped a glazed tart and the others languished in a deep crystal dish of red jelly topped with thick, yellow custard.

'Oh, Bella! You're worth your weight in gold,' Verity praised.

'Susan made the trifle,' Bella said, nodding over at her sulky daughter who was arranging iced buns on a silver cake stand. Oliver's sisters, Rose and Maud, had used their ration coupons to buy them from Whiteley's bakery and had brought them over that morning.

Verity turned to Susan. 'Well done, Susan. It looks delicious. Blaise loves trifle.'

Susan gave a surly nod. She'd had a run-in with Blaise that afternoon, and the last thing she wanted was to please the arrogant brat. He'd had her iron his white evening shirt three times over before he was satisfied. To add to her chagrin, she would have to serve him and his sister's friends at the party rather than joining in the games and dances like the other young people. Curling her lip, she flounced into the pantry to hide her annoyance.

Verity glanced at the kitchen clock above the huge range. It showed a quarter to six.

'Start taking things up just before seven,' she said, 'and I must dash if I'm to be ready to meet our guests, and I still have to do Briony's hair.' She hurried to the basement stairs, feeling rather weary but assured by the spread in the kitchen that the party would be a success.

* * *

Juliet peered into the speckled mirror above the cupboard in her bedroom in the lodging house in Rose Street. Earlier that day, she'd washed her long, blonde hair and plaited it whilst it was still wet. Now that it was dry, she unplaited it and brushed and brushed until it hung about her shoulders in rippling, glossy waves. A smidgen of rouge accentuated her high cheekbones and her shapely mouth. Sadly, the mirror was too small for her to see her full reflection, but she felt sure that the dark-blue chiffon dress she'd bought at the flea market was fitting for the occasion. Once the property of a woman with a much larger income than Juliet's, it was a dress of quality and a few deft stitches had repaired the split underarm and the torn hem. Its nipped-in waist above a tiered skirt and a fitted bodice with a beaded neckline showed off her shapely figure to perfection.

Although Juliet thought that her attendance at Blaise's birthday party might be brief, she wanted to look her best amongst the other girls there, and more so when she approached Mrs Hardcastle. Inside her head, she replayed the words that she had been rehearsing throughout the day then pouted at her reflection, her blue eyes sparkling wickedly.

The dining room at Far View House buzzed with lively chatter as the assembled guests exchanged greetings, Dolly, Florence and Clem with Evelyn and her daughters, Rose and Maud, and Nellie and George with Theo. On the window seat, Briony half-listened as Sarah and two of their schoolfriends admired each other's dresses, and Blaise, Josh and Luke lounged by the fireplace, not talking.

Both Blaise and Briony were feeling on edge, their nerves stretched taut. Had they been able to read each other's minds, they would have been surprised to find that, for once in their lives, they were in tune with one another: Blaise had invited Juliet and – on an impulse – Briony had asked Marc to come to her party when they had met again on Sunday afternoon.

Now, the brother and sister could barely concentrate on anything other than listening for the doorbell to announce the arrival of their special guests. Neither of them had informed their parents of the invitations, the reason being that they expected Verity and Oliver to raise their objections. The unsuspecting couple were at that moment happily circulating the room, making everyone welcome before coming to a halt by the table.

Oliver tapped a spoon against a crystal decanter, and as the chimes rang out, a hush fell over the room. 'Welcome to you all on this wonderful occasion. Has everyone got a drink?' he asked, raising his own. Assured that everyone had, he continued, 'Then let us make a toast. Happy sixteenth birthday to Briony and Blaise.'

'Happy birthday, Briony and Blaise,' the guests chorused.

Oliver then made an amusing little speech about the joys of parenthood, the guests laughing and smiling, and Briony cringing at her duplicity as she listened to his fond words. Blaise sneered inwardly at the sentiments, remembering the times Oliver had chastised him.

Outside, Marc Hendricks hesitated at the gate of Far View House, deliberating whether to go any further. He felt uncomfortable in Dr Maes' evening suit even though it fitted him well, he and the doctor with whom he studied and had travelled to England with being a similar build. Having learned that the Hardcastles were a prestigious family in the Colne Valley, he was unsure of his welcome. He was just about to turn and go back the way he had come when a hackney cab rattled up the hill and stopped by the gate.

A pretty girl with gleaming, blonde hair alighted. Seeing Marc, she gave him a dazzling smile. 'Are you going to the party too?'

'I... I was... I am,' he stuttered, taking confidence from her bubbly demeanour.

'Then let's go,' she chirped, and threading her arm through his, they began walking up to the house. 'I'm Juliet Skeldon, Blaise's girlfriend,' she said. 'Who are you?'

'Marc Hendricks. A friend of Briony's.'

'You're foreign, aren't you?'

'I am... from... Belgium,' Marc replied as, at the door, Juliet yanked on the bell chain. He stood back, amazed by her aplomb and wishing that he had the same self-assurance. He felt puzzled. Although Juliet was dressed becomingly, she seemed rather rough and not at all the sort of girl he associated with Briony and her family.

The bell jangled noisily.

Briony darted across the dining-room floor, but Blaise was ahead of her.

Verity's eyes widened as she watched her son and daughter charge into the hallway. She gave Oliver a questioning, anxious look. He gave a careless shrug, bemused.

Blaise opened the front door. Juliet stepped inside. Marc dithered on the step.

'Juliet,' Blaise exclaimed, reaching for her hand then glancing first at Briony then at Marc in confusion. 'Who the devil...?'

'Do come in, Marc,' Briony urged, overriding Blaise then saying, 'This is my friend, Marc Hendricks. He's a trainee doctor at Royds Hall.' She cupped Marc's elbow and tugged him indoors.

'Blaise?' Juliet snapped, shrugging out of her coat and thrusting it at Blaise. The blasted Belgian had stolen her thunder.

Blaise tossed her coat onto a nearby chair then placed a conciliatory arm around her shoulders.

Oliver strode into the hall, Verity at his heels.

'What the blazes is going on?' Oliver demanded.

Verity's breath whistled in her throat when she saw Juliet. Why in heaven's name was this girl from her weaving shed standing in her hallway in the arms of her son? Tearing her eyes from them, her anger mingled with bewilderment as she stared at Briony and Marc.

'Will someone kindly explain what is happening?' she hissed, conscious that the dining-room door was wide open.

Briony took a deep breath. 'Mother, Father, let me introduce you to Marc Hendricks, a trainee doctor from Royds Hall,' she said, amazed at how calm she sounded and hopeful that they would be impressed by his profession.

Marc clicked his heels together and, giving a courtly little bow, he held out his hand.

'I am privileged to meet you, Mr and Mrs Hardcastle. Thank you for allowing me to attend the celebration of your daughter's birthday.' His smile was shaky.

Still baffled by the turn of events but struggling to regain his composure, Oliver instinctively shook Marc's hand, growling, 'Dr Hendricks.' Verity followed suit.

Briony's sigh of relief was audible. Blaise fumed.

Susan, on her way up from the kitchen with a large teapot, arrived at the head of the basement stairs just in time to hear Blaise snarl, 'You both know Juliet so we don't need to bother with introductions.' Cockily, he made to push past Oliver and go into the dining room.

His mother stuck out a staying hand. 'Not so fast! Why is she here?' she asked bluntly, throwing all proprieties to the wind.

Briony hurried Marc into the dining room. Susan, ears pricked, peered through the crack in the door.

'She's here because I invited her. You did say I could ask a friend, and I chose Juliet,' Blaise sneered.

Susan hared back to the kitchen. 'The brat and his mam and dad are havin' a bloody big row in the hall. There's a lass from the mill there an' all,' she told her mother.

'Oh, Lord, whatever next,' Bella cried, and taking it upon herself to save her kindly employer any further distress, she ordered, 'Start taking the trays up. Give 'em summat to eat till things settle down.'

Up in the hallway, Verity was staring at Blaise in disbelief. *How could he do this?*

Out of the corner of his eye, Oliver saw his

mother and Rose hovering in the doorway. Behind him, he was aware of Bella and Susan carrying trays loaded with savoury tarts, pies, cakes and such.

'Let's not make a scene,' he said, his voice low. 'Miss Skeldon's here now.' He glared at his son. 'We'll discuss this later,' he threatened, stepping back to allow Blaise and Juliet passage then taking Verity's hand. 'Don't let it spoil everyone's evening, darling. It isn't worth it.'

Verity felt as though her heart had been crushed. Holding onto Oliver as though her life depended on it, she went back to her guests who, to her relief, seemed oblivious to the altercation in the hall and were rallying to Dolly's, 'I don't know about you lot but I'm ready for my supper.'

Dolly, having realised that something was amiss, had come to the rescue again, and seeing Verity's wan face, she gave her an encouraging grin. The joy had gone but Verity, feeling deeply grateful to her friend, managed a watery smile in return.

Supper was eaten, the birthday cake cut and games played, everyone but the hostess joining in the merriment. Oliver's gift to Briony of a gramophone and four records caused quite a stir, and a fascinated Josh and Luke took seats either side of the huge brass horn on its large wooden cabinet, eager to set it to work. As music filled the room, George and Nellie and Florence and Clem took to the floor. Evelyn led Maud by the hand, her daughter's vacuous smile heartbreaking as she stumbled over her own feet. Theo asked Rose to dance and as she flirted with him giddily, he gallantly hid his embarrassment.

'Looks like Theo's got himself an admirer,' said Dolly, coming to Verity's side.

'He's welcome to her,' Verity replied. She had no love for Oliver's elder sister. 'And as for that spectacle...' Her eyes were fixed on Blaise and Juliet as, to the tune of 'You Made Me Learn to Love You,' they smooched around the room.

'You have to admit, she looks the part,' Dolly said. 'That dress is lovely. I can see why he's smitten.'

'It's disgusting,' Verity seethed, and Dolly knew she wasn't referring to the slinky, blue dress but to the rapturous look on Blaise's face and the way he held Juliet close.

Juliet was enjoying herself. Like a true coquette, she'd bantered with Josh and Luke, made sheep's eyes at Marc, and acted coyly demure when talking with George and Theo.

It didn't matter that his mother and his grandmother seemed to be giving her the cold shoulder. Juliet was his and Blaise puffed out his chest, proud that his girl looked like an exotic butterfly in a room full of moths.

Briony had taken an instant dislike to Juliet and was keeping her distance. Leaving Sarah and her schoolfriends to dance with each other, she steered Marc to where her father and the older company were gathered. Marc, having overcome his nervousness, acquitted himself with grace, everyone agreeing that he was charming, his manners impeccable.

But for Verity, the evening had been ruined. Unable to hide her disappointment any longer, she quietly left the party. Juliet saw her go. Tugging Blaise by the hand, she urged him to follow his mother.

'Where the...? What the...?' Blaise's head was still spinning with the deliciously naughty things Juliet had whispered in his ear whilst they were dancing.

'We're going to tell your mother about us, let her know we're in love and want to get married when you're old enough,' Juliet gabbled as they entered the hallway just in time to see where Verity had gone.

'Whoa!' Blaise abruptly stopped in his tracks, but before he had time to gather his wits, Juliet was dragging him towards the door of his father's study. She pushed it open and pulled him inside.

Verity spun round, shocked as Blaise stumbled to

a halt in front of her. Juliet stood nonchalantly by his side and gave his mother a gloating smile.

Verity tried to still the thudding in her chest as she stared at them, eyes wide. 'Why are you here?' she asked, her tone cool even though she was shaking inside.

Blaise stared back at her, dumbfounded.

Juliet stepped forward, her head high and shoulders back. 'I'm here to discuss the matter of equal pay, Mrs Hardcastle.'

Blaise's jaw dropped as he looked at the love of his life.

'This is neither the time nor the place, Miss Skeldon,' Verity snapped.

'Maybe you'll think twice about that when you've heard me out, Mrs Hardcastle.'

Blaise flinched at her impudence. 'Let's go back to the party, leave Ma in peace,' he mumbled, reaching for Juliet's hand.

'Not until I've said what I came to say,' Juliet snarled, slapping at his hand before drilling her eyes into Verity's. 'It's like this, Mrs Hardcastle,' the emphasis she put on the name insolent. 'Your son and I are friends – well, more than that, if you know what I mean.'

Juliet's sly expression made Verity's blood curdle.

More than friends? What was this wicked girl implying? What had Blaise been doing with this girl? She opened her mouth to protest, but words failed her.

Blaise, his cheeks crimson, hung his head, unable to look into his mother's face.

'By rights, I suppose he should marry me,' Juliet continued, 'but he's a bit young for that. Still, there's some who'd expect him to *if they knew* the way he's been carrying on. And if there's a baby on the way...' She let the threat hang in the air.

Stunned, Verity looked at Blaise, begging him to refute Juliet's claims. When he didn't, her heart folded in on itself. She reached behind her for the nearest chair and flopped into it.

'Shut up!' Blaise bawled, turning on Juliet and giving her a furious shove. 'You're upsetting Ma and—'

Juliet shoved him back, her face venomous. 'Don't get uppity with me, lad. You've had what you wanted, now I'm telling your mother what I want,' she barked. 'Equal pay, Mrs Hardcastle and I'll say nowt about what your daft son and me have been up to. Equal pay, and everybody will be happy.'

She spun on her heel and flounced out of the study, raced down the passage, grabbed her coat and dashed out of the front door, slamming it behind her.

Blaise, torn between chasing after her and staying with his mother, who by now was sobbing as though her heart would break, decided on the latter. Appalled by how ashen her face was, and the awful sounds erupting from her throat, he went and knelt in front of the chair just in time to catch her as she fainted. He cradled her in his arms, his tears matching her own, and this was the way Oliver found them.

Concerned by his wife's lengthy absence, he'd gone in search of her, and now his heart missed a beat when he saw his son sprawled on the floor with his mother in his arms. At first, Oliver thought she was dead, her closed eyes and the pallor of her cheeks giving her the appearance of a corpse, but as he hurtled to her side and fell on his knees, her eyelids fluttered and she struggled to speak.

Oliver snatched her from Blaise's arms and lifted her in his own. Towering over his son, he roared, 'What in God's name have you done now?'

19

The guests had departed, most of them none the wiser of what had taken place in the study. Blaise had slunk up to his room to drown his misery with a bottle of brandy he had sneaked from the drawing room. Briony, conscious that something was amiss when her parents returned to their guests – her father with a face like thunder and her mother pleading a migraine and apologising for spoiling the fun – had been asked not to question them, and Dolly had had to make do with a similar response. Now, approaching midnight, only Oliver and Verity remained downstairs sitting on opposite sides of the drawing-room fire, their faces gaunt and their hearts heavy as, clutching their drinks, they relived the nightmare that had ruined the party and almost destroyed Verity.

'We have to give in to her demands, Oliver. Otherwise, she will spread her nasty story all over the mill and Blaise's reputation will be ruined.'

'Reputation?' Oliver snorted. 'Reputations are earned, Verity, and our son has proved that he is a worthless, self-seeking brat.'

'Please, Oliver. Don't condemn him. He's young and misguided.' Instinctively, Verity jumped to her son's defence, but then a hideous picture of him cavorting in the arms of the tawdry mill girl swam before her eyes. And she saw it for what it was: unforgiveable. Swallowing nausea and tears, she blurted, 'I'm sorry, Oliver. Forgive me. I'm to blame for this. I'm guilty of loving him too much, and,' she swallowed again, 'and I refused to see what I know is true. He's like my father.' She paused, wiping a trembling hand across her eyes then staring off into space. 'Perhaps if someone had taken Jeb in hand when he was young, he would have turned out differently.' She drew a ragged breath and gave her husband a contrite look. 'I've prevented you from doing that, but not any longer. I'll let you deal with him any way you so choose.'

Oliver gazed at his broken wife, and his mouth twisted in a bitter grimace. *Too late for that, Verity. Too late.* But he didn't voice his thoughts, and Verity, desperate to put an end to the nightmare, continued with, 'As for more immediate matters... we all know that eventually, the Union's demands will have to be met. If we meet them now, we can prevent a strike and save Blaise's future.'

'And you think that will solve the problem? You'll capitulate and be the first mill in the valley to meet the Union's demands for the sake of a young fool who can't keep his trousers buttoned?' Oliver's incredulous roar brought his wife up sharp.

'Oliver! That's a dreadful thing to say about your own flesh and blood,' Verity screeched.

'It may well be, but it's the truth,' said Oliver, glugging at his whisky. 'And shouting about it doesn't help. We need to be rational and talk things through. To my way of thinking, we can bury this debacle by making a few swift moves. You'll sack the girl first thing tomorrow morning, and we'll send Blaise to the school I told you about some time ago. With both of them out of the picture, there'll be little cause for any gossip.'

Verity blanched. Sherry slopped from the glass onto her dress but she seemed not to notice. 'I... I thought we had already agreed that I'm against the idea of boarding school. We could—'

'It's too late, Verity. Blaise needs discipline and out of respect for *your* feelings, I failed to give him that. Besides, a good education will prepare him for university.'

'But what about his work at the mill?'

'He has no real interest in the mill. He'll find a career that suits him eventually.' Oliver emptied his glass and got to his feet. 'It's late. I suggest we go to bed and sleep on it. Things will look better in the morning,' he said, but his voice lacked conviction.

His wife leaned forward in her chair, seeing his pain as she gazed up into his face. 'I don't think things will ever be the same again,' she said, the catch in her voice tugging at her husband's heart. 'But they can't get any worse, can they, Oliver?'

* * *

Verity woke the next morning, her head thumping and her heart in turmoil. She'd barely slept, and as she washed and dressed, she dreaded the day ahead. Oliver was in a similar frame of mind, morose and silent. Blaise, having consumed too much brandy, was sleeping it off, and when his mother looked in on him, she was amazed to think that he could sleep so soundly.

Only Briony had slept peacefully, and as she breakfasted with her parents, she still had no idea of the problems they were facing. She had puzzled over the sudden disappearance of her brother and Juliet, but knowing Blaise as she did, she had come to the conclusion that he had gone with her to dally in something more exciting; in her opinion, Blaise was ignorant enough to abandon his birthday guests in pursuit of his own pleasures. When Oliver commented on what a charming young man Marc was, she agreed with him then announced that she was going to volunteer her services at Royds Hall, reading to the bed-bound and walking those who had lost their sight around the grounds.

'Very worthy, Briony,' her mother said, but just at that moment, she really had no interest in what her daughter was planning to do. The only person uppermost in her mind was Blaise. The porridge soured in her mouth as she recalled the things Juliet had told her.

* * *

The weaving shed at Lockwood Mill thrummed with the clack and rattle of machinery, and as eyes darted from flying shuttles and hands reached for loose ends, soundless gossip flew like mute birds in a churchyard, from loom to loom.

By now, all the women knew that Juliet Skeldon had been at the Hardcastles' party. She'd strutted into the shed first thing and, making a pretence of yawning loudly then muttering, 'Late night,' she'd boasted about what fun she'd had and that she had persuaded the Mill Mistress to agree to equal pay.

Before she could further impress them, the boggle-eyed women's gabble had been curtailed by the blare of the mill hooter. The women had hurried to their looms, bursting with curiosity and envy.

'They didn't invite any of us. Why her?' Lily Cockhill wanted to know.

'She says she's a close friend of a family member,' May Sykes mouthed back.

'Aye, an' we all know who that is,' Maggie Broadbent sneered. 'I heard she wa' mucking about with that lad of theirs.'

'She did say we'll get equal pay afore the end of the week,' Lily mouthed back. 'If that's true, she can muck about wi' whoever she bloody likes.'

Nellie Armitage watched the women's lips. *Was*

Blaise somehow involved with Juliet Skeldon? The very notion shocked Nellie to the core. Blaise was just an innocent young lad like her Luke. *And had Verity agreed to equal pay?* If so, Bert Higginbottom had made no mention of it when she'd spoken to him at the mill gate. Then she saw Verity marching towards her down 'weaver's alley', her eyes blazing and her expression so angry that Nellie was shocked. She'd never before seen her gentle friend so enraged.

Eschewing any of the usual pleasantries, Verity commanded Nellie to send Juliet Skeldon to the office immediately. Then, spinning on her heel, she marched back the way she had come. When she arrived back at the office, Oliver was nowhere to be seen. Cursing him under her breath, she went and stood behind her desk. A bundle of five-pound notes had been left on top of a ledger. Condemning Oliver for his carelessness, she was about to put it in the strongbox when Juliet walked in.

'You wanted to see me, Mrs Hardcastle?' Juliet adopted a casual stance along with a gloating smile.

Verity felt bile rising in her throat. She swallowed audibly.

'You're dismissed, Miss Skeldon. Collect your things and leave immediately.' The words shot out like bullets.

Juliet blinked. Her bright-blue eyes darkened and her lips curled into a snarl. 'You can't sack me. I'll tell everybody what your rotten son forced me to do. His name will be muck by the time I'm finished. I'm not going anywhere.'

Verity looked at the money on the desk. She felt as though she might vomit. With trembling fingers, she lifted the notes and held them out. 'I'm buying your silence, Juliet. Accept it and give me your word that this puts an end to the matter. Leave now and don't come back.' Verity's words grated in her throat.

Juliet's gaze was riveted on the white five-pound notes. There must be two years wages there, she thought. She could do a lot with money like that. She grabbed the notes. Bugger the Union. They could carry on without her. She was off.

'You have my word, Mrs Hardcastle.' Turning tail, she dashed out into the mill yard and through the mill gate.

Verity collapsed into the chair and put her head in her hands. *Oh, Blaise, Blaise. I did it for you.* The phrase pounded in her skull. But what would Oliver say to her paying Juliet to go away? She already knew the answer to that. And where was he when she had needed him?

Just as she thought she could take no more, he bounded into the office.

'Where have you been!' she cried.

Oliver stopped short, appalled by his wife's distress. 'The new hand in the scouring shed scalded himself badly. I had to take him to the doctor,' he explained, stepping up to her and almost lifting her from the chair. 'Why are you so distraught?'

Verity leaned into him, feeling the beat of his heart against her own shattered one. Then, in a low voice, she told him what she had done.

Oliver reared away from her, his face livid. 'You did what!?'

'I did it to save my son,' she shouted.

* * *

Pressure was mounting in the canteen at Lockwood Mill and the air fizzled with anger and dashed expectations.

Bert Higginbottom tried to call the workers to order.

'She can't just sack somebody for making a reasonable demand,' a man from the carding room shouted, even though he hadn't known Juliet.

'Asking for equal pay's not a crime,' Maggie

yelled, disappointed to learn that Juliet's claim was unfounded. She might not have liked the girl, but Juliet had had the guts to face up to the mistress and if that meant more money in Maggie's pay packet, she deserved her support.

Shouting above the racket, Bert said, 'Leave it to me. I've business elsewhere.' He stamped out of the canteen, leaving the mill hands to wonder about his next move. Late the night before, Bert had been at a Union meeting of the amalgamated unions. Blamire's and Lumb's mill hands were threatening to strike, and now with the dismissal of a girl he'd grown fond of, he felt that it was right for Lockwood's to do the same.

* * *

Blaise had eventually wakened with a hangover. Feeling like death, and dreading facing his parents, he'd dressed and made his way to the house in Rose Street. Juliet had called him daft, made him look like fool in front of his mother, and he felt like beating the living daylights out of her. He hammered on the door. Jenny answered it.

'What do you want? If you're looking for Juliet,

her and our Fred have gone to Birmingham. They'll not be back.' Jenny slammed the door in his face.

Blaise felt the pavement shift under his feet. The bitch had run off. He slammed his fist into the stone doorjamb, howling as his knuckles split. Then, like a madman, he ran back home and shut himself in his bedroom. He was still there when Verity and Oliver returned from the mill.

Bella heard their arrival and nipped up the stairs into the hallway to say that tea would be ready in five minutes. Back in the kitchen, she told Susan that the mistress wasn't looking any happier than she had been that morning at breakfast.

'She'll be worrying about the brat. I don't know what it was he did at the party, but summat wasn't right.' She sniffed to show her disapproval. 'An' when I went up to clean his room after he went out, I found a bottle of brandy. Nearly empty, it wa'.'

'That lad's on the road to hell,' Bella said, clattering crockery onto a tray.

Briony had spent the afternoon at Royds Hall reading to a young officer who had lost his sight in France, and helping the nursing staff to serve tea to the other patients. Marc had been delighted when she'd arrived and offered her services, and now as she greeted her parents, she was keen to tell them of her experience.

'Most worthwhile, Briony,' Oliver praised as he led the way into the dining room. 'We can't begin to imagine what those poor chaps have been through.' He frowned. 'But I hope you're not just doing it to impress a certain trainee doctor.' In her father's eyes, Briony was far too young to be romantically attached; she was still his little girl.

Briony burst out laughing. 'Don't be silly, Daddy. Marc is just a friend, and I'm just grateful to him. He rescued me when a bit of gorse got stuck under Emily's saddle and made her skittish, *and* he's found me something to do to help the war effort.'

'That's marvellous, darling,' Verity said distractedly. 'Have you seen Blaise today?'

'He was still in bed when I went out. He shouted at me to go away when I popped into his room. He smelt awful.'

Oliver and Verity exchanged puzzled glances.

'Smelled awful? Of what?' Verity's voice rose a decibel.

'You know, like Daddy does sometimes when he's been drinking whisky,' Briony said innocently as she spread her napkin over her knee.

Verity leapt from the chair she'd just sat down

on, almost colliding with Bella as she rushed for the dining-room door. Pushing past the housekeeper, she ran upstairs and into Blaise's room. It was empty, the wardrobe door and the drawers in the chest hanging open. Discarded clothes littered the bed. She glanced wildly at Blaise's battlefield; most of the soldiers were missing. An ice-cold feeling pierced her heart.

20

Blaise Hardcastle stood on the platform at Halifax Railway Station, his bag at his feet and a lost expression on his face. He gazed up at the heavy, iron arcs that supported the glazed roof. It was clouded with steam from the train that he had just alighted from, and his brain felt just as fuggy. Doors slammed, a whistle blew and the train rattled on to further destinations, but Blaise had no idea where to go next.

He stooped to pick up his bag, pitching forward when someone barged into him from behind. The soldier whose swinging left arm and left leg had knocked Blaise off balance didn't break step as he marched with his squad along the platform and out of the station. Blaise stared at their departing backs, grabbed his bag and hurried after them. They would lead him to where he belonged.

Striding behind the marching soldiers and trying to match his step to theirs, he followed them along Gibbet Street until they came to the Gothic fortress that was the headquarters of the Duke of Wellington's Regiment. Blaise knew all about the 'Iron Duke', Arthur Wellesley, the great Irishman who had led British troops to victory at the Battle of Waterloo. As the squad marched out of sight, he knew exactly what he was going to do. He was going to make his dreams a reality.

It was close on midnight, and Verity, Oliver and Briony were in the drawing room, Briony half-lying on the sofa and her parents slumped in the chairs by the fireplace. Weariness lined their faces, and they made no attempt at conversation. There was nothing more to say. By now, they were resigned to the fact that Blaise had left home, not just for a few hours as he had done in the past, but possibly forever.

When Verity had discovered that some of his clothes and his beloved soldiers had gone from his room, she had known then that Blaise would not be returning any time soon. Even so, they had searched the district, informed the police, and asked all their friends if they knew of his whereabouts. Eventually, tired and heartbroken, they had returned to Far View House.

As last, Oliver broke the silence by asking if Verity would like a nightcap, a small glass of sherry, or should he go down to the kitchen and make cocoa for her and Briony. When they declined, he refilled his own glass with whisky. 'It's late. We should go to bed,' he said.

'I don't think I'll ever sleep peacefully again.' Verity had cried herself dry, but she felt as though her heart had been torn from her chest.

'He'll come back when he realises how hard it is to survive on his own,' Oliver said for the umpteenth time.

'He can't go far. He won't have enough money,' Briony remarked. 'He'll be back when he gets hungry.'

'No, he won't! I feel it in here.' She thumped her chest. 'We've driven him away and...'

Oliver emptied his glass in one gulp. 'We're not serving any purpose going over it all again. We should get some sleep. Tomorrow is another day.' He walked out of the room.

Briony got to her feet, and holding her hand out to Verity, she said, 'Come on, Ma. Pa's right. Blaise'll be back before you know it.'

Verity clasped her daughter's hand and stood. 'And if he isn't, I'll still have you, my darling,' she said brokenly.

But Briony knew she would never take her brother's place. He'd left a hole in her mother's heart that nobody else could fill.

* * *

Bert Higginbottom arrived in a sweat at Lockwood Mill's gate. It was ten minutes to six in the morning. Wiping his forehead, he looked anxiously up the street, breathing a gusty sigh of relief when he saw Joe, the gatekeeper, ambling towards him.

'What brings you here at this early hour?' Joe's surprise was evident.

'I have it on authority that Blamires an' Lumbs are striking today, an' we're comin' out wi' 'em. Keep these blasted gates locked an' don't let anybody in.'

'Nay, the bloody hell! Tha's bringin' nowt but trouble springin' it on 'em like this.'

'It's not as if we haven't been threatening it. Now we're doin' it, an' we'll hold out until the damned bosses cave in.' Bert threw back his shoulders but his heart was palpitating and he felt decidedly unwell. 'Look! Here they come.' He pointed a quivering finger in the direction of a few mill hands at the top of the street. 'Don't open the gates.'

'I'll have to went t'bosses arrive,' Joe blustered. 'I can't keep t'Master and Mrs Hardcastle out of their own bloody mill.'

* * *

At eight o'clock, Oliver was in the hallway at Far View House putting on his overcoat when the recently installed telephone rang. He lifted the receiver, his lips forming a harsh, straight line as he listened to the caller. Verity, thinking that it could be news of Blaise, or better still, Blaise himself, dashed from the dining room. Her tired, grey eyes searched Oliver's gaunt face. Neither of them had slept well. Before her hope could flare, he said, 'That was Blamire. His hands have gone on strike, Lumb's, Brierley's as well. I'd best get to our mill at once.'

'I'm coming with you,' Verity cried, reaching for a coat even though she had intended to go and look for Blaise. Oliver, aware that it was useless to prevent her, went out and started the car.

As they drove to the mill, Verity kept her eyes peeled for signs of Blaise. When Verity and Oliver reached Aspley and drove into the street leading to the mill, they found their way blocked by their workers. A huge crowd had gathered, some waving pieces of cardboard on which they had written *Equal Pay for Women* or more poetically, *Equal Pay for a Hard-Earned Day*. Other placards simply bore, *Support the Strike* or, *No Surrender*. As Oliver brought the car to a sudden halt, Verity stared at the unfriendly faces of the women she looked upon as friends. Her heart felt like a stone. *As if I don't have enough troubles.*

Oliver blared the horn. Maggie Broadbent banged on Verity's window and waved her placard almost threateningly. Oliver opened his door, and standing half-out of the driver's seat, bellowed, 'Out of the way! Let me through!' And sliding back into his seat, he pressed his foot on the accelerator. The car surged forward and the crowd parted.

'Oh, Oliver! Don't kill anyone,' Verity screamed.

Oliver eased up his foot. Slowly, he inched his way to the gates. Joe swung them open and the car raced through. The scattered workers converged again as Joe slammed the gates shut.

Oliver leapt into the yard and Verity followed suit. Together, they faced their employees but there

was little they could do or say against the cacophonous roar that erupted from the crowd. Bert Higginbottom approached them, ready to make his speech.
Shaking his head, Oliver told Verity to go into the
office and, coming behind her, he went straight to the
recently installed telephone. Brief enquiries confirmed that Blamire's, Brierley's and several other
mills in the valley were experiencing the same
problem.

The chanting outside the gate continued, the
noise deafening.

Panic-stricken, her face ashen, Verity looked at
Oliver. 'What are we going to do?'

Oliver picked up the telephone again. 'I'm calling
the police,' he growled.

Verity lifted the nearest chair and ran for the
door. Out in the yard, she set the chair by the gate
then climbed on to it. Nellie gasped in admiration at
her dignified stance. Her features were drawn and
her long, chestnut hair untidy but she still managed
to look magnificent. Last night, Oliver had called at
the Armitage's home to tell them Blaise was missing
and ask if Luke had seen him. She alone out of all
the workers knew the personal strain that Verity was
under, and her heart bled for her friend.

Waving her arms and raising her voice, Verity

yelled at the top of her lungs for quiet. Nellie used her own to quieten those nearest to her.

'I know you're angry. I understand your concerns, but this is no way to settle them,' Verity shouted. Amazed, the mob stopped clamouring, and gradually, some sort of order reigned. When Verity next spoke, it was in her usual mellow tones.

'I've always tried to do my best for you, you know that, but like you, I have rules that I must abide by. Sometimes, in the past, I've broken them and made enemies of my fellow mill owners. This time, I can't afford to do that. Our country is at war. Men are giving their lives so that we might be free. The least we can do is to make the cloth that gives them uniforms to wear, and by doing so, we not only help them but ourselves. If my mill goes under because we can't meet the contracts, your jobs are gone and...'

Mumbling agreement, some workers began to walk away.

'Equal pay! Equal pay!' Maggie yelled. She was joined by dozens of hecklers all bawling their demands.

Verity stood her ground even though her knees were shaking and the chair wobbling beneath her. Again, she shouted for calm.

Oliver came to her side. 'Let her speak,' he bellowed, the veins on his forehead bulging as he placed a supportive hand in the small of his wife's back.

'Believe me, I will plead your case with the other manufacturers and hopefully, we will reach a peaceable solution that satisfies us all,' Verity continued, and suddenly drained of energy, she begged, 'Now, please, go home to your families.'

Her final words were drowned under the clanging of bells that announced the arrival of the police in their Black Maria wagons. Oliver lifted Verity to the ground.

'Oh, Oliver. Stop them! Stop them!' she cried as the women's screams rent the air. Pushing and shoving in order to evade being arrested, the mob began to disperse, the mothers desperate to get back to their children. Wielding their batons, a dozen or so burly policemen cleared the street, but not before several heads had been broken. The Black Maria wagons rumbled away, no doubt to settle other disturbances.

Verity stood in the sudden silence and gazed at her mill, tears wetting her lashes.

'Oh, Oliver. When will all this misery end?' she sobbed, and he knew that she referred not only to the strike but to the loss of her son.

'Soon enough, I hope,' he replied, leading her

over to the car. 'Blamire called to say they're holding an emergency meeting in the George.'

As they drove up into the town to the George Hotel, an establishment favoured by the mill owners for carefree or serious meetings, Verity realised that in the past hour, she'd barely had time to dwell on the fact that Blaise was missing. She wept quietly for the rest of the journey.

* * *

Blaise stretched his length on the bed in the cheap lodging house, his hands behind his head and a grin on his face. He couldn't believe how easy it had been to enlist. Had he known that this was due to the massive casualties the British had sustained in France, Gallipoli and Italy, and that the government were desperate to replace them with new blood, he might not have felt so easy.

When asked for his name and age, he'd replied, 'Blaise Hardcastle, eighteen last month.' The Duke of Wellington's recruiting sergeant had given a wry smile; an arrogant young pup but seeing as the lad looked intelligent and had a splendid physique, he pushed his doubts aside. Blaise had passed the medical with flying colours, and then stood with a few others to be sworn in to defend king and country. The day after tomorrow, he'd go with them to a training camp in Thoresby in Nottinghamshire.

Blaise closed his eyes and gave a satisfied yawn. He'd done with the tedium of learning how to run a mill, and he'd done with women, even though his heart still ached whenever he thought about Juliet's betrayal. Damn them all. He was a soldier, a warrior, and he'd be the bravest and best.

* * *

'We're into the fourth day, Oliver. How much longer can we hold out?' Verity paced the floor in the mill office, unnerved by the quietness. Used to the bustle in the mill yard and the rattle and thrum of machinery in the sheds, she couldn't bear to see her mill standing idle. And where was Blaise? Every night, she prayed for his return, and every morning, her hopes were dashed when she faced another day without him.

Oliver watched his wife's frantic pacing, saddened by how gaunt and weary she looked. She had barely slept or eaten since Blaise's disappearance, and whilst Oliver himself was just as worried, it was imperative that he stayed strong.

'Verity, dearest, you're making yourself ill.' He pulled her into his arms and stroked her hair. She slumped against him, her frenzied movements and thoughts temporarily calmed by his warmth and strength. 'We'll get through this together, my darling, and perhaps today, a solution will be reached.' He let her go, turning her gently towards the door. 'We're due at the George in ten minutes. With any luck, our colleagues will agree on something to bring this debacle to an end.'

'I doubt it,' Verity snapped as she walked out into the yard. 'Lumb and Brierley are intransigent. Without their agreement, we'll get nowhere. And I'm sick of these damned meetings and all the wrangling and shouting,' she groused as she climbed into the car. The mill owners had met every day since the strike, some declaring hell could freeze over before they agreed to equal pay, and others, afraid that their mills would go to the wall if they didn't meet their government contracts, suggesting an overall raise in wages. Verity and Oliver were enthusiastic supporters of the latter.

Outside the mill gates, a despondent gaggle of strikers formed a picket line. Each day of the strike, their numbers had grown fewer, and as the car drove past them, the protesting shouts and placard waving was decidedly unenthusiastic.

'It's well for some,' Maggie snarled. 'Driving round in their posh cars without a care in the world.' She tossed her placard to the ground and lit a cigarette.

'I'm going home. There's no point standing here,' Lily grumbled. 'An' God only knows what I'll give 'em for their dinner. I've nowt put by, an' me rent's due tomorrow.'

'Aye, it's a bugger,' a man from the carding shed agreed. 'We'll have no wages come t'end o' this week...' His misery turned to anger. 'An' it's you bloody weavers to blame for it. I could be working instead of supporting you lot. You're women! You don't deserve equal bloody pay.' He stomped off down the street.

'What happened to solidarity?' Maggie yelled after him, her sarcasm like treacle on her tongue. She turned to the others. 'It's buggers like him that'll break the strike.'

'He has a point,' May said dolefully. 'I know I'll not be able to manage much longer wi' no wages comin' in. Wi' seven mouths to feed, my husband's army pay won't cover it.'

'Have you heard from him lately?' Lily's sympathetic question turned their thoughts away from strike matters.

'His last letter said his feet were rotting inside his boots 'cos he's up to his knees in mud day an' night. He says they do nowt but march from one awful place to another, an' that he misses my cooking. Apart from that, he says he's all right.' May grimaced, but her friends could tell that she was close to tears.

'At least he's still alive.' Lily's tactless remark had the others looking at her askance.

'I wa' only saying!' Lily pulled a face. 'There's three lasses in t'weaving shed lost their husbands in this past two weeks.' She snorted loudly. 'This bloody war has a lot to answer for, and this sodding strike's no better.'

21

On Saturday morning, nine and a half days after the mill hands had gone on strike, Verity was sitting in a smoky room inside the George Hotel with a gathering of mill owners and Union leaders. Oliver was sitting beside her. She was wearing a mauve and grey suit with a slender skirt and a neat, high-collared jacket that showed off her fine figure. Her chestnut hair glowed under a broad-brimmed hat decorated with purple feathers. As the only woman in the Colne Valley to run a mill, she was the only woman in the room. A few of the mill owners were of the opinion that she had no right to be there, that it was unladylike, and that women didn't have a place in business; Verity was aware of this but it didn't deter her.

'You look like a rose amongst thorns,' Oliver jested, nodding to the dark-suited men, many with waistcoats stretched tight across corpulent bellies. Cigars in hand, they were braying and guffawing as they supped their drinks. Joseph Blamire, who was chairing the meeting, called them to order.

The usual proposals and arguments flowed back and forth, voices raised, opinions bluntly delivered and violence threatened as the Union representatives demanded and the mill owners refused. Verity noticed that her own Union man, Bert, made no contribution. In fact, he looked quite ill. Her heart went out to him, but her patience was wearing thin. She got to her feet, her striking presence causing all eyes to focus on her.

'Gentlemen,' she said as her flashing eyes roved their faces. 'It may have escaped your notice, but whilst we sit here wrangling over the same problem day after day, we are all losing money.' A rumble of agreement let her know she had their attention, and in a clear, firm voice, she outlined her proposal. 'It's still short of equal pay, but they might accept it,' she concluded, her eyes drilling into Bert Higginbottom's and then those of the other Union representatives before she turned them on her fellow mill owners, addressing them in cynical tones. 'And it's not as though we can't afford it. We've all reaped the benefit from weaving khaki and flannel, and might I remind you we've already lost our export market. If we fail to meet our government contracts, we'll be penalised, and some of us will be completely out of business.' She paused to let her words sink in. 'Now, consider that and let's settle the matter.'

She sat down, her cheeks flushed and her heart drumming. She closed her eyes and thought of Blaise.

'Well done, darling,' Oliver whispered, placing his hand on hers and feeling it tremble.

The lull that had fallen as both factions cogitated on Verity's words suddenly exploded as heated exchanges bounced round the room.

'She's the silly bitch that gave her mill hands reading lessons and a canteen,' a mill owner sneeringly remarked to his companion.

On hearing this, Oliver leapt from his seat and lunged at the man, grabbing him by his lapels. 'Take that back, you foulmouthed dog,' he roared.

In the ensuing kerfuffle, Verity urged Oliver to let it go; she'd had her say and cared nothing for their opinions. 'Let's get out of here,' she said, clutching at his arm. With her head held high, she marched out, Oliver at her side.

As they left, the Union representatives were huddled together on one side of the room, the mill owners on the other.

* * *

'Thank goodness it's over,' Verity said as she and Oliver walked from one shed to another, visiting all parts of the sleeping mill. It was Sunday afternoon, the day after the meeting they had walked out on. Late last night, a telephone call had informed them the strike was over; the Unions and the mill owners had accepted Verity's advice. The mill hands would resume work on Monday morning.

In the weaving shed, Verity breathed in the smells of oil and cloth that were as familiar as her daily breath, but the surge of happiness she felt was suddenly overshadowed by the feelings she had suppressed during the strike. Blaise wasn't here to share her joy, and she doubted that she would ever again be truly content. Nothing really mattered now that he was gone. She trailed her fingers idly through the dust that had settled on the nearest loom. Her hand fell away, and she pressed it to her mouth to stifle the sobs creeping up her throat.

'Oh, my poor darling,' Oliver said, tenderly brushing the smudges from her face. 'Don't give up hope.'

He had hoped that with the end of the strike, Verity's natural ebullience would be restored, but apart from that one brief moment when her fighting spirit had flared and brought the mill owners and the Unions to their senses, she had relapsed into the distracted, morose woman she had become ever since Blaise's sudden departure.

'I don't seem able to find any,' she sobbed, her face so desolate that Oliver had to swallow his own tears.

'These machines will be rattling and roaring come this time tomorrow,' he said heartily. And softening his voice, he added, 'And our boy will come home, too.'

'I wish I had your faith. I appear to have lost mine,' Verity replied in a hollow voice.

* * *

On Monday morning, the mill yard echoed with the clatter of clogs and relieved voices.

'I never thought I'd say I wa' glad to come to work, but with only a couple of bob in me purse, an' bills to settle wi' the breadman and the milkman, I'm bloody glad of it,' Lily said as she walked with Maggie and May up to the mill gate.

'You're lucky he let you have it on tick,' May snorted. 'When I asked that grumpy old sod in Wallace's grocers if he'd let me pay later, he told me he wasn't letting anybody have owt on credit. He said if he gave it to one, he'd have to do it for everybody, an' me one of his best customers for years.'

'Aye, well, we'll have a pound or two in us pocket come Friday,' Lily chirped.

'We still didn't get equal pay,' Maggie complained.

'No, but what we're getting's a damned sight better than before. It's only short by thirty bob,' May reminded her as Joe swung open the gate to let them and their fellow mill hands clatter into the mill yard.

Oliver was standing at the office door, his mouth set in a grim line. Some of the workers glanced his way and gave sheepish smiles but others looked directly ahead, the tension in the air palpable. Gone was the usual camaraderie between master and employees. And where was the mistress?

Had the mill hands but known it, she was the

reason for Oliver's dour expression, and not due to
them having forced him and the other mill owners
into raising their wages. Verity had taken to her bed,
her energy drained and her mind numbed by Blaise's
disappearance.

As days then weeks went by, Oliver resigned himself to the fact that his wife had lost interest in the
mill that had once so inspired her. Indeed, Verity
seemed to have lost the will to live, and no amount of
encouragement from him or Briony and Dolly could
break the shell of despondence that she now ex-
isted in.

'Why don't you come with me to Royds Hall,'
Briony suggested one sunny afternoon at the end of
April. 'You haven't been out of the house for ages,
and the patients would love to hear you read or walk
around the grounds with them.'

'No thank you, dear,' Verity replied and continued gazing out of the window that overlooked the
drive. She spent much of her day there, and Briony
knew that her mother did so in the hope of seeing
Blaise return.

Biting back the retort, *He isn't coming back,* she
tried another tack. 'We could take a walk to Dolly's.
The gardens at Thornton Hall are lovely at this time

of year, and Dolly would be pleased to see you out and about.'

'Dolly was here yesterday, and I don't think I can bear another day of being chastised by her.' Verity pulled a face and listlessly picked at the cuff of her blouse.

'Please stop doing that, Ma! You're unravelling the threads.' Irritated, Briony put a staying hand on her mother's. 'What Aunt Dolly said was for your own good.'

'It's easy for her to talk. She still has her son.' The bitter remark cut the air.

Dolly, having been sympathetic and comforting in the first few weeks of Blaise's absence, had finally lost patience, and more or less told Verity to snap out of it. 'Hundreds of women have had their sons taken from them forever by this rotten war. At least yours is still alive, and he left of his own volition.'

Verity had been shocked to the core, and although Dolly had made peace with her before she went home, their friendship had been bruised. Yet another reason for Briony to feel angry. Blaise had always caused trouble, and even though she loved, missed and worried about him, he still managed to spawn discontent. She wondered where he was and who, if anyone, was now the victim of his cruelty. Then, conscious that she could never in her mother's eyes fill his shoes, and feeling in need of more cheerful company, she excused herself and departed for the convalescent home.

Once there, and her irritation replaced by the worthwhile feeling of being needed, she read to a group of men whose lungs and eyesight had been affected by chlorine gas, an insidious silent weapon the Germans inflicted on troops in the trenches. As the soldiers wheezed and coughed and tried not to rub their red, ulcerated eyes, Briony related Lord Jim's exploits at sea.

When Marc came to find her, he asked if she would go and comfort a young boy who had lost a leg in the battle at Ypres.

'He is very low in spirit and talking of taking his own life,' Marc told her as they made their way to a ward packed with injured men. 'His name is John Coldwell, the eldest son of a farming family on Marsden Moor. Perhaps you know of them.'

'I can't say that I do, but I'll do my best to help their son,' Briony said, feeling flattered that Marc had such faith in her. But as she approached the lad's bed, her tummy filled with butterflies. John Coldwell lay with his eyes closed, his haggard, young face bitter. His left leg had been amputated below his knee, the stump swathed in bandages. Briony sat down beside his bed. Marc returned to his duties. Briony reached for John's lifeless hand.

'Go away,' he growled, pulling his hand free.

'Hello, John. I'm Briony Hardcastle,' she began and, ignoring the snarl that erupted from his lips, she told him all about herself and her love for horses. Giggling, she related some of Emily's latest funny antics. John opened his eyes, moved his head on the pillow and looked at her. What he saw was a very pretty girl with glossy, chestnut hair and a lovely, warm smile.

'I used to ride on the farm,' he said, his voice low and wistful. His lip curled. 'I'll not be doing that again. I'll not be doing nowt but sitting. That's what cripples do, isn't it?' Tears formed in the corners of his eyes and Briony's heart bled for him. Then she remembered Fred Jackson and she took a deep breath.

'There's a man who works at our mill who has only one leg,' she said. 'He wears a wooden one, and do you know, he moves faster than lots of the men he works with in the baling room.' She giggled. 'One day, when they were walking to the canteen, they saw a pound note lying on the cobbles.' She gave a little laugh. 'Guess who got there first?'

'Your man wi' the wooden leg?' John's eyes crinkled as he gave a wobbly smile.

'Yes! And he shouted, "Finders keepers,"' Briony chirped, her tender heart bubbling when John joined in her laughter.

They were still laughing and swapping stories when Marc came back into the ward.

'Your medicine appears to be far more effective than mine, Miss Hardcastle.'

Promising to visit John again, and receiving a warm thank you, Briony accepted Marc's offer to walk her home. Theirs was a growing friendship founded on shared interests and, as yet, devoid of romance, Marc very aware of the six-year age gap and his precarious position in England, and Briony content to have found a like-minded soul whose company lifted the solemnity of the black cloud hanging over her home and her mother, who waited by a window for her son to return. As Briony and Marc ambled to Far View House, they talked about John and then about Blaise, Briony seeking Marc's advice as to what she could do to ease her mother's misery.

Marc thought of his own mother and how much he missed her. 'Be patient. Give her time. She is grieving,' he said. 'The bond between mothers and their sons is stronger than any other.'

Briony could not disagree.

* * *

The cause of Verity's misery was at that moment excelling himself in the training camp. Blaise Hardcastle was proving to be just what the British army required. Contrary to the discipline he so often flouted at home, he readily obeyed commands, was physically fit to march for miles without tiring or scale the climbing nets and vault over obstacles, and was a crack shot with a rifle. His savagery when plunging his bayonet into a suspended sack of sawdust almost reduced the training sergeant to tears of joy. However, when it came to teamwork, Blaise was only happy when he was in command, and some of the other trainees were wary of him.

Today, they were employed in the brutally mundane task of digging a trench and learning how to repair it, a task Blaise hated, thinking that it was beneath him; target practice and learning how to load a Lewis gun to kill the enemy was more to his liking. Bored, he leaned on his shovel and looked down on

Willie Clegg's bent back. He was packing soil into the bottom of the trench wall.

In peace time, the British army would never have accepted little scrawny Willie, but desperate as they were for boots on the ground, he had narrowly passed muster. Uneducated, and clearly from an impoverished background, Blaise had soon singled Willie out as a butt for his cruel nature and used the poor lad as a lackey. It meant nothing to Blaise that, like himself, Willie had been born and raised in Huddersfield. Willie, afraid of the muscular bully, polished Blaise's boots, made his bed, and suffered in silence when Blaise tormented him. The other trainees turned a blind eye. Blaise's arrogant manner and his desire to dominate had rubbed them up the wrong way, and they steered well clear of him.

Now, Blaise glanced round to make sure the sergeant wasn't looking in his direction. Kicking Willie hard between his shoulder blades, he forced him face down into the foot of the trench then began hacking furiously at the wall. Soil cascaded down, rapidly covering his victim's head. Willie writhed this way and that and Blaise laughed raucously, loud enough to attract the sergeant's attention.

'That man there. What's going on?' At the sergeant's roar, Blaise dropped to his knees and was clearing the fallen earth when Sergeant Hobbs jumped down into the trench.

'Trench wall collapsed, Sarge,' he said, continuing to shovel the dirt until Willie's head was exposed. Willie rolled over on his back, gasping for air. 'He was digging too deep into it. Lucky for him, I saw it, Sarge.'

Willie, still struggling for breath and trembling in every limb, crawled onto his hands and knees, too shocked to stand upright. Blaise stood to attention to await the sergeant's praise.

'Good man, Hardcastle.' Hobbs swung his boot at Willie's backside. 'On your feet, you useless dolt. And think yourself fortunate. Hardcastle's quick-thinking saved you this time. Let's hope he's by your side when you're in France.'

Willie shuddered then staggered to his feet.

22

It was a bright, sunny morning in early June more than two months after the mill hands at Lockwood Mill had gone on strike, and business was back in full swing. Government contracts had to be met and as scourers, carders, and dyers toiled to provide the weavers with the yarns to weave khaki and serge, the sound of frames whirring in the spinning room and looms rattling in the weaving shed was music to Oliver's ears.

But he wasn't entirely happy.

Making the rounds of the mill was something Oliver and Verity had often done together and he was saddened by the loss of all that they had shared. She still refused to show any interest in the mill, choosing instead to sit at home mourning the loss of their son. Standing alone in the mill yard, he was suddenly beset by a flash of jealousy; had she ever loved him as much as she loved Blaise?

The blare of the midday hooter interrupted the awful thought but he stayed where he was, a lost and painful look on his face as the mill hands surged from the sheds and into the canteen. Amy Carter saw him there, and letting her colleagues hurry on, she dawdled until only herself and Oliver were left.

'You look as though you've lost a pound and found a penny, Mr Hardcastle,' she jested.

Startled, Oliver replied, 'Take no notice of me, Mrs Carter. It's just one of those days.'

'I know just what you mean. I have them myself.' She gave Oliver a look rich with sympathy. He acknowledged it with rueful smile.

'You've had it rough this past few months, what with your wife being too ill to help you bear the load, and you must be missing that lad of yours.'

Like all of the mill hands other than George and Nellie Armitage, Amy had no idea that Blaise had run away. They believed that he had gone to boarding school. But this was Amy's opportunity to talk on a personal nature with Oliver, and she wasn't about to let it pass by.

'I have a lad of the same age, and I know how precious they are,' she continued, 'but sometimes, they're difficult to rear.'

'They are indeed,' Oliver heard himself say then found himself listening as Amy warmed to her theme. Her mother had told her about the rumours that had named Oliver as the father of her child and now, as she looked at Oliver's handsome face and his broad shoulders in his well-cut jacket, and the black hair that curled round his ears, she thought, not for the first time, how nice it would be if he was her son's father instead of the scurrilous insurance man who'd scarpered to God knows where when she'd told him she was pregnant.

'It seems we have problems in common, Mrs Carter.' Oliver gave a little laugh. 'But don't let me keep you from your dinner.'

'I feel better for talking to you,' she gushed. 'A problem shared is a problem halved. Any time you feel like talking, I'm ready to listen.'

Amy sashayed towards the canteen. Oliver watched her go, thinking how pleasant she was, and that she had lifted his spirits.

Amy congratulated herself. Gossip in the weaving shed was that Mr and Mrs Hardcastle weren't seeing eye to eye just lately, and if that was true, the time was ripe for Amy to get to work on Oliver, take advantage of the old rumour, get people believing there was more than a bit of truth in it, and that she and Oliver were old friends.

The canteen was buzzing as the women chattered about things their new-found prosperity afforded them.

'I've cleared me rent and me bill at Wallace's,' Lily boasted.

'I got new shoes for all the kids,' a mother of seven announced.

'We had a day out in Scarborough. We went by train. T'Grand Hotel's still in ruins after Germans bombed it in 1914,' May volunteered.

Amy sat down.

'What kept you?' Lily asked.

'I was talking with Oliver,' Amy said carelessly, and bit into her sandwich.

'Mr Hardcastle to you,' May snapped.

'Aye, all right, May. It's just that me an' Olly are such old friends, I forget meself.'

Maggie gave a disbelieving snort. 'Aye, an' my arse smells of roses.'

Amy jumped up and stalked from the canteen. She'd sown the seed.

Maggie sneered and looked at Lily. 'Lying cow,' she said.

'She might not be.' Lily leaned closer to the table and lowered her voice. 'You remember when she fell for that baby, don't you?' she asked the older women. 'Well, everybody said she'd been seen with him, didn't they?'

'Only 'cos the chap she wa' doin' the dirty with wore a hat like Mr Hardcastle's.' May took up the story. 'You see, Maggie, Amy was due to marry George Armitage, but he knew the bairn couldn't be his so he dumped her.'

Maggie, who was too young at the time to know about this, gasped. 'George in the dyehouse? Nellie's husband?'

'Aye, but he wasn't her husband then. An' some nasty-minded folk spread the story about Mr Hardcastle and Amy.' May looked pointedly at Lily.

Maggie decided she'd keep a close eye on Amy Carter and the boss.

* * *

As Verity grieved day after day, night after night and week after week, life in Far View House and in the outside world went on, but it seemed as though she had been reduced to the level where hers was endured without living it. She had drawn away from those she loved, and the mill, and nothing anyone did or said penetrated the shell that encased her.

Oliver, infuriated and exhausted, gave up trying to reach her, but Briony persisted. One evening, after having failed yet again to rouse her mother's interest, she went and rapped sharply on the door of Oliver's study.

He held the door open with one hand and in the other, he held his reading glasses. His hair was ruffled as though he had been running his fingers through it as he struggled with some complex thoughts. He set his spectacles on his nose. The circular lenses framed with thin, gold bands magnified the shadows under his eyes.

'Briony – what is it? What can I do for you?'

'It's about Mother. I... I wanted to talk to you about her.'

Briony's brisk request made him blink and he stood back, opening the door wider. When she was inside, he closed it softly and walked back to his desk but he didn't sit down.

Briony stood facing him, her expression one of abject helplessness.

'I don't think I can bear living like this,' she said. 'I feel as though I've been abandoned.'

Oliver's face twisted as if he'd suddenly felt a stab of pain. He removed his spectacles and rubbed his tired eyes.

'Oh, my dear child, you mustn't feel like that.'

'But I do. Mother is lost in grief and doesn't even see or hear me any more, and you shut yourself away in here to avoid being in her company.' She made an impatient little noise. 'And when you are together, you shout and blame each other, or sit in stony silence.'

Shamed, Oliver stood swinging his spectacles by an earpiece as he struggled with his conscience. Then he looked directly at his daughter. She looked very small and childlike as she watched him, her gaze unwavering. Overcome with remorse, he tossed his spectacles on the desk and took two quick strides towards her, pulling her into his arms and pressing his cheek on the top of her head.

'Oh, my poor darling girl. We've let you down but we never stopped loving you. All this bother with Blaise has completely floored us. We've allowed it to come between us when what we should be doing is pulling together.'

It felt good to be held in her father's embrace and

she breathed in the comforting smell of his cologne and tobacco. She knew that he loved her but she wanted him to show it in the everyday doing of things as he used to, and not like now because they were dealing with a crisis. A stab of annoyance made her pull away from his embrace.

'But how do we do that when Mother won't let either of us help her come to terms with his absence?' Briony said, irritated. 'He's not dead, you know! And Mother acting as though he is isn't doing any of us any good. Blaise is doing exactly as he pleases, and we should pray for his safety and wish him well.'

'How right you are,' Oliver murmured. He caught her by her wrists and looked deeply into her eyes. 'I'm sorry you've had to put up with feeling shut out, and I promise that I'll do all in my power to make your mother happy again.' He pushed back his shoulders. 'We'll work together to bring her out of the doldrums, show her how much she is loved by us both and how much we need her.' His positivity fading somewhat, he added, 'She does love you, Briony. You know that.'

Not as much as she loves Blaise, thought Briony, but feeling better for having aired her misery, she said, 'No more quarrelling and blaming each other then.

You must get her to take an interest in the mill again, and I'll suggest she gets involved in the war effort again and come with me to Royds Hall. She'll be kept so busy, she won't have time to be miserable.'

Oliver threw his arms around her and hugged her tight. 'You are a delightful daughter, one any mother and father should be proud of,' he said, his voice thick with emotion. 'I know I am. And your mother is too.' He didn't say, *And you're all we have left now*, but he thought it. Although he had no idea where his son was or what he was doing, he feared for Blaise's safety. That his impetuosity and belief in his own invincibility might be the undoing of him.

They left the study arm in arm and went in search of Verity.

After a week in which tears were shed, voices raised, and cajoling and pleading became the order of the day, Verity stopped resisting. She dressed and did her hair, and when Oliver came home early from the mill each day, they went for short walks in the countryside. One day, he drove Briony and Verity to Royds Hall. Seeing men whose suffering was far worse than her own, and the dedication of the doctors and nurses, had a profound effect on Verity. She decided there and then to rise up from her slough of despond, but deep inside, she still grieved.

On a day in mid-June, when Oliver arrived home at midday and found her checking a mill ledger on the desk in his study, he inwardly rejoiced. Then, careful not to sound admonishing, he said, 'It's good to see you attending to your work.'

'Do you mean, am I over it?' Verity asked, the pain in her eyes cutting him to the bone.

'I do not.' Oliver's reply emphatic, he reached for her but she drew away. 'It's not something you – we – will ever get over. But we have a responsibility to life itself, you know. To our own lives – to Briony's – we have to learn to live with what has happened. We mustn't let it overshadow the rest of our lives.'

'Yes, Oliver. Life must go on,' Verity solemnly acknowledged, but life without Blaise seemed meaningless and she had resigned herself to living with a broken heart forever.

Amy Carter kept one eye on her loom and the other on Oliver as he slowly made his way down 'weaver's alley'. When she saw that he was about to leave the weaving shed, she knocked out her loom then hurried to find the Mrs Weaver.

'Permission to go to the lavatory,' she gabbled, screwing her face as though her request was urgent.

'Off you go,' said Nellie, her curt reply indicating her dislike for Amy.

Amy raced out of the shed. To her relief, Oliver was still in the yard talking to George. She waited until George headed off to the dyehouse then called out. 'Lovely weather, Mr Hardcastle. I hope life's treating you kindly.'

Oliver turned, his lips parting in a pleased smile. 'Can't complain,' he said, walking towards her. It didn't occur to him why she wasn't at her loom. Although he would never have admitted it, he found himself oddly attracted to her. Their paths had crossed several times in the past few weeks, and each time, they had fallen into easy conversation. Whenever they talked, even though these interludes were brief, she somehow managed to make him feel more of a man – something his wife hadn't done for some time now – and her light-hearted chatter made him laugh – another thing in short supply at home – and he had yet to question the frequency of their meetings.

'How is your boy getting on at Hopkinsons?' Oliver asked. Amy had told him that her son, Philip, had recently found work at the textile engineering firm.

'He's finding it hard,' she said, her face crumpling.

'Well, tell him from me that Lockwood's always has need of a good engineer.'

Amy's heart bounced. Things were working out nicely. 'Thanks, Mr Hardcastle,' she gushed. 'Must dash. Nature calls.'

Oliver laughed as he watched her go running down the yard to the lavatory.

* * *

'Ooh! I really enjoyed today,' Dolly chirped as she settled into the seat in the taxi cab.

'So did I,' Verity replied, flopping into the seat next to Dolly then dropping numerous bags at her feet. They had been shopping for clothes in Rush-worth's Bazaar and then walked further up Westgate to Whiteleys for afternoon tea. 'I'd forgotten how lovely it feels to buy a new dress,' Verity enthused.

'I think you forgot a lot more than that this while back.' Dolly then hastily took the heat out of the con-tentious remark by nudging the bags with the toe of her shoe and listing Verity's other purchases. Since

Blaise's disappearance, their friendship had been precarious and Dolly didn't want to spoil the day. Verity was still very touchy if anyone suggested that her recent behaviour had been overly dramatic.

'You can flaunt your new outfit on your first day back at the mill.' In Dolly's opinion, the sooner Verity resumed her normal way of life, the quicker she would make a full recovery.

'I don't know that I'm ready to do that. The strike caused so much confrontation that I quite lost my appetite for running a mill.'

Dolly knew that her friend was referring to what she thought of as a betrayal of loyalty by the mill hands whose working lives she had tried so hard to improve.

'They didn't strike to hurt you, Verity. They did it to fight an unfair system. Equal pay for equal work isn't a whim, it's a right. If I still worked for you, I'd have been one of the first on the street waving my placard and shouting the odds.'

Verity laughed. 'Oh, Dolly. You're incorrigible. But you do cheer me up immensely.' By now, the cab had arrived at Far View House, and before Verity alighted, she planted a kiss on Dolly's cheek. 'Thank you for today. We'll do it again soon.'

Dolly gave her a quick hug. 'That's my girl,' she

said, and as Verity stepped out of the cab, making a play of being loaded down by her bags, Dolly cried, 'Drive on, good man. Thornton Estate, next stop.'

The cab swung round, and as it departed, Verity stood smiling fondly and feeling grateful for Dolly Beaumont. She regretted having been so awful to her when she had tried to comfort her, and she silently admitted that it was partly because she was jealous; Dolly still had her son, Josh, and Verity didn't have hers. Well, from now on, she wouldn't inflict her misery on anyone. She'd hide her grief.

She gathered her bags and went indoors to show off her new clothes to Briony.

23

On the same day that Verity had been shopping, Blaise was sitting in a trench south of Hebuterne. His squad of trainees had travelled to France with a platoon of 'Dukes' – the name by which the regiment was known – who were returning to the battlefield after being on leave. On the gruelling 100-mile journey to their destination, Blaise, in awe of these battle-hardened men who had already fought for two years on the Western Front, did his best to ingratiate himself in their company. They in turn scared the lives out of the new recruits.

'Tha wants to watch out for Jerry, lads. They creep into t'trenches at night and rip your bowels out.'

'Aye, they eat 'em for their breakfast.'

'I hope you can run, 'cos when a bloody minen-werfer's chasin' thi, tha'll have to run like the clappers else get your legs blown off.'

Most of the recruits were terrified by the gruesome stories and kept to themselves as much as they could, but Blaise loved the banter. These were his kind of men. He boasted about his escapades in Huddersfield when he'd routed German families from their homes, and the soldiers clapped him on the back and told him he was 'a good 'un'.

Crammed into trains that spent long, sweaty hours without moving then when they did, had chugged on at a snail's pace, seemed like a rum deal to Blaise, but in amongst the seasoned fighting men, he bore it stoically. His new pals were two lads aged about twenty from Halifax, Tucker and Bob, and two older men, Seth and Judd, from Huddersfield. They had all worked in the mills before enlisting, and Seth and Judd seemed impressed when Blaise told them his parents owned Lockwood Mill.

At Amiens, they were deposited on a station in a downpour. To pass the time, they played cards, but Blaise didn't dare cheat as he did when playing with his squad. They played for cigarettes, and he lost all his by the time the next train arrived.

An ancient engine puffed into the station and ground to a wheezing halt. Instead of carriages, the train was hauling large wagons with slatted wooden sides.

Seth groaned. 'Bloody hell, it's cattle trucks again.'

The men tramped up the ramps into a scattering of filthy straw and horse droppings. Rammed in, there was barely room to stand, let alone sit. Willie Clegg was crouched in a corner with two lads from the squad. Blaise yanked Willie to his feet and glared at the others. 'Bugger off,' he said, making room for him and his pals to sit down.

They hadn't travelled far when Blaise began wriggling. 'I can't stop scratching,' he complained, delving inside his tunic and raking his fingers under his armpits.

His pals laughed. 'That's summat else you'll get used to, lad. Lice! The buggers are every-bloody-where in this damned country.'

Blaise's stomach turned.

By the time he disembarked from the train, utterly weary, his bones cramped and his skin bitten and scratched raw, Blaise felt as though he was being eaten alive. Fleetingly, he wondered what his mother – a stickler for cleanliness – would think if she knew her son's body was infested with the tiny, black monsters. Just as quickly, he shoved the thought aside.

Then he marched and marched, his greatcoat too heavy when it rained and too warm when the sun shone. His feet were sore by the time he reached Hebuterne, and as he trod in the mud of the trench, he realised, for the first time in his life, that he wasn't invincible. Days of drilling and toiling in working parties repairing trenches compounded his bleak thoughts; this wasn't his idea of soldiering. He'd joined the army to fight, not to labour. Filling sandbags was the task he hated most. It seemed to him that the British army's greatest defence was made up of sandbags. They banked the walls of the trench, they formed the walls of the officer's dugouts, and they became beds to sleep on when there was no alternative. More importantly, they stopped bullets and shrapnel from penetrating the trench.

Sandbagging duty involved the soldiers working in pairs, one filling the jute hessian sacks with earth and the other tying them off. Shovelling being the most arduous task, they'd swap over after a few bags had been filled.

Under the eye of Sergeant Cropper, an irascible man with a shock of red hair who had been a stevedore in Hull before enlisting, the men paired up.

Blaise threw his arm around Willie's shoulders as if they were the best of pals. Willie's heart sank into his boots; he knew for a certainty who'd do the shovelling. Blaise slouched along the trench, pulling Willie with him until they were out of sight of Cropper's steely gaze. He picked up a shovel. 'Get digging, Willie,' he snarled, tossing the shovel at him then lolling against the wall and lighting a cigarette. Willie filled and tied off the sandbags, afraid that Blaise would wreak further vengeance on him if he refused.

But Sergeant Cropper, whose nickname was Carrots, was nobody's fool. He'd soon sized up Private Hardcastle and saw him for what he was: an arrogant young pup lacking in team spirit. It angered him. Wasted potential, that's what it was. Hardcastle had the physical and mental capacity to be a leader but instead, he chose to be an idle bully: not the sort of man you'd want at your side in battle.

Cropper thundered down the trench.

'Carrots's coming, lads,' a voice cried but it didn't reach Blaise's ears. He was sitting on hunkers, dreaming of the day when he'd be on the battlefield killing the enemy. In his mind's eye, he saw himself as the avenging hero firing his rifle and his bullets blowing Jerry's heads off or his bayonet ripping out their guts.

'On your feet, you lazy dog!'

At Sergeant Cropper's roar, Blaise scrabbled to attention. After a furious dressing-down in front of everyone that made him look nothing like a hero, Blaise was committed to latrine duties for the next three days. Shovelling shit reduced him to tears but it also taught him a lesson: he was no better than any other man in his platoon. Three days later, Blaise returned to normal duties humbled by his experience and feeling very low in spirit.

'We're to stand down and go into the village tomorrow for a day off,' Seth told him when he joined his pals that night. Blaise, the stink of the latrines still in his nose and feeling as though he would never feel clean again, received the news with little enthusiasm.

The next day, the soldiers marched to the nearest village and were given a warm welcome by its inhabitants. The local shopkeepers rubbed their hands in glee as homesick men hunted for souvenirs to send to their loved ones. Seth and Bob bought pretty, lace-edged postcards for their sweethearts back home, and Blaise chose one of a church in Hebuterne. It reminded him of All Hallows in Almondbury, and he wondered if he should send it to his Ma. Or maybe to that scheming bitch, Juliet, if he only knew where she was. Let her know he was putting his life on the line to save undeserving tarts like her.

Later, in a yard at the rear of an estaminet, they sat drinking beer and casting speculative glances at the three curtained booths in which women waited to serve the sex-starved men.

'I think I'll give it a try,' said Bob, standing and patting the bulge in his crotch. He joined the end of the shortest queue, and Seth followed him.

Blaise, feeling happier and lightheaded from the beers he had drunk, went and stood in line to wait his turn. He thought of Juliet again. Aroused, he stepped behind the curtain, the buttons of his trousers already loosened. The dimly lit cubicle smelled of cloying perfume and sex. In his urgency, he barely looked at the girl on the bed. Their coupling was quick and lacking in passion.

When Blaise stood to adjust his trousers, the girl was crouched over a douche bowl, the strong smell of vinegar permeating the air. Her head was down, a long tumble of red-gold hair hiding her face. She looked up when a guttural sound erupted from Blaise's throat: Briony! Choking on his cry, he stared at the girl, his eyes wild and his innards roiling as for one confusing awful moment, her pretty elfin features and soft grey eyes had him thinking she was his sister. Bile rose in his throat and he lashed out, swiping the crouching girl hard across her frightened face. She tumbled sideways, the douche bowl spilling its contents over the floor, and her badly split lip spurting blood.

Expecting the girl to start screaming, Blaise rushed from the cubicle then dithered in the yard, unsure where to go next. On legs that felt unsteady, he tottered across the yard to his pals. He slumped on the bench, and when he saw the girl creep away with a scarf covering her face, he was shrouded in remorse. He drowned his self-loathing in beer and had to be carried back to camp.

* * *

Verity felt a mixture of joy and apprehension as she alighted from the cab at the mill gates. The June sun was high in the sky, it being midday, and she paused to gaze with fondness at her mill. She hadn't told Oliver that she was coming, wanting to surprise him, show him she was ready to resume the pattern that had been their lives before Blaise had gone from them.

She greeted Joe and was touched by his hearty welcome. Thinking that she had been foolish to stay away for so long, she walked into the mill yard, the cobbles underfoot familiar and heartwarming; this was where she belonged. Glancing towards the office, its door lying open, she saw that it was empty. Then, adjusting her gaze, she looked towards the bottom of the yard and saw Oliver's broad back. Verity began walking, the sound of voices and the rattle of crockery reaching her ears as she passed by the canteen.

As she drew nearer, she saw that Oliver was deep in conversation with someone. She could tell that it was a woman by the flair of her overall around a pair of shapely legs. She couldn't see the woman's face, but she knew by the tilt of Oliver's head and the soft laughter that he was enjoying her company. Feeling like an intruder, she gave a little cough.

Startled, Oliver swung round, the beetroot stain on his cheeks tearing at Verity's heart.

'Hello, Mrs Hardcastle.' Amy's gloating smile and voice cut like a knife.

Oliver was still staring, red-faced, and stripped of speech. Then, shaking his head as if to dispel a nightmare, he found his voice. 'Verity, what brings you here?'

'I came to see how *my* mill is prospering,' she replied coldly. 'It would appear that it's faring well if the manager and one of my weavers has time to dally by the river.' She spun on her heel and strode back up the yard. Oliver hurried after her, and Amy sashayed into the canteen, smirking with satisfaction.

In the office, Verity and Oliver faced one another.

'What was all that about?'

'Amy was asking my advice regarding her son.' He sounded defensive. 'I'd told her I might give him a job here...'

'You'll do no such thing!'

'He's a textile engineer. She's just looking out for her son and I—'

'Her son? Or is it your son, Oliver? Yours and Amy Dickenson's, as she was then.'

Oliver looked stunned. 'What on earth are you insinuating?'

'I'm not impervious to gossip, Oliver. I am aware of the rumours suggesting that you and she were involved in a liaison, and your little tête-à-tête just now has me thinking that you may still well be.'

'Don't talk such utter nonsense,' Oliver bawled, his protestation making him sound all the more guilty.

'Well, I didn't come here today to discuss your dalliances, Oliver,' Verity said as she removed her hat. 'Now, where is the accounts book?' She sat down at the desk.

Oliver felt like Judas as they perused the accounts. He could not deny that he had nurtured romantic feelings for Amy. She was warm and amusing, and she listened to him.

These days, he rarely got a sympathetic ear at home. He'd even submitted to Amy's grateful kiss when he'd told her he was thinking of offering her son a job at the mill. It had roused his manliness, yet another aspect of his life that had been too long neglected, but his feelings for Amy were shallow when compared with the deep, all-abiding love he had for his wife. He would never love anyone the way he loved Verity.

Swamped in shame, Oliver breathed in the musky smell of his wife's perfume as they sat, heads close together discussing business, and at the same time, he pondered on how to win her love and respect and retrieve all that they had lost.

* * *

Verity resumed her work at the mill, each day fostering the relationship with her mill hands that had been damaged by the strike. They in turn rewarded her kind consideration by producing yards of khaki and serge to the benefit of both parties: increased profit in Lockwood's coffers and bonuses for its employees when contracts were met on time. It was a happy place to be, but in Far View House, the atmosphere was far from pleasant.

'Don't be daft, Verity. There was no truth in those rumours. What would Oliver want from the likes of Amy Carter when he has you?' Dolly scolded as they sat in the garden one evening in late June.

Verity flushed with embarrassment. 'That's just it, Dolly. He doesn't have me – well, not since...' Her voice tailed off. Then, after taking a deep breath, she continued, 'We no longer share a bed, and we don't communicate like we used to. When I was... oh, you know... not myself, I told him to sleep elsewhere and he has yet to come back to our bedroom.'

'Have you asked him to?' Dolly's blunt response brought a wavering smile to Verity's face.

'I don't know how.' She sipped her lemonade, prevaricating.

'Oh, for goodness' sake, woman. You've been married to him for twenty years. You love him, and he loves you. Get over yourself, Verity,' Dolly cried then softened her voice as she added, 'You've been through a lot this while back, but don't let it rule the rest of your life.'

Later that evening, as Oliver and Verity were sitting in the drawing room, he with his nightcap whisky and Verity sipping a sherry, she took her friend's advice. She'd been mulling over it ever since Dolly had left for home. She did love Oliver, and even if he had been tempted by Amy's charms, who could blame him? She wanted, needed, to believe that he would never really betray her, that rumours were just that: without substance. She hadn't believed them in the first place, so why now? Theirs was a love that could not be broken.

She set down her glass. 'Oliver, will you please come back to our bed?' she asked, the tentative request making her voice wobble.

Oliver looked at her as if he hadn't heard her right, then he leapt from his chair and swept her up off the couch and into his arms. 'Oh, my darling girl,' he cried, crushing her against his chest and then kissing her with the same passion as when they were young.

Verity returned the kiss, her passion equalling his own. She might have lost her son, but she was determined not to lose Oliver.

24

On the day that Blaise and his unit were about to leave Hebuterne, he found the crumpled postcard that he had stuffed into his tunic pocket on that shameful day in the town. When the post clerk came to deliver letters from home – none for him, but then he didn't expect any – he scribbled a message on the card then gave it to the clerk.

In the latter part of June, the soldiers marched all around the Somme region from trench to billet and eventually joined the trench line at Authuille. During that time, Blaise tended to keep to himself, spending his free hours reading or mulling over things he had done. Those three days shovelling out the latrines had left its mark on him, and worse still, he was plagued by the memory of his unwarranted attack on the girl at the estaminet who had looked like Briony. In his dreams, he saw her battered face and her soft grey eyes dark with fear and confusion. It made his scalp crawl and filled him with self-hatred. She had only been doing what she had to do to survive in this war-torn country and he, who had been sent to protect her and her people, had betrayed the trust he had sworn to honour. He knew by heart Lord Kitchener's words in the front of his pay-book: *Show yourself in the true character of a British soldier. Be courteous, considerate and kind. Never do anything to injure...* He, who had wanted to be a soldier for as long as he could remember, had done none of those things. That Lord Kitchener had died earlier that month when the ship in which he was travelling to Russia had struck a mine and sunk only compounded Blaise's feeling of betrayal.

'What's wrong wi' you these days, Hardcastle? Tha's like a child what's lost its dummy,' Seth asked as he and Tucker slumped down beside Blaise after a long and arduous drilling session. When Blaise just shrugged, Seth continued, 'Tha's nowt to be mardy about. You're Carrot's blue-eyed boy. He's never done praising you.'

This was true. As Blaise struggled to rectify his

mistakes, he excelled in all his duties. Sergeant Cropper, believing that it was his strict discipline that had brought about the change in Private Hardcastle, was delighted with his protégée's exemplary behaviour.

'I just want to be a good soldier,' Blaise told Seth as Bob dropped down on his hunkers next to them. Bob was acknowledged as the eyes and ears of the squad. Quite how he gathered the information he imparted they neither knew nor cared, but it was invariably correct.

'There's summat big coming up, lads. That's why we're doin' all this preparation,' Bob said. His big, square face was red with exertion. He jabbed a finger at Blaise. 'You're about to get your taste of real fighting, young'un.'

'Aye, it'll be Wipers and Auber's Ridge all over again.' Seth groaned.

'An' don't forget Another Chapel. I thought I'd had my bloody chips there,' Tucker said heatedly.

Blaise smiled at their mispronunciations of Ypres and Neuve Chappelle. And as they recalled the various battles they had already survived, Blaise listened to their tales, his eyes glowing with admiration for the three seasoned campaigners.

'You an' all, Cleggy,' Bob shouted as Willie Clegg

drew near. 'I'm just after tellin' Hardcastle here that you'll be doin' some real fighting afore long.'

Willie dithered. Blaise no longer tormented him, but he was still wary of being in his company. When Blaise gave him a friendly grin and beckoned for him to join them, he went and sat next to Seth and listened as Bob repeated his story that something important was ahead of them and that the 'top brass' were calling it 'the big push'.

So, this was it at last, Blaise told himself, his pulse quickening. This was what he'd been waiting for. Not just the skirmishes they'd had en route where he'd fired his rifle at an unseen enemy, but a major battle face to face with the Huns. He imagined sticking his bayonet into a yielding German then pulling it out dripping with blood, and his excitement faded as common sense told him how easily it might be his blood that was spilled.

* * *

Briony Hardcastle had wakened early, her heart light as she washed and dressed for the day. Now that her parents had settled their differences and life in Far View House had returned to normal, Briony felt as though she had been relieved of a great responsibility. Not having to deal with the dilemma of her mother's grief was a great relief, as was not being the buffer when Verity and Oliver had argued. Whilst she acknowledged that their family life would never be quite the same without Blaise, and that sometimes, she missed him dreadfully, her happiness centred on her home life and her work at Royds Hall. She was even contemplating training to be a nurse or, better still, a doctor.

Down in the kitchen, Verity and Bella were discussing food shortages and rising prices. 'We've just about enough sugar to last to the end of the week, and after tomorrow, we'll have run out of butter,' Bella said as she flipped three rashers of bacon in the pan on the stove.

'Aye, an' I had to queue for two hours last time we got sugar,' Susan grumbled.

Verity, aware of the difficulty in obtaining any of the commodities they had so easily bought before the war, offered to lighten Susan's burden.

'If you just go to Hinchcliffe's and try to buy some meat, I'll go to Wallace's for butter and sugar. In the meantime, Bella, we'll make do with a leek and potato pie for dinner and we'll have strawberries for dessert. Thank goodness for your dad and the kitchen garden.'

She patted Bella's arm in appreciation for the tasty meals her housekeeper concocted then said, 'I'll go and waken my husband. He's having a lie-in this morning.'

As Verity climbed the basement stairs, she heard the rattle of the letterbox in the front door, followed by the soft plop of that day's post hitting the marble black and white tiles. In the hallway, amongst the scattered brown and white envelopes, she saw a post-card with a picture of a church on it. Curious, she picked it up and studied the image then wondering who had sent it, she turned the card over.

Greetings from somewhere in France. Hope all is well. B.H.

Verity's heart was threatening to leap from her body. She opened her mouth, and the sound that erupted from the very core of her lungs would have wakened the dead.

Briony was tying back her chestnut hair with a green ribbon, ready to go downstairs for breakfast, when the ear-splitting wail spiralled up the staircase. She rushed out of her room, her tawny curls bouncing as she took the stairs two at a time.

Her mother stood trembling in the hallway, a

piece of crumpled card pressed to her lips. Her stricken eyes stared into space as though she was seeing something unimaginable.

'Mother! What is it?' She wrapped Verity in her arms, the shudders emanating from her mother's body eating into her own.

Alarmed by Verity's scream and Briony's anguished cry, Bella emerged from the basement stairs. 'Whatever's happened?' she panted.

Seconds later, Oliver came charging down the stairs in his pyjamas, his hair in tufts.

Verity tore herself loose from Briony's arm and, holding the card aloft, she waved it under his nose, her hysterical laughter and the tears streaming from her eyes making them think she had totally lost her mind.

Oliver gripped her in a tight embrace and stilled her frantic movements.

'He's alive, Oliver! Blaise is alive, Briony,' she cried. 'My son, my precious son is alive.' She thrust the card into her husband's hand.

'My God!' Oliver gasped as he read the scrawled message. 'He must have enlisted.'

His face contorting, he passed the card to Briony.

'He always said he would,' she averred, her eyes

meeting her father's as they both acknowledged the danger Blaise was facing.

Verity saw the look and understood what it meant. She let out another wail. 'We must go and bring him home, Oliver. Tell them he's too young to fight,' she urged.

'I doubt that will be possible,' he said, taking her gently by the arm and leading her into the dining room then settling her on a chair as though she were an invalid.

'He wouldn't want you to even if you can.' Briony's words rang with conviction. Oliver acknowledged the truth in them with a dismal nod. Verity covered her face with her hands and moaned.

'Will I serve breakfast, madam?' Bella, who all this time had been hovering helplessly, her kind heart aching for them, didn't know what else to say. But they had to eat, and the porridge would be stuck to the bottom of the pan by now.

'If you will, Bella. Thank you.' Oliver sat down, feeling the full weight of his wife's sorrow. 'At least he's alive, and we now know where he is, darling.' He reached across the table for Verity's hand. 'What you must do, my love, is keep faith for his safety, and like thousands of mothers throughout the country, you'll bear the strain of being parted from him with good grace. Our son is doing his duty to preserve our country's freedom and we should be proud of him.' His voice rich with sincerity, he added, 'I know I am.'

Verity gave a wan smile, and her initial joy at learning Blaise still lived was somewhat revived. And Oliver and Briony were right. Her beloved Blaise was following his dream of being a brave warrior, seeking his destiny, and aspiring to the greatness she had always believed he would achieve.

'Blaise sent us a postcard,' Verity told Dolly as they sat in the drawing room drinking tea that Bella had brought up shortly after Dolly's arrival at Far View House.

Tea from Dolly's cup slopped into the saucer as she put the cup down, amazed by her friend's calm announcement, for Verity had issued the remark as though receiving a postcard from her long-lost son was a regular occurrence.

'Blaise! A postcard?' Dolly exclaimed. 'Oh, Verity, that's wonderful news.' She leaned towards Verity, her eyes wide with curiosity and delight. 'Where is he now?'

'Somewhere in France. We believe he enlisted,'

Verity replied, her heart sinking when she saw Dolly's expression mirroring the look that had passed between Oliver and Briony the previous morning. She drew a sharp breath. 'I know what you're thinking, Dolly. I think it too, and I'm struggling to come to terms with it. I fear for him every minute of the day and night, but more so, I fear for myself.' Verity swallowed noisily, 'I can't... I won't allow myself to be that pathetic, broken woman I was when Blaise went away. I have to stay strong for him... and for Briony and Oliver as well. Blaise is doing his duty.'

Dolly's eyes had moistened. Listening to her dear friend's brave attempt to overcome her sorrow had brought to mind how she herself would feel if it was her Josh out there in the chaos of a war-torn country. She read the newspapers, and the horrors they reported filled her with cold dread. She got to her feet then went and pulled Verity to hers, holding her close.

'You'll get through this, Verity. We all will, and Blaise will come home a hero, just wait and see.' Although her words were strong with conviction, in the back of her mind, she couldn't help but think that the wild, impetuous Blaise of old might try to be too heroic.

Verity gave a wobbly little laugh. 'I know it might

sound silly, but I believe he will.' She smiled wist-fully. 'I have to, otherwise, there would be nothing to live for.'

* * *

Briony could hardly wait to tell Marc the wonderful news that her brother was alive and well. She might not have always approved of the things Blaise did but she loved him; he was her other half, the half that, when they had shared their mother's womb, had absorbed all the impulsiveness and courage that she thought she lacked. She was still toying with the idea of training to be a nurse, her reason for prevaricating due to the fact that Oliver and Verity would be wholly against it.

She admired the dedication of the nurses and volunteers she had met at Royds Hall. Some were members of the Voluntary Aid Detachment, and only a week ago, two of them had left to work in a hospital behind the front lines in France. Briony envied their bravery, but she was far too young to be a VAD and didn't possess Blaise's courage to lie about her age. Besides, her small stature and her girlish features would never fool anybody into thinking she was twenty-one. She would just have to be satisfied with the work she was doing now, she told herself, as she entered the mansion to begin her mundane duties.

Later in the afternoon, having had another encouraging chat with John Coldwell, the boy whose leg had been amputated, she met with Marc to walk round the grounds. Bubbling with excitement, she told him about Blaise's postcard.

'I am pleased for you and your parents, Briony, and I wish your brother well,' Marc said, his eyes darkening as he silently reflected on the savagery of the German soldiers and the atrocities they had committed in his beloved Antwerp.

'And John is to go to Roehampton next week,' Briony said after they had exhausted the topic about Blaise. 'He's never been to London before. He's looking on it as an adventure and he's thrilled to be getting a false leg.'

They continued discussing John until they came to a bench in the shade of an oak tree. Marc suggested they sit down.

Briony's heart fluttered. It was a secluded spot and she wondered if Marc intended them to have a romantic interlude. Uncertain as to whether or not she wanted him to whisper sweet nothings or maybe even kiss her, she perched nervously on the bench.

He sat down beside her, but not too close. The fluttering abated.

'I have news of my own,' he said, sounding rather solemn. 'I am going back to Antwerp. Doctor Maes is of the opinion that we are much needed there. We will leave on Saturday.'

'You're going away?' Marc heard the disappointment in her voice.

'I must. The Germans occupy my country and our people are suffering. Doctor Maes has been my tutor for three years and I must honour his request that I go with him. I will be sorry to leave you, Briony. I have enjoyed our friendship.' His warm, brown eyes were sad.

'I'll be sorry to see you go, Marc. You're a lovely friend, and we will keep in touch, won't we?' Briony knew that she would miss him dreadfully, but she felt a sense of relief when it seemed he wasn't about to protest his love for her.

'On a happier note, I also have news of my cousin, Jan. Up until now, I had no idea what had become of him, but my mother has written to tell me he is in Halifax.' Marc laughed. 'Less than ten miles from here and I did not know. I will introduce you to him before I leave for Antwerp. Perhaps you will be the good friend to Jan that you have been to me.'

Briony agreed to meet his cousin, Jan, then asked, 'But will it not be dangerous to go back to Belgium?'

'It will. We have to enter secretly, but we will have people to help us. Do not worry for my safety. I can look after myself. I will write so you know that I am safe.'

They arranged for Marc to come to Far View House on Friday evening so that he could say goodbye to Oliver and Verity, and introduce Briony to Jan.

As Briony walked back home, she pondered on Marc's leaving and the dangers he faced. *Now I have two people in this horrible war to worry about and pray for*, she thought, quickening her step as the huge, black clouds over Castle Hill threatened a downpour.

25

Blaise sat cross-legged on the ground in the support trench at Sucrerie with his platoon gathered all around him, his eyes and ears fixed on Major Walker as the major prepared to address them. It was early evening, Friday 30 June, a pleasant warmth lingering in the air after the heat of the day that seemed at odds with the icy tension rippling through the assembled troops. From across the distance, they could hear the boom and roar of artillery fire and high explosives.

Leonard Walker stood with his feet apart on top of an ammunition crate, his stance firm and his chin raised. He swallowed noisily, loud enough for Blaise to hear it.

'Men! Listen carefully to what I am about to say. Your lives may depend on it. We are the 2nd Battalion the Duke of Wellington's and we are about to face the enemy. I know that you have been trained to do your duty, but that you may be afraid that was not enough. Do not think like that. Do not be afraid.' The major paused, and as his eyes ranged the lines of men he had come to know well, his features softened. 'We are here to defend our country, to protect our homes, and to fight for freedom! We are not alone. We have each other, and we have the strength of the British Empire behind us. We are the best. We are the bravest. And we will not fail! We know the enemy is dug in, but so are we. They may have more guns, but we have more heart. We will fight with everything we have, and we will win this! Remember your training, remember your brothers beside you, and remember the families waiting for us back home. Tomorrow, we will go out there and show them what we're made of! For king and country!'

The soldiers cheered, and the major turned to the large map pinned on a board behind him. Tapping it with his swagger stick, he indicated where they were. Blaise leaned forward, his eyes glued to the map.

'In one hour, we will march along the Quadrilateral to join our friends in the front line,' the major continued, tracing with his stick to outline the route they would take. 'Our objective is to take Pendant Copse...' a tap of the stick... 'bunker on top of small hill...' another tap-tap... 'a trek of some two thousand yards. The Flying Corps are at this very moment strafing the Huns' defences between Beaumont-Hamel and Serre, and artillery fire is pulverising their batteries and cutting through the wire in readiness for us to burst through the German front line and take Serre.' After giving further instructions, he gave what Blaise thought was a forced, brave smile and concluded with, 'Remember. We are in this together.'

The major jumped down from the box, the rumble of voices rising to a crescendo as the men turned to one another to discuss what they had just heard.

'Two thousand yards. How far's that?'

'From t'chippy on Ward Street to t'Dog an' Gun,' a voice replied.

'What's a copse?'

'It's a little wood. Mebbe we'll have time to catch some rabbits.'

Blaise smiled at the banter, but he took no part in it. Instead, he embedded the major's instructions in his brain and then imagined what to expect and how he might acquit himself when the fighting started.

The hour passed quickly, and the men moved out. Darkness fell as they straggled along the trenches, each man weighed down by a conglomeration of equipment: rifle, gas mask, entrenching tools, and a Mills bomb in each pocket. With every step, the rhythmic clinking and clanking of mess tins against haversacks reminded Blaise of the looms in Lockwood Mill, and Juliet. What a fool he'd been then. An image of his mother, weeping and wailing, passed before his eyes, and he stumbled.

'Are you all right?' Seth asked, catching him by his sleeve. 'Tha nearly fell on your arse.'

Blaise shook him off. 'Never better,' he quipped, but his mind was reeling with thoughts of his family. He recalled his father berating him for his misdeeds, and then how proud Oliver had been when he had shown an interest in the mill. A dull pain throbbed in his chest when he thought of his mother and the love she had for him. Once again, he cursed himself for the ingrate he had been then. And Briony: his sweet little sister, his other half, whose loyalty he hadn't appreciated. She'd rarely split on him when he'd done something dastardly. They had all had to suffer his ignorance. His heart and his tread heavy with remorse, he tramped on, slipping and slithering in the waterlogged tracks where the mud was deep enough to cover his puttees.

The nearer they came to the front line, the louder the roar of aircraft and artillery became. It shook the ground over which the men were tramping and sang in their ears.

'It's like walking into the jaws of hell,' a man carrying a Bangalore Torpedo growled. But Blaise was in a hell of his own making, unable to dispel the thought that he might die before he could return to his family and beg for their forgiveness.

* * *

On that same Friday evening, as Blaise was marching into the unknown, Verity, Oliver and Briony were welcoming the guests that Briony had invited for dinner. Marc then introduced the young man he had brought along. 'This is my cousin, Jan Van Leyden.'

Jan gave a courteous little bow before shaking hands with Oliver, Verity and Briony. He was taller than Marc, and whereas Marc's skin was swarthy, his hair brown and his facial features pleasant, Jan's complexion was fair, his hair dark blond and his face more finely sculptured. Briony thought him strikingly handsome.

Over dinner, Marc and Jan related how they had lost touch with one another when the Germans had invaded Belgium. 'And so, I am amazed to think that we were living so close by and unaware of this until Jan's mother wrote to mine,' said Marc, his smile showing how pleased he was to be reunited with his kinsman then fading as he added, 'But now we will be separated again when I return to Antwerp.'

The conversation turned to his imminent departure and the reason for it. Verity and Oliver told him it was a noble thing to do, and wished him safe passage. Oliver couldn't help feeling rather relieved. He had wondered if the young doctor was romantically inclined towards his little girl, and somewhere deep inside, he did not want that to be the case. However, Briony did not appear overly disappointed, and she too praised Marc for his selflessness and dedication to his career.

Then it was Jan's turn to be the focus of their attention, and Verity and Oliver became avidly interested as they listened to his story.

'When I lived in Ghent, I was a textile engineer. In my work, I analysed and improved the manufacturing process,' Jan told them. This information led to Verity and Oliver asking numerous questions, and Jan went on to describe his work. 'It minimised wastage and reduced costs, and enhanced productivity,' he said modestly then followed it with a sad little smile and a despondent shrug. 'Now I am simply a loom weaver. My new employers do not wish for me to use my skills.'

'Oh, but we do!' Verity cried, her enthusiasm making her cheeks bloom. She looked at her husband, her head cocked to one side and the glimmer of a smirk curving her lips. 'Did you not say a short while ago that you were considering setting on an engineer, Oliver?'

'Indeed, I did,' he replied rather too heartily, her barbed question piercing his sensitivity. She still hadn't completely forgiven him for Amy Carter, and he had told her he was going to offer Amy's son a position at the mill as an engineer. He cleared his throat before addressing Jan. 'I like the sound of your ideas, and after my wife and I have discussed the matter, I think we might be in a position to offer you work at Lockwood Mill.' He sat back, hopeful that he had cleared the air.

'I don't need to think about it,' said Verity, keen to avail her mill of Jan's knowledge. Jan, just as eager, accepted their offer and said he would leave Halifax and find lodgings in Huddersfield by the end of the next week.

When the evening drew to a close, Briony bade Marc a fond farewell, promising to write back to him once he was settled. Marc thanked her again for her friendship and told her to keep up her good work at Royds Hall. As she said goodnight to Jan Van Leyden, she had to restrain herself from showing how delighted she was that he would soon be living and working near enough for them to develop a friendship.

Later, as Briony undressed, she reflected dreamily on the evening, and began drawing parallels between herself and Jane Eyre. Jane had been instantly attracted to Mr Rochester, just as she had to Jan Van Leyden. She wondered if she was falling in love, and giggling at the notion – she didn't know what love was – she climbed into bed and immediately fell into a dreamless sleep.

* * *

It was after ten o'clock when Blaise's platoon trudged into the front-line trench. Troops from the King's Own were already in situ and they gave the Dukes a typical soldierly welcome.

'You took your bloody time. We thought you'd forgotten to come.'

'Aye, Jerry's waiting for thi.'

'We wa' getting dressed for the party.'

'We didn't want to get here afore he lit the candles on the cake.'

'And when he does, we'll blast his bloody cake to kingdom come,' yelled Blaise, laughing as he joined in the banter. He slumped down against the trench wall to rest his aching feet and opened his mess tin. Munching on corned beef, cheese and jam, he talked with Seth, Tucker and Bob, and the 'Koylis' as the King's Own Light Infantry were generally known. Seeming oblivious to the rumble of big guns and the incessant screeching of shot and shell, the men laughed and joked, but Blaise knew that like him, they were doing it to hide their fear. They would not have made so light of things had they known that the artillery had failed to pulverise the German batteries, and had they known that the Germans were expecting them, they wouldn't have laughed at all.

Several hours before the troops had assembled in the assembly trench, a party of Hull 'Commercial' had cut lanes through the British wire into no man's land. Shortly after that, the Sheffield City Battalion had crept out to lay lengths of white tape, pathways to guide the British soldiers to the German trenches. As the artillery continued their onslaught on the German batteries, the Germans replied with a fusillade of machine-gun fire, and as Very lights flared and the sky lit up with flashes from the enfilade, the white lines of tape were glaringly obvious. The Germans knew they were coming.

At midnight, a stone gallon bottle of rum was delivered to the trench where Blaise and his companions rested. Loud cheers met its arrival, the men holding out their tin cups for Sergeant Cropper to fill. Blaise, wanting to keep a clear head, took a sip then gave the rest to Bob. Bob glugged it down at one go. The rum had a soporific effect and the men quietened down, talking in hushed voices. Further down the trench, the army padre began to sing, and to the soft sweet strains of 'Abide with Me', Blaise fell into an uneasy sleep.

He was dreaming of his bedroom at home and his tabletop battlefield of soldiers when a rough shake and a harsh voice ordered him to get to his feet.

'W... what time is it?'

'After seven,' Sergeant Cropper growled and moved along the line of sleeping men.

Blaise rubbed his hands over face and head,

willing the blood to rush to his brain and keep him alert. All around him, bleary-eyed men were standing up, stretching and shaking their cramped limbs. Blaise arched his aching neck and gazed up into a sheet of perfect blue sky: a perfect day for a perfect battle. He peered cautiously over the parapet of mud and sandbags and saw a dense cloud of smoke drifting over Gommecourt Wood. He remembered that Major Walker had told them that this was a planned distraction to confuse the enemy. He pointed it out to Seth and Tucker.

'I hope that's enough to take Jerry's mind off us when we're going to Pendant Copse.'

'I'd be happy if I thought he'd forgotten all about me,' Tucker moaned. 'I'm beginning to think I made a bloody big mistake when I joined up. I'd have been done for at Another Chapel if Seth hadn't shot that bastard German that wa' going to shoot me, but I've a nasty feeling me luck's run out.'

Blaise felt shaken by Tucker's confession. The sturdy man from Bradford had survived two years of fighting battle after battle. Blaise wondered if he would survive his first. The thought made his mouth dry as if he'd been eating sand, and to hide the feeling of dread, he fiddled with his rifle, patted his pockets to check for the Mills bombs and shook his water bottle, although he already knew it was full.

Major Walker, the officers and the NCOs scurried up and down the line giving orders and after a lengthy time in which Blaise's heart rate had quickened and his palms grew clammy, they were given the order to stand to.

Major Walker moved down the line, repeating the Duke of Wellington's motto, 'Fortune favours the brave,' his voice abruptly drowned out by a massive explosion that rendered the air asunder. Blaise felt the ground beneath his feet tremble. The mines under Hawthorn Ridge had gone off. 'Another distraction,' he muttered to nobody in particular as the mighty rumbling faded and was replaced by the rattle of German guns. In the minutes that followed the thunderous fulmination, Blaise saw the Air Flying Corps wheeling overhead low enough for him to smell the fumes of fuel, and the artillery ceased its rigorous bombardment of the German batteries. A strange, eerie quietness fell over the foul air, and the men who smoked lit up their pipes and cigarettes for what they thought might be the last time.

A frisson of expectancy flurried down the trench as the order came to move out. Pipes and cigarettes disappeared and packs were lifted and shoulders squared.

'This is it,' Blaise said over his shoulder to the man behind. Willie Clegg gave him a wobbly grin. He too had been weighing up his chances, and although he had no fondness for Hardcastle, he had reached the conclusion that if he wanted to stay alive, he needed the protection of a man who excelled in all the life-saving tactics they had learned in training.

He'd stick by Blaise Hardcastle through thick and thin.

'Do you think Artillery'll have blown Jerry out of Pendant Copse by now?' Willie asked, his breath warm on the back of Blaise's ear as they shuffled along the trench.

'That was the intention. Any strays left behind, we either kill 'em or take 'em prisoner.'

'Is it all right if I stick wi' you, Hardcastle?' Willie's voice was barely a whisper.

Blaise turned his head and grinned. 'Be my guest, Cleggy.'

The whistle blew and a blur of bodies scrambled up the ladders. Blaise and Willie rolled over the top of the trench and out into the unknown territory that they must cross to get to Pendant Copse. The order was to walk with rifles held at port arms, and as wave after wave of men left the trench alongside Blaise, he thought how foolish it seemed. If he'd been in charge, he would have attacked at night, not in broad daylight, and he would have ordered the men to run and crawl, rifles at the ready. Across the far distance, through the mist and smoke, they could see the huge, subterranean fortresses that the Germans had built between Serre and Beaumont-Hamel, and in the near distance their goal: Pendant Copse.

'Two thousand yards,' Blaise told Willie.

The Dukes and the Koylis began walking over the rolling, chalky ground, and Blaise wondered if the noise in his ears was gunfire or the beating of the hearts of the men alongside him. His own was thudding like the clappers.

They had walked no more than one hundred yards when a hail of machine-gun fire rained down on them. Blaise dropped to the ground, pulling Willie with him. Bullets hissed into the chalky soil and the air was foul with the stench of explosives. They lay face down in the muck and watched chaos ensue as men they had been talking to only a short while ago were blown off their feet, limb from limb, heads shattered, and the chalky, white earth was stained red with their blood.

'Looks like Jerry's still in occupation,' Blaise growled.

'The swines! They told us he'd be gone afore we got here,' Willie grunted.

The survivors gathered into a ragged group, stepping over their fallen comrades as they moved forward. Blaise's heart missed a beat as he recognised Tucker lying with a gaping hole in his chest and his eyes wide open. They pushed on until they were right into the enemy's barrage of shells, shrapnel, and fear-inspiring whizz bangs. By now, the soldiers were utterly disorganised, their officers either dead or out of sight. From deep inside the bunker in Pendant Copse, the Germans kept up the bombardment. It became clear to Blaise that they had to be taken out. He felt for the Mills bombs in his pocket.

'Cover me, Cleggy,' he shouted before he set off running like the wind.

Willie's scream alerted the others nearby. 'Cover him!' Willie yelled, aware that his own rifle skills were sadly lacking. Rifles at the ready, the men watched as Blaise zigzagged up to the sloping ground. At the top of the slope, he dropped to his knees then crawled until he was right up against the side of the bunker. Delving in his pockets, he took out the Mills bombs. Then wriggling slowly upright, he inched towards a loophole.

'Surprise, surprise,' he said, laughing hysterically as he pulled one pin then the other and tossed the grenades in through the loophole. And still laughing, he hurled himself down the slope, rolling wildly until he bumped into something that blocked his passage. Lying on his side, Blaise watched as the devastating explosion inside the bunker shook its walls and smoke poured from the loopholes, its guns silenced. Letting out a mighty whoop, he staggered to his feet, only to realise that his cascading roll had been stopped by a dead body. The Dukes and Koylis surged forward to take the copse, but a volley of gunfire stopped them in their tracks.

'There's more o' the buggers up there,' Sergeant Cropper yelled. 'Up and at 'em, lads.'

In the fighting that ensued and lasted until darkness fell, twenty or so German soldiers had been killed or taken prisoner. In the lull that followed, Blaise was much vaunted by his pals and Sergeant Cropper. In their opinion, he had performed a supremely self-sacrificial act, and whereas the 'old Blaise', as he now thought of himself, would have boasted about it and accepted their praise with arrogance, he just modestly shrugged it off. But later, huddled at the foot of a tree in the captured copse with only his thoughts for company, his insides roiled with the fear of what might have happened.

Orders came the next morning to move forward, and as they approached the fortress that was Serre, Blaise was horrified by what he saw: torn bodies hanging in the entanglement of barbed wire, screaming for help when there was none, and lads who had lost their minds cringing in shell holes, crying for their mothers.

'They never told us it 'ud be like this,' Willie said as they crouched in a shell hole, waiting for the opportunity to attack the formidable barbed-wire defences.

'Well, now we know they lied, Cleggy.' Blaise sounded far more nonchalant than he felt.

'Aye, an' we've no chance of getting through that bloody stuff. It's thicker than t'gorse on Scammonden Moor,' a beefy, ruddy-faced lad commented.

Blaise smiled at the mention of the moors near home. Corporal Horace Beavers came from Huddersfield and his family had a farm on the moor. Blaise wondered if he or Beavers would ever walk them again.

The minutes dragged by, and the weary, hollow-eyed men, too tired even to tell jokes, waited with heavy hearts for the signal to move. Lieutenant Ramsey McEvoy, the most senior officer in charge, told them they would attack the wire at the first opportunity. Impatient, Blaise let the rattle of machine guns and loud explosions fill his ears. He did not immediately hear Lieutenant McEvoy's command, and when he realised that he was alone in the shell hole, he sprang to his feet and raced after them without thinking. He had almost caught up with them when a hail of bullets swarmed from the German fortress. He stumbled and pitched forward, stunned as the ground came up to meet him. Then he was being dragged over the morass, a voice gasping, 'I've got you, Hardcastle. I've got you.' The last thing he felt was a dead weight landing on top of him.

26

'What was that you said?' Verity glanced up from the newspaper spread out on the dining-room table. She had been scanning the obituary columns in the *Examiner*, something she did every day since she had learned that Blaise was fighting in France.

'I'm going to the mill. Will you come later?' Oliver put on his bowler hat, relieved that his wife had not found what she was looking for.

'Not until after lunch,' she replied, 'and when we're on our way home, don't let me forget to buy a copy of the *Halifax Courier*.'

Oliver sighed. Reading the lists of fallen soldiers had become an obsession. Not only did she search the columns in the newspapers, she went each day to the Drill Hall to peruse the list that was posted there. Although Oliver was just as anxious for Blaise's safety, he was fearful that Verity might be heading for another bout of manic depression.

'Darling, we'd have received a telegram if all wasn't well,' he said gently.

'We might not. Have you seen how lengthy the columns are? They grow by the day. So many young lives lost. How can they possibly keep track of every man out there?'

'They have ways of checking on everything.'

'Ugh!' Verity snorted. 'It doesn't seem like it. Less than two weeks ago, the papers were reporting the glorious victory our troops had had in the thing they're calling "The Big Push". They must have got that information from the high-ups in the army after they'd done their checking,' she jeered. 'Then two days later, we're reading that it had been an absolute massacre, thousands dead and wounded and the British Army in chaos.' Her tear-filled eyes looked directly into Oliver's. 'They don't know what's going on any more than we do, Oliver.'

'Please, darling, don't let your imaginings distress you.' Even to his own ears, he sounded pathetic. 'I'm as anxious as you for Blaise's safety, but we mustn't lose hope.'

* * *

Shortly before the shift in the weaving shed was due to clock off for dinner, Oliver left the office to ask Nellie if the latest batch of khaki yarn was up to standard. As he approached the shed, the door opened and Amy Carter burst out into the yard, slamming the door behind her. When she saw Oliver, she flew across the yard and accosted him angrily. Utterly taken aback, Oliver fended off her flailing hands and shouted, 'For God's sake, woman, calm yourself.'

'Calm myself,' Amy sneered. 'It's easy for you to say. You never acknowledged our son, and now it might be too late.'

Oliver looked mystified. He swallowed, and Amy saw the hard knot of anger slide down the strong column of his neck.

'He's been conscripted and it's all your fault,' Amy spat.

So that was the cause of her distress. 'I'm sorry to hear that, Amy.'

Then, the desire he had once felt for her turning to pity, he gentled his voice and said, 'Amy, we both know Philip isn't my son. Why keep up this pretence? What do you hope to gain by it?'

Like a burst balloon, Amy's body sagged, the fight

gone out of her. She began weeping copiously and Oliver, afraid that somebody might see them, hustled her into his office and pushed her into a chair. Then he stood looking down on the pretty woman who had once stirred his manliness, and curious as to why she wanted him to admit to something they both knew had no substance, he said, 'Tell me what this is all about, Amy. Why am I to blame for Philip being conscripted?' He dragged a chair from behind the desk and sat down.

In her diminished state, Amy could barely speak. Her tears still flowing, Oliver gave her his handkerchief and she buried her face in it. Gradually, her shoulders stopped heaving and her sobbing petered out. She looked up at Oliver, the same pain breaking across her face as he had seen in Verity's when Blaise had run away. He shivered. Amy drew a deep breath.

'It all started with that rumour people were putting about. They said I'd been seen with you, and you must be the father of the baby I was carrying.' She raised her eyes to meet Oliver's. A flush of embarrassment coloured her cheeks. 'I... I thought if I could get enough people to believe it was true then... you'd be forced to do something about it.'

'Like what?' Oliver stared at her, incredulous.

'Well, if you'd taken him under your wing, the

gossips would have thought you were just doing what was right and they'd have lost interest. Scandals are soon forgotten when a new one comes along,' Amy said artlessly.

Oliver was staggered by her naivety. 'That is the most ludicrous thing I've heard in a long time,' he exclaimed.

Wearied by the ridiculousness of it all, he unfolded his powerful legs and stood up. Amy had the frightening impression of a bull pawing the ground. She cowered in her chair.

'Go home, Amy. Put this nonsense behind you. *Your* son, like mine, is serving his country. Let us both hope and pray that they will return safely.' He strode to the office door and opened it. 'Goodbye, Amy.'

On legs that appeared to be unsteady, Amy ducked past him and ran for the gate.

Oliver breathed a huge sigh of relief then crossed the yard to the weaving shed. After a brief word about the khaki yarn, he said, 'I saw Amy Carter leaving a short while ago.' His comment sounded casual enough but his nerves were on edge.

'Aye, I let her go early. She's upset. Her son's been conscripted and she wants to see him off.' Nellie's elfin face creased with compassion. 'I know how I'd feel if it was our Luke. And how you and Verity get through each day is beyond me.'

By now, it was common knowledge that Blaise Hardcastle had enlisted and that he was somewhere in France. The mill hands had met the news with admiration and sympathy, and both Oliver and Verity appreciated their concern.

'We have to accept it, Nellie.' Oliver then followed his solemn reply with a nervous cough and his cheeks reddened. 'By the way, talking about Mrs Carter. Has there been any silly gossip linking my name with hers? I... I...' He floundered and Nellie quickly came to his rescue.

Nothing much that happened in the mill got past Nellie. She knew about his little assignations with Amy, and had been keeping a close eye on things. She'd told Dolly about it, and whilst neither of them liked Amy, they had felt a sneaking sympathy for Oliver when Verity had blamed him for Blaise running away then banished him from her bed. 'Amy's up to her old tricks and he's a man with his brains in his trousers,' she'd said at that time. Now she made light of the matter.

'Oh, aye, there was some talk about you being her lad's father, but nobody believed it – well, a few might have – but it's an old story.' Nellie's deprecating tone put Oliver at ease, and he even managed to laugh when she said, 'Anyway, they've found something else to gossip about now. In fact, most of them are worrying too much about their own sons to care about who fathered hers.' She wiped her hands on her overall as if she was washing them clean of the subject.

The mill hooter blared, and thanking Nellie for her time, Oliver walked back to the office feeling far happier than he had when he left it.

Not long after Oliver had left to go to the mill that same morning, Dolly and Theo had arrived to take Verity into the town. Theo had business with the farrier, and Verity and Dolly were going to the rooms on Lord Street where Mrs Blamire and Miss Siddons organised the packing of comforts to be sent to the troops. Mrs Blamire was a magistrate and the wife of Joseph Blamire, a prominent mill owner. Miss Siddons was a college governor and a Poor Law guardian. Both were formidable women, one who sat in judgement and decided the fate of miscreants, and the other administered the workhouse and oversaw the provision of food, clothing and lodgings for the poor within the parish. Dolly and Verity secretly mocked them.

'Mind you don't put more than one bar of chocolate in a parcel this week, Verity,' Dolly admonished, imitating Miss Siddons's waspish voice as they walked along Venn Street to the Drill Hall so that Verity could read the bulletins listing the latest casualties.

Verity giggled. 'I thought she was about to pull down my bloomers and spank me,' she crowed as both of them burst into fits of laughter at her mistake.

Outside the Drill Hall, their merriment ceased as they stopped in front of the boards to read through the list of names written in alphabetical order. Verity's eyes darted to the names beginning with H. The surnames were written in heavy capital letters. Hackett, Haigh, Hall, Hampton, Hardcastle. Her heart missed a beat. Her hand flew to her mouth as a wail escaped.

Dolly peered at the board. 'Verity! It's not Blaise,' she cried before reading out loud, 'Hardcastle, James, thirty-five, Meltham.'

Verity sagged against her friend. 'Oh, Dolly. For one awful moment, I thought he'd...' She dared not say the words. She wiped her hands over her face. 'How foolish I am.'

'Not foolish, just a worried mother who loves her son,' Dolly said. 'Now, let's go and send the brave lads some comforts.'

The room in Lord Street was busy with women sorting through the items to be packed: tobacco, socks, mufflers, games, sweets and chocolate, wedges of fruit cake and soap – things that brought comfort to the deprived men in the trenches and let them know they were not forgotten.

'In his last letter, our Tom told me he cried when he got a bar of soap in his parcel. He said he'd not had a proper wash in weeks and his feet were sticking to his socks,' Verity heard a woman saying as she took her place at one of the long trestle tables.

She was putting a pouch of tobacco into a package when Mrs Beavers came up to her. The farmer's wife, whom Verity knew lived on Scammonden Moor, placed a gentle hand on Verity's arm. 'Mrs Hardcastle, how are you, dear?' Her voice was thick with concern.

Verity ignored the heaviness in the question, thinking this was the way the woman she didn't know very well always spoke. 'As well as can be expected,' she replied breezily. 'I've little to complain about.' She gestured at the parcel she was filling, her unspoken words indicating that its recipient had far more to worry over.

Ida Beavers blinked her surprise. Was Mrs Hardcastle being very brave, or was she ignorant of the facts? Judging by Verity's smiling face, she decided on the latter.

'I... I'm glad to hear it,' Ida murmured, and giving Verity's arm another motherly pat, she went and stood at the far side of the room, thinking that maybe she had misunderstood what her son, Horace, had written in the letter she'd received that morning. Taking it out of her handbag, she read again.

Dear Mother and Father,

You will be happy to hear that I am well and now safely resting away from the fighting. I hope the shearing went well and that the fat lambs brought a good price at market. We here have had a rough time of it and I must admit that the first day of July was the worst I have ever experienced and the saddest. My dear friend, Simon Sykes, lost his life. No doubt you will visit his parents to offer your condolences. Another casualty was the son of the Hardcastle family, who own Lockwood Mill.

The letter went on to say how much Horace missed the farm and her home cooking, but Ida didn't bother to read that. Her fingers trembling, she stuffed the letter back in her handbag. It wasn't her place to say anything to Mrs Hardcastle. She would hear the awful news soon enough. She looked across the room. Verity was laughing at something her friend Dolly was saying. Ida felt sad. The poor soul. *She'll not have much to laugh about in the next day or two.* Feeling like a traitor, Ida found couldn't stay in the room a minute longer.

27

In the Casualty Clearing Station at Heilly, it was business as usual. Nurses and VADs washed the wounded, changed dressings, emptied bedpans and held the hands of the dying. Stretcher-bearers came and went, and doctors shouted for assistance and equipment in their attempts to save lives. The air reeked of unwashed bodies, blood and putrefaction, and the sharp smells of acriflavine and carbolic acid.

Blaise Hardcastle had no memory of how he had got here. He couldn't recall the hair-raising journey over bumpy ground as the field ambulance had transported him to the hut, and the bed he was now lying in. He'd regained consciousness to find himself surrounded by beds in which lay moaning, groaning, crying men. He didn't care where he was. They'd been ordered to march into gunfire and shellfire, told to walk slowly, and been fooled into believing that the Germans had already been vanquished. That much he did remember.

He raised his head then tried to roll over onto his back. A dart of pain like a shard of broken glass shot through his shoulder and he was forced to stay on his side. He closed his eyes and must have dozed for when he next opened them, a pretty nurse in a grey and white uniform was smiling down at him.

'Private Hardcastle,' she said, glancing at the head of his bed, and in a distinct Scottish accent asked, 'How are we feeling today?'

Blaise smiled at the 'we'. 'I don't know how you're feeling, but I'm feeling pretty ropy,' he croaked, the sound of his own voice surprising him.

It was her turn to smile. 'You took a bullet through your shoulder. It made quite a messy hole. Now, I'm going to change your dressing. It might hurt a little.'

Blaise liked the way she rolled her 'r's. He looked at a trolley with kidney dishes, bottles and swabs on it.

Gently, she eased him onto his front. He groaned and swore. She began peeling away the blood-soaked, stinking dressing. Blaise winced as the sticky tapes tugged at the hairs on his skin, and as she swabbed his wounded shoulder, he gritted his teeth and tried not to cry out. A pungent smell like creosote brought back a memory of Bert Medley and the rear garden at Far View House.

'What is that stuff?' he asked.

'Lysol,' she said, soaking another gauze swab then dabbing it into his wound.

'Stinks like the stuff they paint fences with,' he said, wincing as it bit into his flesh.

'There, there,' she said with a flourish of 'r's. 'All done, private. You were very brave.'

I'm not brave, he told himself as he stemmed his tears, *but I'm alive*.

The nurse applied a clean dressing and made him comfortable then moved to the next bed.

For the rest of that day, and maybe another, he intermittently slept, suffered having his wound cleaned and dressed, and wondered where he would go from here.

At some point, when more in charge of his faculties, he opened his eyes to find Ramsey McEvoy standing by his bed. It took Blaise a few moments to recognise the young officer.

'Good to see you made it, Hardcastle. We thought we'd lost you,' McEvoy said.

Blaise nodded. Then clearing his throat, he asked, 'What happened?'

'We were closing in on the wire when the Hun spotted us. You were bringing up the rear when they opened fire and let us have it. A few of us were lucky enough to get out with our lives. You have Private Clegg to thank for saving yours,' McEvoy said before adding sombrely, 'Sadly, it cost him his own.' He went on to describe what Willie had done.

Blaise felt as though he had been gutted and filleted. Little Willie Clegg, who he had tormented and belittled, had covered his body with his own and taken the full blast. Blaise felt the spiral of self-loathing rushing into his throat. McEvoy handed him a kidney dish just in time. Afterwards, when the officer had moved on to another casualty, Blaise pulled the sheet over his head and sobbed until he was empty. He hated himself.

The next day, he was transported by train to the base hospital at Abbeville. Shrouded in remorse and regret, Blaise determined that the most honourable thing he could do was to make a quick recovery and rejoin the Dukes. That way, he could take his revenge on Jerry, and he'd do it for Willie Clegg.

* * *

In Lockwood Mill, work went on as usual, but in many of the sheds, there was an air of solemnity. In the weaving shed, the women kept sharp eyes on their flying shuttles and caught at loose ends to maintain the parallel perfection of the khaki and serge winding its way up to fattening cloth beams, but their hearts weren't in it. If indeed they did sing whilst they wove, it was hymns rather than the catchy tunes of the day. The war, which had been met with patriotic fervour and national unity, had lasted too long.

These days, too many of them of them were grieving for the loss of loved ones.

'I'm sick of weaving this sludge-coloured stuff, an' all for what?' Maggie mouthed to Lily.

Maggie's brother had been killed at Pozieres, leaving a wife and two small children, and Maggie's parents had had to take them in now that her sister-in-law had no means of support.

'So that bloody Jerry can rip it to shreds wi' his blasted bullets,' Lily mouthed, her face twisted in pure hatred.

The hooter signalled dinner time and the looms fell silent. The women trudged to the canteen, hungry and glad of a break, but the conversations were no happier there.

'My heart nearly stopped this morning when t'telegraph boy knocked on my door,' a woman from the spinning shed exclaimed. All eyes turned on her. 'Thank God, he'd got wrong house,' she told them.

'Aye, but some other poor soul 'ud get it,' said May.

'It wa' Fanny Birkhouse in Fountain Street,' Isaac, the old loom tuner informed them.

'Eeh! She has five kids an' another one on the way,' the spinner squeaked.

'Aye, her husband wa' home on leave afore Christmas,' Isaac continued, 'but he copped it on the Somme an' died of his wounds when they were bringing him back to England.'

The women stopped talking and reflected sadly on Fanny's problems before recounting the deaths of the husbands, sons and brothers that so many of the mill hands had lost. This too petered into a thoughtful silence.

'I paid fourpence for a pound of margarine from a chap what does black market,' Lily said a few moments later. 'Fourpence! An' it tastes like engine grease.' She screwed her lips.

'Aye, it's nowt like butter. An' bread made wi' potato flour's awful.'

'An' shop-bought bread's that dark these days, it's like eating burnt sawdust.'

'It's not bad if you spread condensed milk on it.'

'Aye, but conny onny's nowt like real milk,' said Isaac, using the local term for the sticky, sweet milk substitute. 'It tastes rotten in tea.'

The dismal complaints went on, the airing of their hardships and restrictions on everyday life compounding their disillusionment with the war.

'The only good thing to come out of this rotten war is us getting better wages and plenty of work,' Maggie declared.

'An' that'll not last. When this bloody war's over an' the men come home wanting their jobs back, the bosses won't need us women like they do now an' you'll see your wages cut to nowt, mark my words,' the woman from the spinning room spat.

'A lot of those brave souls won't ever be coming back,' Isaac said, his lugubrious reminder causing the spinner's cheeks to redden.

'Aye, that's true, an' what's goin' to become of a young lass like me when there's no young lads left to marry? You hardly see a chap under fifty these days,' a pretty teenage weaver wanted to know.

'You'll end up like me,' Maggie told her. 'Twenty-two an' I've never had an offer.'

'That's because she's too bloody gobby,' Lily sneered, the contentious remark drowned by the hooter's blast and another cause for misery averted as Maggie, oblivious to the slur, linked arms with Lily as they left the canteen. Lily, regretting the callous remark, squeezed Maggie's arm and said, 'I'll bet you a pound to a penny you'll be married afore you're twenty-five, Maggie.'

* * *

One young lady didn't actually have marriage in mind, but she was sure that she had fallen in love at first sight. Briony Hardcastle was thrilled whenever hers and Jan Van Leyden's paths crossed, and she cleverly and frequently manipulated these occasions, by visiting the mill, something she had rarely done before.

It was a balmy evening in August and she had just taken a short walk on the riverbank with Jan before going back to the office where her parents were winding up the day's business before she would travel home with them. When she entered the office, her cheeks were flushed and her head filled with romantic notions. Jan, as usual, had seemed delighted to see her, and their conversation had been about their likes and dislikes and their childhoods. He told her about the canals in Ghent and the beautiful bridges. Briony told him about her pony, Emily, and her interest in suffrage. In fact, Jan enjoyed her company as much as she enjoyed his. He had been instantly attracted by her elfin features and sweet nature, and although he was nine years older than Briony, he was a patient man content to let the relationship develop at its own pace.

'That's the third time this week that you've come to the mill,' Verity said, noting the sparkle in her daughter's eyes as Briony climbed into the rear of the car. Oliver turned in the driving seat, his puzzled look compounding her mother's curious tone.

'It makes sense that I should show an interest in what we do,' she told them. Oliver showed his surprise by asking what had become of making a career in nursing.

'Oh, that was just a girlish dream,' Briony replied. 'With Blaise away and not keen to be a manufacturer when he is here, it's only right that I learn the business so that eventually, I can carry on your good work.' She sounded supremely innocent and sincere.

Verity gave a little laugh. 'Are you intending to

put us out to pasture? Do you think we're too long in the tooth to run the mill?' She sounded scornful, but secretly, she was excited. It would be history repeating itself. She pictured herself as the young girl who had taken over a bankrupt mill and how she had struggled to make it prosperous. Of course, Briony wouldn't be faced with that problem. 'I think it's an absolutely marvellous idea, darling,' she said. 'What say you, Oliver?'

Oliver kept his eyes on the road, his hands tight on the steering wheel. Whenever he had given thought to his precious daughter's future, it had little to do with the mill other than that in time, she would benefit from its wealth. He had silently objected to the idea of her making a career in nursing, and instead had envisaged a marriage to a man who met with his approval and who would make Briony happy.

'I must admit, you've taken me by surprise,' he said.

'It's not that surprising,' Briony chirped. 'Mother became the Mill Mistress when she was not much older than me, and saved it from bankruptcy. And you taught her all there was to know about how cloth is manufactured, so why not teach me?'

'But in your mother's case, it was a necessity to

save the mill. You don't have that problem.' Oliver wondered why he was being argumentative.

Briony continued to state her case, and it sounded so innocently sincere that her father buried his doubts. Had he known that his sweet little girl was planning her future with a man who also had a future in manufacturing cloth, Oliver would have been even more surprised.

As the Hardcastles made their way back to Far View House, Susan was descending the stairs into the hallway, a tin of polish and a duster in her hands. She had just finished giving the master bedroom a good clean. Seeing a scattering of envelopes on the floor behind the front door, she put the tin and cloth on the hallstand and gathered up the post: the second delivery of the day. A buff-coloured envelope with a green cross on it let her know that it had been sent by a soldier serving abroad; her cousin's husband who was in France used the same sort of envelopes. Sniffing her contempt for the person she presumed had sent this one, she set it on top of the pile, picked up her cleaning tackle and went down to the kitchen.

'There's a letter from the brat,' she told her mother.

Bella glared at her. 'You shouldn't call him that,

not when he's fighting for our freedom and serving king and country,' she protested.

Susan sniggered. 'You sound like one of them posters. An' I'll call him what I like,' she said, washing her hands at the sink then helping herself to a sliver of ham on the chopping board and crying, 'Ouch!' when Bella rapped her hand with the back of her knife.

'Aye, well, keep your opinions to yourself.'

'I will, but I've not forgotten how rotten he was to me, an' if he's half as nasty when it comes to dealing wi' them bloody Germans, I suppose we should be thankful,' said Susan, sneaking another bit of ham when her mother's back was turned.

At the sound of the front door opening, Bella said, 'They're back. Wait for it.'

Only a second, and Verity's squeal of delight bounced off the hall's ceiling. Gazing through misted eyes at Blaise's sloping scrawl then clasping the buff envelope to her heart, she recovered the power of speech sufficiently to say, 'It's from Blaise. Go into the drawing room. We'll read it there.'

Oliver and Briony followed Verity into the room. Standing in front of the fireplace, she carefully opened the envelope and withdrew a single sheet of paper, her fingers trembling. Clearing her tensed throat, she began to read out loud.

Dear Ma, Pa, and Briony,

I'll start this letter by apologising for the trouble and grief I must have caused you in the past. Fighting this war has made me realise the error of my ways, and I deeply regret being that foolish fellow who failed to appreciate the love you gave me. I give you mine and miss you all, especially you, Ma.

I am well, as I hope you are. At present, I am writing this letter in a resting place away from the front line. Thank you for the soap and chocolate and socks. They are much appreciated (Briony made a fair job of the socks even though they are for two left feet).

Briony giggled, and Verity gave a little smile then continued reading.

This next bit is specially for you, Ma. I have an important favour to ask of you. I want you to visit the address I have written on the reverse of this page, and when you do, I want you to take an enormous box of groceries and other such supplies to Mrs Clegg with my deepest regards. You might consider making this a regular thing, especially at Christmas. I thank you in the certainty that you will do this for me.

I remain yours respectfully,

Blaise.

Verity continued to stare at the page, disbelief constraining her joy, and the depths of her emotions making her feel confused. Then, moved to tears by the letter, she ran her fingertip over the paper, tracing Blaise's scrawl.

The letter was all that she had hoped for and so much more. He was sorry for the hurt he had caused them – that he loved and missed them, her especially – and that he was safe and well. *Oh, Blaise, my dearest darling.* God was smiling on her at last and she felt as though her heart might explode. She scanned the brief missive again, puzzled by his strange request. Who was Mrs Clegg?

Oliver took the letter from her hand and silently read the first paragraph, the lump in his throat threatening to choke him. *The lad who had run away had become a man, wise and brave enough to say he was sorry.* His body filled with a warm glow, he read to the end and said, 'It's possible that Mrs Clegg is the mother of one of his comrades. Perhaps his friend made Blaise aware of their circumstances and he wants to do them a kindness.'

'Going to war seems to have changed my brother beyond all recognition.' Briony made the comment without derision, and although her mother's heart and mind were filled with boundless joy, she frowned.

'I'm sure my darling Blaise is no longer the boy we called our own,' she said wistfully. 'How could he be after all he's seen and done?'

'But he's safe and well by the sounds of it, and thinking of others less fortunate,' said Oliver with pride in his voice.

Bella tapped the door to announce dinner was ready, and ignorant of the fact that their beloved son and brother had written the letter whilst lying in a hospital bed waiting for his wounds to heal, they went into the dining room to eat ham and cabbage.

28

HUDDERSFIELD, DECEMBER 1918

It was Christmas week, and what a Christmas this was going to be. The war that had prevailed for four long, bitter years was at an end, and the celebrations that had welcomed the cessation of the fighting showed no signs of waning. Each day brought with it a reason for being joyful as husbands, brothers and sons returned to their loved ones and back to a life many of them had thought they might never see again.

Or at least, that was how it appeared to be for many of the families in Huddersfield. Behind closed doors, there were mothers and wives and children whose lives would never be the same. Their men were not coming home. They were lying under foreign soil in places too far way to even go and shed tears, pay respects and put flowers on their graves.

For those with something to celebrate, the rejoicing had begun on 11 November at eleven o'clock in the morning when the war that had been dragging its tail for weeks like a dying serpent crawled into the armistice. Bells rang out, bunting went up, street parties were organised and singing and dancing heralded a new future.

At Lockwood Mill, the mill hands had formed a conga line and danced round the mill yard. Afterwards, at a celebratory tea in the canteen, Lily had remarked, 'If all it took was for them in charge to meet on a train and decide it was all over, why the bloody hell didn't they do it years ago?'

On a more sombre note, Verity, Oliver, Briony and Jan had attended the memorial service in St Peter's Parish Church. Verity had said a prayer asking that the good Lord send Blaise home soon. There had been no more letters from him, but she felt sure that it would not be long before she would hold him in her arms again.

Now, with only two days left before Christmas Day, she still held fast to that belief. She had just paid her third visit to Mrs Clegg, taking with her a huge hamper filled with Christmas cheer. As usual,

Marian Clegg had received it with gratitude. Over a cup of tea, the women had shared their relief that the fighting was at an end, but the conversation hadn't been easy. Both women, still oblivious to the real reason for the bringing and receiving of the gifts, had come to a common agreement that their sons must have been the closest of friends. As Verity had wished the Clegg family all the best for the season, she had been overcome with a feeling of deep sadness that the Cleggs would never again share Christmas with their son, Willie. And as she rode in the hackney cab that was taking her back to Almondbury, she prayed once again that Blaise would be home before the big day.

When she arrived back at Far View House, Verity found Briony in the kitchen with Bella and Susan. They were discussing arrangements for the Christmas Eve buffet. The war might be over, but food was still scarce and with twenty or so people to feed, Bella was making useful suggestions as to how they could manage it with panache, for it wasn't just any old family-and-friends get-together to welcome in Christmas; it was a party to celebrate the engagement of Briony to Jan Van Leyden.

Jan had declared his love for Briony at a summer party in 1917. She had then told him that she had fallen in love with him at their very first meeting when Marc had introduced him to the Hardcastles. Since then, they had spent a great deal of time together at the mill or elsewhere, and Verity and Oliver had accepted that their precious daughter was no longer a little girl but a woman who knew her own mind. When Jan had asked Oliver for Briony's hand in marriage, he'd given his consent with the caveat that they waited at least two years before the wedding.

'They're recreating what we started, darling,' he had said to Verity that night as they sat in the drawing room drinking a nightcap after what had been a rather momentous day. 'Jan's a wonderful young man. He's full of ideas for making the mill prosper, and Briony's just as interested in learning from him every day.'

'Like I did with you, my dear. Learning how to run a mill and falling in love,' Verity had replied dreamily as she swirled the sherry in her glass, its amber glow catching the light from the fire. 'Perhaps we should change the name from Lockwood Mill to Lovers Mill.'

They'd both laughed at that.

Now, Verity and Briony, satisfied that Bella had everything in hand for the party, went up to the drawing room to talk some more, the air filled with the excitement that accompanies romance, Christmas and a world at peace. Mother and daughter had never been closer, and Verity thanked the Lord for giving her a second chance to appreciate how precious Briony was. This, of course, led to rueful thoughts as she silently admitted that she had neglected Briony in her devotion to Blaise. And as they talked and laughed, she hoped with all her heart that he would soon be present to share all this love.

Verity was still in high spirits the next morning and was happily arranging sprigs of holly and trailing ivy on the mantelpiece in the drawing room when the doorbell rang. She hurried out into the hallway, calling out, 'I'll get that, Bella.' Her house-keeper had enough to do preparing for the party that evening.

'Too many to put through the letterbox,' the postman said when she opened the door. He handed her a rather large bundle of post. 'Merry Christmas to you and your family.'

Verity took the bundle and told him to wait a moment. Then nipping into the dining room where her handbag was, she scattered the post on the table, took some coins from her purse and, back at the door, she handed them to the postman. 'Merry Christmas, and thank you for your good service throughout the year,' she said.

'Thank you, Mrs Hardcastle,' he replied, smiling at the generous Christmas box, and pocketing the coins with a cheery salute, he went off down the drive.

Verity dithered, torn between returning to the holly and ivy or dealing with the post. She knew that the latter would mostly be Christmas greetings from friends and business associates, and feeling no urgency to open them, she went back into the drawing room. Briony joined her a short while later. She'd slept late, the excitement of her forthcoming engagement party denying her a restful night.

'There's fried eggs in the warming dish and toast on the table, but the tea might be stewed by now,' Verity told her. 'You can make do with that for breakfast. We don't want to interrupt Bella.'

Never one to make demands, Briony trotted off to the dining room. A few moments later, Verity heard her shout, 'Can I open the post?'

The answer being, 'Yes, please do,' Verity then heard her daughter give a little whoop, and curious, she scurried to see what had caused it.

'It's a card and a letter from Marc,' Briony said.

'Congratulations on our engagement.' Marc and Dr Maes had made it safely back to Belgium in 1916 and, working secretly with the partisans, had saved many lives since then, even though their own lives were at risk from the German invaders. Now, Marc was writing to say they were setting up practice in Antwerp.

'Such brave men,' said Verity, sitting down and helping herself to a cup of tepid, stewed tea. 'And to think, if you hadn't met Marc, you would never have met Jan.'

'I've Emily to thank for that.' Briony laughed as she recalled the day her pony had behaved badly, and Marc had rescued her. 'Do you think I should have her as a bridesmaid at my wedding?' she asked, lifting an unopened envelope that lay face down on the table and drawing a sharp breath when, on turning it over, she recognised the handwriting. She handed it to her mother. 'It's from Blaise,' she said.

Verity took hold of the envelope and gazed at it, her eyes eloquent of something Briony could not decipher. She waited for her mother to open the envelope, but Verity continued to stare at it. Blaise wasn't coming home; she knew it in her heart. Steeling herself for Briony's sake – nothing must spoil today – she opened it and withdrew a beautiful card edged with snowy-white lace around a picture of mistletoe and holly and the words, *Joyeux Noël et Bonne Année*.

Her eyes bleak with dissolving hope, she said, 'He wishes us all the best of the season. He's spending his in Paris. He's been promoted. He's a corporal now,' she said, her voice hollow and the feeling of having been kicked in the pit of her stomach spreading through her body. She handed the card to Briony.

'I'm sorry, Mama,' she said, feeling her mother's disappointment and swallowing her own. She would have liked for her brother to be home to celebrate her engagement but, knowing him as she did, Briony's hopes had not been tempered with the fervency of those that her mother had clung onto as Christmas approached.

In fact, Blaise had thought long and hard about going home for Christmas, but when he reflected on how badly he had hurt them, his courage had failed him; he wasn't ready to face them yet.

Verity, her hopes cruelly dashed, forced herself to stay strong, and later that day, dressed in her best grey suit, she arrived at the mill to perform her annual duty. With Oliver carrying the trays, Verity visited every part of the mill, personally handing each of her employees a packet containing a Christmas bonus. To shouts of, 'Merry Christmas' and the chanting of, 'She's a Jolly Good Fellow' ringing in their ears, Verity and Oliver made their way back to the office.

'You were marvellous, darling,' he said, taking her in his arms and pressing her to his chest. From the moment she had stepped into the office, he had seen the pain clouding her beautiful eyes above the brave smile. He had been deeply saddened to learn that their son was not coming home, but it was more for his wife's sake than his own. He had never expected him, had never looked through rose-tinted spectacles at their son as did his mother. And Blaise being the self-centred lad that he was, Oliver now assumed that he had chosen to celebrate the festive season in the company of like-minded young men, and perhaps women, and strong drink, because Blaise was no longer a boy. Christmas spent in the confines of Far View House would be far too restraining for a man who had fought a war, survived against the odds, and now, as Blaise always had, was dictating his own happiness.

'He's most likely not yet been released from duty,' he said as a means of comfort. 'We're just one of the many families still waiting for loved ones to come home. And now he's a corporal, he probably has extra duties,' he added with false heartiness.

'I know. I know, Oliver. It's just... I'd put too much store by...' Verity fumbled for words as she moved out of his arms. 'And we'd better get moving. We have a party to host. This is Briony's special day, and we mustn't let anything mar the occasion.'

* * *

Lights flooded from the windows of Far View House, spreading their glow on frost-covered lawns, trees and flowerbeds under a velvet sky loaded with brittle stars. The air was still, no breath of wind, and as Briony and Jan stood in the doorway to greet their guests, she wondered, was this how it had been on that first Christmas night as the shepherds and kings came to pay homage?

First to arrive were Evelyn and her daughters, Rose all giggles and teeth as she introduced Ernest Hollingworth, a rather careworn, middle-aged man she hoped was The One. Maud smiled vacuously at everyone and clung to her mother's hand like the child she would always be. Then came the Beaumonts and Armstrongs, Florence and Clem with them.

'Isn't this just grand?' Dolly said as she hugged Verity. 'But I must say, it makes me feel like an old woman now that Briony's engaged to be married.'

'I can't quite believe it,' Verity replied, 'and yes, it does make me feel old. I just hope I'm older and wiser.'

'You've always been wiser than this one,' said George, giving his sister a playful nudge.

'Let's not go down that road,' Clem told his children. 'We're here to celebrate.'

'Doesn't our Briony look a picture,' Florence said, as on Jan's arm, her granddaughter was circulating the room, introducing him to Sarah and the three schoolfriends she'd invited, and generally making everyone feel welcome. Briony's amber, silk dress, with its tiered skirt and ribboned waist, showed her diminutive figure off to perfection and enhanced the colour of her chestnut hair.

Luke Armstrong recalled the time he'd fostered romantic notions for Briony, and whilst he still thought she was lovely girl, she didn't match up to Polly Oldfield, a girl from the weaving shed he was walking out with. You couldn't beat a mill girl, in his opinion. Look at Mam and Auntie Dolly. And Mrs Hardcastle. They were women to be reckoned with.

'Aye, she's no longer our little girl,' Oliver mused, his proud smile denying any misgivings.

'Our children are only lent to us for a time then we have to let them go,' Theo opined, smiling in the direction of his son, Josh, who was looking very grown-up as he stood talking with Luke, a young man now as broad as his father. 'He's settled in well at university. He won't be a land agent, like his old dad. He's destined for better things.' Theo let his eyes slide to meet Verity's. He knew that she was finding Blaise's absence hard to bear. 'They all do their own thing in the end, and we have to accept that because we love them, no matter what.'

Verity swallowed the lump that had crept into her throat and gave him a grateful smile. Theo was right. Blaise would always be her son, and wherever he was, she would always carry him in her heart.

Oliver asked had everyone got a drink, and as friends and family clustered round Briony and Jan to toast the happy couple, they were all thinking much the same thing. Together, they had struggled through trying times and come out the other side. Now, on Christmas Eve, they were gathered here to celebrate the engagement of two lovely young people and at the same time, were hopeful for rosy futures for themselves. Their hearts were still filled with joy that the war was over – the war to end all wars, so it was being called – and as they exchanged proud, happy smiles and raised their glasses, they believed it.

'To Briony and Jan,' Oliver said, his voice rich with sincerity. 'May the years ahead bring them the same happiness that Verity and I have shared. My beautiful daughter and this fine young man deserve nothing but the best.'

'To Briony and Jan,' Verity echoed, 'and to all of you here and to those who cannot be with us tonight,' a sad little smile flickered across her face, 'with all my heart, I hope that life smiles kindly on all of us and,' she raised her glass higher, her eyes twinkling mischievously as they met Briony's, 'on Lockwood Mill.'

* * *

MORE FROM CHRISSIE WALSH

The next instalment in the Lockwood Inheritance series from Chrissie Walsh, *The Mill Girls at War*, is available to order now here:
https://mybook.to/MillGirlsatWarBackAd

ACKNOWLEDGEMENTS

First and foremost, I would like to thank the wonderful people who continue to support me in my writing. I would be nowhere without them. Many thanks to my agent, Judith Murdoch who, twelve books ago, took a chance on an absolute beginner. Her wise advice and encouragement got me this far. And where would I be without my fantastic Boldwood editors, Sarah Ritherdon and Emily Ruston? Words simply cannot explain my gratitude. Thanks also to my copy editor, Emily Reader, and my proofreader, Rose Fox, for lending me their sharp eyes and brilliant minds. Clare Fenby and her marketeers for their super covers and promotions. I am extremely grateful to them and the rest of the brilliant team at Boldwood for their friendly guidance in all matters.

I've always wanted to write about my home town and Gordon and Enid Minter's 'Discovering Old Huddersfield' was invaluable for research and anecdotes. I also found Hazel Wheeler's 'Huddersfield:

The Old Days' very useful, as were E. A. Hilary
Haigh's 'Snapshots in Time' and 'Huddersfield: A
History & Celebration' by Lesley Kipling & Alan
Brooke. I learned a lot from these authors and pho-
tographers. Finally, thanks to Roberta Walker who
hosts the brilliant site 'Old Photographs of Huddersfield'. Roberta and her team do terrific work, and I
gathered some very useful information from them.

Huge thanks as usual to my wonderful family
whose love keeps me going.

ABOUT THE AUTHOR

Chrissie Walsh was born and raised in West Yorkshire and is a retired schoolteacher with a passion for history. She has written several successful sagas documenting feisty women in challenging times.

Download your exclusive bonus content from Chrissie Walsh here:

Follow Chrissie on social media:

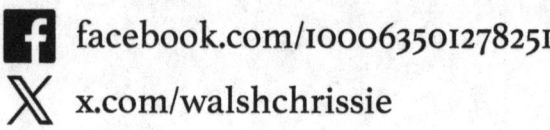
facebook.com/100063501278251

x.com/walshchrissie

ALSO BY CHRISSIE WALSH

The Weaver Street Series

Welcome to Weaver Street

Hard Times on Weaver Street

Weaver Street at War

The Lockwood Inheritance Series

A New Dawn for the Mill Girls

Trying Times for the Mill Girls

Standalone Novels

The Midwives' War

The Orphan's Heartbreak

The Workhouse Lass

Sixpence Stories

Introducing Sixpence Stories!

Discover page-turning historical novels from your favourite authors, meet new friends and be transported back in time.

Join our book club Facebook group

https://bit.ly/SixpenceGroup

Sign up to our newsletter

https://bit.ly/SixpenceNews

Boldwood

Boldwood Books is an award-winning fiction publishing company seeking out the best stories from around the world.

Find out more at www.boldwoodbooks.com

Join our reader community for brilliant books, competitions and offers!

Follow us
@BoldwoodBooks
@TheBoldBookClub

Sign up to our weekly deals newsletter

https://bit.ly/BoldwoodBNewsletter

www.ingramcontent.com/pod-product-compliance
Lightning Source LLC
Chambersburg PA
CBHW010656100726
47900CB00010B/2684